“The Earth-Mind i[illegible] powerful that its dreams have become reality for us, and our entire world is contained in the dream-images of its ages-long sleep. There are many paths within the dream, and men have the power to choose between them, but the very fabric of our world and the paths themselves are formed by the Earth-Mind.” Jordan paused and Cai nodded in agreement. “The Earth-Mind is a single entity,” he added, “upon whom we all depend.”

A few moments passed in silence, then Jordan went on, reciting words which Cai knew by heart, but which now sounded even more ominous.

> “Remember the Dream
> And whence it comes.
> Madness for the One
> Is death for all.”

Panic fluttered like a trapped bird in the wizard’s heart. Ideas rose up in his mind that would have been inconceivable only a short while ago. He fought against them, but their inexorable logic drove him back. So many of the pieces fit now.

“The Earth-Mind is going mad,” he whispered.

VOLUME III

The Unbalanced Earth Trilogy

THE AGE OF CHAOS

Jonathan Wylie

BANTAM BOOKS
NEW YORK • TORONTO • LONDON • SYDNEY • AUCKLAND

For JM . . .
Dear love, for nothing less than thee
Would I have broke this happy dream.
It was a theme
For reason, much too strong for fantasy,
Therefore thou wak'd'st me wisely; yet
My dream thou brok'd'st not, but continued'st it.
—John Donne,
The Dream

All characters in this publication are fictitious, and any resemblance to real persons, living or dead, is purely coincidental.

This edition contains the complete text
of the original hardcover edition.
NOT ONE WORD HAS BEEN OMITTED.

THE UNBALANCED EARTH TRILOGY, VOLUME 3: THE AGE OF CHAOS
A Bantam Spectra Book / April 1990
PRINTING HISTORY
Corgi edition published January 1989

ISBN 0-553-28454-1

Published simultaneously in the United States and Canada

Bantam Books are published by Bantam Books, a division of Bantam Doubleday Dell Publishing Group, Inc. Its trademark, consisting of the words "Bantam Books" and the portrayal of a rooster, is Registered in U.S. Patent and Trademark Office and in other countries. Marca Registrada. Bantam Books, 666 Fifth Avenue, New York, New York 10103.

PRINTED IN THE UNITED STATES OF AMERICA

RAD 0 9 8 7 6 5 4 3 2 1

part 1

THE IRON CHASM

chapter 1

The steel floor was clearly visible, hundreds of paces below the narrow walkway on which he stood. Yet he did not see it. He had become fascinated by his own left hand, staring at it as though mesmerized.

My hand. If I tell it to, it moves. He demonstrated that fact by spreading his fingers, then turned his hand over so that he looked at the palm. Perspiration glistened on the delicate ridges and whorls that marked his skin.

My hand.

It looked soft and vulnerable. *Human.* He trembled at the thought, and waves of anxiety washed over him.

He glanced at the metal band that had been sealed around his wrist, and which could not be removed. His name was inscribed there, beneath the endlessly flashing panel that gave his position within the grid-map. It ensured that the Center always knew where he was, and could send him a message at any time, commanding instant obedience. The tiny red light above the panel showed all that was functioning properly. Everything was just as it should be.

And yet this gave him only a momentary reassurance. As he stared at the lines on his hand, he was assailed by terrible doubts.

K207M, he thought, looking once more at the metal band. *That is my name.*

From somewhere far away, perhaps from long ago, came the echo of a memory. *My name was Ardath.*

No!

He stared at the engraving on the circlet, repeating his

number over and over again in furious, fearful denial of the ideas that were developing in his mind.

K207M. That is my name. Thus I know my place within the grid. K207M. That is my name . . .

The litany faltered. It was no good—a crack had appeared in the structure of his existence, and it was widening, threatening to bring the whole edifice crashing to the ground. He shuddered, then tore his gaze from his treacherous hand and looked around.

Metal gleamed all about him: iron, steel, lead, and others he could not name. K-level was one of the lower orders within the grid; he had been taught little of metallurgy, and nothing at all of the secrets of power. He operated within the Communications Section, a huge, multi-level group whose complexity and hierarchy were beyond his understanding. He just did what he was told. It had been enough for him—until now.

He studied the network of pipes and girders, meshes and spirals, and saw them as if for the first time. Power pulsed within the great labyrinth of steel, the air hummed with the vibrations of energy, and heat rose from hidden depths. Lights flared and died within the stark illumination provided by the blue-white panels that lined the interior walkways and the roofing far above. Beneath him was one of the well shafts within the giant complex. The walkway on which he stood crossed the shaft two thirds of the way up, a tiny strand of steel strung across a gaping void many stories high.

K207M had walked across this gantry countless times during his endless cycle of journeys within the complex. He had never felt any fear, and had not even been aware of the vertiginous drop on either side. The bridge was merely part of his designated route, planned out for him within the grid-map according to his assigned task. Never before had he stopped to look about him.

In the distance, far above and below, men and women went about their business, like tiny insects within a gigantic metal hive. The sight of their industry, their sureness and obvious contentment, made him feel desperately inadequate.

Why can't I be like them? I don't want to see things differently! His hands clutched convulsively at the rails that protected each side of the bridge. Fear and utter confusion rose up within him, and he closed his eyes to try to shut out the disturbing sights.

But his thoughts could not be quelled so easily. He was alone, suspended in midair in the center of a complex that was but one small part of the city that was his whole world.

It was not always my whole world.

The idea came to him unbidden and unwelcome, and brought with it a rush of images that made no sense. He cowered before them and felt a cold wind blow through him, tearing away the last warm shreds of his protection.

I came from afar.

He remembered the long arduous journey from his home to this strange place in the south, the joy and camaraderie he had shared with the others who had been called. He recalled the song that had been in everyone's ears, everyone's heart, drawing them ever closer to their goal. He saw again the chaotic arrival of his group at the embryonic city and the explorations that had followed. They had all been so eager then.

Barriers inside his mind were falling; he could feel them crumbling, opening the floodgates of horror.

At first, their work had been simple; massive construction projects overseen by a few men and women, the élite, who had the ear of the Great Leader and who were privy to his schemes and strategies. Yet the labor had been a pleasure, and Ardath and his fellows had been overjoyed to see the city grow at an astonishing rate. The grid became the universal chain of command, enabling everyone to know his role within the grand design. None of the workers could even begin to understand the whole plan but knew that great advances were being made. The Great Leader told them so. He announced discoveries almost daily—miracles of medical advancement, of food cultivation and of ever more sophisticated technology, were quickly taken for granted. And it was hinted that powerful weapons were being developed to ensure that the Great Leader's plans would be unopposed throughout the entire world.

Then the problems started. Several of Ardath's companions had been taken ill and disappeared without trace. All he could discover was that they had gone for treatment. He never saw them again.

A huge explosion had ripped part of the city to shreds and this meant months of arduous labor while the damaged sector was repaired. Many of those involved in the rebuilding became ill, and they too disappeared.

K207M opened his eyes and looked again at the metal band around his wrist.

The tracking devices had been introduced soon after the explosion. At first, they had been presented as a safeguard and were used only on those who were a potential danger to the city and its inhabitants. However, it became clear before long that the Center was intent on making sure that *everyone* wore them, for their own "protection." Few had objected, and even those who did accepted them within just a few hours of fitting.

But it's not working now!

K207M focused his gaze on the metal circle. He felt sick, knowing that something was horribly wrong and wanting nothing more than to retreat back into the cocoon of warmth and contentment that was being denied him by this flood of unwanted knowledge.

Why?

The patterns on the flashing panel changed suddenly, demanding his attention and querying his current actions.

I have been still for too long, he thought, desperate now. *The Center has found me*. Terror engulfed him. What should have been his greatest comfort was now the source of fear. He tried to conceal his thoughts, to hide them away as though the treacherous memories could be expunged by an act of will.

But he failed. The dam had been breached, and he was powerless before the flood.

He remembered that something else had followed after the fitting of the bracelets. Something terrible.

A bleep startled him. The sharp, insistent sound came from the band on his wrist. He stared at it uncomprehendingly, then a movement at the end of the walkway caught his eye, and he looked up.

Inhuman figures were gathering there; they stared at him with invisible eyes set deep within masks of steel.

Ardath was filled with revulsion and he looked down again at his hand, seeing it for an instant with unbearable clarity. He could see every single hair, every tiny wrinkle; his nails reflected lines of light, and every morsel of skin revealed the living flesh, bone, and blood beneath.

None of the things about him made sense anymore. The number on his band meant nothing.

They have stolen my soul.

Slowly, fearfully, he raised his hand. Soft, vulnerable fingers probed the space where his face had once been and encountered the ultimate horror of cold metal.

His mind snapped.

Vaulting over the rail, Ardath plunged into the iron chasm, screaming as he fell into the ravening depths—until the steel floor far below granted him the ultimate respite.

"Another of the K20's has malfunctioned," the controller said tersely as he studied the panel of flashing lights.

"Medical Control will have to check the process again," his superior replied, a touch of annoyance in his voice. "The Great Leader will be angered by such evidence of failure. If they cannot make a simple wrist implant work consistently, how can they expect the mind-screening to be effective?"

The controller felt it wiser not to reply.

"Instruct them that there must be no more mistakes in future. If they do not improve, make progress, they are themselves failing. That should not be hard to understand."

"I will tell them."

"What news of Mendle?"

The question came suddenly, startling the communications operative. As always, the approach of the Great Leader had been unheard and unseen.

"We still cannot contact him," the young man replied, rather nervously. "He has not answered for some hours now—I think his equipment must have been damaged somehow. I can't even get confirmation that our signals are being received."

The operative waited tensely for the instructions that he knew would follow.

"Mendle is dead," the Great Leader said emphatically. "He was always overconfident. Even so, he must not go unavenged." He paused, as if considering his options.

"Send the fliers," he ordered, then turned and strode from the room.

part 2

THE AGE OF CHAOS

chapter 2

The sun rose on the first day of a new age.

Thin beams of light slanted through gaps in the window drapes, and dust motes danced in the quiet morning air. From his chair beside the window, Arden watched the room about him. He saw an ordinary chamber, with plain furniture, bare stone walls, and a dusty wooden floor. It was the most wonderful place in the world.

As a ray of sunlight moved slowly across the pillows of the large bed, Arden watched as it caressed the hair of the woman who lay there. Fire seemed to sparkle from the short, disheveled red locks; everything else in the room seemed to shrivel into insignificance by comparison.

Arden smiled as she shifted without waking, turning her head from the light.

Sleep on, my love, he thought. *You deserve it*.

He thought back to their reunion the previous day.

His search of the great metal tower had proved fruitless. It was entirely empty of life; if Gemma ever had been a prisoner within its echoing walls, she was there no longer. Arden knew that there was only one place left to look, and he swore violently.

"We should have tried there first!" he muttered.

He started back down the seemingly endless stairs, heading for the base of the tower and the underground chamber that was guarded by a pulsing blue screen.

"We still don't know how to get in there," one of his companions told him, when he realized where Arden was heading.

"We'll see about that!" Arden called over his shoulder, then went on, taking the steps three at a time.

A short while later, he stood before the elemental wall, breathing heavily and trying to summon all his courage and determination. Behind him, the others entered the room quietly but held back, not wanting to disturb his fierce concentration.

You have encountered these creatures before, Arden told himself sternly. *You know that they respond to friendship. This screen is only a mass of such beings—all you need to do is cast aside your fear*.

He recalled the extraordinary sensation that had flowed through him when he had been enveloped by one of these strange ethereal creatures while in the Lightless Kingdom. It had reacted to his firm resolve and hopeful friendliness, but that fluid being was very different from the cold, pulsating barrier that faced him now.

Cast fear aside. Easier said than done! he thought. *Oh well, whoever said it was going to be easy? Gemma is in there! Isn't she worth a little effort?*

Throughout the months during which they had been unwillingly separated, Arden had come to realize just how strong his feelings for Gemma were. His longing to see her again had grown, becoming overwhelming. Now that he was so close, *nothing* was going to keep them apart.

Then another memory flashed into his mind. At the time, the cat's words had been just one more aggravating aspect of Arden's enforced stay in the floating city, and had provoked an angry denial from him. But now he grinned as he recalled the enigmatic riddle. "Now is the time for you to become a wizard. And then again, perhaps you always were one."

If I can get through that, he thought now, *I'll have a hard job convincing anyone I'm not a magician*.

The flickering blue screen had remained impassive all this time, as though daring him to attempt to breach it. All previous approaches had been repelled, sometimes violently, before the attacker could even touch the shimmering surface. But all such attempts had been made in fear or anger. With an insight born of his earlier experience, Arden knew that he would never succeed that way.

He stepped forward, and uttered his invocation.

"I am your friend."

There was no response, and he took another slow step forward, trying to clear his mind of everything except feelings of happiness and welcome. Although he could not suppress the yearning of his love, and a tremor of anxious anticipation, fear and anger were banished completely.

Another two paces brought him within an arm's length of the screen. He could not look at it closely, because the bright, swirling patterns moved too quickly for normal sight. Arden sensed the enormous power behind it, but also its constraints. The ancient masters who had created this chamber had hemmed it in with implacable skill and cruel precision, knowing that their work would inspire awe and even terror, and thus become impregnable.

I am you friend. Help me.

Arden's silent plea was not answered.

There was life within you once, he argued. *Warmth and joy and love. Can't you remember?*

Images of Gemma sprang unbidden into his mind. Flame-red hair and soft gray eyes; her face growing even more beautiful when she smiled; the teasing and the laughter they had shared; the bemused friendship that had turned at last to love.

Stretching out a hand, Arden stepped forward, unaware of the astonished gasps behind him as he slid into the elemental mesh.

He could feel its pressure on every fraction of his skin; for a few moments, he was blind, caught up in a maelstrom of fleeting visions. He sensed the pain of the elementals' eternal imprisonment and was filled with pity for them. As they reacted to his unexpected presence, he felt a little hope.

And then he heard Gemma's voice.

"This book has been changed once. And it can be done again!"

Joy and relief washed over him, sweeping aside all other emotions. She was there!

He stepped forward, moving freely now, and found himself in a marble chamber. Gemma was standing beside a table at its center; as she looked at him, the horrified expression on her face made Arden's heart sink.

"Wasn't once enough?" she cried, her voice cracking with misery. "Why must you taunt me with these demons?" She closed her eyes. "Your games mock me—and him. Return to your proper state."

Arden could not even begin to understand what she was talking about. He was horrified by the misery in her tone—so different from the greeting he had expected.

"Gemma, my love, I'm no demon," he said quietly, his own voice hoarse with emotion.

She looked at him again then, tears brimming in her eyes, and he saw the tiny flicker of hope light up her face. He forced himself to remain still as Gemma walked slowly toward him, somehow knowing that she had to exorcise her own ghosts. She stretched out a shaking hand and placed it on his chest, trembling at the touch, then looked up at his face, her eyes wide in disbelief.

"You *are* real," she whispered, then fell sobbing into his welcoming arms.

"Of course I'm real," he replied softly, holding her tight and wondering what ordeals she had been through to make her act this way. "You're safe now, my love."

"Safe for now," she breathed, a few moments later. "But it's not over yet. Arden, we have to go to the far south."

They had drawn apart a little, though they still held each other's hands, and as Arden looked into her eyes, feelings stronger than he had ever known in his life rose up within him.

"I don't care *where* we have to go—to the far south, even to hell itself—as long as we're together," he told her. "If you decide on any more crazy kite flights, you'll be taking along a passenger this time!"

They laughed together, a sound not heard in that marble chamber for centuries.

"Thank you," Gemma said.

"What for?"

"For living, for being real, for bringing the light back into my life."

They kissed. Long moments passed, then Gemma pulled away and burst out laughing.

"Is my lovemaking *that* funny?" Arden queried, taken aback but unable to suppress his own smile.

"Just the opposite," she gasped. "Ed asked me if I could still breathe. He sounded so worried!"

Arden looked beyond Gemma for the first time, and saw the meyrkats gathered by the table. Each pair of bright black eyes stared back at him, their sharp little noses sniffing inquisitively.

So Wynut was right! Arden thought, remembering the wizard's advice about the important role the meyrkat clan would play. There was so much he and Gemma had to tell each other—but not now.

"Can you breathe?" he asked, grinning.

"Oh, yes!" was her happy reply.

When they finally drew apart from a second, even longer kiss, the meyrkats had obviously overcome their initial concern and had moved to joint the two humans.

"What are they saying now?" Arden asked. He knew that Gemma could converse with the meyrkats through mind-talk—or telepathy as some called it—and wished at that moment that he shared her gift.

"Ox asked me if what we're doing is a mating ritual," Gemma answered, a sparkle in her tear-bright eyes.

"What did you say?"

"I said yes, of course!" Her attempt at bravado was only slightly marred by the rising color in her cheeks.

They were silent for a few moments, both thinking the same thoughts; come what may, it would not be long before their love was granted its fullest expression. Although in the past they had spent many nights together, they had always been chaste. *This* night would be a new beginning.

As they realized this, wonder and happiness were reflected in their eyes. Then they recalled their present situation, and their expressions became grave. They started to speak at the same moment.

"There's so much—" Gemma began.

"The others are waiting . . ." Arden hesitated, and Gemma went on.

"There's so much to tell you!" she exclaimed. "I don't know where to begin."

"It will have to wait for now," he replied softly. "We must get out of here—the others are waiting."

"But first I have to show you this," Gemma insisted, taking his hands and pulling him toward the table. The meyrkats capered around them, chirruping happily, but Gemma's expression remained serious. She pointed to the large book that lay open on the table.

"Read from there," she instructed, pointing to a particular passage.

Arden obeyed, wondering what could be so important in a book. At first, the letters seemed to jump and waver before his eyes, but eventually he saw the words clearly, and read aloud:

"'The signal marking the beginning of the change was the return of the Bringer of Destruction to the Apex City and his accession to its highest power.'"

"The Bringer of Destruction is the book's name for Mendle," Gemma put in.

"Mendle!" Arden was taken aback—he had thought that Mendle had been killed some time ago.

"Yes. *He* was the unnamed Overlord who built the tower," she went on, gesturing toward the ceiling. "He's dead now."

"You're sure?"

"Yes." Her eyes showed that there was much she was not saying, but Arden did not press her.

"The Apex City is Great Newport," he said, feeling that he had heard this somewhere before.

Gemma nodded and indicated that he should continue reading.

"'Although the actions of his associates achieved nothing except an orgy of bloodletting, he was nonetheless able to build a secure, seemingly impregnable fortress of steel. From there, he set in motion the experiments and processes that would lead to the new age.

"'Only one power could have opposed his progress, and that nearly failed through ignorance and clinging to outmoded ideals. However, the Servants of the Earth achieved a temporary victory when the Key to the Dream . . .'"

"That's me, believe it or not," Gemma said, in answer to Arden's unspoken question. He went on.

"'. . . who had been imprisoned in the steel fortress, was able to reassert the doctrines of magic and turn the Bringer of Destruction's power upon himself.'"

Arden looked up at her.

"You did that?" he whispered.

"Only with the meyrkat's help," she replied. "I would have been powerless without them. And I still can't understand how they got in here."

"*I* brought them!" Arden said gleefully. "Wynut told me to."

Gemma looked at him in amazement.

"You're even more wonderful than I'd thought," she said at last.

"Oh, it's just natural talent," he remarked, grinning happily. "But *how* did you defeat him, and what exactly is the Key to the Dream?"

"You're not going to like this," she answered, smiling to herself now. "It concerns magic." This subject had long been a source of friction between them; until Gemma had literally stumbled into his life, Arden had had no time for anything but practical matters. Arcane phenomena were no concern of his. However, recent events had forced him to reconsider.

"I'm a wizard myself now," he commented nonchalantly. "I can handle a little magic. No trouble."

Gemma was speechless, wondering if he was teasing her. Arden merely smiled and motioned for her to continue.

"Since The Leveling," she told him, "magic works in groups, circles if you like. There are hundreds of circles, but they all intersect at one point—and one point only."

"The Key to the Dream," he said.

"Me," she agreed quietly. "Mendle's tower was a receptacle for power, and his plan was to let all the circles feed their magical energy to me so that he could then syphon it off."

"Leaving him with complete power," Arden put in.

"And destroying all of us—and magic itself," Gemma concluded.

"So how . . . ?"

"The meyrkats are one of the circles," Gemma explained, "which is why I can talk to them."

"And they were *inside* the tower," Arden said.

"You catch on fast," Gemma replied, genuinely surprised. Arden had never before showed any understanding of or inclination toward the principles of magic.

"We wizards do," he answered, with almost unbearable smugness.

Gemma suddenly remembered that she had caught a fleeting glimpse of Arden amid the faces that had streamed through her thoughts during that terrible battle with Mendle. *So he* is *in one of the circles*, she thought. *Can he be serious?*

Seeing her puzzlement, Arden explained.

"The cat in the floating city informed me that I am a wizard," he said. "And then again, who would believe *him*!" He grinned. "The point is, you won!"

Gemma's face fell.

"Only temporarily," she replied. "Read the next bit."

Arden obeyed, his heart in his mouth.

"'However, this setback merely spurred the forces of the far south to even greater efforts, and their influence soon spread throughout the world. The old order was destroyed.

"'The Age of Chaos began.'"

chapter 3

It was Arden who broke the silence.

"Wait a moment," he said, shaking his head in confusion. "I don't understand. Just what is this book?"

"I don't know exactly," Gemma replied, "but *somehow* it has recorded the history of our world—and the future."

"That's imposs—" Arden began. Then he remembered the libraries in the floating city. "It's hopeless," he said quietly.

"No." Gemma's voice was firm now. "When I first saw this book, it described how Mendle succeeded in destroying magic. He used that account to taunt me."

"But—"

"It's changed," she insisted.

"It changed *itself*?"

"Yes. And having done it once, it stands to reason that we can change it again," Gemma concluded triumphantly.

"I don't think *reason* has anything to do with it," Arden responded. His head was spinning again. Just when the world had seemed to be making sense—in spite of all this *magic*. "What is the Age of Chaos, anyway?"

"I think I'd prefer not to find out," she replied. "But we know where it stems from."

"And that's why we have to go to the far south."

Gemma nodded.

"Can't we read any more of the book, and get help that way?" Arden wondered.

"No. Try it and see what happens."

So he turned over one of the heavy pages and tried to read what was written there. After a few moments he gave up and rubbed his eyes. The words had jumped, jumbling themselves before his gaze. Just when he thought he could decipher a particular word or phrase, it slid away, becoming unintelligible once more. The following pages were even worse.

"See what I mean?" Gemma asked.

Arden nodded. "Yes—and I have the headache to prove it," he added ruefully.

"But what has been written about the past is perfectly clear," she told him. "There's a whole section devoted to my childhood—and it gives a very accurate picture."

"So you were important even then," he stated softly. The full implications of Gemma's role in these momentous events were beginning to sink in, and as they did so, Arden's face grew so solemn that Gemma was worried.

"Whatever it is that makes me special," she began, taking his hands in her own and pleading for understanding with her eyes, "I'm still *me*, I'm still Gemma." *I'm still human.*

Arden met her gaze calmly.

"I love you," he said, dispelling her fears.

"I know," she replied, smiling. "I love you too."

They paused to renew their mating ritual, then Gemma said, "I had such strange dreams about you. Where have you been?"

"It's a long story," he replied, "among many long stories, I suspect! But first we must get out of here—the others are waiting outside. There'll be time to fit the pieces together later."

Something else occurred to Gemma.

"How did you get through the screen?" she demanded suddenly.

"I told you. I'm a—"

"Don't say it!" Gemma ordered, holding up a hand to ward off his flippant claim. "I thought you were an apparition—like the last time."

"What?"

"It was when I was with Hewe and Ashlin," she told him, "on the coast road between here and Altonbridge. You—or what looked like you—appeared in front of me." She shuddered, remembering how her jubilation had turned to horror and despair. "But when I got close you . . . it changed, became an elemental and flew away."

"Gods," Arden breathed, imagining the effect such an

incident would have had on her. "That must have been the elemental who touched me in the Lightless Kingdom."

It was Gemma's turn to look bewildered.

"Where?" she asked.

"Not now," he answered firmly. "Let's go."

"You still haven't told me how you got through the screen," Gemma protested. "I'm not sure I have enough strength to open that door again."

"All it takes is friendship," he replied enigmatically.

Hand in hand, they walked toward the pulsing blue wall, the meyrkats trailing behind them like a miniature guard of honor.

As dawn had broken on that fateful day, Great Newport was in chaos. There was fighting in many streets and several buildings were damaged or burning. Looting was commonplace. Only a few people were attempting to stem the tide of violence, and they were meeting with little success. For decades the Guild, the ruling body of Great Newport, had kept the city and the land of Cleve in a state of constant deprivation. Under the brutal tyranny of the Overlord and his colleagues, this governing body had ensured that a privileged few led pampered lives of luxury, ease, and power, while the majority were condemned to subjugation and abject poverty.

Recent events had allowed those downtrodden people their chance of revenge, and now it seemed that a bloodbath was inevitable.

For many years, the secret organization known as the underground had been planning to overthrow the Guild, but even they had been unprepared for this sudden upheaval and were therefore unable to prevent the ensuing carnage. They were now working hard to try and bring some sort of order to the city—and hope for the future—but they were also preoccupied by another devastating threat to Great Newport and its citizens.

In the center of the city, a gigantic steel tower had arisen, holding the entire city in thrall with a truly awesome display of power. Beams from the great tower had already destroyed two sections of the city wall and had killed hundreds of people. The leaders of the underground knew that the *real* enemy was no longer the divided, fearful Guild, but the nameless Overlord, the sole occupant of that monstrous metal growth.

Knowing that the tower was impregnable above ground, they had besieged its underground entrance. At first, nothing had been achieved, and they sacrificed many good men and women, seemingly in vain. But then, in the early morning, the tower had inexplicably opened its doors; the guards inside had gone insane, killing each other and themselves.

But when the underground had been able to search inside, they found that both the Overlord and Gemma—whom they had known to be a prisoner within the stronghold—had disappeared. Only the blue-flame chamber at the tower's base remained—and only Arden had been able to attempt an investigation of that mysterious room.

That he had succeeded in entering had astonished the onlookers. However, he had been inside for a considerable time now, and several people were expressing concern.

"What should we do?" Hewe wondered aloud. The bear-like man was standing at the front of the group, his scarred face frowning in puzzlement.

"What *can* we do?" Jordan replied. "Except wait?" He was the leader of the underground, and was feeling his responsibilities acutely. There was so much that he should be doing but, for the time being, his attention was commanded by whatever might be happening beyond the blue-flame wall. He turned to his lieutenant. "They're a resourceful pair. After all, they both got in there . . ."

Then Jordan turned to address a group of warriors who were standing in the deepest shadows of the room. These soldiers were all slim and tall, and their entire bodies were covered in a shiny black material that gave them a distinctly sinister air. They were the control group from the subterranean realm that Arden called the Lightless Kingdom. He had lived with them in their dark and wondrous world for several months.

"Any ideas, D'vor?" Jordan asked.

"Arden won the trust of the elemental in the Hall of Winds," the control-group leader replied. "Perhaps this barrier is formed of similar beings. We find it difficult to look at it directly, in spite of our protective coverings," he added by way of explanation, "but we believe it could be so."

Just at that moment, a dual shadow appeared within the shimmering barrier and all conversation ceased as the onlookers held their breath. The screen bulged, then, in a shower of sparks, Gemma and Arden appeared, hand in hand. As the meyrkats followed them, making their characteristic peeping noises of excitement and pleasure, the onlookers stared in amazement.

Noting the astonishment of their audience, Gemma and Arden were seized by the same impulse and, still holding hands, they bowed low. The clan recognized this action from their traveling days with Gemma, and so made their own obeisance—with varying degrees of success. Some of them fell over in the attempt, and the effect was so comical that, when Gemma and Arden straightened up with the wide grins on their faces, the others burst out laughing.

"Bravo!" Jordan exclaimed.

"I told you she should be on stage," Hewe remarked casually. "Now she even has her own company."

An hour later, Gemma's "company," together with Jordan and Hewe, were ensconced in the underground's old headquarters, a comfortable room deep beneath an enormous rubbish tip in one of Great Newport's poorer districts. This headquarters was part of a labyrinth of tunnels that ran beneath the streets of the city, and that had been the province of the underground for a long time.

The Lightless Kingdom group had not joined Gemma's party—in spite of their curiosity about her. D'vor had explained that, even with the protective layers of silkfish tape, his people were now beginning to suffer from their continued exposure to many forms of light. So they had been led to the darkest area of the tunnel network and left there to remove the restrictive bindings and recover in more amenable surroundings. Gemma had been fascinated and a little afraid of them at first, and had much that she wanted to ask, but Jordan insisted that she tell her tale first.

She repeated what she had told Arden, adding details and clarification where necessary, and explained her theory about the book in the blue-flame room. When she finished, Jordan was silent for a while, his face thoughtful.

"You're sure the Overlord was Mendle?" he asked eventually.

Gemma nodded. "He told me so. And even though his face was covered with the metal mask, I would have recognized him. I'll never forget that voice as long as I live."

"And you're certain he's dead?"

Gemma had skimmed over his death during her story; she still felt guilty about the way she had forced him to throw himself from the very top of the tower. Not even the man's irredeemably evil nature seemed justification enough to her now. She was glad that he was gone, but she had never wished to use magic in that way and regretted her actions.

"Yes . . ." She hesitated, then went on. "He fell from the top of the tower."

Hewe whistled quietly. The Overlord's edifice had been at least forty stories high.

"I made him do it," Gemma said. "It was when the magic of all the circles was flowing through me. I had so much power! I couldn't do it now—I wouldn't even want to."

For a few moments, nobody spoke, then Jordan said firmly, "The magic obeyed its own instincts."

"No matter how you feel about it now, you've done us a great favor," Hewe stated.

"I never want to have that much strength again," Gemma told them. "It was terrifying!"

The rest of that day was spent bringing Gemma up to date with recent events. And she listened in wonder as Arden told her of the Lightless Kingdom, of his months of illness and injury within the crystal-lit caves, of the fair-skinned, huge-eyed people who lived their lives underground, and of their kindness and eventual acceptance of himself. He told her of C'tis, the healer of the control group now in Great Newport, who had labored for so long to save his life. He described the prophets, the spiritual leaders of that underground realm, whose eyes were entirely black from eating the sacred fungus, raellim. Through his eyes, Gemma saw the endless maze of tunnels, caves, and underground waterways—and suffered with him as he described the pollution that was driving his new friends from their homes. His words made sense of her dreams.

Then Arden went on to tell her of his encounters with the elementals and the meyrkats, of his capture by the fanatical Gray Raiders—who were at war with the subterranean people—his subsequent rescue and eventual return to the surface.

Jordan took over the story then, and described how Arden had led him into the Lightless Kingdom, and of the pact he had made with the underground people, promising to try to find a solution to their problems in return for their help with the struggle against the Guild.

"In the meantime," Arden put in, "I'd gone to the valley to look for you—only to find that Hewe had beaten me to it!"

The two men grinned at each other.

"Then I got caught up by the floating city," Arden went on. "And Wynut told me of the importance of the meyrkats, and got me to Newport in time to bring them in."

"The rest you know," Jordan concluded. "The Guild's been shattered and Mendle's dead, but the city is in a mess. We've got an incredible amount of hard work ahead of us."

Jordan's words were to be borne out by a messenger arriving a few moments later. The work of establishing a new society had already begun, and this was just the latest of several interruptions by members of the underground seeking orders or advice.

"Egan wants to know what to do about the entrances to the tower," the messenger reported. "The citizens are getting very curious."

"Tell him to seal them up for now," Jordan replied. "We don't want anyone wandering in there and blowing up half the city by accident. We'll examine it carefully later, when we're more organized. There are too many other things to worry about right now."

The messenger nodded and started to leave.

"Ambros!" Jordan called after him. "Make sure that everyone knows the tower no longer represents a threat. It's empty."

"Right."

"Are you *sure* there's no more danger?" Hewe asked a few moments later.

"No," Jordan replied, unabashed. "But we'll never get anything done if people are looking over their shoulders the whole time."

As the afternoon wore on, both Gemma and Arden grew visibly tired. Jordan noticed their state, and turned to Hewe.

"Are there any safe houses with room to spare?" he asked.

"We could try the Black Horse," his deputy replied, naming one of the city's many taverns. "It's the nearest."

"Go and get some rest," Jordan told them. "You've done more than enough for one day!"

* * *

"We'll see that you're not disturbed," Hewe said. "Sleep well." He closed the door behind him, leaving Gemma and Arden in the plainly furnished but comfortable bedroom. The meyrkats had refused to leave Gemma, so they were there too; the creatures immediately made for a dark corner, huddling together for comfort.

Arden took Gemma in his arms and kissed her. When they drew apart, he saw the utter weariness in her eyes, and felt a moment's uncertainty.

"Don't even ask!" she ordered, smiling. "I'm not *that* tired."

After that, words were no longer necessary.

The meyrkats observed discreetly, glad that the human's mating ritual had at last reached the proper—and highly satisfying—conclusion.

Arden awoke several hours later. When he saw Gemma's face close beside him, a flood of happiness surged through him, making further sleep impossible. Being careful not to disturb her, he rose, wrapped a robe about him, and sat by the window, watching over his love. She was still fast asleep, breathing steadily and deeply, pale with exhaustion from the ordeals—and pleasures—of the previous day.

As the sun rose on the first day of a new age, Gemma and the meyrkats slept on, leaving their guardian alone with his thoughts.

When she finally awoke, it was to the terrifying sounds of skyravens howling overhead. The screaming thunder of the gigantic metal birds was accompanied by the crump and roar of tremendous explosions.

"What's happening?" she asked, her voice groggy from sleep, her eyes wide with sudden fear.

"Skyravens," Arden replied, looking out of the window. "They're destroying the tower."

chapter 4

"Now we'll never know its secrets," Jordan said regretfully as he surveyed the ruins of the tower.

Hewe shrugged. "I'm not sure those were secrets I'd care to know," he replied. The big man's sentiments were shared by the vast majority of the citizens of Great Newport. The tower had been a source of terror and destruction, and most people were heartily glad that it was gone. Few had believed that it represented no threat just because it was unoccupied. So the general opinion was that, for once, the dreaded skyravens had done them all a favor.

The attack had been swift and devastating. Huge explosions had ripped the metal shell of the tower to shreds, flinging molten steel into the sky and deafening anyone unfortunate enough to be in the vicinity. Luckily, casualties had been very few. Their business complete, the skyravens had flown away to the south. As they left the city, further explosions rocked the southern districts, but this seemingly spiteful action caused little noticeable damage in a city already in turmoil.

Now all that remained of the tower was a mass of smoking, twisted metal.

"There was so much power there," Jordan remarked almost wistfully. "Perhaps we could have harnessed it for good rather than evil."

"It was *designed* for evil," Hewe told him. "You might as well try to turn a vulture into a songbird."

"You may be right," Jordan admitted. "But why did they *do* it? I can't understand the skyravens wanting to do us any favors."

"If Mendle was part of the same organization," Hewe

suggested, "it's obvious that whatever he was trying to do had failed. And perhaps they punish failure rather severely." He grinned. "Either way, we're better off with that tower gone. At least now we can concentrate on getting the city organized without worrying about half of it being blown up or disappearing!"

They were both assuming a connection between the tower and the skyravens. Each had displayed awesome powers beyond the comprehension of the two men.

"So Gemma was right about the far south?" Jordan wondered.

"Could be," Hewe said.

"Do you get the feeling someone's playing a game with us?"

"Some game!"

"I'm serious."

"Even if *they*—whoever *they* are—are as powerful as it would seem," Hewe stated firmly, "we've still got more than enough on our hands here. The far south will have to take care of itself for a while. We've got too much work to do as it is."

Jordan looked at his friend.

"It's a good job there are people like you around," he said eventually. "If the world was left in the hands of dreamers like me, we'd be in an even worse mess!"

"If you were *just* a dreamer, you'd never have accomplished as much as you have," Hewe retorted. "The whole city is looking to you for leadership."

"Gods! I'm not ready for this." Jordan shook his head.

"You'd better be," his lieutenant replied. "You're speaking to them in Colosseum Square this afternoon."

Jordan was speechless.

"We've already spread the word," Hewe added, "and it should be quite a good turnout." He paused. "Come on, Jordan. You wouldn't want to disappoint your public, would you?"

The six members of the control group from the Lightless Kingdom sat together in the corner of the underground hall where their people were resting. They had been a team for a long time now and, though two of their number had been lost in earlier battles, their replacements had been chosen carefully and had fitted in almost immediately. Back in their own world, the job of the control party had been to survey the hostile regions of the southern cave systems, monitoring the pollution that was spreading there. Each member had grown to trust and rely upon the others completely during such hazardous work, and it was only natural that they should stay close now.

The make up of a control group was a matter of great importance. The necessary combination of differing skills meant that members were often of widely varying temperaments and abilities, and this group was no exception. C'tis was a healer, blessed with an ability to look *within* another body, and thus diagnose and remedy some ills by the force of this awareness. She was also an expert in the more conventional applications of medicine. Her gentle hands were matched by a gentle nature. Even so, none could doubt her strength and determination. She had nursed Arden for several months, earning his eternal gratitude and, more recently, had brought herself to the edge of exhaustion by treating the wounded of this latest conflict.

V'dal was the group's guide. His phenomenal memory and instant recall of all their home tunnels and caves was invaluable. While the others all shared a basic knowledge of the remoter regions of their realms, it was V'dal they relied upon to plan routes and estimate timings. Beyond the confines of the Lightless Kingdom, his skills were of necessity greatly reduced, but his agile mind was welcome in any decision-making process. His personal philosophy allowed him an important sense of history and a profound concern for his fellow men—be they members of the Lightless Kingdom or not.

The same could not be said of J'vina, who was a warrior, pure and simple. Her tall slender frame disguised immense physical strength and agility; her outlook on life was straightforward. She reveled in her combat abilities and, while she did not always agree with her companions' reasonings, was nonetheless fiercely loyal to them. She could state an awkward truth or admit her own shortcomings with an equally ruthless honesty. No one would ever be in any doubt over where they stood with J'vina.

By contrast, T'via, the third female in the group, was quiet and reticent. Her role was basically that of an observer and a representative of the prophets. She spoke on their behalf when necessary and would report back to them on her return from Great Newport. She seemed reserved, and spoke with authority only when interpreting religious or spiritual matters. As one of the new members of the control party, she still had to be coaxed into expressing her views.

The other relative newcomer was C'lin. Like J'vina, he was a soldier and, though he could not match her fighting expertise, he was also skilled in the many practical matters necessary for survival in the remote and dangerous places they visited. He was strong and of a practical nature.

The man entrusted with holding this diverse group together was D'vor. He was older than the others, but believed himself to lack the special skills that entitled him to the position of leader. He often wondered why he had been chosen by the prophets, and at times the responsibility weighed heavily. Yet his colleagues would have been able to give him a wide variety of reasons as to why he enjoyed their faith and loyalty. However, asking for such reassurance was completely against D'vor's nature, and as a consequence, he was always striving—in his own mind—to justify his authority.

This group was resting now, recovering from the rigors of their journey and the subsequent conflict. For the first time since they had left the Lightless Kingdom, they felt it safe enough to fully remove their restrictive bindings of silkfish tape. Beneath this protective covering, their skins were far more sensitive than those of the people who lived above ground.

The hall in which they sat had been chosen because it was one of the largest chambers beneath the city, and because it was lit only indirectly from the corridor that ran alongside. Although it was damp and musty, to the newcomers it was as near to home as could be found, and they were able to relax, stretch unfettered limbs, and look about them with uncovered eyes.

At first, their vulnerability had worried J'vina.

"They'd only need a couple of those diabolically powerful lamps," she complained, "and we'd be helpless!"

"We're always going to be at some risk in the upworld," D'vor replied. "Jordan has assured us that the enemy is nowhere near here, and he's posted guards, just to be on the safe side."

"How do we know we're safe with *them*?" she demanded.

"Jordan may be trustworthy but his people are upworlders, after all."

"It's pointless worrying about that now," V'dal commented. "If we're to have any chance of our two races working together successfully, we *have* to take them on trust, and accept the risks as worthwhile."

"And just being able to get out of the tape is certainly a relief," C'lin added.

"That's true," J'vina admitted.

"Lie down and relax," C'tis advised. "We all need to rest."

The warrior complied, albeit reluctantly.

J'vina's suspicions were understandable. Until Arden's unexpected arrival, their only contact with upworld people had been with the fanatical warrior sect known as the Gray Raiders. This ferocious group had considered the underground dwellers to be inhuman vermin and had killed any they met without compunction. The only other thing bequeathed to the Lightless Kingdom by the upworld was deadly poison. So it was hardly surprising that prejudice against upworlders was deeply ingrained. But if their mission here succeeded, there was at least a chance that they would receive help with both their problems. The very existence of the Lightless Kingdom was threatened, and that was surely worth an attempt to reconcile the two societies—however risky it seemed.

With that in mind, D'vor decided to treat this journey like any other that the control group had previously undertaken. The next morning, after their night's rest, he gathered them together.

"We'll need to report everything back to the prophets in due course," he began. "Let's have your appraisals so far. V'dal?"

"Well, I already have a fair understanding of the underground ways beneath the city," the guide answered. "At least the parts we've seen or been told about. Above ground is a complete unknown—I can't even imagine what it looks like." He paused, considering the absurdity of an entire city, thousands of people, living *above* ground. All he had seen when approaching Great Newport in the dead of night was a dark silhouette of the city walls, and his imagination balked at the idea of what was inside.

"Could you find the tunnel we entered by?" D'vor asked.

"Yes."

"And outside? Could you take us back home, unaided?"

"I could do *that* blindfolded," V'dal claimed, to general amusement. They had traveled overland at night, protected by a single layer of silkfish tape over their eyes. This had filtered out enough of the star- and moonlight to make the upworld bearable, while at the same time leaving their vision unimpaired.

"J'vina?"

"What can I tell you?" she replied dismissively, but before D'vor could reprimand her, she pulled herself together. "You already know my worries about our tactical situation, but I accept the fact that the enemy is not believed to be within striking distance." She managed to sound only a little doubtful. "So far, from a military point of view we've performed well. We've had an acceptable number of casualties, and we're still fully armed. Without knowing what else we're likely to have to face, there's nothing more for me to add."

D'vor nodded, then turned to T'via.

"The prophets will be pleased," she said quietly. "We have been instrumental in helping Jordan's people overcome a great threat. With him and Arden arguing our case with the upworlders, we have every hope of a mutually beneficial relationship." She hesitated. "Gods," she whispered. "I sound as though I'm giving a lecture."

"True," J'vina remarked, "but you spoiled the effect by admitting it. The prophets are *supposed* to—" A warning look from D'vor stilled her tongue, but T'via had not taken offense. She merely looked thoughtful.

"I've often wondered—" she began, then stopped, looking around at her expectant companions. "It doesn't matter," she ended lamely, then added as an afterthought, "I have a good feeling about our being here."

D'vor was reassured by her words. The ones chosen to represent the prophets were often sensitive to stimuli beyond the scope of most people. He had long since ceased to question such invisible forces and trusted T'via's instincts as much as he had those of her predecessor, L'tha.

"C'tis?"

The healer looked up wearily. For her, the most arduous tasks had come after the fighting, and she had been reluctant to admit to her weariness. However, once she stopped working, she had immediately succumbed to exhaustion, and one night's rest had not been enough to renew her strength. Now she sounded irritable.

"Two men are dead," she stated, "but they were an *acceptable* number of casualties, and I was unable to help them." The bitterness in her voice stung J'vina into a response.

"It happens," the warrior said, unabashed. "We were lucky we didn't lose more."

The two women stared at each other for a few moments, and D'vor wondered whether to intervene.

"I'm sorry," C'tis said eventually. "I find it difficult to be objective about such things."

"Our group would not be very effective if we all thought in exactly the same way," V'dal reassured her.

J'vina sat up and grinned. "You can say that again," she said. "I think *you're* all crazy, you all think *I'm* crazy, so we have to work even harder to protect each other." She lay down again, apparently pleased with her reasoning.

"I never realized that before," C'lin remarked, rolling his eyes and distorting his face in such an absurd manner that everyone began to laugh.

"It's an interesting philosophical theory—" V'dal began with feigned solemnity.

"No more lectures, *please*," T'via interrupted, smiling broadly. It was the first time she had felt comfortable enough to join in their banter, and her own gentle self-mockery was noticed—and appreciated—by the others.

D'vor was glad that the awkward moment had passed, but genuinely needed a report from C'tis. In this alien environment, her skills were more important than ever.

"No more speeches," he agreed, holding up his hands for quiet, "but we must hear what C'tis has to say." He turned to look at her.

"Even if we *are* all mad?" she asked mischievously.

"Definitely."

The healer grew serious once more.

"Apart from our two losses, the wounds inflicted during the fighting are not serious," she reported. "They will heal, given time, though we must watch for infections. I have no idea what could be lurking in a place like this." She paused, weighing her next statement. "What worries me most are the odd aches and pains that I can't explain. I won't be able to tell until I have the energy to do some proper tests, but I *think* they may be caused by the effects of the different sorts of light. It's possible that the tape may only give us partial protection, so prolonged exposure could be serious."

They were all quiet now, feeling and testing the truth of her words in their own bodies.

"What do you recommend?" D'vor asked.

"Continued vigilance," C'tis replied. "That's all we *can* do until I know more. We should restrict the total removal of tape as much as possible, however uncomfortable it is. And we already know that we must avoid full sunlight at all costs. It would be fatal."

"Anything else?"

C'tis nodded, but seemed reluctant to speak again. "Some of our party are in a mild state of shock," she said eventually. "They don't realize it themselves, but it could affect their actions."

"Why?" J'vina asked quickly.

"Because it clouds judgment and delays reaction times."

"Great! Just what we need in a fight!" The warrior was disgusted. "Perhaps that's why F'val . . ." Her voice died away as she remembered the death of one of her companions.

"What's causing it?" D'vor queried. "Do you know?"

"I can only guess," the healer replied. "Although our party was carefully chosen, none of us could have been prepared for the upworld. I think the shock of being in such open *space* for so long on our way here has unnerved some of us. Those affected feel lost . . ." She hesitated. "It shook me too," she added softly.

"It shook all of us," V'dal said.

They sat quietly, remembering the traumatic moment when Jordan had led them from their world into his. Even though they had tried to prepare themselves, physically and mentally, the simple fact of being able to see for such inconceivably long distances had filled them with awe. And to be able to look up at the stars, unimaginably far above them, and surrounded by so much *nothing*, was indeed an exercise in madness.

After that amazing beginning, their journey had been a series of revelations, interspersed with hardship and anxiety as they searched for protection from the terrible fire that Jordan warned them would rise in the eastern sky. Trees, flowers, the gently rolling, grass-covered hills, the glimpses of human habitation in the distance, animals, and the movement of wind and clouds—these were all sources of wonder and not a little fear. But it was the infinite dome of the night sky that forced their biggest mental readjustment. It was hardly surprising that some of their number found it difficult to cope.

"The rest here will do us good," C'tis said, gesturing at the dark, confining walls around them, "but we must prepare ourselves for *outside* eventually."

They were silent for a while. D'vor's request for information had provided him with more than he had bargained for. However, he knew that he had no alternative but to complete the round.

"How are the supplies, C'lin?" he asked, trying to sound as businesslike as possible.

"Fine," the soldier replied promptly, recognizing D'vor's intention. "We've plenty of food and water—even if the food *is* peculiar stuff. As far as C'tis and I can judge, it's perfectly safe and nutritious."

"No one's suffered any ill effects from it so far," the healer added.

"You just need to get used to the taste," V'dal grimaced.

"You've eaten worse in the past," J'vina responded. "We didn't always have B'van to cook for us."

There was a moment's silence. The death of their former colleague in an earlier battle still weighed heavily upon them. Not only had he been an expert cook, but his unfailing humor and honesty had made him an invaluable friend. C'lin, who had replaced him in the control group, cleared his throat.

"Well, you're stuck with me now, I'm afraid," he said. "So it's lucky that we don't have to do our own cooking. We're dependent on our hosts for that, as well as for our lodgings at the moment. But if we had to, we could cope."

"Good," D'vor concluded. "Anybody got anything else to add?"

"Yes, actually," J'vina answered. "What shall I do about the snake that's just come out of that hole in the wall?"

chapter 5

Horrified, the group turned to look. The snake was an ugly yellow, and as thick as J'vina's wrist. Only the upper part of its body had emerged so far, and that reared up, surveying the room as though selecting its first victim. Small malicious eyes gazed out from its flat, hooded skull.

J'vina rose smoothly to her feet, her sword hissing from its scabbard, and advanced slowly. The snake watched her for a moment, then withdrew into the darkness.

"You mean we've slept here all night with *him* in there?" C'lin shuddered as he spoke.

"Could we block the hole?" C'tis suggested.

"Yes, but there'll probably be other entrances," V'dal replied.

"Well, we can't watch every crack," the healer said wearily. "How will we get to sleep tonight?"

"Perhaps *we* can help," a woman's voice said from the doorway.

They looked round to see a man and a woman silhouetted in the entrance; around their feet were several smaller shadows. As Gemma and Arden came forward into the hall, treading carefully in the half-light, the meyrkats capered around them, their claws scratching on the stone floor.

Did you see the snake? Gemma asked them silently.

We have her scent, Ox answered for the clan. *Curve-food will be good*, he added in a tone that made it clear that he had not been happy with their recent diet.

Won't it be dangerous?

In the small-burrow, yes. So we will try to chase her out

into the open. The clan leader sounded as though he relished the prospect.

As the humans watched, the meyrkats split up, searching for other entrances to the snake's lair. They found two, and a pair of animals promptly dived into each.

"What's going on?" D'vor asked.

"The clan are hunting," Gemma replied. "They like snake meat—they call it curve-food—and it'll solve your problem."

"They've got their work cut out for them, then," J'vina stated. "That thing's much bigger than they are." Even standing on their hind legs, the meyrkats only came up to her knee.

"They work as a team," Gemma replied, but she watched the holes anxiously.

A few moments later, Ed's voice sounded in Gemma's mind. *Curve-food comes*.

She barely had time to warn the others when the snake emerged amid a volley of snarls and hisses. Ignoring the onlookers, it turned back to face its tormentors. Two meyrkat faces, fangs bared, appeared in the hole, and those left in the chamber ran up to divert the serpent's attention. It was soon surrounded by the entire clan, each meyrkat darting in to bite or claw, keeping the snake off balance, turning this way and that in an effort to escape. The war of attrition eventually began to take its toll, and the snake tired visibly.

"I can finish it now," J'vina said, her sword still in her hand. Her voice was full of admiration.

"Be careful," Arden warned. "It could spit poison into your eyes."

J'vina moved forward cautiously, and picked her moment well. In one clean movement, her blade separated the snake's head from its body—which twitched a few times, then lay still. The meyrkats made peeping noises of approval.

Gemma smiled at the fair-haired warrior.

"The meyrkats have named you clan-friend," she told her.

"I am honored." And J'vina sounded as though she meant what she said.

"They wish to know if you would like to share the kill," Gemma went on.

"Thank them for me," the other answered, after a moment's reflection, "but it is they who deserve the prize. They make an impressive team—I've never seen anything like it!"

Gemma relayed the soldier's message, then watched as the meyrkats disappeared once more through the hole in the wall.

"More snakes?" C'lin asked.

"No, just eggs," Gemma replied.

"Don't let them hatch!" V'dal said hurriedly.

"Not much chance of that," she responded. "The meyrkats are eating them."

For countless years, the city of Great Newport had been a center of corruption and the home of innumerable vices. It had housed both outrageous decadence and indescribable poverty. While a few had lived in luxury on their ill-gotten gains, many had been forced to scavenge amid the piles of stinking refuse of the poorest districts. Now all that had changed.

Now *everyone* was in the same situation. Nobody's future was certain; people were living from moment to moment, grateful for each mouthful of food, each respite from fear, each new breath.

A fortunate few had fled the city, taking with them whatever they could carry, but many more—either through greed or sheer stupidity—had clung to the symbols of their wealth and power, refusing to see the truth of the revolution. Several members of the Guild had been killed by raging mobs, as had members of their families and their servants. Countless guards had suffered the same fate, paying dearly for their past service to hated masters.

But after the first wave of fury and revenge had passed, and the tower had been destroyed, people began to look about them, and a few even began to ask, "What happens now?"

They saw a city in ruins. Two sections of the perimeter wall and nearby buildings had been reduced to piles of rubble. Many other houses were derelict—or smouldering embers. And yet, to those who had the eyes to see, Great Newport still contained many marvels. Ancient stone structures still stood, mocking the chaos about them; broad thoroughfares produced sweeping views of the city. Yet other districts were made up of mazes of streets and tiny alleyways.

Within these thoroughfares, all manner of things could once have been purchased—for a price. And that price was usually wealth or influence. And, given human nature, it would all be available again soon. What remained to be decided was whether Newport would be ruled by a new form of authority or whether it would revert to the ruthless law of the wild. The strongest among them knew the ways of self-preservation, while the majority cowered in silence, awaiting guidance.

Into this silence, word came that the underground was coming forward to meet the challenge. Rumors spread like wildfire, fearful whispers and scornful derision mixing fact with fiction. But one name stood out above all the gossip, a name that almost everyone knew, though few could claim truthfully to have met him face to face.

That would be remedied, this afternoon, in Colosseum Square.

Jordan was to speak.

Gemma had spent several hours in conversation with the people from the Lightless Kingdom. Their mutual fascination had been fueled by their partial knowledge of each other, and sparked by Arden's enthusiasm.

They had told her about their subterranean realm and the poison that was threatening to destroy it. Gemma and C'tis had discussed their respective healing abilities and methods. The meyrkats and Gemma's link with them had led to a description of her greater role within the scheme of magic. And, quite naturally, future plans had been the subject of much speculation. But, more than anything, the meeting had been an exploration into each other's worlds, and it ended with expressions of mutual regard.

"You're every bit as special as Arden claimed you were," T'via said. "The prophets send you their thanks and hope that you will be our lifelong friend."

"Arden is somewhat biased," Gemma replied, "but for my part, I echo the prophets' wishes. If I *am* special, it is only because of people like you. I never knew there were so many wonders in the world."

She looked around at her new friends, seeing their pale, almost ghostly skin, their huge eyes, and pale hair. *How strange I must look to them,* she thought, bringing a hand up to touch her own short red locks.

All tall-ones-shed-skins are strange, Ed commented, using the meyrkats' term for humans.

Gemma had almost forgotten that the meyrkats were there. They had long since reemerged from the holes, pronouncing the area clear of snakes, and had finished their meal of curve-food. The clan were now huddled together in a corner, and most of them were contentedly asleep. Only Ed and Av remained on watch.

You have a point there, Gemma replied. *Even we think so!*

That is why you have such long names, Av said. The meyrkats always gave long names to things they did not understand. Gem-ma and Ard-en implied a lack of self-knowledge that the little creatures could not comprehend.

"What are you grinning at?" Arden asked.

"The meyrkats are telling me how strange we humans are," Gemma replied.

"They have a right to that opinion," J'vina said. "I've never seen any group of humans work together as a team as well as they do."

"We could learn a lot from them," V'dal agreed.

"I already have," Gemma added.

"We'd better go now," Arden said. "Jordan will be speaking soon, and he'll need all the friends he can get."

Gemma and Arden left, promising to return with news as soon as possible. As the meyrkats stirred themselves and followed, they were watched by many pairs of large eyes.

The silence lasted until they were out of earshot.

"She's like a flame," C'lin said, unexpectedly lyrical. "All heat and light . . ."

"But so frail," V'dal added.

"And so much seems to depend on her," D'vor said.

"Everything," T'via agreed solemnly.

Colosseum Square was thronging with people when Gemma and Arden got there. As they looked out over the milling crowd, she glanced at Arden, recalling the day when he had spoken to a similar crowd, trying to enlist their support for a remote and beautiful valley.

"I hope Jordan does as well as you did," Gemma said.

"He won't have flocks of geese to help him." Arden replied, then hesitated. "Or will he?" he asked, eyebrows raised.

"What I did then was instinctive," she answered. "I'd help

Jordan if it became necessary, but this is one argument he really should win on his own."

Arden nodded. "Anyway, convincing the people here didn't do us any good in the end," he said.

"No, but we found *other* ways to save the valley," she reminded him, and they smiled at each other, remembering.

It was behind the imposing facades of the buildings that surrounded the square that much of the Guild's business had been enacted. The debating chamber, the courts of law, and many offices of administration and trade had been housed there. The basic structures had been too solid for angry crowds to destroy, but marks of violence were apparent in several places, and many of the rooms inside had been ransacked. Nevertheless, the square still represented the heart of the city.

Jordan was to address the people of Newport from the monumental Judges' Seat. This stood at the center of the northern side of the square and was constructed of the same light-colored stone as the government buildings. It rose dramatically above the arena; at its midpoint was a single stone bench, long enough to seat up to seven judges. In front of the bench was a solid stone table, and to each side of it, the platforms where past petitioners had addressed both adjudicators above and the crowd below. Arden and Gemma knew from bitter experience that the Guild's scales of justice had been unfairly weighted, but in Jordan's case, the decision would be made by the people alone, without the dubious expertise of the Guild's judiciary.

In the past, these public trials had been festive events, with many people betting openly on the result, and with many more shouting advice or heckling the speakers. Today, however, the mood was somber, and there was little conversation. Men looked suspiciously at their neighbors; many were armed.

"Gods, I hope he can convince them," Arden whispered as he and Gemma made their way closer to the stage. "It wouldn't take much for this lot to get out of hand."

"I'm glad the meyrkats decided to stay underground," Gemma replied quietly. The image of the clan sleeping peacefully in their own "burrow" helped calm her nerves a little.

As they moved on, they found a way opening up before them. Arden had the look of a man not to be trifled with, but it was Gemma's appearance that eased their passage. Red hair, so uncommon in this southern continent, had long been associated with magical creatures from the mysterious northern isles—and superstitions died hard, even in times of massive upheaval. Gemma heard several people whisper the word "witch," and noticed that a few made the hand signs meant to ward off evil. A mixture of emotions welled up within her.

They were only a short distance from the platform when there was a stir among the throng. Jordan had climbed up on to the Judges' Seat and now stood upon the stone table so that everyone could see him. Hewe, Egan, and several other men and women ranged themselves behind him. Jordan's dark face was calm but he radiated an obvious excitement as he surveyed his audience with bright eyes.

"My friends!" he called out, his deep voice carrying easily across the square. "My name is Jordan, and I come to you today to speak on behalf of what used to be called the underground."

Ragged cheers came from some sections of the crowd, while there were mutterings elsewhere.

"I say *used to be,*" Jordan went on, "because we no longer need to hide. We are in the open now!"

More shouts of approval echoed round the square. It was clear that the speaker had many friends who were intent on making their presence felt.

"Most of you will know that we in the underground had dedicated ourselves to the overthrow of the Guild." The noise level rose once more, but Jordan continued, raising his voice again. "Although we cannot claim all the credit, I tell you now that the Guild has been defeated, utterly destroyed. And I know for certain that the Overlord is dead."

He paused, waiting for the noise to subside.

"But we have no time for rejoicing!" he roared, taking the crowd by surprise. Silence spread over the square.

"Look about you!" Jordan cried. "You have all seen the destruction and bloodshed, the hunger and the homelessness. You know what challenges we face. The only way to face them is to do so *together.*"

They were listening now, even if all were not convinced.

"If we continue down the path where each man only looks out for himself, we will simply replace one form of tyranny with another. There is wealth enough in this city to provide each and every one of us with a decent life—a roof over our heads, food and drink on our tables, quiet sleep at night, and peace of mind. Is that so ridiculous a goal? We have the opportunity to make that dream a reality. But refuse it now, and it will not come again. This is our only chance."

A voice was raised above the muttering of the crowd.

"How are you going to pay for all this? Bread and meat don't come free."

"Newport has wealth in abundance. Cleve is a rich country—surely it is not beyond our abilities to see to it that every citizen benefits from that."

Yet another voice intervened.

"If a man works hard for years to earn a little luxury for his family, why should he give it up for those who have done nothing?"

Angry shouts and accusations followed from various sections of the crowd.

"No!" Jordan yelled above the clamor. "The just rewards of hard work or talent should never be denied. All I ask is that no man lie idly amid a surfeit while others starve. We *need* trade. We *need* our diverse skills. But there is work enough for all. Just rebuilding the parts of the city that have been destroyed and keeping our people fed and healthy will take up all our energies for a while."

The crowd were all listening intently now, and Jordan seized his advantage. He went on to tell them about the underground's practical plans; the centers they were establishing for food distribution, the building cooperatives, the appointment of guardians for each sector of the city, and the planned hospitals. He emphasized the need for volunteers in all areas and described how the work had already begun in some places. He received several shouts of support from those members of the audience who had seen these plans in operation, and for a time all seemed to be going well. Then a loud voice stilled the growing enthusiasm with a single question.

"What's to stop you forming a new Guild, with *you* as its Overlord?"

"What's to stop it?" Jordan replied promptly into the sudden hush. "*You* are! All of you. Do you think the people of Great Newport would stand for that after all they have suffered? Even if you don't trust me, don't belittle your fellow citizens. From now on, anyone who works for you will be answerable to *you*."

His impassioned words touched a chord with the crowd, who could sense his sincerity, and a roar of approval swept round the square. Jordan descended shortly afterward, gathering together volunteers to implement the beginning of his plans.

In the crush, Gemma and Arden could not get near him, so made their way from the square alone.

"He didn't say anything about the Lightless Kingdom—or the far south," Gemma said thoughtfully.

"He'll tell them when they're ready," Arden replied. "It would have just complicated the issue today. He won't be able to do anything unless he wins the people here first."

"You're right," she admitted, "but they'll have to know sooner or later. All the rebuilding in the world won't do them any good if . . ." Her voice trailed away. She was unwilling to share her premonitions.

chapter 6

For everybody in Great Newport, the next three months passed in a blur of activity. Many suspicions and hatreds were gradually overcome as more and more citizens felt the benefits of leadership by the underground. And as those benefits became increasingly obvious, the weaker among them grew strong, helped by cooperation and trust. Confidence grew, and with that came an added willingness to volunteer help for the various projects that the underground had set in motion. It became harder for the cynical to remain aloof; they grew increasingly isolated, and their numbers dwindled.

With patience and luck—together with the aid of numerous friends and allies—Jordan was gradually making good his word. Order *was* emerging out of chaos.

Of course, things did not all progress smoothly, and there were a number of setbacks and frustrations. Violence and robbery were commonplace at first, and it took much effort—and many unpleasant punishments—to establish the authority of local "wardens." These were men and women recruited from the general populace, but because so many people had suffered at the hands of the corrupt guards in the past, it was a long time before their replacements were accepted by the majority.

Beyond this, the major concerns were health, housing, and food. Building work and repairs were hampered by a lack of materials and by the relative inexperience of much of the newly recruited workforce. Organization was a nightmare, and there were many disputes over supplies and priorities. During the early days, Jordan and Hewe took it upon themselves to arbitrate personally, and they needed all their common sense and ready humor to remain diplomatic—and sane! However, as time passed, they were able to leave more and more in the hands of their colleagues as each found the role that best matched his talents.

The disruption of trade caused by recent events had also badly affected the food supply. Because the meager area of farmland immediately surrounding the walls of Great Newport could not support huge numbers of people, the city relied upon imports to sustain its community. The few farmers in the region had kept away from the city, for obvious reasons, making the situation even worse. But, as stability returned, local produce became readily available again, and Jordan made the reopening of the coastal road a priority. This enabled goods to be brought in from the more fertile regions to the east and west; it also meant that the underground could gather news from the other great ports of the province, Altonbridge and Clevemouth. At first, this news was patchy, but eventually, the information came through that the Guild's malign influence had been destroyed in those cities as well. The remnants of their organization had surrendered; some former members and employees were even permitted to join in the reconstruction work. Their threat had gone forever.

Altonbridge reported that ships from neighboring lands had ventured into the harbor. This was encouraging—and yet another sign that confidence was returning, and that trade would follow. One of these vessels was from the faraway country of Quaid, and when Gemma heard this, she felt a jolt of secret pleasure. The ambiguous footnote she had read in one of the floating city's libraries had become fact.

Jordan had made a public statement that no one would starve, and he kept that promise. For a time, many went short, but desperation was always kept at bay. However, the initial scarcity of food contributed to the most worrying of all the city's problems. Great Newport had never been the healthiest of places, even in calmer times, and now the upheaval and hot summer weather had combined to produce epidemic conditions. Infections spread quickly, and efforts to rid the city of the omnipresent garbage and the vermin that came with it were only partially successful. In one area, however, an unexpected alliance brought notable results.

The meyrkats were often in danger of being mistaken for rats, and were therefore very keen to show their usefulness by helping to clear the underground passages of the noxious pests. Gemma explained their duties to them, but as she had tasks to perform elsewhere, they were left to work with the soldiers of the Lightless Kingdom, who were also particularly suited to this dark though unpleasant task. J'vina especially relished the hunt, and took great pride in her growing understanding of and fellowship with the clan. She wished fervently that she could share the telepathic communications of these energetic little creatures, but made every effort in its absence to familiarize herself with their habits, teamwork, and audible communications. For their part, the meyrkats readily accepted the warrior as a clan-friend and gave Gemma glowing reports of their exploits when she had the opportunity to pay them a brief visit. On one such occasion, Gemma received a surprising insight into the lives of both the meyrkats and the people of the Lightless Kingdom.

. . . and then the fat-squealer ran into the burrow, Ed reported. Fat-squealers was the clan's derisive term for the rats.

Where the curve-food ate them, Ox added with evident satisfaction. The snake had done their work for them.

We chased out the curve-food, Ed went on eagerly, *and J'vee bit it with her hard-claw.*

The meyrkats could not come to terms with J'vina's full name, finding it much too long and full of self-doubt. However, they had definite respect for the powers of her hard-claw—or sword.

Clan-friend fast, Av concluded. *Move with us.*

What do you mean? Gemma asked.

The clan found this difficult to answer. It was Ox, their leader, who eventually replied.

Clan fight, J'vee fight. Moving inside the same.

Piercing black eyes regarded Gemma curiously. The clan obviously knew exactly what Ox meant, but they wanted their friend to understand as well. They were still unsure of the meaning of human facial expressions, and so watched her very carefully.

Gemma was mystified at first, then felt a possible glimmer of understanding. She turned to J'vina.

"How did you know the snake would come out of the burrow . . . the hole, I mean?"

For several long moments, the warrior did not answer.

"I just knew," she admitted hesitantly. Seeing that this was not enough, she added, "I've watched the clan often enough now to be able to predict what they're planning. I suppose I must have interpreted their calls and the noises from inside the hole."

"So you were acting on instinct?"

"Not exactly." J'vina paused again. "Something inside me *told* me to move. I just knew what to expect."

Moving inside the same, Gemma thought to herself.

"It happens sometimes within the control group," the soldier went on. "I suppose it's because we know each other so well. That's why we're a team—like the meyrkats."

The echoes of magic, Gemma mused. *Why is it that only some groups can put it to its full use?* Then her thoughts were interrupted.

"But not as good?" D'vor said, grinning in the gloom.

"We'll never be as good as them," J'vina replied seriously. "They're incredible."

"There are things we can do that they can't," V'dal pointed out.

"Those are only physical limitations," she argued. "As a team, they act as one, as though the entire clan had just one mind. We'll never be able to duplicate that."

Don't be so sure, Gemma thought, but said nothing. Ideas were beginning to form, but they were not yet ready for general consumption.

"Being in the same mind as you would be unnerving, to say the least," V'dal teased. "I'm not sure I'm ready for that!"

"Nor me," C'lin added. "We might find out what you *really* think of us!"

"I've told you that often enough," J'vina retorted, abandoning the attempt to remain serious. "You're a bunch of clod-hopping incompetents who've only got this far because I've been here to protect you."

She glared about her, defying them to disagree.

"You speak the truth, O Great Warrior," C'tis declaimed, bowing deeply in mock obeisance. J'vina accepted both the comment and the bow with a nonchalant wave of her hand, but she was soon laughing; the meyrkats, recognizing the healer's gesture, and noting J'vina's, tried to copy both, with comic results.

"See! Her tribe bows down before her," T'via exclaimed

between giggles. "And waves in worship. Better not let the prophets hear about this idolatry!"

"Be quiet, all of you," J'vina retorted as several meyrkats picked themselves up off the floor. "Or I'll set the clan on you!"

C'lin and V'dal cowered in mock terror, their laughter louder than ever.

The camaraderie of the control group rolled over Gemma like a wave, and she began to see the sense of Ox's words. *Moving inside the same.*

"Come on, C'tis," she said, as the laughter subsided. "We can't stay here all day. Time to get back to work." She said good-bye silently to the clan, and received their multivoiced response.

Happy-lies-all-know are good? Ed added to the chorus.

Yes, Gemma replied. *In times like this a sense of humor is very valuable—it's sometimes the only thing that keeps us going.*

You are weary, Gem-ma, Av said solicitously. *Rest in your burrow.*

I will, Gemma replied, but she smiled then, thinking of her "burrow" and the time she had been able to spend there with Arden. Those hours had been too few and very precious—and had not always been spent resting.

The two healers left, C'tis hurriedly refixing her silkfish protection. All those who had a healing skill—whether magical or mundane—had been in great demand in the ravaged city, where all kinds of disease and injury had to be treated. Gemma had thrown herself into the work wholeheartedly. Although the relentless work had drained her of energy, her only regret was her lack of contact with Arden, who was equally busy with other tasks, and the fact that she was unable to see much of the meyrkats. She occasionally found herself thinking of their long-term goals, and the mystery of the far south, but she accepted that nothing could be done until Cleve was healthy again—in every sense.

C'tis was also working incredibly hard, in spite of her difficulties with the increased light. She was aware, from her treatment of Arden, that her people and the upworlders were fundamentally the same, and she gave her time and effort unstintingly. She compared notes with Gemma, and they found many similarities in the ways that their powers and senses worked. While each worried about the other's health and possible exhaustion, they nonetheless spent long hours giving all they had—and became firm friends in the process.

At first, many of C'tis's patients found her appearance unnerving. However, she soon dispelled the doubts of all but the most timid or prejudiced with her calm competence and undeniable effectiveness. Gemma noted her dedication and came to understand Arden's high regard for her.

C'tis was the most visible of all the people of the Lightless Kingdom, and her appearance helped dispel many of the wilder rumors about the alien warriors. Even so, their reputation was still enhanced by endless gossip. Among the most common stories were the tales of *invisible* soldiers who could approach unseen and strike silently, and of the black giants who could see in the dark—even though they had no eyes.

Those who knew the truth—though they were still in a minority—corrected the fallacies and confirmed the facts. This minority was deliberate; Jordan saw no harm in having reputedly invincible allies and had not wanted to complicate events in the city by making general knowledge of the plight of the Lightless Kingdom and his pledge to help them. As a result, he told the full story to only a few trusted individuals and depended upon their discretion. The riddle of the far south was known by even fewer people. *That* was something that would be faced in due course, but which would now only be a distraction from more pressing matters. Panic and despair would be less than useful at the moment.

Fortunately for the underground's parochial concerns, the city was blessed with external peace for some months. There were no further attacks by skyravens, and therefore no visible reminder of the power to the south. In addition, the blue-flame wall to the west of Clevemouth seemed to have stabilized. Although it had been approaching the city steadily, though slowly, it now appeared to have stopped. So yet another external threat had lessened, allowing the citizens of Cleve and its cities to concentrate on their own concerns. Few people were farsighted enough to see that the whole world was under threat—and, for the time being at least, that was probably a good thing.

chapter 7

In that hectic period of Gemma's life, two events stood out for her. The first of these was the departure, just over a month after her battle with Mendle, of the men and women from the Lightless Kingdom. Their decision to return to their own realm had been inevitable; D'vor and T'via had to report to their people and the prophets, V'dal was needed for his guidance, and both C'lin and J'vina—as well as many others in the group—wanted to return to a more familiar world. Out of all the control party, only C'tis really wanted to stay, knowing that her special skills would be sorely missed. However, she could not countenance either splitting up their group or remaining on her own. And in her heart, she saw the necessity of their return.

Before they left, they held extensive discussions with Jordan and others, and plans were laid for future contact. D'vor agreed that as well as telling the prophets of their upworld exploits, he would try to persuade them to send research parties into the dangerous, poisoned regions of the southern caves. The purpose of this would be to try to locate the source of the pollution; if possible they would also attempt to pinpoint where this was *above ground.* That way, when an expedition from Cleve was finally mounted, there would be a definite target. Jordan could not promise when this would be, but assured them that it would be his first priority once the "local difficulties" were resolved.

Several volunteers from the underground agreed to go to the Lightless Kingdom with their guides, in order to help with the search for the pollution, and also to strengthen the links between their two races. Gemma and Arden were sorely tempted, but knew that they were needed in the city.

"I'll see your world one day," Gemma vowed.

"I hope so." C'tis's reply was soft—and fervent.

"You will be welcome at any time," D'vor added warmly. Like all his party, he had been impressed by this flame-haired woman, whose delicate beauty could not disguise her inner strength.

"We'll be back," V'dal told her, "as soon as we have any news worth reporting."

"And if the meyrkats ever get fed up with this place," J'vina put in, "send them to us—they seemed quite at home the last time. And I'm going to miss them."

"I'll tell them," Gemma promised, knowing full well that, much as she herself would miss the meyrkats, there would probably come a time when she and the clan would have to part. "The giant burrow will be their second home."

And then it was time for them to go. Their journey began with a walk through the tunnels and out under the city wall. A starlit night greeted them as they emerged, farewells were exchanged, and then the people of the Lightless Kingdom and their new colleagues slipped away into the darkness.

"I hate to see them go. It makes me so sad," Gemma said.

"Partings are always sad," Arden replied, putting an arm around her shoulders. "And they've come to mean a lot to us."

Gemma nodded, and said nothing about her ill-defined worries for the future of the Lightless Kingdom.

The meyrkats grew depressed by the absence of their hunting partners, and, as Gemma could spend little time with them, the clan decided to leave the city. Settling into the holes near the dry river bed where Arden had first met them, they enjoyed being out in the open again, in terrain more suited to them. The barren plain outside Newport was the next best thing to their native desert.

There is no stinger-food, Ox complained when Gemma asked him if there were any comforts she could provide for their new home.

Well, I'm not becoming an importer of scorpions, even for you! she replied, laughing.

The second event of importance occurred almost a month later and was even more traumatic. Unlike the first, it could not have been foreseen.

It was Hewe who saw them first. He had been watching the eastern approaches to the city from the tower that surmounted the main gate. A large shipment of supplies was expected from Altonbridge, and he wanted to be sure it was distributed as quickly and effectively as possible once it arrived. The food and medicine were needed urgently, and, even though he knew the convoy would be well guarded, he was always nervous on such occasions. Three supply caravans had recently been waylaid on the coastal road.

His spirits rose as he saw dust rising from the hooves of several horses, but as the riders drew nearer, his hopes turned to alarm. Waiting only until he was quite sure that the riders all wore the sinister clothing of the Gray Raiders, he sent an urgent message to Jordan, who joined him quickly. Together they watched the party approach.

"How many?" Jordan asked, squinting into the harsh sunlight.

"Thirty," Hewe replied. "Forty at most."

"No real threat then."

"Not directly."

They were both thinking that even a small number of the gray-robed fanatics could present quite a problem.

"What do you think they want?" Hewe asked, but Jordan only shrugged in reply.

They found out later that morning, by which time half the city—Gemma included—were aware of the new arrivals. She had particular reason to be concerned by the presence of the raiders. They believed that all their world's ills were to be blamed on the newcomers from the northern isles, whom they described as "demon-spawn"—and whom they frequently killed. As a red-haired "enchantress" from the far north, Gemma was to them the personification of evil. She had been captured by them once, kept alive for reasons that had never been explained, and had escaped only by a combination of unexpected help and good fortune. She had no wish to fall into their hands again.

Her opinion of them had also been lowered—though she had not thought such a thing possible—on learning of the raiders' deadly and unreasoning enmity toward the people of the Lightless Kingdom.

This group of raiders was setting up a temporary camp

some three hundred paces from the city wall. They were watched by several interested onlookers.

"I've never seen that many of them together out in the open like that," Hewe commented.

"What does it mean?" Gemma asked, unable to hide her anxiety in spite of the present security of her position.

"I think we're about to find out," Arden replied, pointing.

Two raiders were now riding toward the city gate. Once within hailing distance, they halted, looked around at the derelict area where the shanty town had once stood, then turned their gaze to the group on the tower.

"We come in peace!" one of them called. "And unarmed. We also bring you a gift. Will you permit the two of us to enter as envoys?"

Jordan's expression remained impassive, while those about him exchanged puzzled glances.

"Ride to the gate!" he called back, after a few moments' deliberation. "It will be opened." He turned, then stopped, glancing back at Gemma and Arden. "You two stay here," he ordered. "I don't think this is a trick, but I'm not taking any chances. Hewe, come with me."

As the two men began their descent of the stone steps, Gemma called after them, "Be careful!"

Hewe grinned up at her. "Careful is my second name," he said, then pretended to trip over his own feet, only "saving" himself from falling down the stairs at the last moment.

"Idiot," Gemma whispered, grateful for his attempt to distract her with laughter.

"There's nothing to worry about," Arden reassured her, smiling. "Those two are more than a match for any Gray Raiders." His contempt for the fanatics, at whose hands he had also suffered, was obvious.

Less than an hour later, a messenger came to ask them to join Jordan in his old underground room. Jordan's various bases had necessarily expanded and now covered several parts of the city, but he still used his original headquarters for meetings of a delicate nature.

When she and Arden were ushered into the room, Gemma could not prevent a slight shiver when she saw that the two raiders were still with Jordan and Hewe.

The eyes of both gray-clad men widened perceptibly at

her entrance, and the younger one paled visibly. For a few moments, no one moved or spoke.

"This is Gemma and Arden," Jorden said eventually, his deep voice as smooth as ever.

The raiders nodded in acknowledgment, but their eyes showed that the introduction had not been necessary.

"These gentlemen are Galar and Tomas," Jordan went on calmly. "They have been telling me of a change of attitude within their organization. It seems that enlightenment has at last dawned upon some, and travelers from the north are no longer their automatic enemy."

So you've decided to test their resolve by presenting them with me! Gemma thought, not sure whether to be angry or amused. She did not speak.

"As a token of friendship, they have brought something that may interest you, Gemma." Jordan indicated a bag that had been placed on a low table, but Gemma did not bother to look inside. She already knew what it contained.

"Dragonflower seeds," she said quietly.

The younger raider, Tomas, began to explain, gabbling his words in his haste.

"They are an invaluable aid to healing," he began. "Used with . . . properly . . . used properly they can . . ."

"I know their uses," Gemma interrupted, her voice stronger this time. Arden had used a paste of the seeds to soothe Gemma's burns after finding her wandering in the Diamond Desert. "I also know how they can be abused."

In excessive doses the seeds caused exotic dreams and wild hallucinations. In Great Newport's earlier, degenerate days, the drug had been widely used by the rich and decadent for just that purpose. What was more, Gemma believed that the Gray Raiders had been instrumental in supplying this market. Now Galar spoke.

"It is true that in the past we were guilty of profiting from such abuses," he said evenly. "But that will never happen again. Many things have changed within my sect—and this is just one of them. We offer you this gift in good faith."

He went on to explain that the Gray Raiders' organization had been purged of certain undesirable elements.

"They had lost sight of our original goals and were using us only for personal gain. Now that things are changing in Cleve we can no longer tolerate such behavior."

Arden snorted.

"So you've give up trading on other people's misery!" he spat venomously. "So what! Your *original goals* were to kill as many innocent travelers as you could. Is that what you're going back to? And are we supposed to congratulate you for it?"

Gemma felt him trembling with rage at her side. He glared at Galar.

"No!" Tomas burst out, then was silenced by a gesture from his superior.

"I will not deny that your accusation has some validity," Galar said.

"That's big of you!" Arden returned sarcastically.

"Please hear me out," Galar begged. "I know that you two have suffered at the hands of the Gray Raiders, but I—and others like me—have always been against the obscene violence that many of our number advocated."

"Then why are you still a raider?" Gemma asked sharply.

"Because I *still* believe that the power calling travelers like yourself to this land is evil," he replied earnestly. Hearing this statement from such an unexpected source gave Gemma and Arden pause for thought; considering the Gray Raiders as potential *allies* was something new to them. They glanced at each other, then waited in silence for Galar to continue.

"What we should have been doing all this time was searching for the *truth*. That will never be found by killing. I believe that those who are called here are the innocent victims of the *real* enemy. And I have been able—at last!—to persuade most of my colleagues of the reality of that fact."

"And the others?" Arden demanded, steel in his tone.

"We have gone our separate ways," the raider replied. "They are renegades now, outlaws persisting in idiocy."

"Which group is Aric with?" Gemma asked suddenly.

"Aric is dead." Galar answered, knowing that it had been this man who had captured Gemma. "However, his deputies, Wray and Yarat, escaped, and they are among the outlaws. What we need to do now," he went on, "is to work together, combining our knowledge and resources in order to defeat our common enemy. And that is what we have come here to offer."

As soon as Hewe had escorted the two raiders out of the room, Gemma turned to Jordan.

"Can we trust them?" she asked.

"I'm inclined to think we can," he replied solemnly, "but I'm not about to do so without taking necessary precautions."

"Gods!" Arden burst out. "Just like that? They walk in here and say—we're *awfully* sorry, we were wrong, everything will be different now—and you just accept it?"

"No," Jordan replied with infuriating calmness. "I shall naturally require further proof of their good intentions. But the omens *are* encouraging. They came here unarmed, with a genuine peace offering. What could they hope to gain if they were planning treachery? They have been open with me, and I have given nothing in return. And just think—if their offer is genuine, what an opportunity it represents. Can we afford to pass it up?"

"That's a big if." Arden was sullen now.

"True."

"And what did they say to you about the Lightless Kingdom?" he asked, burning with resentment on his friends' behalf.

Jordan smiled.

"I think I put our case across reasonably well," he said wryly. "Galar agreed to cease hostilities and will begin their immediate withdrawal from the caves."

Arden was astonished.

"I'll believe that when I see it," he breathed.

"So will I," Jordan said. "And only then. If he keeps his word, it will be evidence of their real intentions."

"It seems too good to be true," Gemma said quietly, slumping down into a chair.

"Let's hope not," Jordan replied.

In the days that followed, all the evidence pointed to Galar's sincerity. More gifts were received, no violence was reported, several outlawed raiders were brought in for trial, and, best of all, messages came from the Lightless Kingdom to say that the soldiers were indeed leaving the desert caves.

Gemma accepted the dragonflower seeds—and was grateful for them. In tiny doses the drug was remarkable in the way that it could speed recovery and restore flagging energies, so necessary to the healing process. Yet she still could not help a shudder of apprehension whenever she caught sight of a gray-clad warrior and shied away instinctively from the images they produced in her mind.

However, she was soon preoccupied with even more disturbing visions.

chapter 8

Her dreams began innocently enough, but their recurring themes soon began to disturb her. She woke in the night regularly, interrupting the sleep she so desperately needed. At first, the sight of Arden's peaceful, sleeping face so close to her own was enough to calm her fears. But later, when the dreams turned to unfathomable nightmares, she needed the greater reassurance of his arms about her. Arden never objected to being waked in those dark hours and held her closely.

"What's the matter?" he would ask sleepily.

"Nothing. Just a dream," was Gemma's standard reply.

However, Arden began to see the fright and fatigue in Gemma's eyes, and he eventually made her tell him as much as she could remember about her night-visions.

"This can't go on," he said firmly. "You have to share your problems. That's what I'm here for." He smiled crookedly at her, but Gemma said nothing. "You need some decent sleep," he went on. "We both do. If you're not careful, you'll exhaust yourself completely."

"I'm always so tired in the dreams too," Gemma admitted. "Just moving is an effort."

"You're working too hard," Arden said flatly. "I don't care *how* much you're needed, you've got to start thinking of yourself."

"Soon," she replied, "but not yet. I can't give up on the children now." Her special concern in recent days had been a ward of youngsters, some little more than babies, who had contracted a vicious disease that threatened their eyesight and, in the severest cases, their lives. Long hours of patient effort and hard work had yielded a cure for some, but in several cases, Gemma's own special powers had been vital. The epidemic was waning now, but its final defeat was still some time away. Until then, she would not stop—and Arden knew it.

"All right," he conceded. "But make sure you get as much help as you can. And tell me what's been bothering you all these nights."

Gemma was silent for a while, gathering her thoughts.

"At first it was very similar to the dreams I used to have of you in the Lightless Kingdom," she said eventually. "But then I kept going back to that cave with the fungus. What did you call it?"

"Soulskeep."

"With the picture on the wall of the god—"

"The God Beneath. Rael."

"In my dreams the picture started moving, and then it became *real*. It was huge, and it moved until it was looming over me. It was terrible—as if the Earth-mind had waked up and was watching me, engulfing me. I felt so small, so helpless . . ." Her voice trailed away, and she swallowed hard before continuing. "But what happened next was much worse. Rael broke into pieces, flying in all directions, and leaving a huge, gaping black void. That made me feel awful, as if *I* was empty too." She shuddered.

"Why didn't you tell me about this before?" Arden asked quietly, stroking her hair.

"Because I didn't think dreams could hurt me," she replied, deliberately not looking at him. "It didn't make any sense and, besides, you needed your sleep as much as I did. You said so," she added weakly.

"Idiot," he said fondly. "Do you really think I could be so selfish where you're concerned?"

"No, but—"

"No buts," he interrupted. "I don't know what those images mean, but just talking about them might help. And maybe someone else *will* know."

"Who?" Gemma asked hopefully.

"T'via," he suggested. "I'll ask Jordan to contact her."

"I hadn't thought of that," she admitted.

"You're not the only one round here with brains," he replied, grinning. "Now go back to sleep."

"I haven't told you everything yet."

"Then get on with it!"

"In the dream . . . in the caves . . . I heard the siren song."

Arden stiffened.

"You're sure it was in the dream, and not real?" he asked anxiously.

"Yes. I haven't heard the real call since I've been here—you know that."

"Thank the gods for small mercies," he sighed.

"But why should I hear it down there?" Gemma was puzzled. "Why should it be connected to the Lightless Kingdom?"

"It all links together somehow," he replied. "You told me that yourself. All you have to remember is not to give in to it."

"But in the dream I *can't* fight it," she told him. "I always turn south immediately."

"Oh."

"I can't help it," she protested defensively. "And that's when I meet you."

"That should help!" He smiled.

Gemma did not respond. If anything, she grew even more distressed.

"It *would* do if you were real," she said quietly, "but as soon as I touch you, you turn into an elemental and fly away." Tears began to form in the corners of her eyes, and she shook with misery. Arden tightened his arms about her, snuggling close.

"I'm real," he whispered into her ear. "I'm real."

After a few moments, he asked, "Anything else?" He wanted to ensure that her confession was complete.

"Just one thing," Gemma replied, "and it's even more confusing." She paused. "I've seen little Gemma, Mallory's daughter, several times."

"But she hasn't even been born yet!"

"I know, but all the same, I *have* seen her. The really odd thing is that while I'm in the caves, she's in the mountains . . . or is it the other way round? . . . but somehow we're still together." Again Gemma paused, frowning now.

"That's easy enough to interpret," Arden responded confidently. "You want to go back to the valley to see the baby born."

Gemma looked at him, new hope dawning in her eyes.

"We'll go as soon as you can leave the children safely," he stated firmly. Happiness welled up within Gemma. "Now get some rest."

Within moments, they were both fast asleep, safe in each other's arms.

Now that the idea was there, the thought of returning to the valley became a touchstone for Gemma's flagging spirits. Whenever her constant tiredness threatened to spill over into exhaustion, she would wallow in anticipation of the time of rest and beauty to come. Even so, the dreams continued to plague her and she often grew irritable. Arden spent more and more time at her side, finding a deputy for his own duties; he became a proficient nurse and a firm favorite with the young patients.

The relief of knowing that the end to her toil was in sight and the comfort of Arden's support kept Gemma going. To her delight, Jordan wholeheartedly approved of their plans.

"You've done more than enough here," was his opinion. "More than we can ever thank you for. The valley will do you both a lot of good—and I'd welcome some news from that part of the world." He paused before adding, "In any case, Gemma, I think it's important that you be there when your namesake is born."

"I think so too," Gemma replied, returning his smile.

Soon after that conversation, they received another pleasant surprise.

"I'm coming with you," Hewe told them, grinning. "I promised Mallory I'd get you back in time, and I *daren't* break my word to her."

"That's wonderful!" Gemma exclaimed, giving the big, bearlike man a quick hug.

"Careful," he responded in a stage whisper. "Arden will get jealous."

"Of you?" Arden retorted. "That'll be the day!"

"And we'll be able to visit Adria on the way," Hewe went on. "We haven't heard from her for a while, and it'll be good to catch up with her news. And at least *she* appreciates my true worth."

Gemma's spirits rose another notch. *The latentor*, she thought. *What secrets will she reveal to me this time?*

* * *

Gemma had been in Great Newport for just over three months, and summer was turning slowly to autumn when she finally conceded that the children no longer needed her. Her decision was still a difficult one, but once made, the feeling of relief was almost overwhelming.

Jordan had asked whether they'd need an escort for the journey, but both Arden and Hewe preferred to travel light.

"Besides, we have a witch to protect us," Hewe explained with a grin.

However, the trio did not leave Great Newport unaccompanied. Gemma had explained her plans to the meyrkats, and the clan, knowing that the valley was not for them, decided to accept J'vina's earlier invitation and return to the giant burrow. They would thus journey together to the entrance of the Lightless Kingdom, then the humans would ride on alone.

It took them three days of leisurely traveling to reach the rock-strewn valley. Bidding farewell to the clan was painful for Gemma, but the animals were in high spirits, and she herself was longing for the peace of the valley. They had no doubts that they would meet again. Gemma watched in silence until the last of their tails disappeared into the labyrinth of stone that hid the entrance.

"They mean an awful lot to you, don't they?" Hewe said, as they turned eastward.

"Yes. I know now why the wizards on my home isle were so attached to their familiars." Gemma glanced at Arden, but he made no comment. "There is something very special about being able to communicate like that. I can't explain it properly."

"I don't think I'd like to have someone knowing what I was thinking all the time," Hewe remarked.

"Oh, but you keep your privacy," she told him. "Only projected thoughts can be heard properly, and anything else comes through just as vague feelings—if at all. It took me a long time to feel comfortable with it."

They talked for a while as the horses plodded slowly onward, cutting across the northern tip of the Diamond Desert and heading for the coastal road.

"You're very quiet," Hewe told Arden later.

"I'm just thinking," he replied, summoning up a smile.

"About the Lightless Kingdom. I wish we'd heard from T'via before we left."

The messages that *had* been received were encouraging, reporting that the Gray Raiders were leaving, and giving the general progress of the expedition to the south, but there had been no word about Gemma's dream-images.

"They have too much to worry about without trying to interpret my nightmares," she said.

"I know, but—"

They were interrupted by Hewe.

"What on earth is going on over there?" he exclaimed, pointing ahead.

As the others looked, they saw in the distance two men on horseback. They were riding back and forth, galloping a few paces, then rearing up, their horses' hooves skidding in the sand, before setting off in another direction—only for the cycle to repeat itself. Faint echoes of their angry shouts floated over the desert. The whole spectacle was so ridiculous that Hewe and Arden began to laugh, but Gemma had seen something that they had not; a strange, miragelike flickering that danced around their horses. In addition, the riders were wearing gray—and looked unpleasantly familiar.

"Raiders," Gemma warned.

Arden's eyes narrowed.

"I've seen the thin one before," he said, serious now.

"It's Wray, isn't it?" she replied.

Arden nodded.

"The other one is Yarat," Gemma went on. "They are dangerous men!"

"I don't think they're paying us much attention at the moment," Hewe remarked, watching the whirling dance. "All they're trying to do is stay on their horses! Should we get a bit closer?"

They rode forward cautiously, intrigued in spite of their misgivings.

"There's something—" Hewe began.

"I see it!" Arden exclaimed. "An elemental?"

"No. This is different," Gemma stated. She was quite sure that the flickering image was not a product of an elemental creature, but felt an inexplicable reluctance to find out what it really was.

They were close enough now to see the sweat slick on the

horses' coats, their foaming nostrils, and the wildness in their eyes. The riders were hanging on for dear life as their mounts bucked and turned, but at last they caught sight of the newcomers. Their reaction was—to say the least—odd.

Yarat's eyes rolled heavenward, and he screamed as though in mortal agony. As his horse reared up, the fat man fell to the ground, landing awkwardly amid a whirl of apparently disjointed limbs. Wray fared better, being both lighter and more agile, but he screamed obscenities at them, then pleaded frantically.

"No more! No more!" he sobbed. "Kill us, demon—put an end to it." Taking one hand from the reins, he pointed at Arden, and shouted, "I cannot kill you again! Why torment us so?"

His horse bucked again, but Wray managed to control his fall, and slithered to the ground unharmed.

Before they could react, something happened to the air in front of them. What had been nothing suddenly became hazy and *squirmed*. An image formed there slowly, becoming more and more real as they watched. This time it was their turn to be horror-struck.

Arden was face to face with himself.

chapter 9

"Who *are* you?" Arden breathed.

"That's what I'm trying to find out," the other replied, sounding very matter-of-fact.

Gemma trembled at the sound of the quiet voice. It was Arden's, but hollow somehow.

Wray looked up from the ground, stared for a moment, then laughed like a maniac.

"There's *two* of them!" he gasped.

Arden turned to Gemma and Hewe.

"What *is* it?" he whispered. But neither of them could find enough voice to answer.

The apparition spoke again.

"I've been trying to find out who I am," he repeated, "but I'm already fading." He held up his right hand. "Look! I can see right through it. Unless I find out . . ." He paused, then pointed an accusing finger at the fallen raiders. "*They* know me, but they won't tell. So I followed them." He sounded resentful now. "The horses ran away. They *always* run away from me. Even the first ones, just after the fog cleared . . ." He looked at each of the trio in turn as their mounts shifted uneasily beneath them. "Can *you* help me?"

"You're sure it's not an elemental?" Hewe asked softly. The answer came, unexpectedly, from Wray.

"Of course it isn't! Do you think I couldn't deal with a single elemental?" He sounded genuinely disgusted.

"Then what—" Hewe began, but was interrupted—the explanation for the unnerving apparition had occurred to his friends simultaneously.

"The floating city!" Arden exclaimed.

"When it moved you in space but not in time," Gemma finished for him.

"Wynut *said* there might be complications later," Arden remarked.

"Looks like he was right," Hewe commented dryly.

"What are you talking about?" the spirit-Arden asked suspiciously.

"If I told you who you are, would you be happy to go in peace?" Gemma replied.

The ghost nodded slowly, hope shining in the unnervingly familiar eyes.

"You were once a man called Arden," Gemma told him. "But he is gone from this time now." She went on, unaware of the strange looks that she was receiving from her companions. "It is right that you should fade, and you will be much happier when you do. You already know that time and space do not constrain you."

The apparition nodded again, then looked embarrassed.

"Was I a good man . . . when I was real?" he asked softly.

"The best," she responded, with a lump in her throat.

He smiled, relieved. "I wondered . . . when the horses ran away from me."

"Go now," Gemma said. Her voice was kind, but firm.

"Thank you." He smiled.

And the image dissolved before their eyes. This was no elemental transformation, but something infinitely more basic. The second Arden had been confronted with the impossibility of his own existence, and so was fading away into a timeless nothing. The air above them was soon clear once more, and only one last, faint, windblown echo remained as the ghost repeated his own name. Then that too faded into oblivion.

Gemma swallowed hard, fighting back her tears, while Arden shivered convulsively. Hurriedly dismounting, they fell into the comfort of each others' arms.

"Are you all right?" he whispered.

"I think so. Are you?"

"I feel very peculiar," he admitted. "It's not often you meet your own ghost."

Hewe had also dismounted and was now advancing on the fallen raiders, sword in hand. When he reached the inert form of Yarat, he called over his shoulder, "What shall we do with these two?" When he received no reply, he bent over the still body. "His neck's broken," he reported, then turned to Wray. "Perhaps I should finish this one off too."

"No!" Gemma called, not sure whether Hewe was serious or not.

Wray lifted his head and looked at Arden.

"You're *real*," he said slowly, madness flickering within his eyes.

"I wish people would stop sounding so surprised when they say that," Arden remarked facetiously.

Wray suddenly scrambled to his feet, and Hewe tensed, his sword at the ready.

"You're no match for me!" Wray screamed. "That *thing* might be able to survive a sword through the heart, but *you* can't." He sounded exultant. "You've done my work for me!"

"Aren't you forgetting that there are three of us, and only one of you?" Hewe asked.

"That's where you're wrong!" the raider yelled. "I have friends!" He raised his arms dramatically and shouted, but made no attempt to draw the sword that hung from his belt. Wisps of blue appeared from the sand all around him, filtering into the air, then dancing. Within moments, the elemental circle was complete.

"I am invincible!" Wray cackled. "And I can dispose of you as I choose." Turning his back on Hewe, he advanced menacingly toward the others; the elementals moved with him like a giant blue shield.

"I should have killed the two of you before," he gloated, "but I'll enjoy it even more now. Kneel and beg for mercy—or my elementals will destroy you."

To Wray's utter astonishment, Arden just laughed.

"I think not," he said calmly, then stepped forward, Gemma at his side.

"Death to the demon-spawn!" Wray shrieked. "Burn!"

Gemma and Arden were totally unafraid as they stepped into the blue flames. They sensed at once the resentment that the elementals felt toward Wray's power over them, and knew that they longed for friendship—something the raider would never understand.

They stopped only a few paces from the now bewildered Wray, and Arden smiled.

"These creatures are my friends," he said quietly. "And I set them free."

A rush of joy and warmth swept through him, and the elementals began dancing wildly, soaring into the sky, away and back again, before disappearing completely.

"No!" Wray's agonized voice cracked. "Come back!" He tried to reach for his sword, but felt the tip of another come to rest lightly on the back of his neck.

"I wouldn't, if I were you," Hewe advised, his voice as cold as his steel.

The raider's knees gave way and he fell to the ground, where he lay sobbing, a broken and exhausted man.

Hewe took his sword from him.

"Traveling with the two of you is even more exciting than I'd hoped," he commented dryly. "I haven't seen a show like that since . . . since . . ." His memory failed him.

"And this is only when we're on our holidays," Gemma said brightly. "Just think what we'll be like when we *really* get going."

"I wouldn't mind the rest of our journey being a *little* more restful," Hewe replied. "In the meantime, what shall we do with *this*?" He prodded the sniveling heap with the toe of his boot.

"Let him go," Gemma answered.

Both men looked at her in astonishment.

"He'll be no threat to anyone now," she explained. "Just look at him."

"But he would have killed you," Hewe pointed out.

"He didn't, though."

"Yes, but—"

"What can he do now?" she asked. "He's alone and friendless. Yarat's dead and even the elementals he was so proud of have deserted him. If he doesn't see sense and try to make his peace with Galar, he's not going to last long. And if he does, who knows? He may even be of some use."

Arden was skeptical.

"How could we ever trust him?" he asked.

"Just threaten to come back and haunt him again," she replied, grinning. "That should sort him out!"

At their feet, still desolated by the mind-numbing loss of his self-esteem. Wray squirmed at her suggestion.

"I'll do anything," he mumbled.

"Leave him here," Gemma said. "Unarmed."

Wray looked up, his face wet.

"Not here, not in the middle of the desert. Please."

"You're only half a league from the coast road," Arden replied disgustedly. "And you might be able to catch one of those horses."

"Where can I go?" He started crying again.

Sickened, Arden turned away.

"Do you really think he could be useful?" Hewe asked Gemma.

"He has some skill. Perhaps he can be taught to put it to better use," she replied.

"All right." Bending down, Hewe pulled Wray up by his collar and glared at him, their faces only a handspan apart. Fear showed clearly in the raider's eyes. "Listen, you little dung heap. You don't deserve this, but we're going to give you a chance. You're to go to Great Newport, tell Jordan and Galar that I sent you, and offer to help with anything they suggest. Understand?" The question was accompanied by a good shaking, which emphasized Wray's answering nod. "I'll be back there soon, and if I hear *anything* bad about you, you're dead. Do I make myself clear?"

Wray nodded again.

"How do I get to Jordan?" he whispered.

"I'll give you a note," Hewe replied, then shoved him away hard. Wray sat down with a bump.

"Is that wise?" Arden queried.

"It'll be in code," Hewe replied. "If he uses it, Jordan will have the whole picture, and not just what Wray might want him to know. If he doesn't, he won't even get inside the city walls."

As Hewe walked over to his horse to write his message, Wray sat perfectly still, looking at his three conquerors nervously, as if unable to believe his good fortune. Hewe returned and pushed the letter into his hand.

Then he and his friends mounted and rode away without a further word. When they were some distance away, Arden glanced back and saw Wray trudging slowly after the runaway horses.

"What do you think he'll do?" he asked.

"He doesn't have any choice," Hewe returned.

"I hope he *does* go to Jordan," Gemma put in. "Whether we like it or not, he's in one of the circles of magic—and in the end we'll need *all* their help. Every single one of them."

chapter 10

It took them another eight days of traveling—uneventful this time—to reach Adria's isolated cottage. The whitehaired old lady was standing outside her front door, watching as they approached. As they drew closer, she peered at them with bright eyes.

"About time too!" she grumbled, then turned on her heels and hobbled inside, leaning heavily on her stick.

Arden raised his eyebrows. "Are you sure we're welcome?" he asked uncertainly.

Hewe, who knew the old lady's ways well, smiled.

"If she greeted us with sweet words, I'd wonder what was wrong," he said as they dismounted. "She may seem prickly on the outside," he went on loudly, "but inside, she has a heart of gold."

He was answered by a single word from within the cottage. It shocked Arden, but Gemma and Hewe burst out laughing.

"You two go on in," Hewe ordered, grinning. "I'll see to the horses."

"Are all latentors like this?" Arden asked.

"How would I know?" Gemma replied. "She's the only one I've ever met." She grinned, seeing his reluctance to enter, and asked, "You're not scared, are you?"

"Of course not! It's just that she's . . . not quite what I'd expected. You described her as being wise—and gentle . . ."

"And so she is," Gemma put in. "Come and meet her."

Gemma had gone to some pains to explain to Arden that latentors were individuals who, while lacking any appreciable magical talent themselves, could recognize it and occasionally enhance it in others. It was Adria who had finally given Gemma the beginnings of confidence in her own abilities. Arden had been impressed by the description, but found it difficult to reconcile it with the crusty old woman he had just encountered. Feeling like a nervous schoolboy, he followed Gemma inside.

They sat down side by side on a comfortable divan while Adria settled herself into an armchair. The parlor smelled of herbs, and a small fire burned in the grate, in spite of the day's heat.

"Adria, this is Arden," Gemma began.

"I know who he is, child," the old lady said, her voice sharp but not unkind. "One look at the two of you and it's obvious you're lovers."

Arden felt even more uncomfortable.

"Are we *that* transparent?" Gemma asked, smiling.

"Why is it that each generation believes it's the first to ever experience love?" Adria muttered, a twinkle in her eyes. "I may be old, but I'm not blind." She raised a wrinkled hand and pointed at Arden. "You are very lucky, young man. There must be something wonderful in you for Gemma to love you so. She is a remarkable girl—you'd better look after her properly, or you'll have me to answer to. Among others."

"I swear to cherish her," Arden responded promptly and with feeling. "On any power you choose."

"He'll do," she said.

"*I* think so," Gemma replied, taking his hand and squeezing it gently. "We were kept apart for long enough to be sure of each other."

"And you're making up for lost time now," Adria commented.

"What do you mean?" Arden asked, embarrassed, but feeling that he had to ask.

Adria looked at him from under lowered brows.

"You know perfectly well what I mean! And I don't suppose you've even given the consequences any thought," she commented dryly.

"*What* consequences?"

The old woman looked heavenward in exasperation. "Children!" she said. "It wouldn't be altogether convenient if Gemma were to become pregnant just now, would it?"

It was Gemma who broke the ensuing silence.

"You're right. Neither of us even considered it," she admitted, wondering at the direction the conversation was taking. The physical expression of their love had seemed only natural—undeniable and unquestioned. The possible results of their enraptured thoughtlessness now seemed all too obvious.

"Well then, it's a good thing you can't," Adria said.

"Can't?" A second anxiety replaced the first in Gemma's heart.

"You pay a price for the magic in you," Adria replied calmly. "Surely the wizards told you that?"

Gemma nodded slowly, remembering the time in her childhood when one wizard had gone to incredible lengths to renounce his magic, thus enabling himself to father a child.

"But there's . . . nothing *wrong* with us?" Arden asked quietly.

"No. You're lucky, young man. You'll get all the fun and none of the responsibilities."

At that, Arden leaped to his feet, his face suddenly dark with rage.

"No!" he cried. "You're wrong! You know nothing of me if you can think that. I *do* have responsibilities—to Gemma, and to myself—and I'll never shirk them. Just because she . . . we can't have children . . ." He stopped abruptly, and let out a sigh of exasperation as he stared at Adria. The old lady was shaking with silent mirth. He gradually regained his composure, and after a few moments, he smiled.

"Have I passed the test?" he asked softly, sitting down again.

"Oh, yes," Adria replied, still chuckling. "Oh, yes. It *is* rather convenient though, isn't it?"

Gemma and Arden found that they daren't look at each other; soon all three were laughing.

When they were calm again, Gemma asked, "Will I ever be able—?"

"Who knows?" Adria replied. "Only time answers such questions. You have more than enough in your future not to feel the lack of babies. To tell you the truth, I'd have jumped at the chance of something like this when I was your age. For a start, I wouldn't have been lumbered with those two great oafs that call themselves my sons."

"You know perfectly well," Hewe said, carrying a tray into

the room, "that those *oafs* have brought you a great deal of joy."

"At a cost," she retorted. "Like *all* gifts from men."

Hewe passed round the drinks.

"With a little nutmeg in it," he told their hostess. "Just how you like it."

Adria refused to be impressed.

"I suppose every man has a few good points," she remarked, sipping from her mug." Even those that are all brawn and no brain—like this one."

"Flatterer," Hewe responded, unperturbed. "What were you talking about while I was working?"

"You would find it inconceivable," Adria replied. As Gemma and Arden groaned at her awful pun, she added, "You're the biggest gooseberry I've ever seen."

"It's a sacred duty," Hewe said, catching on. "If I wasn't around to keep an eye on them, they'd be too exhausted to travel."

"Please!" Adria returned. "You're embarrassing them!"

"No chance of that," Hewe replied. "They're shameless. It's quite touching, really." He pretended to wipe a tear from the corner of his eye.

"Stop it!" Gemma exclaimed, laughing. "The pair of you!"

They stared at her, wide-eyed and innocent. It was obvious that Adria and Hewe were very fond of each other—despite their continual battle of words.

"So tell me what you've been doing since you last disturbed my peace," Adria demanded. "That's what you've come for, isn't it?"

And so they told her of their travels, of Arden's sojourn in the Lightless Kindgom, and of the conflict in Great Newport. Adria had already heard parts of the story, but insisted on hearing the whole thing at first hand. When it came to the battle with Mendle and the involvement of the circles of magic, she made Gemma go over some of the details again and again. Eventually, her understanding was complete.

"Fascinating!" she whispered. "You remembered what I told you, then?"

"Every word," Gemma replied. "I even *understand* some of it now," she added, smiling.

"I *knew* there was something different about the source of your energy," Adria went on, "and now I know what. But I'm still not sure why your use of the circles' energy does not diminish them—there's still a piece of the puzzle missing."

The others were silent for a while, giving her time to think. Eventually she asked them to continue their story. She was told of the slow rebuilding of Great Newport and of Gemma's unsettling dreams. Gemma had hoped that Adria might be able to throw some light on the ominous imagery, but the old woman only agreed with the ideas that Arden and others had put forward; she had nothing further to add. Then she was told of their decision to return to the valley and of their encounter with Arden's "ghost." This episode amused her greatly.

"I can just see those stupid men," she chuckled, "confronted by someone they've tormented in the past, but who is invincible now—and who insists on making their lives a misery. Poetic justice!"

"It wasn't exactly enjoyable, even for us," Arden said.

"I can understand that," she replied seriously. Then she grinned wickedly, and added, "That'll teach you to accept rides from strangers."

"But it was only because he was helped by the floating city that he was able to get there in time and bring the meyrkats in," Gemma pointed out.

"It left his double *out* of time," Hewe said thoughtfully.

"You did well to persuade the spirit to go gently," Adria said. "It could have made things *very* confusing."

"That's putting it mildly!" Arden said. "The elementals were bad enough—"

"Speaking of which," Adria interrupted, "you appear to have some magical talent yourself, young man."

Arden was taken aback and unwilling to accept this. "It's just being friendly," he insisted.

"Don't underestimate that ability," she replied. "Come here. I want to examine you."

Arden glanced worriedly at Gemma.

"I know I *said* I was wizard," he protested, "but I was joking!"

"Go to her," Gemma told him. "She won't hurt you. Don't you want to find out more about yourself?"

"No," he answered defiantly.

"Typical male!" Adria muttered.

"Humor her," Hewe said. "It's quite harmless—honestly."

"How do—?"

"Oh, Adria looked into me years ago—and soon gave up in disgust," the big man replied with a grin.

"Hewe is too tied to practical things," Adria put in. "The energy's there, but he won't find it in this life."

Gemma gave Arden a gentle push and he reluctantly knelt in front of Adria's chair. He felt horribly self-conscious while the old lady placed paper-dry thumbs on his temples and rested her other fingertips below his ears. Adria shut her eyes, then grew very still.

Time passed slowly. Eventually, she took her hands away and slumped back in her chair. A long, weary sigh escaped her.

"Well?" Arden demanded.

"You're too slippery for me," she replied weakly. "I came close to grasping something, but it kept sliding away. And I thought *Gemma* was a mystery!"

"What do you mean?" he asked, bewildered. "You can't just leave it like that!"

But Adria could. She had fallen asleep and did not even stir as Hewe carried her upstairs to bed.

chapter 11

Gemma went to talk to Adria early the next morning, as she had on her previous visit. The old lady was already awake and was sitting up in bed as though expecting visitors. She smiled as Gemma entered the room.

"How did he take it?" she asked, a mischievous gleam in her eyes.

"Not very well," Gemma admitted. "I've been up half the night trying to make him see sense."

"Sometimes, putting up with men who won't see sense is the price we have to pay for love. All women find that out, sooner or later."

"I'll pay it gladly."

"We all do," Adria sighed with resignation. "And yet somehow it gives *them* an excuse to call us the weaker sex—and feel justified when they do so!"

"Don't you like men at *all?*"

"Nothing could be further from the truth!" the old woman exclaimed. "I just see them—and the workings of their minds—rather more clearly than most."

She noted Gemma's quizzical look and added, "Oh, I'm not so old that I can't remember what it was like to be young and in love. I was as blind as anyone when it came to my man. It's only looking back now that I can see all his faults." She paused, remembering. "His worst was that he couldn't be bothered to stay alive long enough to keep me company in my dotage." There was a look in Adria's eyes that brought a lump to Gemma's throat, but the old woman stirred herself, and when she next spoke, she sounded quite cheerful again.

"And I'm not too old to answer a few questions," she

stated. "You didn't come here to listen to my ramblings. What did Arden say about last night?"

"He said he'd felt a strange tingling all over his body and that he saw flashes of light."

"And?"

"He couldn't explain any more. Just odd feelings, he said. But when I pressed him to *try* to explain, he just got annoyed." Gemma shook her head and smiled wryly. "He was rather sullen for a little while and ended by saying that *nothing* had happened. It was as if he wanted to deny the whole episode."

"Well, that's about standard," Adria commented, "but in all honesty I can't blame him for being confused. There was *something* there, but I'd never encountered anything like it. And as he's built a lot of defenses to protect himself from whatever it is, then perhaps it's better that it stays hidden."

"What do you mean?"

"Well, his experiences with the elementals point to a powerful instinctive reaction. So far, he's put that reaction to good use. It may be that meddling with his self-knowledge could harm that."

They thought about this in silence for a few moments, then Adria went on, "His mind's energy is too random—there's nothing to focus on. And he's become adept at screening things off, hiding them even from himself . . ." She hesitated, seeing Gemma's worried expression. "You know more of his story than I do, child. I'll not pry." Then the kindness and concern in her face were replaced by a wicked grin.

"We'll just have to *pretend* we know what's going on," she said. "After all, we have a reputation to keep up!"

"All right. I'll just smile knowingly and try to avoid the subject," Gemma agreed, grinning back.

"From the sound of it, he'll avoid it for you."

Gemma nodded, and then something else occurred to her.

"This *something* of Arden's" she asked, "do you suppose it could be earthwild—from when he ate all that raellim? His body may not be clear of it yet."

Gemma remembered C'tis's description of earthwild; *part substance, part energy, part dream-image—and wholly enigmatic.* It was a force that moved within anyone who ate the Lightless Kingdom's sacred fungus, producing strange visions and even stranger abilities.

"I don't know," Adria replied honestly. "I've never encountered it before, so I'd have no way of recognizing its effects."

That seemed to bring to an end their discussion of Arden, and their talk turned to more general matters. Gemma left Adria in good spirits some time later and went to rouse the still slumbering men. They made their farewells shortly afterward and set off on the last stage of their journey.

As Adria had predicted, Arden made no attempt to discuss his experience, and Hewe had enough sense not to raise the subject.

Three days later, they approached the northern side of Raven's Crag. This imposing rock wall was broken only by a sheer-sided chasm, from which the valley's river emerged in a series of waterfalls and boulder-strewn rapids.

"It looks impassable," Arden commented. Although he had visited his beloved valley many times, he had never approached it from this direction.

"You're right," Hewe answered. "It was only because we were so bloody-minded that Dale and I were able to find the way up last time."

From below, the precipitous trail that zigzagged its way up the cliff was completely invisible, further evidence of the way the valley protected itself from the outside world.

Arden had been back to the valley only once since the events that had restored the river, and that had been only an overnight stop. Now he could not wait to see his friends again and to revel in the tranquillity and beauty of this very special place. When they reached the top of the crag he could not restrain his eagerness and led Gemma and Hewe down the relatively gentle slopes into the valley at high speed. Once within its invisible boundaries, though, he reined in his mount and breathed deeply. The green-gold patchwork landscape of the valley stretched out before them in all its glory, rimmed by mountains and filled with peace. All manner of trees, flowers, and shrubs flourished here, and there was an abundance of wild animals and birds, living peacefully with their domestic brethren and the human population.

The trio rode on slowly, savoring every moment of their return. They needed no words to describe their feelings of joy or fast-growing contentment; indeed, none of them could have explained just what it was that filled them with such delight.

Mallory's sons, Vance and Jon, were the first to see them as they approached the farmhouse late that afternoon. The boys had evidently been perched in the branches of a tree and had thus had a good view down the track that led from the northern end of the valley. They dropped to the ground and ran into the house, yelling, "They're here! They're here!"

Then they came running to meet the newcomers, shouting with glee. A few moments later, Mallory followed them at a more leisurely pace, on the arm of her husband, Kragen. The riders dismounted, and were greeted warmly.

"Please note that I am a man of my word," Hewe remarked, kissing Mallory's cheek. "I've brought her back in time."

"But only just, from the look of you," Gemma added, looking at Mallory's enlarged belly.

"Revolting, isn't it," her friend replied, laughing.

Gemma thought that she had never seen Mallory look more radiant, and said so.

"Thank you for those kind words," her friend responded, "but I feel as big as the farmhouse! Still, it won't be long now. Will you look at her for me?"

As Gemma reached out and held Mallory's proffered hands, the others grew quiet. She closed her eyes and let her special inner sense take her within her friend's body, noting its health and vitality. Gemma was astonished at the sense she had from the child within—of how impatient she was to make her entrance into the world. It felt as though she were making every effort to be ready ahead of time; even before the child was born, it was obvious that she would not lack determination.

"She's beautiful," Gemma breathed.

"Takes after her mother then," Kragen commented, but Gemma did not hear him. She had experienced a surge of awareness that transported her into what was at first a familiar scene; the image of the child to be as she looked down upon the world from a great height. It was as though she were standing on top of a mountain. Gemma had seen the same thing several months earlier, and subsequently in her dreams, but this time the vision did not fade. In the valley below the mountain, a vast chasm opened up, spewing forth fire and molten rock. Then the child waved a tiny hand, and the flames disappeared. Now the valley was filled with water, a serene, fathomless blue lake that stretched into the hazy distance. All this flashed through Gemma's mind in an instant, and its suddenness left her shaken. She could not recover quickly enough for her friend to miss her momentary disquiet. There were questions in Mallory's eyes, but she did not ask them. Instead, she simply asked about her baby's health, and Gemma was thankfully able to reassure her; the rest could wait until they had a chance to be together in private.

"Let's go inside," Kragen suggested. "There's a meal waiting."

"What wonderful timing!" Hewe applauded. "Traveling always gives me an appetite."

"The timing was easy enough," his host replied. "We knew you were coming—Winder saw you riding down from Raven's Crag. 'Galloping as if they had demons behind them' were his exact words."

"We've seen our share of *those* right enough," Arden laughed, "but not here."

"We'd have come to meet you, but—" Mallory patted her stomach.

No one questioned the fact that Winder's sighting of the newcomers had so quickly become common knowledge in the valley. The community shared a sort of special mental osmosis that they called "knowing." If a piece of news was of interest to them, only one person needed to learn of it, and in less than an hour, everyone else knew it too—without any conventional communication. It was not mind-talk such as Gemma shared with the meyrkats, but something less specific, more universal. This shared knowing was yet another facet of the valley that made it such a special place.

The meal was a celebratory occasion, with beer and wine to wash down the delicious food. As always, they ate no meat; the valley people preferred to share their home with the animals and lived instead on the plentiful and varied produce of their land.

It seemed at first as if Gemma and Arden would have to spend all evening talking, but Hewe eventually interrupted the flow of questions, explaining that he would have to leave the next day.

"Why can't you stay longer?" Mallory protested.

"You know you're more than welcome," her husband added.

"Thank you, but I have to get back," Hewe replied. "I need to spend some time in Altonbridge, and Jordan can't spare me for too long. Perhaps these two can tell you all about their exploits after I've gone. But before I go, I'd like to know how things are here in the valley. Jordan wanted a full report, and if I'm going to remember anything you tell me, I'd better hear it before I have any more of this." He lifted his half-empty glass and grinned. "So—what's been happening since I was last here?"

"There's fish!" Jon exclaimed with a five-year-old's enthusiasm. "Big pink ones and small silvery ones. In the river," he added by way of explanation.

"He doesn't want to know things like that, silly," Vance said scornfully, showing off the experience of his greater years.

"I want to know *everything*," Hewe told the younger boy tactfully. "But perhaps your mum and dad could help me now, and you can show the fish to Gemma and Arden tomorrow."

Both boys seemed satisfied with this arrangement and waited in polite silence for their parents to begin.

"The news is good," Kragen said in his slow, calm way. "And the best of all is the river. It's still running strongly, though we're well into autumn now. In previous years—before the drought—it would have just about dried up by now, and it *certainly* wouldn't have been deep enough for fish." He smiled at his sons.

"Of course, it's not as full as it was in spring," Mallory put in, "but if it keeps on like this, we'll have enough water stored for a whole year!"

"Even if the previous pattern is reestablished, and the river only flows every other year—" Kragen said.

"Which would mean it drying up at midwinter," Mallory interrupted.

"—we'll still be all right for *next* year," Kragen concluded. "Our reservoirs are full, and the irrigation systems are working better than ever."

Gemma's thoughts wandered to the rocking stone at the center of the Diamond Desert. *Will it move when the other meyrkat clan sing this year?* she wondered. *I hope so.* Then the mountain would move, and the river would switch from the valley to the Lightless Kingdom. Until the next year. *Can it really be almost a year since I restored that spell?*

Lost in thought, she missed some of the conversation, and when she started listening again, Mallory was talking.

"There are some long-term effects of the drought that need more time to heal," she said, "but on the whole, we've had a wonderful summer."

"It was a good harvest," Kragen confirmed, "and when it's ready, this year's vintage should be the best ever."

"Remind me to visit you again then," Hewe said.

"I'll do that," the farmer replied.

"There's every sign that our health is returning to its former state," Mallory went on. "Even the old ones are energetic again. Of course, we'll never be able to replace those who died prematurely—"

"But a few of those who left the valley when things were at their worst have returned," Kragen added. "They were ill, but are recovering now."

"The knowing is back to full strength," Mallory said thoughtfully. "It was only when it started faltering that we began to appreciate just how important it was to us."

"How's Kris?" Arden asked.

"He's fine," Mallory replied. "Still a little confused about that vision of Gemma he shared with you, but apart from that, he's his usual self."

"It shook me up, too," Arden said, looking at Gemma, the relief that his love was safe showing in his eyes, "but at least now we know how to explain it."

"I'd like to talk to Kris," Gemma said. *About a lot of things.*

"He's on his wanderings at the moment," Mallory answered, "but I wouldn't be at all surprised if he didn't come visiting soon."

"Good."

"So all is well," Hewe concluded. "That's the sort of news I shall enjoy taking back to Jordan." He paused, then drained his glass. "What were the *older* vintages like?" he asked innocently.

chapter 12

Hewe left the valley the following morning, happy in the knowledge that all was well there. His two friends were already beginning to benefit from its tranquil atmosphere.

"Don't even *think* of coming back until you're ready," he told them. "You've earned your time here. If anything happens and we need you desperately, we can always get a message through."

"Thanks for everything, Hewe," Gemma replied. "Safe journey."

"It's going to be very boring without you two along to stir things up," he responded, grinning, then turned to Mallory and Kragen. "Thank you once again for your hospitality," he said. "And thank you for the care I know you'll take of these two."

"You're more than welcome," Mallory answered. "Come back soon."

"I intend to."

"When?" she persisted. "Gemma will be here for at least a month and a half. She's got to see her namesake born, remember?"

Gemma was puzzled by this—she felt sure that the baby would not be that long in coming—but said nothing. This was not the place.

Hewe's scarred face was screwed up in concentration as he pretended to consider Mallory's question.

"When did you say this year's vintage would be ready?" he asked eventually.

"Not for several months," Kragen replied, smiling.

"Expect me then," Hewe decided. "Farewell."

He rode away amid a chorus of good-byes, the two boys running alongside his mount for a short while.

"Now," Mallory said, turning to Gemma, "We have some serious catching up to do!"

"So you see," Gemma concluded several hours later, "it's not over yet. We've won a battle, but the war goes on. Whatever it is that's threatening from the far south, we haven't beaten it yet."

"As soon as Jordan gets Cleve on a secure footing," Arden added, "then he'll be able to spare people to help us try and solve the mystery. But he's got months of work to get through first."

Their audience had been spellbound from the start. Even the two boys, normally so active, had been content to sit and listen to this story of magic, battles, great cities, and the monstrous metal tower.

"No wonder Hewe said you'd earned your time here!" Kragen remarked. "That's the most incredible tale I've ever heard." He shook his head in disbelief.

"I liked the part about the meyrkats best," Jon said brightly. "I *wish* we could meet them." He and his brother had always been fascinated by the exploits of Gemma's small furry friends.

"We all wish that," his father said, smiling. "Come on, boys. The day's almost gone and we've still got work to do. The farm won't run itself, you know."

"Have you finished the story?" Vance asked quickly, anxious not to miss anything.

"We've finished," Arden replied. "Come on. I'll give you a hand with the chores—that way they'll get done quickly."

As they went out, the boys were peppering Arden with questions—and advice about the tasks he was to perform.

"They've grown," Gemma said fondly, remembering the small, pale children she had met on her first visit to the valley.

"Haven't we all?" Mallory replied, resting her hands on her swollen midriff. She had been very quiet for a while, and now her smile seemed a little forced. Gemma said nothing, knowing that she had to wait for her friend to speak.

"The most amazing part of everything that happened," Mallory began eventually, "is that none of it affected us at *all*.

Ever since the river returned, the valley has been as peaceful and lovely as it ever was. And yet all these earth-shattering events were taking place outside."

"That isolation is one of the reasons why this place is so very special," Gemma replied.

"Yes, but aren't we just hiding ourselves away? It seems that sooner or later the world will catch up with us—it's already tried to. How long can our serenity last?"

"I don't know," Gemma said, serious now. "But I *do* know that there are a lot of people—not just me and Arden—who will fight to keep the valley as it is."

"You've already proved that," Mallory said. "I don't doubt the two of you, or the others like Hewe, but there are so many other problems now—the Lightless Kingdom, all of Cleve, and the far south. It seems so unjust that with such violent upheaval all around us, we just carry on happily in our private, perfect haven. It makes me feel very guilty."

"Perhaps you *will* be drawn into it, in time," Gemma admitted, "but that's all the more reason to appreciate the beauty of what you've got now. I certainly intend to!"

But Mallory was not to be sidetracked.

"The far south," she said thoughtfully. "That's where everything's coming from—the poison under ground, the sky-ravens, Mendle's powers—"

"Yes, and probably the dam that deprived you of the river."

"And the siren song?" Mallory asked quietly.

"That too."

"But how can this evil power, *whatever* it is, produce a song of such beauty?" Mallory had only heard the unearthly music once, in the mountains, and never in the valley, but it still sang in her memory. "You must think seriously about this connection, Gemma. After all, it was what drew you to our land in the first place."

"I know," Gemma replied. "And I intend to find out why. But it can't bother me here."

"Have you heard it at all recently?"

"Only once, on the way to Great Newport with Hewe and Ashlin." Gemma paused. "Since then, I've only heard it in my dreams."

"What was that like? It must have been terrible." Mallory was aghast.

"Better than when I'm awake!"

They were silent for a while.

"I was so sorry to hear about Ashlin," Mallory said softly.

"I know. If I hadn't let him come with me—"

"It was his choice."

Gemma nodded sadly. "They told me he died bravely, trying to save me. I must go and see his family tomorrow."

Mallory maneuvered herself to her feet. "I'd better get some food ready. They'll be ravenous after working in the fresh air."

"Let me do it," Gemma protested. "You should be resting."

"I'm not an invalid!" her friend replied. "There's a while to go before this little lady makes her appearance."

"Not as long as you think," Gemma told her.

"What do you mean? I *can* count, you know."

"Well, I think little Gemma might be in a bit of a hurry," Gemma said. "I could sense her impatience."

"How long will it be then?"

"A month, maybe less."

"Is that *all* you sensed?"

Gemma hesitated, but realized that further prevarication was impossible. So she described her mountaintop vision.

"What does it mean?" Mallory wanted to know.

Gemma shrugged.

"I know she'll be special, somehow. Beyond that, I'm as mystified as you."

"Special . . . for good or ill?" the mother-to-be wondered.

"No child of this valley—more especially, no child of yours—could be a force for anything other than good," Gemma stated firmly. "You need have no worries on that score."

Mallory nodded, though she was not wholly convinced.

Then the two women busied themselves preparing food, taking refuge in the necessities of daily life. As the evening drew on, Arden and the others returned. They were in high spirits, the boys full of their exploits and their plans for the days ahead. The meal and conversation helped Gemma and Mallory relax, and they began to anticipate events with pleasure, not just uncertainty.

The valley wove its familiar magic about them all.

* * *

The next morning, Gemma went to see Ashlin's parents. They were devastated by the news of their son's death, and though Gemma was generous in her praise of him and of his courage, nothing could assuage their grief. They had not been able to understand why he had gone in the first place, and now could not understand why his life had been wasted on a conflict that had nothing to do with the valley. There had at least been a reason for his earlier travelings, they said. He had helped bring the river back. But this was senseless.

Harsh and unforgiving words mingled with their tears, and Gemma could say nothing to bring them consolation. She knew herself to be guiltless of Ashlin's death, but saw how it must appear to his family. She was glad that Arden had not accompanied her. He would have been angered by their accusations and defended her too vigorously—with possibly disastrous results. As it was, she left their house feeling utterly wretched and was glad to see Kris approaching. If anyone could help them, he could.

Gemma waved as the crippled man made his steady but erratic way toward the house. Kris returned her greeting, but did not stop and, much as Gemma wanted to talk to him, she was glad.

They need him more than I do, she thought sadly, and went on her way; it did not even occur to her to wonder at his timing.

She found Arden sitting on the riverbank with Vance and Jon. The water was still flowing strongly.

"There's one! There's one!" Jon shouted excitedly as she approached. Gemma ran to join them and saw the sheen of a large fish beneath the surface.

Arden glanced up at her and saw the pain behind her smile.

"All right?" he asked gently.

She nodded and took his hand in her own, squeezing it tightly.

Arden pulled her toward him and kissed her.

"You should have let me come with you," he whispered in her ear.

"No. I had to do it alone. And Kris is with them now."

"Good. We'll talk about it later."

Gemma felt the color rise in her cheeks as she saw the

boys regarding them with intense curiosity. Grinning, Arden released her.

"Vance, didn't you tell me that there were fox cubs near here?" Arden asked.

The boy nodded. "In the woods," he replied, still looking at Gemma. "I expect they'll be quite grown up by now," he added uncertainly.

"I'd like to see them anyway," Gemma said, as eagerly as she could. "Will you show me?"

The expedition set off, and the boys were soon their usual lively selves once more. Gemma and Arden followed more slowly, enjoying the youngsters' antics and relishing the fact that they were together and in such a lovely place. He took her hand, and she smiled happily.

Kris arrived at Kragen's farmhouse that evening in time to join their meal. Each home in the valley always kept a spare place at table and a bed for Kris, in case he should arrive unexpectedly. Although he stood no taller than a child and his spine and limbs were badly distorted, there was nothing at all sad about him. He invariably brought a sense of warmth and happiness to those he was with, and it was for this, as well as his ability to create visions and occasionally foresee the future, that he was so respected.

After the meal, Gemma managed to talk to him and Mallory alone. Kris already knew most of her story, but she wanted to ask some specific questions of him. Kris could not speak, and communicated with the valley people through hand signs, which Mallory would be able to translate for Gemma when necessary. However, before Gemma could begin, Kris leaned forward in his chair and took both her hands in his. She felt joy surge through her, so intense that she almost cried out. Images filled her head of a group of people gathered together in celebration; among them were Ashlin's parents, happy and smiling. Kris was showing their future forgiveness.

Gemma looked into his strange slit eyes and thanked him silently. *No wonder they love you so*, she thought. As Kris withdrew his hands and relaxed in his chair, Kragen appeared at his side and handed him a glass of wine, then gave two more to the women.

"Don't worry," he said. "We'll leave you in peace." Mallory smiled at him as he returned to the kitchen.

Kris, his glass held awkwardly in crooked fingers, drank with obvious pleasure.

"I know you may find this unpleasant," Gemma began, "and I'm sorry for that. But would you tell me about the vision you showed Arden?"

Kris looked momentarily uncomfortable and did not answer. Then he very carefully put down his wine, and his hands fluttered so quickly that Gemma missed some of his meaning.

"He says there is a very strong bond between you and Arden," Mallory translated. "The vision of you came from that bond. But there must have been a higher power involved, because that was the only vision Kris had ever had of something *outside* the valley."

"*What* higher power?" Gemma asked.

Kris shrugged and shook his head, gestures that needed no interpretation.

"Do you know of the circles of magic?" Gemma asked, changing the subject.

The birdlike hands spoke again.

"The valley is like a circle?" Gemma guessed, looking to Mallory for confirmation. "But have you truly never seen anything else beyond the valley?"

"No. That was the only one," Mallory said, watching Kris's fingers. "Ever."

"Oh." Gemma's hopes fell. Then she described the image of little Gemma on the mountaintop and asked Kris about the far south and its siren song, but he could not enlighten her. He reported that he had seen nothing unusual in Mallory's future, or in her child's. The fragments that Gemma had seen were a mystery to him, as was the entire subject of the far south. He seemed downcast by Gemma's obvious disappointment, but as they passed on to other, more pleasant topics, his cocoon of warmth and contentment was soon complete once more.

"Kris said there was a strong bond between us," Gemma told Arden as she lay in his arms that night.

"Tell me something I don't know," he replied sleepily. "After all we've been through together, how could it be otherwise?"

"Mmm." She snuggled closer.

"Do you want to formalize the bond?" Arden murmured.

"What *do* you mean?"

"There's a council in Lower in a few days' time," he

replied. "And in the valley, that's when marriages are celebrated."

For several long moments, Gemma was speechless. The idea of marriage had never occurred to her. She had merely been basking in the relief and warmth of their longed-for reunion, and so was doubly touched by Arden's words.

He drew back a little to look at her.

"Say something!" he demanded. "I know I should really be down on my knees . . . but I'd rather be in here with you. I know I haven't got much to offer—"

"Shut up, you idiot!" Gemma interrupted, laughing. "Of *course* I'll marry you!"

chapter 13

Twelve days later, the village of Lower was crowded with people attending the council gathering, and the atmosphere was festive. Although the day was cool, the sky was clear, so the brief business matters were concluded in a meeting held in the open air. Then they passed to the *important* reasons for the council. First, two newborns were introduced and named by their proud parents, and then came the event that had brought people from even the remote corners of the valley.

Gemma and Arden were regarded as heroes by the majority of the population, and that, together with the fact that they were the first outsiders ever to be married in the valley, meant that the ceremony was a source of great interest.

Although it was not a formal rite, by the standards of the outside world, the solemn yet joyful exchange of vows was listened to in reverent silence by everyone present. When it was over, a great cheer went up, and then the *real* business began.

As Arden had told Gemma, the valley people were always glad of a reason to celebrate—and they had been provided with an especially fine one. Not only was the valley literally blooming once more, but the two people most responsible for that miracle were safely back at last—and celebrating themselves. The festivities lasted well into the night.

Caught up in this swirl of joyous activity, Gemma could not remember ever being happier. She caught a glimpse of Ashlin's parents, laughing and talking, and when they made a point of speaking to her later that night, their friendliness told of the forgiveness in their hearts.

Even Mallory managed a slow dance.

"At least you can't tread on my toes this time," she told Arden. "You couldn't even reach them!"

When the celebration finally came to an end, Kragen took them slowly home in the farm cart. Gemma was tired, but her eyes were still shining as she sat with Arden's arms around her. Beside them, Vance and Jon were fast asleep, nestled into their mother's ample form. As they drove along, Gemma and Arden listened to Kragen's seldom-heard singing voice. It was a slow and simple song, timed to fit in with the horse's stately pace, and told of the joys of the countryside.

In winter we sleep,
In spring we sow,
In summer we reap,
In autumn we grow.

As the last deep notes faded away, Gemma shifted her head drowsily on her husband's shoulder, which seemed, as always, a perfect fit.

The valley is like a circle, she thought. *Entire and complete. Long may it remain so.*

With the natural perversity of many babies, Mallory's daughter chose to make her entrance into the world in the bleakest time of the night—the period just before dawn that the people of Gemma's home isle called the wolfing hour.

Gemma had been asleep, but when her dreams were invaded by images of blood, she woke up, feeling confused and a little frightened. She sat up, not noticing the chill night air. Beside her, Arden stirred.

"What's the matter?" he mumbled.

"The baby," she realized. "It's coming."

She leaped out of bed and was hurriedly dressing when there was a knock at the door, and Kragen came in.

"She's started—" he began, then saw that Gemma was already up.

"I know," she said. "I'm coming."

"Can I help?" Arden was alert now.

"Would you go to the boys' room?" Gemma asked. "They're bound to wake up, and I don't want them getting scared."

Arden looked relieved and clambered out of bed. Gemma smiled as he yawned hugely. She and Kragen went out into the corridor, and the farmer made for his own room. Gemma stopped him, putting a restraining hand on his arm.

"Will you go and fetch Clare?" she asked.

Kragen looked puzzled.

"But you know Mallory doesn't want any other healer except you," he said slowly. "Why—?"

"I know, but I've never acted as midwife before," Gemma told him. "Clare has, and I may be glad of her help. To tell the truth, the way I'm feeling at the moment, I may not be much use at all."

"Why? What's the matter?" Kragen looked worried now.

"I don't know," she replied, trying to work it out for herself. She was being bombarded by a maelstrom of images and emotions. "My head is spinning." This was a far-from-adequate description of what was happening, but it was the best she could do for now.

Kragen put two large hands on her shoulders, and stared at her intently.

"Are you going to be all right?" he asked. "Shall I get Arden?"

"No, I'll be fine. Just go and fetch Clare. I'll stay with Mallory."

After a moment's hesitation, Kragen left, taking the stairs three at a time. As Gemma approached Mallory's room, her head was full of questions. Questions she could not answer. Questions she was not even aware of asking!

Is it time? Is the waiting over?

Faces, old friends and new, unknown and familiar, human and animal. Voices, young and ancient, deep and tremulous, songs of the hearth and the wild.

Is it complete? Can we begin?

Light and dark. Cold and heat. Desert tracts and mountain walls. Sunlight on water, starlight on snow.

Are you leaving us? Is this the end?

Joy and sadness. Love and anger. Time passing, through generations. Circles within circles.

Stop it! Gemma screamed silently. *I am in the valley!*

The clamor in her head receded slightly, becoming less insistent. It was a small relief. At the door to Mallory's room, she paused, her fingers on the handle. It took every last ounce of her determination to open it and step within.

Mallory's eyes were wide with pain and effort.

"It won't be long now," she gasped, forcing a smile. "You were right . . . she *is* impatient!"

Gemma went to her friend's side and took her outstretched hand. At that first touch, Mallory sighed peacefully and relaxed visibly as Gemma's instinctive powers reached out to help her.

"I'm so glad you're here," she said. "Everything will be all right now."

"What are those noises?" Vance was puzzled.

"That's your baby sister being born," Arden replied. "Your mother has to make noises like that—it helps her." He hoped he was right.

"Can we go and watch?" Jon asked hopefully.

"No. We'd just get in the way. Your father and Gemma are already with her."

"*That*'s all right then," Jon said, displaying his obvious confidence in Gemma's abilities.

Clare was not at all annoyed by being waked so early, and dressed quickly. She was the most knowledgeable healer in the valley and also an experienced midwife, so she reacted calmly and managed to soothe the anxious farmer. They hurried back to the farm; by the time they got there, Clare had all the information she needed.

When they entered the room, Mallory was breathing deeply and noisily, her contractions both frequent and powerful. But she was smiling as she felt the life within her struggle to claim its independence. Gemma still held her hand, and stood unmoving, a faraway expression on her face.

So Clare took over, all competence, talking to Mallory, encouraging her, and guiding her breathing. Kragen wiped the sweat from his wife's brow and kissed her, then looked at Gemma.

"Are you all right?" he asked, but she did not react.

"Gemma?" Kragen was worried and made to move toward her.

"Leave her!" Clare ordered. "She's taking Mallory's pain. And the baby's coming."

Gemma's mind reeled in confusion. One part of her could "see" the baby's progress and was able to screen Mallory from the worst of the pain. Her healer's instinct had come to the fore—and was the only part of her that remained sane. All the rest was madness.

Is it now? Is it time?

Flashes of light. Eternal fires.

Is it her? Are you protecting her?

Love and anger.

Leave her alone! Gemma cried. *She is not ready!*

Eyes peering. Lips parting. Tongues weaving spells of sound. Fading into obscurity. Disappointment and fear.

Leave us alone!

Circles.

In some far distant world, she felt the new life begin, heard the cry of protest and welcome. Her hand opened of its own accord.

Silence.

Gemma sighed deeply and fainted clean away.

Clare placed the newborn infant in her mother's arms and pushed Kragen to her side, then went quickly to attend to Gemma.

"Is she all right?" Mallory asked, exhaustion and anxiety mingled in her voice.

"She's fainted," the valley healer reported, "but she'll be all right soon. She might have a bump on her head, though."

"It all happened so quickly," Mallory went on. "I don't know what I would have done without her. When she took my hand—"

"She has a remarkable talent," the midwife said thoughtfully, "which makes it even more peculiar that she should have reacted like this. If she could control your pain, why not her own condition?"

"I'll get Arden," Kragen said. "We'll put her to bed." He kissed his wife gently as he left.

Mallory gazed into the deep brown eyes of her daughter.

"Well, little Gem. I don't know what you did to my friend," she whispered, "but you'd better be ready to explain yourself when she comes round. She's not someone to be trifled with!"

The baby regarded her solemnly, as if already considering her defense.

chapter 14

"I thought it was men who were supposed to pass out at things like that." Arden smiled, glad to see the color returning to Gemma's cheeks.

They were alone in their room. Kragen had gone to introduce his sons to their new sister, and Clare, satisfied with the progress of *all* her charges, had gone downstairs for a rest and a hot drink. Gemma had recovered consciousness soon after being put to bed and now, apart from a dull headache, was feeling more or less herself again. She was still confused, though, and found it difficult to explain what had happened.

"I know," she said now. "A fine healer *I* made, fainting like that." She shook her head, and instantly regretted the motion.

"Clare was very impressed. She said you shielded Mallory from the pain," Arden responded. "Perhaps that's why you blacked out."

"No. That part was easy." Gemma paused, remembering what she could from the confusion in her mind. "I'm glad I was able to help Mallory—that was the whole point of my being there, after all! It was the voices that made me faint."

"What voices?"

"Asking questions. So many questions!" Gemma looked at him, wide-eyed.

"You're not making any sense, my love."

"I know. Nor did they." After a moment, she tried to explain. "It was like that time on the tower, with Mendle—when all the circles of magic were open to me. Only *this* time, the images weren't clear, they all blurred into each other. And *all* of them asking questions."

"What about?"

"Time. Beginnings and ends. Little Gemma, I think."

"The baby?"

"For some reason, she's very important to them–but it's too soon! She's not ready yet!" Gemma was agitated now, almost shouting.

"Calm down," Arden said, trying to soothe her. He took her hands in his own. "The baby's fine. She's safe—nobody can reach her here."

"That's what I thought," Gemma replied, "but now I'm not so sure. We're in the *valley*, Arden."

"I know that," he said, smiling in spite of her earnestness.

"But don't you see what this means?" she persisted. "The circles of magic—if that's who it was—shouldn't be able to reach me here. The valley has always been a shield—against Cai, against the siren song, everything like that. So why not now?"

"You're asking *me*?"

"You know the valley better than any outsider," Gemma insisted.

"Yes, but I'm hardly an expert on magic!"

"Not so long ago, you were claiming to be a wizard," she accused, grinning despite her concern.

"And you believed me?" he asked, raising his eyebrows. "Do I *look* like Wynut or Shanti?"

Gemma laughed.

"No. Thank goodness!" Then she saw him frown. "What is it?"

"I'm trying to remember something those two told me," he replied, his forehead creased in thought. Gemma waited impatiently.

"They were explaining about the survival of magic," he said slowly. "Wynut said that you were the present key, and that the other—Mallory—*represents the future*."

"The future Key to the Dream?" Gemma whispered. "The baby?"

Arden shrugged as more came back to him.

"He went on to say that you were both crucial—his exact word—but that your influence could be either for good or for ill."

"Oh." Gemma was taken aback. "Why didn't you tell me this before?"

"With everything else that happened, I just forgot. We

have had quite a lot on our minds since then," Arden protested.

"I'm sorry," she said quietly, recognizing the truth of his statement.

A few moments passed in silence.

"You said yourself that little Gemma would be special. Perhaps just having the two of you together during her birth was so strong a force that the circles were able to break through the valley's defenses," Arden suggested.

"It's awfully confusing," Gemma complained, "but I hope you're right."

Arden nodded, understanding her apprehension. If his explanation was wrong, then it could only mean that the valley was no longer the haven so necessary to them all. The implications of *that* were not something he wished to consider.

"Don't worry about it now," he told her gently. "Do you feel well enough to come and see her?"

"Of course."

Arden helped Gemma out of bed, and they walked arm in arm to Mallory's room.

Gemma's last wish before going inside was that, whatever fate awaited her namesake, she would at least be able to grow up in the peaceful home that should be hers by right. The alternative was too awful to contemplate.

The baby—whom everybody called little Gem, taking their cue from her mother—had been born a month after Gemma and Arden's arrival in the valley. It had been an idyllic time for them; they had enjoyed to the full the incomparable beauty and serenity of the place and the unstinting hospitality of the people. They had reveled in their escape from the responsibilities of the outside world and enjoyed being together as never before.

Although they had known that it must end some time, neither was prepared for the abrupt and sickening way in which this would happen. In retrospect, it was as though Gem's birth had acted as a trigger for the disasters that followed. At the time, however, all had seemed well. The baby was resoundingly healthy; Mallory and Kragen were delighted with her, and the two boys, far from feeling jealous, were inquisitive but very loving and protective toward their tiny sister. Gemma suffered no more visions and recovered her strength quickly.

Another month passed in comparative calm. Gemma spent a lot of time with the baby, watching her grow and looking into her wide, brown eyes, wondering what was going on inside that little head. Fate did not seem to be hanging heavily on Gem.

But when she was just over a month old, news came that all was not well. Several people living in the upper reaches to the south of the valley reported feeling ill. This in itself was unusual, because the valley people generally kept in extraordinarily good health. What was worse, though, was that the local healers could not discover the source of the sickness. It was some time before they realized that all of the victims lived next to the river; by then there were other, more obvious, symptoms of the valley's malaise.

The night after hearing of the mysterious illness, Gemma dreamed of the caves and the god Rael for the first time since reaching the valley. She lay awake and fearful for some time.

By the next day, the disease had worsened and was spreading fast. Everyone in the valley suffered to some degree. The cause of the epidemic was a mystery; an outbreak like this had never been known before, not even during the time of the drought. Gemma and Mallory cast many an anxious glance at the children and were thankful that, for now at least, the worst effects of the illness were confined to the south.

It was Jon who brought home to them the full horror of what was happening. He had been playing with his brother beside the river, which still flowed strongly, even though midwinter's day was less than half a month away. The boys spotted a large fish, then realized that it was not like the others they had seen. There was something wrong with it.

Jon, who had been fascinated by these elusive, silvery creatures, waded into the water to get a closer look. The fish bobbed sideways on the surface of the river and made no attempt to swim away. Jon put out a tentative hand and caught hold of its tail, then lifted the unresisting thing out of the water. It still did not move.

"It's dead," Vance commented from the bank.

"Its eyes are all funny," Jon said. "Milky."

He poked at the fish with his free hand and a few scales fell off, to be carried away by the current.

"It must have eaten an awful lot," he remarked, looking at the creature's bulging stomach.

"Bring it here," Vance told him.

"We'll take it home to show Arden," Jon decided. "He knows about strange animals." He waded ashore, and the two boys set off across the fields.

"It smells nasty," Vance said, as they approached the farmyard. "You'd better not take it inside."

Jon saw the sense of this and put the fish down on the ground before running into the house.

"Come and see what I've got!" he yelled, and in a few moments Arden, Gemma, and his mother followed him outside. He pointed to the fish.

"It doesn't look so nice now," he said sadly. "It was all shiny."

Before the adults had a chance to comment, Jon picked up a stick and prodded his prize—as if punishing it for not being beautiful any more. As he stepped back with an exclamation of disgust, the others saw what had so revolted him.

The stomach of the fish had burst open, spewing forth its guts in a vile fountain. The innards were a phosphorescent green.

Arden had to fight to keep himself from throwing up. He gulped for air, seeing once again the poisoned stream in the Lightless Kingdom, the dead fish floating by, the remorseless spread of the pollution.

"No!" he screamed. "Not *here*! Please, not here!"

Jon ran to his mother and began to cry.

"Keep away from it!" Gemma told them, her face white.

"Vance, go and fetch your father," Mallory ordered, and her elder son did as he was told.

"Don't let anybody touch it," Gemma instructed, calmer now. "Get a shovel, put it in a container, then bury it deep." She could feel the emanations of evil, even from a distance; all her healer's instincts were revolted.

"That won't help." Arden turned to her, his face haggard. "Don't you see? It's the river! If the river is poisoned, then the whole valley is doomed."

Huddled within his mother's arms, Jon cried even harder.

Over the next few days, the valley was stricken with a catalog of woes. The illness spread; plants near the river turned brown and died; trees began to rot where they stood. The dead bodies of fish and animals could be seen floating down the river.

The community did what they could. They sealed off their reservoirs in order to preserve their supplies of fresh water and moved whole families away from the river to the upper slopes. Beyond that, however, there was little they *could* do, except hope that this evil would pass—or that the river would run dry at midwinter—now only a few days away—so that the valley could recover.

Arden alternated between fury at his own helplessness in the face of this ghastly threat and a deep depression at the thought that the valley he loved so much might be doomed after all. He wanted to go into the mountains, to the river's source, or return to Newport and enlist Jordan's help—or ask advice from the Lightless Kingdom. He wanted to do *something*. But his ideas turned to ashes, and he stayed, helping where he could.

Gemma's talents were naturally much in demand, but, while she could alleviate some of the symptoms of the green-sickness, she could not cure it, nor could she understand its cause. She labored tirelessly, but her heart was heavy, and she returned home every evening expecting someone in Mallory's family to have become the epidemic's latest victim. Jon caused her the greatest concern, but four days after finding the fish, he was still healthy—though unusually pale and quiet.

Gemma came down from his room one afternoon to talk to Mallory in the kitchen.

"The boys are fine," Gemma whispered, not wanting to disturb little Gem, who lay asleep in her cot near the fire. "I wish I could say the same for everyone else."

"Is it getting worse?" Mallory asked.

Gemma nodded, and was about to say more when the problems of the valley were thrust from her mind. She stared at Mallory and saw the same thing reflected in her friend's expression. Rapture and horror were equally mixed.

The siren song rang in their minds, unutterably sweet, full of longing and invitation, but now with overtones of terror and dread.

The valley was no longer a haven.

As the minds of the two women fought for understanding,

part 3

A LIGHT FROM THE NORTH

chapter 15

There seemed nothing very remarkable about the lone passenger who came ashore from the trading vessel; the city-port of Altonbridge, in eastern Cleve, had certainly seen more unusual comings and goings in recent days. It was almost five months now since the Guild had been overthrown, and the underground, following the example of their colleagues in Great Newport, had begun to reorganize the city's government. The initial chaos was over, but there were still signs of turmoil everywhere. The newcomer was just one tiny thread in a huge and ever-changing tapestry, and no one paid him much attention.

Even if they had, his appearance would have caused little surprise. He was young, with the boyish good looks that so many women found attractive. His brown hair was straight, cut longer than was the custom in Cleve. He was of slight build and carried only a small pack, slung over one shoulder, and a curiously constructed wooden box.

On closer inspection, however, an observant onlooker might have noticed something interesting. The traveler's youthful face was marked with care lines that seemed incongruous in one so young. His green eyes looked old, and they held a secret sadness; some would describe them as haunted. And—most unusual of all—his box was emitting a faint buzzing noise.

The man stood uncertainly on the quay for a few moments, looking around at the dockside bustle, the nearest buildings—some of them still in ruins—and the throng of people. It seemed almost as if his sole aim in life had been to reach this place, and now that he had finally arrived, he had forgotten his reason for coming. A momentary bewilderment joined the melancholy in his eyes.

But then he visibly pulled himself together and set off at a brisk pace, carrying his burdens with an ease that belied his slim frame. Asking directions from a passerby, he marched straight to the nearest tavern and took a room, without even checking to see whether it was suitable. He was exhausted after a very long journey and was sorely in need of rest. Although the solid ground beneath his feet was taking some getting used to, the thought of a bed that would not tip and sway was irresistible. Now that—at last!—he was truly in the fabled southern continent, he felt he could put off his search until tomorrow.

Although it was still only early evening, the traveler dropped his bag on the floor, placed the box carefully on a table, then undressed and climbed into bed. As he relaxed beneath the sheets, he cursed, remembering that he had forgotten to lock his door. In this unknown city, far from home, he knew he should guard against unwelcome visitors, but the warmth and comfort of his bed were already lulling him to sleep. He stared at the key, scowling, then mumbled a few words and made a small gesture with his hand.

On the other side of the room, the key turned slowly in the lock, there was a loud click, and the stranger relaxed. He laughed.

Having spent all these years denying your talent, you finally go and use it for something as trivial as that. What a waste! he thought. *And what's more, I don't care!*

He was still smiling as he fell asleep.

Cai had known Gemma since she was a little girl. They had been great friends even then, and the wizard had been a firm favorite with the young princess. He was always willing to play games and to talk about things that the other grown-ups did not understand or would not explain; his swarm was also a constant source of fascination. Everyone knew that all wizards had familiars, but Cai was unique in that his consisted not of one single animal, but of an entity made up of the many individuals within a group. He communicated with the *swarm*, not the separate bees. Most people found the creatures unnerving, even terrifying, but Gemma thought that was silly of them.

For his part, Cai found that his young companion was remarkably entertaining and surprisingly observant. At the time, he had taken great pleasure in the intimate company of numerous rather more mature women, but he always found time for Gemma, and on one famous occasion had had good reason to be more than grateful for her devoted friendship. During the course of a dangerous but vital magical experiment, the swarm had reacted to their wizard's mental state and had lost control, terrorizing the palace while Cai lay unconscious. Though she was only seven years old, Gemma had calmed the maddened, tormented bees and had returned them to their master, thus enabling him to survive—and to complete the magical process.

They had discussed those dramatic events very soon afterward, and part of that conversation remained clear in Cai's mind even to this day.

"I wouldn't be at all surprised if you became a wizard yourself one day," he had told her.

"Would you marry me then?" was her immediate response.

It was not the first time the little girl had asked him that question, but it was to be the last. Her days of innocence were numbered, and the terrible upheaval of The Destruction had changed everything. For Cai, it brought to a tragic end his faith in magic, and he refused to think of himself as a wizard any longer.

As Gemma grew into a beautiful young woman, this subject was the only cause of friction between them. She could not understand why all the *good* that wizardry could achieve must be lost when its potential for *evil* had been destroyed. He explained that all magic had two sides to it, and that because it had been put to such vile use once, they must never use it again—at all. He grew angry when she pointed out that he still used his powers to heal, that he did not age as other men did, and that the bees had remained with him. Cai defended himself as best he could, rationalizing these inconsistencies to her, and despising himself while he did so. Now, he had finally realized that he had been wrong, and this knowledge was a source of deep and bitter regret. So many things could have been different. If only . . .

In spite of their disagreements, the two had remained constant companions, and often had been mistaken for lovers.

Cai's body was that of a lithe and handsome twenty-year-old, even though he was actually twice that age. Indeed, Cai *had* come to love Gemma, but had never admitted it, even to himself, until it was too late. They had been great friends though, and he had shared many of her hopes and desires.

Because of this closeness, he had been bitterly hurt by her secret departure. She had left him feeling angry, betrayed, and very lonely, unable to take any comfort in the company of others. He became a dual personality; by day he was outwardly happy and slightly absentminded, loved by everyone at court, but by night he became a wizard again, no matter how strenuously he tried to deny it to himself. He had always been plagued by dreams and forced to relive certain tragic events from the past. In Gemma's absence, these dreams grew even more painful. As months passed and she did not return, he spent more and more time in his remote mountain retreat, longing for peace.

And then, one heart-shattering night, his world had been turned upside down by a new, even more vivid dream. Gemma had appeared like a ghost in his lonely room, and he had been enveloped by fear until he realized how far away and yet how powerful she had become. He was helpless, but his weakness became a gift to her—the only thing he had left to offer—as she took from him the secrets he had hidden for so long. Even in his dream, though, he had been unable to tell her that he loved her.

After that, the contacts with Gemma had been infrequent, but very real—waking experiences in which he could speak to her—even if he could not always say all he wanted. She became a constant, yet terribly remote, presence within his mind—except for the times when she disappeared into that "secret place" which, to his anguish, kept her hidden. Even so, the times when he *could* communicate directly were few and far between—and thus very precious.

The first of these had been when she used her special talent—which Cai knew to be more powerful than his own had ever been—to heal two sick children. He had guided her then, seeing that her knowledge did not match her power. He was able to convince himself that this was not *real* magic, just healing—and therefore something that was obviously worthwhile.

The second time had been infinitely more frightening. Gemma was flying in a kite, just as she had done with him in earlier days, but her journey now was suicidal. Cai had stayed with her for as long as he could, but eventually he had been seized by desperation, convinced that she was going to die. So he left her, saying many things that he later regretted. But he meant every word of his last message.

"Make them all proud of you. As I am. I always loved you, Gemma. Don't remember me too badly."

His forebodings seemed to have been borne out by the fact that Gemma's "presence" disappeared completely for several months. Cai had almost given up hope, when, without warning, he had a vivid and unmistakably happy dream about Gemma and, on the very next day, found that he was able to talk briefly to her reawakened spirit. It was then that he learned of the secret place and of the latentor from whom she had learned so much.

"You could have taught me," she had said, half in accusation, half regret.

He had denied it, citing his shattered belief, but Gemma had persisted, asking whether it could never be renewed.

"Perhaps *you* can do that," he had replied—and even began to believe in the possibility himself.

But it was the last two visions that truly brought him renewed hope—and emphasized his terror.

In the first, she stood before a blue-flame wall of ancient, arcane power. Cai knew that he was not alone with her and had felt confident in offering the help he knew was there. Her reinforced willpower, strengthened by Adria's teachings, had enabled her to breach the wall, but then, to his dismay, she had been lost to him entirely, until the fateful battle that had taken place on a tower high above an unknown city. There he had once again been able to offer his help, and, in spite of her insistent refusals, had forced aid upon her—just as all the other participants had done. However, he soon became aware that something was terribly wrong. He grew confused and afraid, and the swarm had taken to the air, buzzing round his head in an angry cloud. Madness had threatened as he grew suddenly weak, but then, as mysteriously as his power had drained away, it was returned. He knew that Gemma had survived, but everything else was shrouded in mystery, and he longed in vain to be able to speak with her once more.

And so he finally made the decision that had been tugging

at his heart for many months. He would travel south, and try to find her.

Now, nearly five months later, after innumerable delays and a voyage that had taken him to almost every other island in the known world, he had finally reached the land where—if anywhere—he would find his lost pupil.

His only worry was that for the past month Gemma's presence had again been denied him.

How will I find you if you can't talk to me? he wondered. *This land is vast.*

Abandoning the problem until morning, Cai sent a soothing message to the bees in their traveling hive, then fell into a deep, dark sleep.

chapter 16

The nightmare began in the wolfing hour, though Cai would not realize that until later, when he lay sweat-soaked and afraid, watching the light return to the world outside his room.

Brief, undefined images of blood were replaced by an overwhelming sense of confusion. Cai knew that Gemma was central to his dream, even though he could not see her clearly. Everything was blurred, out of focus and out of reach. Important events were taking place, but were hidden from him. He grew desperate, shouting questions into the night, anxiety slicing through him like a blade.

Conflicting emotions roiled within him. Then, in a single moment of clarity, he saw his bewilderment mirrored in Gemma's face. He cried out to her, and although he could not hear what she replied, it was obvious that she was angry. He withdrew, frightened and ashamed.

Now there was another woman in the dream. The images of blood and pain were coming from her, but Cai felt Gemma take that burden upon herself. He wanted to save her from the agony, but he was helpless. As Gemma spurned his presence once more, Cai realized that the dream was not his alone. The others were there again, as they had been on the tower. But they were as remote and as confused as he was. The revelation lasted only a moment.

He heard a cry of protest and welcome; a cry that filled him with foreboding.

And then silence.

And a black void, as still and empty as death.

He woke feeling like a rag doll that had been washed in icy

water, then put through a wringer. Although he was bathed in sweat, he was shivering. His heart was pounding, and he was so weak that he could not move a muscle. He lay still, reviewing every image of the awful night-vision.

Gemma's rejection had shaken him to the core. In the past she had seemed to welcome his remote presence—surely she could not have faked those earlier joyful responses. So what was different this time? He felt lost, depressed. If Gemma did not want or need him . . . Had his long and arduous voyage been for nothing?

Blood and pain. In his head, he heard again the baby's cry and was swamped by a wave of conflicting emotions—wonder at the new life, love for the child, hate and jealousy for the father. Then he realized that the child was not Gemma's. Whose was it—and why was its birth so important? What was Gemma's connection to it?

Cai longed to feel her presence once again so that he could at least have the chance of talking to her—but there was nothing.

A black void, as still and empty as death.

The denial rose within him, unbidden. Gemma is *not* dead! And his certainty was not just an irrational yearning; the contact, however disturbing, had been real. He realized then that Gemma must be within her "secret place," where events were not *meant* to be seen by the outside world. That was why she had been so angry—why she had sent them all away!

His mood swung wildly, and he almost laughed. The very fact that he had seen her at all became a symbol of how close she must be. He had not journeyed in vain.

"If this land holds you, Gemma, I will find you," he promised aloud.

Then something else occurred to him, and he calmed down, thinking it through. Whatever had happened that night was an indication that powerful forces were at work. Magical forces. There was more at stake here than the fate of one runaway princess.

Cai smiled wryly. He had spent the last fifteen years resisting the idea that magic still existed, and had dismissed his own powers as meaningless anachronisms, the remnants of a time of great evil. Gemma had been the only one to disagree with him openly, and their arguments had often been bitter. He had tried to force his world into a mould that it did not fit—the shape *he* wanted, not the shape it *was*. He knew that now, had known it in his heart since that first traumatic dream of Gemma, but it had taken the battle on the tower to make him face the truth.

It had been a bitter and difficult admission, and had cost him a great deal. He had been desperately unhappy during much of his voyage, appalled by the thought that magic was alive in the world again—and that he was a part of it. Nevertheless, he forced himself to recall his former skills and found a certain amount of relief in practicing wizardry once more. The unrealized potential of his mind had weighed heavily upon him during the intervening years, and now that burden of denial had finally gone.

Cai sent a silent message to the swarm. They emerged from the small holes bored in their mobile hive and flew round the room. The wizard watched them, a glint of happiness in his eyes. At least now he could stop feeling guilty about communicating with the bees. When his search began, they would be with him openly, as a familiar *should* be.

Cai smiled and got out of bed. Although he still felt weak, and shivered in the chill of the early morning air, there was a new determination in his heart. He dressed quickly, eager to begin his search.

This time, the citizens of Altonbridge took note of the newcomer. His own appearance had not changed, but he was accompanied now by a small black cloud that hovered above his head, buzzing ominously. The swarm was not dangerous in any way, but some people moved away quickly nonetheless. Those who took the trouble to look more closely at the swarm's master saw the steely determination in his green eyes. Some even saw the sparkle of humor there. For the first time in many years, Cai was enjoying his association with the bees—and the effect their presence was having.

He strode purposefully through the early morning streets, a black cape protecting him from the thin, chill mist that rose from the harbor. The landlord of his tavern had suggested that he contact a man named Chad, and had given directions to his house. Apparently, this man was a leading member of a group known as the underground. According to the landlord, the underground was the nearest thing the city had to a government.

The underground, Cai thought. *Are they the people that Gemma was going to help? Or are they the ones she was intending to oppose?*

He wished now that he had let her tell him more, but those early contacts had been painfully brief. Instinct told him that the underground were Gemma's allies, but he had no way of proving this. He had been told something of Altonbridge's recent power struggle by his host, but one man could not be expected to give him the whole picture.

Tread carefully, the wizard warned himself.

He reached the house he was looking for and knocked boldly. The door opened after a few moments, and a man peered out. He had a slice of bread in his right hand and was chewing heartily. When he saw his visitor, his jaw stopped, and he glanced suspiciously at the swarm.

Cai smiled broadly. "Are you Chad?" he asked.

The man nodded, still looking up.

"My name is Cai. I'm a wizard from the northern isles." Cai's smile widened. *This is how I tread carefully!* he thought with some amusement.

Chad swallowed and lowered his gaze to the newcomer's face.

"I can make them go away if they bother you," Cai said. Chad did not reply. "May I come in?" Cai asked. "I have several questions I need answers to, and I've been told you might be able to help."

Chad recovered his poise.

"I'm sorry," he said. "I'm not usually so slow in my welcome. Come in." He waved Cai inside with the piece of bread. "But leave the bees outside."

"Of course."

Cai walked past his host into a dimly lit room. Food was spread upon a plain wooden table.

"I was just having my breakfast. Will you join me?"

"No thank you," Cai replied. "I've already eaten."

"You rise early," Chad remarked, indicating a chair for his guest. "Please excuse me for a moment."

He went into an adjoining room, and Cai heard a brief whispered conversation, though he could not make out what was being said. Then there was the sound of a door opening and shutting quietly, and Chad came back into the room.

"Do you mind if I finish my meal?" he asked, sitting down at the table. "I'm expecting other visitors soon."

"Go ahead."

"What are the questions you need answering?"

"I know something of recent events here," Cai began, "but I'd like to hear more from someone who was in the forefront."

"Hardly that," Chad demurred.

"You *are* a member of the underground?"

"Yes, but I'm a foot soldier, not a general."

"You're being too modest, I'm sure," Cai said, but Chad only shrugged. "I hear there was a crucial battle in the big tower," the wizard probed.

Chad took a mouthful of food and chewed slowly, then swallowed and looked at Cai with real curiosity.

"That was in Newport, not here," he said.

"Forgive me. I'm new to this land," the wizard replied. "Where *is* that?"

"Great Newport, the capital of Cleve. It's about seventy leagues west of here," the other replied. "Along the coast road."

"A woman named Gemma was involved in that battle, wasn't she?" Cai asked, his heart beating faster.

"What is Gemma to you?" Chad asked, suspicious now.

"A friend," Cai replied, light-headed with joy, in spite of the other man's wariness. This man knew Gemma! Cai felt at last that he was among friends—her friends—and that he would soon find her.

"I've known her since she was a child," he went on. "Do you know where she is now?"

Chad shook his head.

"But you could help me find out?"

"Why do you *want* to find her?"

Cai did not give the reply that sprang into his mind. Instead, he told Chad what he had told himself in order to justify his voyage.

"Great events are happening in your land. Gemma is central to them—and so is magic. As her friend and as a wizard, I have a part to play, but I must find her first. I have come such a long way . . ."

He was interrupted by a knock at the door.

"Come in!" Chad called, looking almost relieved, and a

slim, wiry man entered the room. He pushed back his damp hood, nodded to Chad, then turned to face Cai, who rose from his seat.

"So you're the wizard?" the newcomer said.

Cai nodded. "I am."

"He claims to know Gemma," Chad put in. "Says they grew up together."

Not exactly, Cai thought, but did not correct the understandable mistake.

"I've told him nothing that isn't already common knowledge," Chad stated, slightly defensive.

I can't blame them for not trusting me, Cai decided, but he was frustrated nonetheless. *So near and yet . . .*

"Forgive us, but we have had reason in the past to be suspicious of strangers," the newcomer said, as though responding to Cai's unspoken words. "My name is Dale."

"I'm Cai."

"I've heard of you."

"Then you know Gemma?" Cai exclaimed.

"I may do." Dale was wary still; he could not remember Gemma ever talking about Cai during their journey from the valley to Altonbridge, but the name had come up in a later conversation with Hewe. He racked his brains to recall what had been said, but without success.

"Please," Cai said. "Can you tell me where she is?"

Dale responded with a question of his own.

"Can you prove that you are her friend?"

The wizard sighed. Gemma's defenses were indeed formidable.

"I can tell you all about her early life," he said. "I was the one who taught her how to fly in a kite. And I know that she has used that talent since arriving here."

Dale considered him appraisingly.

"I know nothing of her life before she came to Cleve," he said. "Describe her to me."

"She has red hair," Cai began.

"All men know that," Chad muttered, but Dale waved him into silence as Cai went on.

"Her skin is fair and freckled. Her eyes are gray. She's twenty-one years old, nearly twenty-two now. And she's beautiful."

Dale nodded.

"How do you know of her exploits here?" he asked.

"Our minds link up sometimes," the wizard replied. "Not often, and only briefly. But I saw part of her flight from the mountains, and saw her go through the blue wall. And that battle on the tower . . ." He thought back. "And healing the children in Keld."

"Those stories are common enough," Dale replied, showing no surprise. "You could have picked them up in any tavern."

"Why *should* I?" Cai asked in despair. "What could I hope to gain by claiming falsely that I know Gemma? And what will it take to convince you that I am her *friend*?"

The other did not reply, so the wizard tried again.

"There was another time," he said. "After she'd seen the latentor."

"What?"

"The old woman who helped her. Adria."

Cai noted Dale's momentary discomposure, and gained hope from it. "She showed Gemma how to use her magical powers," he went on. "This happened soon after Gemma left what she calls her special place." He watched his inquisitor closely, yearning to be accepted by him. Long moments passed in silence.

Dale was thinking hard. He and Hewe had been with Gemma when she visited Adria, and as far as he knew, they were the only ones aware of that encounter. In spite of his suspicions, he was beginning to feel impressed.

"Can you prove you're a wizard?" he asked abruptly.

Cai thought for a moment. "I don't like to use magic frivolously," he said, "but I suppose this is a good cause." He snapped his fingers and a lifeless candle on the table sprang into flame. He waved a hand and it was snuffed out again. Chad gasped, but Dale remained impassive. *Let's see what you make of this then*, Cai thought with a touch of malice, beginning to tire of their suspicions. He had seen that one of the windows was open, and now sent a message to the swarm. A few moments later, the bees began to stream into the room. Chad and Dale dived for cover, unnerved by the swarm's angry buzzing, which was magnified by the confines of the small chamber.

The bees slowly gathered together on one wall, and the noise dropped to a low hum. The two members of the

chapter 17

Dale led Cai briskly through the maze of city streets, the swarm flying overhead. He had many responsibilities needing his attention, and, prompted by the wizard's final demonstration, had seen an opportunity to kill two birds with one stone while still guarding against treachery. He had instinctively warmed to the northerner, but had seen too much deceit in recent years to take anything—or anyone—at face value.

"Where are we going?" Cai asked. They had left Chad's house quickly, with no explanation as to where they were heading.

"There's someone I want you to meet," Dale replied. "She works at our headquarters near the center of the city."

"Does she know where Gemma is?" the wizard asked quickly.

"No more than I do," Dale replied.

"Then how can she help?"

"Because she wants to find Gemma again as well."

"Again?"

"Zana arrived in Cleve on the same ship as Gemma, part of the same group. They were separated soon afterward, but she's been badgering me for months to let her go and see Gemma."

"Then you *do* know where she is!" Cai exclaimed, excited and annoyed at the same time.

Dale shook his head.

"Let me explain," he began patiently. "Gemma stayed in Great Newport for some months after the battle in the tower, but the last I heard was that she had gone away to rest."

"Where to?" the wizard asked, sure that it must have been to her secret place.

"I don't know," Dale replied. *Although I could probably guess*, he thought. "I was told that Gemma and Arden were in a safe place, and they weren't to be disturbed except in a case of dire emergency."

"Who's Arden?"

"A close friend of hers. Saved her life once, I believe."

Cai was filled with an emotion he refused to recognize as jealousy; he pushed it aside, and asked,

"Where did you get this information?"

"From a colleague of mine, Hewe. I think he's in Great Newport at the moment. And that's where I'm sending you and Zana."

Ah, well, progress of a sort, Cai thought. He wondered briefly if Dale was keeping anything from him.

"In any case," the southerner went on, "it's nearly a month since Hewe was last here, so it's possible that Gemma may even be back in Newport by now."

That idea cheered Cai considerably.

"And if she isn't, you should at least be able to get news of her," Dale concluded. *And if you're not who you claim to be, Jordan and Hewe will sort you out soon enough*, he added to himself. He had no intention of leading the stranger to the valley, where Gemma would be without the powerful protection of the underground.

Their headquarters in Altonbridge were in a warrenlike building that had once been the offices of the Guild, the recently overthrown government and trade organization. Dale ushered Cai into a small room, which was almost filled by a huge desk behind which sat an attractive, dark-haired woman in her early thirties. She was talking to a young man who stood beside her.

"No. No. No!" she said. "They should go *there*." Her forefinger stabbed at a paper on the desk, emphasizing her words. She glanced up at the newcomers, acknowledging their presence, but went on talking. "The Reel Street crew won't need roofing tiles for two months, but if those houses in the north quarter aren't covered soon, they'll be rotting by spring. Go and tell Bevin, and make sure he knows where to go."

The young man hurried out, smiling apologetically at the two men.

"I hope you're bringing me reinforcements," the woman said to Dale. "No one in this place has the faintest idea how to run a city."

"What would we do without you, Zana?" Dale grinned.

"A lot less, probably," she replied, shaking her head but smiling. "Who's this?"

"A friend of Gemma's."

"Oh." Zana stared hard at Cai. "Not reinforcements then?"

"I don't think I'd be much use in an organizational capacity," Cai said.

"He's a wizard," Dale added, by way of explanation.

"Oh," Zana said again. There was a pause. "Anything else I should know?"

"Yes," Dale told her. "You're going to Newport with him."

Four hours later, Cai and Zana met, as arranged, in a nearby tavern. Dale had explained the situation briefly to Zana, then left them to make their own plans. She had leaped at the chance of going to Newport, seeing in it a way of escaping the endless toil involved in the reconstruction of Altonbridge, as well as a way of contacting Gemma again—something she had been wanting to do for some time. Dale had spoken to her privately, explaining his misgivings and asking her to keep a close eye on the newcomer, but this had not dampened her enthusiasm.

Cai was already there when she arrived soon after midday. The barkeeper greeted her warmly and poured her a drink without being asked. Zana waved to several other customers as she made her way over to the wizard's table.

"Your health," she said and sipped appreciatively. "The best wine in the city." She relaxed into her chair and eyed Cai curiously. "Where are the bees?"

"On the roof," he replied. "I didn't think the landlord would appreciate them in here."

"You have a point," she agreed, and they smiled at each other.

"When do we leave?" Cai asked.

"You're in a hurry," she commented.

"I've come a long way—and I should have come sooner."

Zana nodded thoughtfully.

"Well, it'll take me a couple of days to get things

straightened out here," she decided. "I can't leave just like that," she pointed out, seeing his crestfallen expression. "It'd be chaos." She paused. "Or rather, worse chaos than it already is. In the meantime, we might as well get to know a bit about each other. Where are you staying?"

"At the Dolphin. It was the first place I found."

"You were lucky," she said. "Most of the inns near the harbor are pretty rough."

"You seem well informed . . ." he said.

"I was in the trade," Zana explained. "I ran my own tavern on Haele before I came here."

"So that's where you got your business training."

"Hah! Helping rebuild a city is just a *bit* different."

"Dale said you came on the same ship as Gemma."

"Yes. She was part of a group who called themselves the Swallows. I helped them find a ship—not that it *was* much help, as it turned out."

"Why?"

Zana told him of the death of their drunken captain, and the subsequent shipwreck that had stranded them on a deserted part of Cleve's coastline. She went on to describe the trials of their search for shelter, and of Gemma's mysterious disappearance.

"For months I thought she was dead, but then I heard rumors of her through the underground. She's quite famous now." She told Cai what she had learned of Gemma, and he recognized much from his own remote contacts.

"I'll wager there's been some embroidering in the telling," Zana concluded, "but, even so, there's obviously something rather important about my traveling companion."

Cai nodded. He needed no convincing on that score.

"When I found out she was alive, I wanted to go and see her straight away," Zana went on, "but by then I'd become involved in all this." She waved her hands to indicate the city around them.

"Why did you come here in the first place?" Cai asked. "Did you feel the same call as the Swallows?"

"No. My reason was much more mundane," she replied, with a rueful smile. "I have no family, and the only man I ever really cared for had already sailed south—he *had* heard the call. In the end, I decided to follow."

"And have you found him?"

"No—and I don't suppose I ever will now. Even if he's still in Cleve, and hasn't gone even farther south, this place is just too big—I could search for years and still not find him. It's not like the islands."

"I'm sorry." Cai wanted to tell her that it was love that had brought *him* to the southern continent, but could not bring himself to speak. Even so, it was an unspoken bond between them; they had both arrived in search of someone else.

"It was a foolish idea, anyway," Zana said. "I realized that before I even got here."

"Foolish is not the word I would use," Cai said quietly. "Human, maybe."

"It amounts to the same thing," she replied. "Look at what's happened in this country. If that doesn't demonstrate humanity's foolishness, I don't know what does."

Over another drink, she told Cai of her arrival, with the remnants of the Swallows, at Altonbridge. She had lived for months in the squalid shanty town outside the city walls, trapped there by her poverty. The remaining Swallows had drifted away soon after their arrival, leaving Zana alone and friendless. Then she had been approached by the underground, and found in their cause a distraction from the hopeless search for her lost lover. Her intelligence and abilities meant that she soon became an important member of their organization, but her skills had really come to the fore after the revolution. Someone had to try to bring order to the shambles that was Altonbridge, and she took on the task willingly, working long and hard. Her grumbling was only for show.

Zana spoke modestly about herself, but Cai saw behind the self-deprecation and humor to her obvious keen intelligence, and was not surprised at the progress she had made. He also saw her pain, and wondered about her past. *I have no family*. He would have liked to help her, to heal those inner wounds, but knew that he was too much in need of healing himself to be of use to her. For all his newfound determination, Cai was not blind to his own limitations.

"Getting rid of the Guild and its vile corruption was the best thing that could have happened to this city," Zana concluded, "but it's a terrible shame that it took bloodshed and so much suffering to achieve it. The least *I* can do is to help with the recovery, in my own small way."

"You value yourself too low," Cai told her seriously.

Zana shrugged.

"That's enough about me," she said. "Tell me about yourself, wizard."

Cai winced.

"No one's called me that for years," he began, then, seeing her discomfort, added, "It's my own fault. I introduced myself to Chad in a rather dramatic fashion, hoping that he'd take me to someone who could help me."

"Well, are you a wizard or aren't you?" she asked, amused.

"I am. But I'd rather you didn't use the term in public." Long years of denying his wizardry had left Cai with an aversion for the title, even though he now accepted his powers.

"All right. Tell me about your life before Gemma left."

Cai was silent for a while.

"Did she say much about it, about me?" he asked eventually.

"Not really," Zana replied. "But then, none of the Swallows talked much about their past. They were all obsessed with the future, with getting here—the gods know why." *I wouldn't have been in such a hurry,* she thought to herself, *if I'd been leaving behind a man as attractive as you.*

"I've known Gemma since she was a little girl," Cai began. "I was the resident . . . expert in her father's court on Heald."

"Her father's—?"

"She's a princess, though it never seemed to mean that much to her. Her brother still rules the island—or what it became."

"In The Destruction?" Zana's surprise was obvious.

"Yes. That catastrophe changed many things, not least the shape of the land." Cai's memories of that time were extremely painful.

"In Haele too," Zana said, remembering the days of terror as the volcano had erupted and the island had been forced out of the sea, becoming twenty times its former size.

"After that," Cai went on, not mentioning his own and Gemma's intimate involvement in that cataclysmic event, "we were companions, good friends. We only ever quarreled about one thing."

Zana raised her eyebrows in mute question.

"Magic," he said softly. "I insisted that it was dead, and she wouldn't accept that. In the end, that's what drove her away." Zana's heart went out to him—he looked so sad.

"And now you've changed your mind?"

"Yes."

"Why?"

"Her leaving came as a great shock to me, and it forced me to reassess many things." Cai lost his solemn expression, and he grinned. "I brooded, swore at helpless, inanimate objects, and generally made a complete idiot of myself. Then events persuaded me to admit the truth. Even so, it took me an awfully long time to summon up the courage to leave. Gemma had to force that upon me, too."

"What do you mean?"

Cai explained his dream-link with Gemma and his conviction that important events were brewing.

"The least I can do is try to help," he ended. "In my own small way."

They smiled at each other across the table.

chapter 18

"You're quite sure that you're happy to go with him on your own?" Dale was concerned, and he wanted to be sure that Zana was comfortable with the arrangement.

"Yes," she reassured him. "I don't think we'll be bothered. The road is much safer now. And besides, you know you can't spare anyone to escort us."

"I was thinking more of the danger from *him*," her colleague said.

"I like him," she responded simply. "I'll take the chance." She and Cai had met several times during the past two days, and she had never felt threatened in any way. His manner had always been kind and gentle, and there was fire in his eyes only when he talked about Gemma. He had even introduced Zana to the swarm, so that she was no longer nervous with them—or at least, not much.

"We're all very fond of you," Dale said, uncertain still. "I'd hate anything to happen to you."

"It's nice of you to be concerned," she replied, smiling, "but I'll be all right." Privately, she decided that Dale was probably worried more about the loss of his capable administrator than about her as a person. He thought only of his work—and had never given any sign of thinking of her as a woman. *At least Cai has noticed that!* she thought. He had complimented her on her appearance several times. To hear this, even when she felt tired and careworn after a long day's work, was very pleasant. It was only a little thing, but one that she appreciated.

"Besides," she went on, "if he's a wizard of any real power, a few armed men wouldn't be much use!"

"All he's done so far is a few tricks," Dale pointed out.

"You can't have it both ways!" Zana said, laughing now. "If he's only a showman, then he's no real danger and I'll be able to take care of myself. If he's a powerful wizard, then a guard wouldn't help me at all."

"All right. All right." Dale held up his hands in defeat. "Just be careful, that's all, and remember that you're the one who'll lead him to Gemma. Make sure he realizes that. He won't get near Jordan or Hewe unless you vouch for him."

"I'll be careful," Zana promised. She didn't point out that a real wizard would achieve his purpose whether she helped him or not.

Now that the decision had been reached, Dale grew businesslike once more, giving Zana messages for Jordan, recommending places to stay along the way and where to shelter when they were beyond the reach of any village.

"Your horses and equipment are all ready," he finished. "We can't spare more than two, so you'll have to take it steady."

Zana nodded. She was thinking of the nights to come and imagining the starlight reflected in Cai's green eyes. She saw again the melancholy that was never far from the surface, for all his smiles. And for the first time, she began to question her own motives for so readily agreeing to the journey.

"Will you show me some magic?"

"No."

Cai's instant, angry rebuff left Zana feeling hurt and uncomfortable. Her suggestion had been a lighthearted one, prompted by an ever-increasing curiosity and by their deepening friendship. They had been traveling for four days now, and were almost half way to Great Newport. Tonight would be the first without a roof over their heads, and the isolated nature of their campsite had encouraged Zana to make her request. Now she stared into the campfire and wondered if she had misjudged the wizard. Their days together had passed quickly, enlivened by conversation and his inquisitiveness. However, Cai always managed to steer away from topics concerning his past, coaxing her instead into telling him more about the land they were traveling through. He had listened diligently, asking many astute questions that somehow clarified Zana's own thoughts about Cleve. Cai was interested in everything about the region: its politics and history, its geography, and its people. He was fascinated by their religious beliefs and the more outlandish cults, and Zana told him all she had learned about the Gray Raiders, the blue-flame sect, and the ancient Abbey. She often regretted that her own experience was so limited, and had to remind him from time to time that she was a northerner like himself, and that the facts she related were secondhand.

Cai was especially intrigued by her description of the elementals.

"I hope we meet some on the way," he had remarked.

Zana did not share his enthusiasm at this prospect, but kept her thoughts to herself.

Throughout their journey, Cai had treated Zana with consideration and tact, keeping the swarm out of sight while they rested at village inns, and making sure that his companion was as comfortable as possible. She had begun to believe that he must like her—at least a little.

Yet now she seemed to have spoiled all that by her clumsy, instantly regretted words. *This is not how I imagined it*, she thought bitterly as she wrapped her cloak more securely around her. The sky was clear, with stars shining far above, and the night was cold. She huddled closer to the fire.

"I'm sorry," Cai said quietly. He had noticed her discomfort, but had been unable to put his feelings into words. Zana looked up at him, but said nothing, and the hurt in her eyes forced him to try to explain.

"Magic should never be used for trivial things," he said quietly, recalling with secret embarrassment a key turning slowly in its lock. "It's too serious, too important for that. If we misuse it, terrible things can happen." He paused. "I didn't mean to snap at you. It's just that I've denied magic for so long that even talking about it is difficult."

"Forgive me," Zana whispered. "I didn't understand."

Paradoxically, her unquestioning acceptance of his words meant that Cai felt obliged to explain further, and he found himself talking about wizardry, something he had once sworn never to do again.

"Magic is a form of energy," he told her, remembering, his own lessons, so many years ago. "It's stored in here," he went on, tapping his forehead. "Every human mind is capable of far more than it is used for normally."

"You mean *anyone* can become a wizard?" Zana asked, surprised.

"Perhaps not," he replied. "You do need to have a particular aptitude and capacity. But everyone has magic in them, it's just that most people can never harness it in any meaningful way. The wizard's trick—" he smiled ruefully at his choice of words "—is to store and then direct enough energy to have a noticeable effect on the outside world. That takes an awful lot of knowledge, patience, and hard work."

"So *I* could possibly do some magic, but it would be so small that nothing would really change?"

"The world is full of magic, but most of it isn't seen, precisely for that reason. Think of it like a hammer and a nail. Rest the hammer on the nail, and nothing happens. Bring the hammer down hard, and the nail is driven in. Yet it's the same hammer, the same nail. Only the amount of energy involved has changed."

"You'd make a good teacher," Zana remarked.

Cai remembered Gemma's words—*You could have taught me*. The recollection brought with it a reminder of his own uncertainties.

"At least, that's how it used to be," he told Zana soberly.

"What do you mean?"

"Well, there's something *new* now," he replied. "All the old wizards are gone—except for me. I don't know why I should have survived, or why I've retained my powers."

"There are *no* wizards left in the islands? None at all?"

"Not in the sense that I knew them," Cai answered. "Everything changed with The Destruction. Perhaps Gemma will be able to explain it."

"The *only* wizard?" Zana breathed. "Doesn't that make you feel rather—?"

"Lonely?" Cai said. "Yes."

There was silence again for a while, as Zana sought unsuccessfully for some words of comfort. Then Cai went on. "Especially because I hated everything wizardry once stood for, seeing only the evil it had brought, and refusing to admit that there could still be a positive side to it."

"Poor you," Zana said gently. In the firelight, with his eyes downcast, Cai looked so young and so dejected that she longed to hug him to her, comforting him as a mother would her son. Then the images in her head changed, and she shied away from them, forcing herself to remember her reason for coming to Cleve, and wondering if her old lover could still be alive.

"It was my own stupid fault," Cai admitted in disgust. "I should have listened to Gemma."

"We'll find her," Zana stated confidently. *We have to*. Ensuring Cai's future contentment had suddenly become very important to her.

They rose early the next morning, emerging from their separate tents as the sun rose over the eastern horizon. They ate a quick meal, then broke camp, and were about to mount their horses, when Zana groaned.

"My body isn't used to all this riding," she complained. "I ache all over."

"I'm sorry," Cai said, immediately solicitous. "I should have thought of that." He walked over to her. "Take my hands."

Zana did so, wondering what he intended. Their eyes met as the wizard's power flowed into her body, warming cold limbs and soothing her aches and soreness.

"Better?" he asked after a while.

She nodded, struck dumb with amazement. She felt healthier, more alive, better than she had in years.

"Come on, then," he ordered, and helped her into the saddle.

By the time they had ridden the short distance back to the coast road, Zana had recovered her composure.

"That was amazing," she said. "Thank you."

"It's simple enough, really," he replied, grinning. "I just helped your body do what it would have done anyway—eventually."

"As far as I'm concerned, you've just proved that magic can definitely be used for good," Zana stated, smiling back at him. "The beneficial effect has been *very* noticeable!"

"I haven't been flattered like that in a long time," Cai laughed. "I think I rather like it."

"That wasn't flattery," she replied. "I meant every word. And, in any case, I'm sure all the women have nothing but praise for you."

"Oh, it was like that once," he answered, "but a long, long time ago."

Zana glanced at him curiously then.

"That's one thing I've been meaning to ask you," she said. "You told me that you were already a wizard when Gemma was a child, but—"

"I'm not as young as I look," he interrupted. "Wizardry has its conceits, you know! Whether I wanted it to or not."

Zana felt pleased that Cai could joke about it, but she was still confused.

"I'm twice as old as Gemma," Cai explained. "Looking the way I do is one of the fringe benefits."

"Oh." And Zana felt the color rise in her cheeks.

They rode on that day under a clear, pale sky. They had passed the salt swamps, and were now approaching the arid sea where the coast road skirted the Diamond Desert. The wind was from the southwest—directly over the desert—so the cloudless sky was no surprise.

They were both preoccupied. Zana was keeping a wary eye on the rocks and sand dunes, knowing that it was around here that the Swallows had encountered first elementals, then the deadly Gray Raiders. Cai was aware of her unpleasant memories of the area, but he was feeling distinctly uncomfortable himself. Ever since noon, something about the air had made him increasingly tense. Somehow, it seemed to constrict his chest, and his heart was beating wildly. Had the idea not been so patently absurd, he would have guessed that a violent thunderstorm was on its way. He looked about anxiously, but could see nothing to explain his peculiar foreboding.

When the skyravens suddenly roared over their heads like a thunderclap of doom, both Cai and Zana started so violently that they nearly fell off their horses. But by the time they had managed to calm their terrified mounts, it was obvious that the enormous metal birds had no interest in them. Instead, the skyravens were flying far out to sea, traveling at an incredible speed, their sound now only an unpleasant drone.

"They're heading toward that cloud," Zana said, peering into the distance.

Cai said nothing, stunned by his first sight of the awesome skyravens.

"There's something funny about it," Zana went on. "The

cloud, I mean. It wasn't there before—and there are blue flashes inside it, like lightning."

Cai stared hard and saw that she was right.

"But lightning wouldn't normally appear in one isolated cloud," he replied. "And we haven't heard any thunder."

"The skyravens *are* going to it!" Zana explained. "Look!"

They watched in silence as a burst of yellow light blossomed below the cloud. Then the sky flashed once more, casting lurid shadows all around the cloud. Long moments passed, then the sounds of the explosions washed over the disbelieving travelers.

"What's happening?" Zana whispered, but Cai did not answer. All his attention was focused on the distant battle.

The skyravens were almost invisible, but he could just make them out, buzzing round the cloud like angry insects. More explosions followed. Then, without warning, a huge ball of bright orange flame enveloped both the cloud and the three skyravens. Cai and Zana covered their eyes, sheltering from the impossible brightness. It lasted only a few moments.

They looked up again as the sound of the biggest explosion yet rolled over them. In the far distance, the cloud appeared unchanged by all the mayhem, but there was no sign of the skyravens.

Cai and Zana were distracted for a few moments as they calmed their horses, but then they looked at each other, seeing fear and bewilderment reflected in each other's eyes.

"These are powers beyond my understanding," Cai said. "I want no part of this."

"Nor me," Zana agreed breathlessly. "Is it over?"

"I hope so!"

So they resumed their journey, casting many a sidelong glance out to sea. Half an hour passed before either dared put into words what they had both realized.

"It's getting closer," Zana said, fighting down her terror.

"I know," Cai replied, sounding calmer than he actually was. "I can't understand it—it's traveling in the *opposite* direction of the wind." He was overwhelmed by a sense of foreboding.

"Can we avoid it?"

"I hope so. On its present course, it should pass in front of us. We'll wait here for a while, and let it go."

They dismounted, petted their still-nervous mounts, then

sat quietly on the ground and watched the cloud. The eerie blue flashes were still there and were easy to see now.

They both realized what was happening at the same moment and looked at each other in horror. There was no need for words. Leaping into their saddles, they urged the restless horses into a wild gallop. Somehow, the cloud had changed course and was heading directly toward where they had been sitting. Unless they could outrun it, it would probably pass directly overhead—a prospect neither of them relished.

The horses pounded on, driven by their own fear as well as that of their riders, but their efforts were in vain.

"It's coming!" Zana yelled above the rushing of the wind. Above them, the cloud loomed large, blotting out the sun; the day seemed suddenly cold.

"Keep riding," Cai shouted back. "Maybe we can still outrun it." But the next instant proved him wrong.

One moment they were galloping along, the next they were plucked from their saddles by invisible hands and whirled, terrified and screaming, into the air. The earth beneath them swirled in a giddy circle as Cai and Zana were pulled into the sky. And then the earth disappeared.

They were *inside* the cloud.

chapter 19

They were swallowed by the cloud, but held within the gray mist for only a few moments. Then, completely disoriented, Cai and Zana found themselves in the hallway of an elegant, old-fashioned mansion. Their abrupt arrival had not brought with it the expected jolt of landing—there had been only a sort of slippery, popping noise—but they were both shaking and wide-eyed with shock. Instinctively, they reached out and held each other tight. Zana closed her eyes, shutting out the impossibility of what she saw around her, and buried her face in Cai's shoulder. The wizard looked about him in amazement while trying to bring his stunned brain back to life. His heart was beating like a drum, but the sense of oppressive foreboding had left him. It would appear that this was what he had been waiting for, and his only choice now was to face it as best he could. *This is certainly wizardry,* he told himself, *but more powerful than anything I could ever aspire to.*

A familiar buzzing noise distracted him, and he glanced up, immeasurably gladdened by the fact that the swarm had been transported with him. He sent them a message of reassurance. The bees' reply both surprised him and helped calm his shattered nerves.

This hive is wholesome. The swarm is content.

Indeed, the bees were behaving as though nothing strange had happened. They were not flying erratically or making the angry sounds that normally indicated their displeasure or discomfort.

The cells are complete, but not whole, they added enigmatically. Cai questioned them, but could not get a clear idea of what they meant.

The wizard looked around at the large tiled hall, empty save for Zana, himself, and the swarm. Several wooden doors led from it but they all appeared fast shut. A curving staircase led up to a balcony with wooden railings. Other doors were visible in the shadows of the upper floor.

Helped by the warmth of Cai's arms, Zana's trembling had subsided a little. He looked at her carefully as she lifted her white face.

"Are you all right?" he asked softly.

"Of course not!" she replied, her voice high-pitched and over-loud. Then she laughed nervously. "Where are we?"

"I have no idea. But whoever brought us here must have had a reason for it."

"That sounds ominous," she said. She was calmer now, but her voice still quavered.

"The bees aren't afraid," Cai reassured her. "That's always a good sign."

Zana looked up hopefully, willing to grasp at any promising straws.

Come on! Cai ordered himself. *You're a wizard. Start acting like one!*

"Shall we have a look round?" he suggested aloud.

"All right," she whispered.

She was reluctant to leave the comfort of his arms, and though she pulled away, their hands remained joined.

"Where shall we start?" Cai asked.

"I don't—" Zana began, but she stopped and gave a small scream as one of the doors was thrown open violently. Terrified, she hid behind her companion.

The sound of laughter came through the open door and was followed by two outlandish figures. The first stood a head taller than Cai, while the second was little more than half his size. In all other respects, they were identical. Both wore shapeless brown robes and enormous, droopy leather hats. They had long pointed noses, and their bright eyes shone in the gloom under the rims of their hats. The strange effect was completed by unruly gray beards that fell almost to their waists. The smaller of the two men carried a book in his long-fingered, knobbly hands, but he was not studying it now. He was too busy laughing.

"Like moths around a flame!" the tall one exclaimed.

"An *invisible* flame," the other retorted, and they roared

with laughter again. "Shooting their pathetic little fireworks at *us*. What a waste of their time!"

"A waste of *no* time!" This comment brought about such a gale of mirth that both men doubled up, holding their sides and gasping for breath.

"And then they hit each other!" the small one shrieked. "Whoosh! Bang! All gone."

The two men flung their arms round each other and danced a kind of jig, then separated and tried to calm down, wiping the tears of laughter from their cheeks.

Cai and Zana watched this extraordinary performance in speechless amazement. They knew that they would be noticed as soon as the hilarity subsided.

"Er—" Cai began, clearing his throat.

The newcomers turned to look at him.

"By all the tomes of eternity," the tall one said. "You've got here at last!"

"And about time too," the other added tetchily. "We've *needed* a real adept."

"I *told* you he'd turn up."

"Well, I'm just glad your research finally paid off."

This bickering was the last straw, and Cai's self-control snapped.

"Who *are* you?" he yelled.

The others regarded him with apparent surprise.

"I am Wynut," the tall one said. "And my fellow-mage is Shanti." His tone was suddenly formal.

"I'm—" Cai began.

"We know who you are," Shanti snapped, his irritation showing. "We've been chasing you about all over the place."

"Me?"

"Yes, you! Why are you so surprised? You *are* the last wizard, aren't you?" The spark in those half-hidden eyes grew brighter.

"I . . . I suppose . . . I could be," Cai stammered, unnerved by this irate demand.

"What we don't know," Wynut put in, "is who *that* is." He pointed to a spot behind Cai.

"This is Zana, my friend and guide."

"Can she be trusted?" Shanti asked sharply.

"Of course!" Cai was angry now. "Can you?" he half shouted.

His rash question had greatly differing effects on the two mages. Shanti's face turned first red, then purple, and he seemed on the verge of a seizure, but Wynut, after a moment's startled hesitation, just chuckled happily.

"That's a good question," he remarked. "We can—and I hope we can prove it to you."

"Right," Cai said immediately. "You can start by explaining why we've been abducted in this ridiculous manner. We could have been killed! And where are we?"

"And when can we go home?" Zana whispered in his ear. Cai was glad to hear her sounding relatively normal, and turned around to give her a smile.

"I apologize for your abrupt arrival," Wynut replied, serious now. "Unfortunately, it was a matter of necessity. We cannot always control the exact nature of the interface."

"You're a wizard, aren't you?" Shanti put in. "You should know about such things." Although he sounded distinctly grumpy, his face had returned to its normal color.

"I have never used wizardry to transport unsuspecting victims against their will," Cai retorted. "What kind of magic is that?" Zana squeezed his arm encouragingly, and his confidence rose another notch.

Shanti subsided, looking sullen.

"What's an interface?" Zana asked suddenly, and the three men looked at her in surprise.

"It's the border between time scales," Wynut answered. "The plane separating the past from the future, or in this case, your time and no time. You see, *this* place is adrift in time." He spread his arms wide, expecting his answer to satisfy her.

"I wish I hadn't asked," Zana whispered.

Cai smiled, then returned to his earlier question.

"Why have you been chasing me?" he demanded.

"You mean you don't *know?*" Shanti looked as if he would explode with exasperation, but his colleague remained calm.

"We have already answered too many of your questions," Wynut said evenly. "As an adept, I am sure you will realize the consequences of what could be construed as meddling."

And the mage held up a hand before Cai could respond.

"Please," he said. "Come with us. We will explain all we can without the need of further questions from you. It will be better that way."

chapter 20

Zana held Cai back for a moment.

"This must be the floating city," she whispered. "You remember—I told you about it. Those two men helped Gemma and Arden."

"Let's hope they can help us," he replied softly. "Do you really think they can?"

"The underground has been on the lookout for this place for ages," Zana went on. "There are libraries here, with books full of history that hasn't happened yet. I mean, all the things that *might* happen . . . I think." She frowned. "I never quite understand that part. Some of the rumors about this place are pretty wild."

"I'm not surprised," Cai remarked dryly.

"Time may not pass here in the conventional sense," Wynut called from the adjoining room, "but that's no reason to waste it!"

"Come on," Zana said, giving Cai a gentle push.

They entered a room lined with books from floor to ceiling; the only furniture was a large desk, surrounded by several comfortable chairs. The whole was lit by bright globes that hung from the rafters. Cai looked at the endless rows of books and wondered which past—or future—they represented.

Shanti pulled cushions onto the chair behind the desk, then sat there while Wynut took one of the armchairs and waved Zana and Cai into others. When they were all settled, Wynut began to speak. His voice was slow and calm, as though explaining something to a child, but there was still an undeniable undercurrent of excitement in his tone.

"Please hear me out, and resist the temptation to ask any questions," he began. "Believe me, it *is* necessary." He paused and waved his hand to indicate everything about them. "We are an anomaly here," he stated. Then he added, "When the Age of Chaos began and magic came to an end, we were cast adrift by forces stronger than those that had formed our world. As wizards, we could not exist—and yet we did. There was no time to which we could belong, so we ended up *outside* time.

"As you can imagine, this caused us much inconvenience, but we eventually saw the opportunities that were available. We have traveled far—in all senses—and have acquired much knowledge. We have always hoped that we could turn the tide and restore magic, thus returning ourselves to the world. It is no small task, however, when the infinite branches of time divide at every moment."

"Get on with it," Shanti snapped. "We don't need a lesson in chronology. The scales are becoming more unbalanced every moment they are here."

"It's a risk we must take," Wynut shot back. "Need I remind you that a mistake now would mean the end of everything?" There was no answer, so he carried on, his tone measured once more.

"You will realize, of course, that there are limits imposed on the ways in which we can interfere with the world in real time. These limits are strict—and that is why your questions are dangerous, both to you and to us. If we went too far, it would rend the very fabric of time and space, and the consequences of that are unthinkable—literally. So we must proceed with great caution. Our contacts have thus far been limited only to minor actions by a few important people. Each action carries with it a multitude of possible repercussions, not all of which can be foreseen, and which, until now, have only been rearguard actions, delaying the inevitable, final conflict.

"It's different now. The whole future of the earth is in jeopardy, and the decision must be made soon. That's why *you* are here."

"It's rather appropriate, don't you think?" Shanti remarked scornfully. "The last wizard to start the last battle."

At first, their words made no sense. Then Cai understood, and was horrified. He could not *possibly* be the one they wanted! He was not important; all he was here for was to find

Gemma. He wanted to voice a passionate denial, but his throat had closed up. He found it hard to breathe.

"A great threat hangs over the world," Wynut said. "The threat of destruction on a terrible, unprecedented scale."

The Destruction, Cai thought. *It can't happen again!*

"But this time," Wynut added, as if reading Cai's mind, "no one will survive."

Cai stared at him, his mental anguish numbed and exacerbated at the same time by that impossible statement. *No one?*

"No one except—possibly—us," Shanti said. "And our immortality would be a curse more painful than the worst of deaths." The mage's voice was filled with an unbearable sadness; it was a strange contrast to his earlier tetchiness.

Cai heard a sob and turned to Zana. She stared at him with horror and disbelief reflected in her eyes; tears were streaming down her ashen cheeks. He tried to smile, but his face was frozen. The bees had left their temporary perches and were flying in all directions, mirroring the wizard's turmoil.

"But, surely—" Cai began, then stopped as Wynut held up a hand, signaling for silence.

"There *is* still hope," the taller mage said, restoring a little sanity to the chaos in Cai's mind. "But it grows less each day, and only by knowing the full extent of the evil you face can you hope to defeat it."

Me? Cai thought desperately. *It can't be so*. And yet he forced himself to remember that there was hope. He had believed Wynut from the beginning; if defeat was a foregone conclusion, there would have been no point in the mage telling him anything. He struggled to put aside his apprehension, ready to listen once more.

"Although there is a chance that the destruction we fear may never actually take place," Wynut said, "that alone will not save us. The very fact that the threat is *there* may be enough to doom us all. You must prevent not only the execution of the threat, but also the *possibility* of it ever happening."

Questions flooded into Cai's mind, but he held his tongue, knowing that he must not ask them.

Shanti spoke then, reciting what was obviously a quotation; Cai could not even guess at its source.

Remember the Dream
And whence it comes.
Madness for the One
Is death for all.

As the words rang in Cai's ears, he knew that he would hear them always; they would be seared in his memory until the final moment of his life.

Silence settled upon the room. Zana had stopped crying, and the bees were settled peacefully once more.

There must be more! Cai thought, looking back and forth between Wynut and Shanti. *You can't leave it at that!* Yet neither showed any sign of speaking again, and Cai could not find his tongue to ask for the help he so desperately needed. Not so Zana.

"What are we supposed to *do?*" she burst out. The three men looked at her, their expressions showing varying degrees of shock.

"There must—" she tried again, but was interrupted by Shanti, who roared, "Quiet!" The diminutive wizard had risen and was now standing on his chair behind the desk. He would have looked utterly ridiculous had it not been for the obvious seriousness of the situation and the intensity of his feelings. "Your foolishness will destroy us all!" He turned to Cai. "Can't you keep her under control?"

"It's not fair," Zana complained in a hoarse whisper. "There must be *something* you can tell us. All you've given us so far are riddles."

"Zana, please," Cai begged softly. "There's nothing else they can do."

"Anything," she persisted. "Just one small fact that we can hold on to."

Wynut and Shanti exchanged anxious glances. A moment later, they made their decision—and flickered out of existence.

"No! Come back!" Zana screamed in frustration, then crumpled up in her chair and started crying again. Cai went to her and put a consoling arm around her shoulders.

"I'm sure they've told us everything they can," he said gently. "It's not their choice to make."

"I suppose you have to be a *wizard* to understand," she replied bitterly, brushing aside her tears and scowling.

"I *don't* really understand," Cai admitted, "but I know they're telling the truth."

"But what they said made no sense," she objected. "It all sounded so frightening—and then they say it's up to you to go and make everything all right—but they don't tell you how!" She was angry now. "Is that what they call help?"

"Perhaps it'll become clearer later on," he replied, hope and doubt mingling in his voice. "I know so very little about this land—perhaps when we discuss it with Gemma—"

"You're pinning all your hopes on that poor girl," Zana commented. "Isn't that rather a lot for one pair of shoulders?"

Cai had no answer to that. *And suppose you don't find her*, he told himself. *What then?* He had begun his long voyage almost in desperation, but over the weeks, his hopes had grown steadily. Everything seemed to be going his way—but this unexpected intervention had renewed all his doubts and added new terrors. *The last wizard to start the last battle*. Once more, he shied away from the implications of Shanti's statement, and took refuge in action.

"Come on," he said firmly. "Let's get out of here."

"Oh, we can just walk out of the front door, I suppose?" Zana retorted sarcastically. "We're in a *cloud*, remember?"

Images of their dizzying ascent flashed before his eyes, and he stood for a moment looking lost and uncertain. Zana's mood changed from frustration to fondness for her bewildered companion. Amidst the insanity of what was happening, here was something real, something human—something she could cope with.

"Are you sure you're as old as you say?" she asked. "Right now, you look just like a little boy."

Cai shook his head, smiling weakly.

"Let's go back to the hall," he suggested. "That's where we arrived, so perhaps if we go back there, we'll be able to leave."

Zana refrained from commenting that such logic did not seem relevant to their current experience, and stood up. They left the library slowly, treading carefully, almost as if they expected to sink through the floor at any moment. The doors swung closed behind them of their own accord. The swarm droned placidly overhead, but otherwise the hall was silent.

"All these doors have symbols carved on them," Zana observed. "Except the large ones over there."

So they walked round the hall, studying the carvings: an

acorn, a clover leaf, a rose, and a falcon. A draught blew through the cracks around the unmarked doors, but they dared not touch the handle.

"Now what?" Zana asked, but Cai held a finger to his lips. Muffled voices could be heard from above. As they turned to look at the stairway, a door on the balcony opened and Wynut walked out. He looked over the banisters, curling his long fingers around the top rail. However, before he could speak, Shanti's voice sounded from the room behind him.

"He's supposed to know that already!" he shouted angrily. "That *can't* be what's holding us up. Your calculations must be wrong." He began muttering crossly.

Wynut ignored his fellow mage and spoke to the pair below.

"Thaumaturgy was never Shanti's strong point," he remarked with a resigned shrug. "I apologize for the delay. Something is preventing your return to the world, and we're not sure what it is."

"Wonderful," Zana breathed.

"But we're working on it," Wynut continued. "Please bear with us." Turning, he strode back into the chamber. "Normal service will be resumed as soon as possible." He chuckled as he went.

"I don't know what you're laughing at," they heard Shanti say, then the door closed, and the hall was silent once more.

"They're mad," Zana said. "Completely, utterly, *mad!*"

"I don't think so," Cai replied cautiously. "They just see things differently from us."

"You can say that again," she said, shaking her head in bewilderment. Then she cleared her throat. "I don't know about you, but I could do with a stiff drink." This was said with feeling.

"Try this, my dear," a voice said cheerily. "It'll bring the color back to your cheeks."

Amazed, they spun around to face the newcomer, a plump, matronly looking woman. She was carrying a tray on which stood two glasses, amber liquid glinting from within.

"It's good," she insisted, smiling encouragingly. "Though I do say so myself. Wine with a little something extra—something special."

Cai recovered first from this latest bout of speechlessness.

"May I ask who you are?" he asked, taking a proffered glass.

"Me? I'm just the housekeeper," she laughed. "No one of importance."

"Do you know anything about what those two have been telling us?" Zana asked, glancing toward the balcony.

"Goodness me, no. They're always messing about with magic and other such nonsense. They get so wrapped up in it they'd forget to eat sometimes if they didn't have me to look after them. Enjoy your drinks."

With that she turned on her heels and waddled away.

"Don't go!" Zana cried, but the door had already closed behind the housekeeper. Zana tried to follow, but the door would not open.

"This is delicious," Cai remarked. "Try some. You're our drinks expert, after all."

"I'm sure I wasn't brought here to be a wine taster!" she retorted, but took a sip from her glass nonetheless. The drink was cool, fragrant, and very strong. "On the other hand," Zana said, taking a larger mouthful, "a drink might help improve my understanding of this place."

They smiled at each other, both glad that they had recovered a little composure. Then, by unspoken agreement, they walked across to the stairs, sat down on the bottom step, and carried on drinking.

"I wonder what happened to the horses," Zana said.

"They must have been as terrified as we were when we flew off like that."

Cai studied his glass. The liquid within seemed to be disappearing awfully quickly.

"They may not even have noticed," he said thoughtfully. "After all, while we're here, we're out of time."

"Don't *you* start," Zana complained.

"That's why it wasn't affected by the skyravens," the wizard went on, as if explaining it to himself.

"Perhaps we should get everybody to come and live here, then," she suggested. "Hiding from the skyravens is not quite so easy in the real world." She had seen the devastation caused by them in Altonbridge. Her glass was nearly empty. She held up her free hand and clicked her fingers. "Waiter!"

Their laughter was stilled by an answering, inhuman cry,

and they twisted round to look up at the latest surprising inhabitant of this strange place.

The large tortoiseshell cat was sitting on one of the top steps, its tail curled nearly around its feet. They had just had time to take in its appearance when they realized that the animal's meow had not faded away as it should have done, but instead was echoing and evolving, growing in complexity and modulation with each moment. They stared wide-eyed at the impassive animal as its cry gradually turned into comprehensible speech.

"A sense of balance is important in all things. And then again, falling over is just another way of *regaining* one's balance."

The bees hummed around them in surprised agitation, but Cai and Zana were speechless. The cat glanced at the swarm, but obviously considered them no threat. It meowed again, then licked a forepaw and began to clean its face. Once again, the long, drawn-out call evolved into clear speech. Even though Cai and Zana were prepared for it this time, the effect was still the strangest thing they had ever heard.

"The key will open the door," it said. "And then again, locks can be changed."

Cai and Zana looked at each other, nonplussed.

"What does *that* mean?" Cai wondered aloud.

"More insane riddles," Zana muttered disgustedly, as the cat cried out again.

"Age may talk to youth. And then again, innocence is power."

Zana clapped her hands to her ears; her glass dropped to the floor and shattered.

"I can't stand this!" she screamed.

Cai, on the other hand, was fascinated. The cat's words meant little to him, but something was stirring in his mind. He was about to ask another question when he heard Shanti's voice raised in triumph.

"You see! We're moving again. So much for your calculations."

Wynut muttered something in reply but, by then, Cai was no longer listening. The walls, the floor, everything about them dissolved, and their surroundings became misty and unreal.

"Wait!" he cried out to the unmoving cat. "Don't go!"

But it was too late; the mansion disappeared, and Cai and Zana were left suspended, weightless in a mist that was filled with mysterious blue lights.

As daylight appeared, Zana screamed. Far, far below, the earth revolved madly as they plunged toward it.

In those flickering, terrifying moments, they were both convinced that they were going to die. In fact, they were placed gently into the saddles of their racing horses, who galloped on as though nothing had happened.

They managed to keep their balance and brought their fretting, wild-eyed mounts under control. Looking up at the cloud, they saw that it was moving away to the southwest.

When they dismounted, Zana's legs gave way beneath her, and she sat down in the dirt with a bump. Cai's legs felt just as unsure of themselves, so he staggered over and joined her.

"We're back!" she whispered, as if unable to believe their good fortune.

He nodded, as relieved as she was.

"Did it really happen?" she asked.

"If it didn't," he replied, "we've both got drunk on nothing more than air."

Zana grinned.

"Not possible," she said emphatically. "And I speak as one who knows. It's a pity we couldn't bring that wine back with us—I could *really* do with some now."

They made camp there and then, too exhausted to travel or to worry about concealment. They lit a fire and cooked a meal, but tasted little. They talked for hours, trying, unsuccessfully, to make sense of their experience. They both knew that it was important, but neither of them knew what to do about it.

They slept that night in the same tent, grateful for the companionship and warmth.

In his dreams, Cai was back in the floating city, running from door to door and wrenching them all open. The same scene greeted him beyond every threshold, but still he kept running, endlessly running, hoping that the next one would be different.

At last, exhausted and afraid, he came to the final door, the last possibility. The symbol carved into the wood was a pair of scales, unbalanced by what looked like a fish. For some reason, this made Cai's heart sink even further. He put out a trembling hand and opened the door.

But it was just like all the others. The library had vanished and in its place stood a devastated landscape. Ash and smoke were everywhere, drifting over broken and blackened rock. Fires roared in the distance, and molten earth spewed skyward to meet somber dark clouds. The desolation was complete. It was a scene totally devoid of life.

He woke sweating and distraught.

"No," he moaned. "No!"

"What's the matter?" Zana asked, genuine concern in her voice.

"I've seen the end of the world," he gasped.

chapter 21

Five days later, Cai and Zana reached the city of Great Newport. Zana immediately made herself known to the gate watch and asked that they be taken to see Jordan and Hewe. She no longer had any doubts about Cai, and trusted him completely. She had letters for Jordan, but it was Hewe whom she and Cai most wanted to meet. It seemed that he had accompanied Gemma and Arden to the "secret place," and was therefore the most likely to know her current whereabouts.

They were led through bustling streets toward the center of the city. Because of the bees, they were the subject of considerable interest for a while, but the people of Great Newport had witnessed many strange spectacles in the past few months and soon returned to their business.

Zana was impressed by the progress the city had made, after the ravages of the recent conflict. Perhaps because of the integral role it had played, Great Newport's recovery was more advanced than that of Altonbridge. Zana had heard of the vast destruction meted out by both the enemy tower and the skyravens, and so was even more surprised at just how much had been achieved. New buildings were rising everywhere, and she knew from personal experience just how difficult mass construction was to organize.

But the most impressive thing of all was the obvious sense of purpose in the people around them. No one appeared idle, and there was a heartwarming air of cooperation in many of the activities. Even though she could see only a tiny part of what was going on in Newport, Zana was delighted and impressed. That such a transformation could take place in a city that had once been so divided and oppressed was a tribute to the achievements of Jordan and his underground.

They were taken to one of the imposing buildings on Colosseum Square, and their guide took Zana's messages and left them to wait in the entrance hall. Cai's impatience was obvious, and the bees grew agitated. They had settled on the high ceiling, but even so, their droning sounded loud in the confined space, and there were many anxious glances cast at the wizard's unusual familiar. Even Zana, who was used to them by now, found herself a little nervous. Cai did not appear to notice anything untoward. He was too intent on the next stage of his search, and so did not hear the small boy approach.

"Are those your bees, mister?"

The child tugged at Cai's sleeve with one hand, while the other pointed upward. His head was tipped back so that he could watch the progress of the insects.

The wizard looked down, then glanced at the ceiling almost uncertainly, as if he was not sure that they *were* his bees. His mind had been elsewhere, and it took a few moments for him to realize where he was.

"Yes," he said eventually. "They're mine."

"Noisy, ain't they."

"I suppose they are." Cai had not even noticed. He sent a calming message, and the buzzing died down a little.

"Did you do that?" the boy demanded, obviously impressed.

"Yes."

"Make them do something else."

"What's your name?" Cai asked, amused by the boy's enthusiasm.

"Marc."

The bees began crawling purposefully on the ceiling, and a few moments later, Marc's name was there for all to see, spelled out in letters of black and gold.

"Wow!" The boy's eyes lit up as he gaped at the swarm. "Wait till I tell the others about this!"

He took one last look at the bees, stared at their master for a few moments, then ran out of the building as fast as his little legs could carry him. Cai watched him go, thinking fondly of another small child who had once been entranced by his familiar.

"Very impressive," a deep voice commented from the

other side of the hall, and Cai turned sharply. He saw a tall, broad-shouldered man, whose black skin was dark even for these southern climes.

"Are you Jordan?" he asked.

"Yes." The man stepped forward and put out a hand in greeting. "You are welcome here, Cai." Dark eyes appraised the wizard from head to toe, then Jordan turned to Zana.

"And you too, Zana. Dale has told me great things of you. You are doubly welcome."

"You look as though you're doing quite well yourselves," she replied, and shook his hand.

"Maybe. But we still have an enormous amount to do."

"Let me know if I can help," she said, smiling. "It was silly of me to believe that I could really get away from building work!"

"You must have time to rest first," Jordan assured her. "We have made *some* progress, after all—"

"Like teaching that little boy to read?"

"Hospitals and schools have been a priority," he answered simply. "Our children are the future." He paused, then added, "When you are ready—but only then—there will be a job for you to do. Expertise such as yours will be a great help to me. But first I want to hear your news and to talk to Cai."

And I to you! the wizard thought. *At last!* Jordan's manner and bearing commanded respect, and his calm demeanor had made Cai reluctant to give voice to his own impatience. He could see why the underground's leader was held in such high regard.

"Come with me," Jordan told them. "I'm sure you're tired and hungry after your journey. I've arranged a meal for you."

They followed him along a gloomy, dark-paneled corridor and up some stairs, then turned into a light and spacious room. A simple meal was laid out on a table by one of the many windows, and Jordan ushered them into their chairs. The bees settled on a nearby wall.

"Is Hewe coming?" Cai asked, finding it impossible to think of food just yet.

"I've sent him a message," Jordan replied. "He'll join us shortly."

"Do *you* know where Gemma is?"

"In theory, yes."

"What does *that* mean?" Cai demanded, a small flash of anger showing in his eyes.

"She is not here at the moment, though we expect her back quite soon," Jordan answered calmly.

"How soon? Where is she now?" Cai's spirits rose immeasurably.

"I don't know exactly when she'll be back," the other went on. "At the moment, she's in the valley. But I don't know where that is—I have never been there, and could not find it alone."

"But Hewe could?" Cai persisted.

"Perhaps."

"But—"

"Why do you want to find her?" Jordan asked, cutting off Cai's objection.

The wizard hesitated. *How many times do I have to go through this?* he groaned inwardly.

"Didn't Dale tell you that in his letter?" he asked.

"Yes," Jordan said, "but I'd like to hear it from you. Dale's caution does him credit, but he obviously found some of the things you said a little hard to believe."

Cai was silent for a moment, considering this. *So I still have to prove myself*, he thought bitterly. His emotions were swinging from one extreme to another.

"Zana's safe arrival here is a point in your favor," Jordan continued, "and it appears that she has given you her trust, but I would like to know you better myself. Gemma has been the best of friends to us, and we wish to protect her from any possible danger."

Jordan left it at that, letting the implication of his words hang in the air.

"Surely you can't believe I wish her harm!" Cai exploded, half rising from his chair and glaring across the table.

"Forgive me," the dark man answered softly, his face giving nothing away. "I know nothing of you. And I wish to learn."

Forcing himself to relax, Cai sank slowly back into his chair. He took a deep breath and began to speak. In less than an hour, he had told Jordan of his background as a wizard, his relationship with Gemma, his recent voyage, and, most important of all, his terrible forebodings. The detailed accounts of his remote contacts with Gemma clearly made an impression on Jordan, and the black man nodded many times, as if agreeing with some of the wizard's conjectures.

Eventually, Cai reached the encounter with the floating city, and Jordan's interest immediately doubled. He obviously attached great importance to this, so, with Zana's help, Cai told him of their extraordinary adventure. He repeated every word of the conversations they had had with Wynut and Shanti, and the enigmatic statements of the cat.

When he had finished, Jordan was silent for a long time, chilled by the mage's words. *But this time*, no one *will survive*. There was much that was not clear, and he could not explain them anymore than his companions could—although he had one or two ideas.

"*You must prevent not only the execution of the threat, but also the* possibility *of it ever happening*," he quoted. "That's difficult enough even when you know what the possibility is."

Then Cai told Jordan of his dream. There was room in Jordan's philosophy for both the practical and the arcane, and he was not about to dismiss the wizard's vision just because it came in the form of a nightmare.

"Even The Leveling did not achieve such devastation," he said slowly, then pulled himself together and added, "Now it's my turn to tell *you* a few things." As he spoke, he realized that Cai had gained his confidence. The only way that the visitor could be false would be for him to have constructed a vast and intricate tissue of lies, requiring an incredible amount of knowledge as well as a more than vivid imagination—and the necessity of placing Zana in thrall to his treachery. Jordan could not believe that he would allow himself to be duped in such a manner. *And if I can, we're all doomed*, he decided. *In the final analysis, only Gemma can vouch for him—and she won't be here for a while*. He decided to accept the judgment of his subconscious. He moved over to the wall and pulled on a bell rope that hung there.

Going back to the table, he looked thoughtfully at Cai for a moment.

"Gemma believes that there is a threat to us all, and that it is coming from the far south," he began, then went on to tell them of her discovery of the timeless book in the blue-flame room beneath the tower and of its prophecies of doom. He added quickly that their actions had changed the book once, and that Gemma believed it could be done again.

There is still hope, Cai remembered.

"It seems logical," Jordan went on, "to believe that this threat is the same as the one the mages spoke of. Yet it is hard to believe that the weapons that must come from the south—the skyravens and the tower's rays—devastating though they are—could produce the annihilation you saw in your dream. After all, the weapons appear to be man-made, not the product of some evil magical force."

He was interrupted as Hewe came into the room. He was dressed in his usual black, and there was a grin on his scarred face.

"You rang, sir?" he said.

"Hewe, this is Cai and Zana," Jordan said. "Come and join us."

"Zana and I have already met," the bearlike man replied, pulling up a chair. "It's good to see you again."

"Do you know where Gemma is?" Cai asked.

"I know where she *was*," Hewe replied. "But I don't know if she's still there." The very fact that he was in the room showed that Jordan had decided to trust Cai.

"In the valley?"

Hewe nodded.

"Will you take me there?" Cai's tone was urgent.

Hewe looked at Jordan, who replied, "Going to the valley may not be your wisest course," he said.

"Why not?"

"Gemma reached the valley about . . . a month and a half ago." Jordan looked for and received confirmation from Hewe. "And in all that time, we've heard nothing from her."

Neither have I, Cai thought.

"But still, we have no reason to believe that there is anything to worry about," Jordan went on. "The valley is a self-contained community, with very little contact with the outside world. However, Gemma went there not only to rest but to attend the birth of a friend's baby."

The baby? Cai remembered his last vision of Gemma, that confused and confusing dream of blood and pain—and her angry rejection of his interference. *Of course!*

"Who is this friend?" he asked.

"Mallory," Hewe answered. "Arden has known her for many years."

Cai flinched inside at the sound of Arden's name, but said nothing.

"The baby should be due soon," Jordan put in.

"Any day now," his deputy confirmed.

It was born twelve days ago, Cai thought, but did not speak.

"Gemma told us that she'd return here after making sure that Mallory and the child were all right."

"How long would it take for her to get back?" Cai asked quickly.

"About ten days or so," Hewe told him.

"My point is," Jordan said, "that if you leave now, you may miss her. You'd probably be better off waiting here. We can always send a messenger to her, just in case."

This made sense to Cai. If the baby *had* been born twelve days ago, as he believed, then Gemma would almost definitely be on her way back.

"I must confess that I have an ulterior motive for suggesting that you stay," Jordan admitted. "We have in our organization here several people with some sort of magical talent. You will forgive me if I say that if you really *are* the wizard you claim to be, then their abilities would be small indeed compared to yours."

The last wizard, Cai thought, surprised that he was not angered by Jordan's seemingly doubtful words.

"Wizardry as you know it is alien to this land," the black man said. "And if you would be prepared to help us, we could learn a great deal from you."

You could have taught me. Cai winced as he recalled Gemma's regretful words. He still did not speak.

"Specifically," Jordan went on, "I'd like you to have a look at the blue-flame chamber. We haven't been able to get in there since Gemma left, and if we are to plan an expedition to the far south, I need to see for myself what this book is currently saying."

Cai had been very interested by the sound of the blue-flame room, and Jordan hoped that it might tempt him to stay in Newport. He believed that there was much they could learn from the wizard.

"So you're already planning to travel south?" Cai asked.

"Yes. I promised Gemma that as soon as the city was in reasonable shape, with things running smoothly, we'd head south," Jordan replied. "And that's another reason to be sure that she'll return soon." He paused. "There are *other* reasons for the expedition, which I'd like to explain to you."

"I'll stay," Cai decided abruptly. "Will you send a messenger for me—today?"

"I'll see to it," Hewe said, and went to make the necessary arrangements.

Jordan was smiling broadly. He picked up a glass and raised it in a toast.

"Welcome to Great Newport and to our branch of the underground," he said formally. "May our friendship be long and mutually beneficial."

Cai picked up his own glass and drank. He was suddenly very hungry, and as he began to eat, Jordan and Zana grinned at each other.

chapter 22

"This is Wray," Hewe said. "He's a sniveling little wretch, but he has his uses."

Wray's eyes had the look of a cornered animal, and he flinched as they approached. Although he no longer spent much time with his former comrades in the raiders' camp, he still dressed in gray. It was his only act of defiance toward a world that now treated him with disdain.

Wray had arrived at Great Newport nearly a month and a half ago and, though the underground's initial reaction to him had been less than cordial, the coded message from Hewe allowed him to enter the city. He had made contact with Jordan, confessed to his earlier fanaticism, and pleaded for a chance to make amends. There were many people who were still suspicious of the Gray Raiders, in spite of their continued cooperation under the firm leadership of Galar, and they warned Jordan that Wray was not to be trusted. The full extent of his earlier crimes would never be revealed, they argued, and he was known to have been involved in violent activities, as well as trading in the dangerous dragonflower seeds and abduction. It was suggested that such a man had no place in their organization.

Jordan, however, judged Wray's penitence to be genuine. His recent humiliation at the hands of Arden, Gemma, and Hewe, and having been made an outcast by his former colleagues, had broken his spirit. Even his ability to control elementals—the talent with which he had risen to power—had been stripped from him. His self-esteem was in tatters; he was, almost literally, scared of shadows.

A large group of Gray Raiders had set up a permanent

camp to the west of Great Newport, using this as their headquarters now that they had left the desert caves of the Lightless Kingdom. On several occasions, they had proved themselves to be genuine allies, acting as scouts and protecting supply convoys along the coast road. Many people still found their sinister appearance and barely veiled intensity unnerving, but the raiders had done much to overcome their reputation for violence and unreason.

Enlightenment had come to Galar and his young deputy, Tomas, as well as to many of their colleagues, and this group now held their wilder brethren in check. However, many of the raiders were frustrated by a lack of action. Having no one to fight, now that the travelers from the north were no longer the enemy, they yearned for the day when they could march south. It was there, everyone agreed, that the real enemy lay.

Their camp was often a rowdy, noisy place, fermenting with passionate arguments, but they kept to themselves for the most part and gave their strength to the city only when it was requested.

Jordan had not wanted to expose Wray to this atmosphere, which might revive the former raider's fanaticism, and in which Wray himself might become the object of considerable resentment, and so decided to trust his own judgment. On learning that Wray had been able to control elementals, he had instructed the all-too-willing man to study the blue-flame wall beneath the ruins of the tower. No one had been able to enter that room since Gemma left it with Arden and the meyrkats, and Jordan longed for the chance to read more from the mysterious book within.

Wray had jumped at the chance, in spite of his loss of faith in his own powers. While his initial attempts had been unsuccessful, this had made him even more determined, and he buried himself in the city's archives, seeking out ancient references to elementals, the secret chamber, and anything remotely connected with its mystery. He would return regularly to the shimmering wall and test a new theory but, so far, his efforts had all been in vain.

Now he had been summoned to meet Hewe and a stranger to the city in the room beside that pulsating barrier. While he waited, he tried out his latest discovery, gleaned from a so-called chart of power that he had found in a centuries-old tome. The wall remained impervious, however.

Hewe spoke again, having made Wray jump with his first words. The bearlike man always made Wray nervous, but this time there was more menace in his speech than in his imposing physical presence.

"This is Cai. He's a wizard—from the northern isles."

"I . . . I never meant them harm," Wray gabbled. "I was misguided, misled. I know now that the true enemy is to the south. Northerners are our friends!"

Cai looked from the frightened man to Hewe.

"He wasn't always quite as sensible as this," Jordan's deputy explained. "The gods know what he was guilty of before he saw the light."

"Nothing. Nothing!" Wray protested shrilly.

"Perhaps I should get Cai to read your mind," Hewe suggested, smiling. "Then we could see what your memory *really* holds."

Panic showed in Wray's eyes, while Cai watched, wondering what possible use this pitiful creature could be to them. The wizard was also trying to keep his horror at Hewe's suggestion from showing on his face. The big man obviously knew little of the tenets of magic; tampering with the mind of another human being, except with their express permission, was unthinkable."

"Don't worry," Hewe said cheerfully. "Cai won't be wasting time or energy on you. He's here to get in there," and he pointed at the blue-flame wall. "Have you made any progress?"

"No!" Wray shouted back, not sure whether to be thankful or resentful about the wizard's usurping of his task. "They hate me!"

"Who hates you?" Cai asked.

"*They* do," he replied, his face twitching. "The elementals in there. They're packed in so tight, and they're so cold and hard . . . I can't touch them."

"He's been down here for days, and has got nowhere," Hewe said. "Still, I suppose it keeps him out of mischief. I'll leave you to it. You won't give Cai any trouble, will you, little man?"

Wray shook his head wildly.

"Let me know if you need anything," Hewe told Cai, then went on his way.

The others stood in silence for a while, Cai studying the

fluid, powerful swirling of the barrier, and Wray watching the wizard.

"They tell me you used to be able to converse with elementals," Cai said eventually.

"Not these," the Gray Raider replied. "I could control the free ones outside, though." A touch of pride crept in, but vanished with the next statement. "That's gone now."

"I've never seen a free elemental," Cai said, still looking at the pulsing screen. "Tell me about them."

Wray gazed at the wizard in amazement, as if Cai had just admitted that he had never seen rain fall from the sky. Elementals had always been a part of Wray's life, ever since the time when, as a child, he found he could frighten the other boys by getting one of the strange creatures to follow him.

"They're beings of pure energy," he began hesitantly. "They can move faster than sound, and can take any shape they choose." He went on to tell Cai everything he could about the enigmatic creatures, amazed that the wizard should listen so intently. Surely *everyone* knew all this!

"So they're associated mainly with the areas that were most affected by The Destruction . . . The Leveling?" Cai asked.

"Yes. But they can go anywhere."

The wizard was deep in thought.

"Tell me again how you used to control them," he said.

"By force of will," Wray answered promptly, gaining confidence now. "Not everyone can do it. I just had to let them know who was master, and then it was easy."

"Easy?"

"Well, they squealed a bit at first," Wray admitted, "but eventually they *had* to obey. That's how it worked."

Cai nodded absently, his mind apparently elsewhere.

"But these?" he asked, gesturing at the blue wall.

"Nothing," Wray replied. "They're immovable. At first I thought they must use another form of power, but all the old references I've found prove that it *is* made of elementals. The force that must have been needed to meld them so thoroughly is beyond belief!"

Cai walked slowly toward the shimmering barrier. Close up, he found it impossible to focus on the bright, swirling patterns, but the sense of enormous power was unmistakable. The ancient masters who had created this chamber had hemmed it in with implacable skill and cruel precision. And yet it was not impregnable. Gemma had been able to enter it. So had Arden.

How?

As the antagonism Cai felt toward Gemma's unknown companions rose in his mind, the screen before him pulsed even more vividly. He felt the pressure of its rejection in his chest.

They squealed a bit.

Lost within his speculation, Cai had not noticed the arrival of the swarm. They had come in response to his unspoken need, leaving their hive and following his trail deep into the maze of tunnels beneath the city. Wray was terrified and fled to a doorway in the far corner of the room. He watched in awe as the bees circled the head of the unperturbed wizard.

It is meant to inspire fear and hate. That is its strength, Cai thought. *What if—?*

He reached back into his memory for what he sought and found it in the laughter of a little girl, long, long ago. The swarm picked up his thoughts and amplified them, clarifying his images of the past. They too had fond memories of Gemma.

Cai stepped forward. He encountered such a wave of resentment and hate that he almost faltered. His own emotions were mixed and threatened to overpower the joy he found in his recollection of the young girl. Then the bees bolstered his memory once again, and as the pressure on him lessened, he was able to study the feelings emanating from the trapped elementals. He stepped forward once more—and found himself inside a marble chamber.

Cai turned round to study the blue screen once more, aghast at the savage cruelty implied by its very existence.

Those are living things!

He found the thought of their eternal imprisonment almost unbearable.

No wonder the fear and hate is so strong.

The last of the bees had now joined him, popping through the barrier like bubbles rising from under water. Together, they moved to explore the room.

chapter 23

The chamber was almost bare, its beautiful stone cut in clinical lines. The only furniture it contained was a marble table, which stood at the far end of the room. On it lay a large book. Cai felt a strange reluctance to read those forbidden pages and walked around the edge of the floor, pretending to study the construction of the walls. The bees knew better; they flew straight to the table and congregated there, settling in an intricate, crawling pattern on its upper surface. The wizard gave in and approached the book with fear in his heart.

Do I really want to read this? What if it tells of Gemma's downfall? Or my own? Is it better to wait, unknowing, for the blows of fate, or face them squarely, with a tiny spark of hope?

He glanced at the pages that lay open before him, and read the description of Gemma's battle on the tower that had once stood above this room. For the first time, he realized the importance of the conflict—and saw how close Gemma had come to defeat. He still did not understand exactly how she had managed to turn the tables, but could see that his own remote participation had not been a factor.

"'Only one power could have opposed his progress, and that nearly failed through ignorance and clinging to outmoded ideals,'" he read.

That had an uncomfortable ring to it. Cai steeled himself and went on.

"'However, the Servants of the Earth achieved a temporary victory when the Key to the Dream . . .'"

Echoes awoke in the wizard's mind. Unwanted memories rose up and tried to claim him, but the phrase that resonated loudest was "the Key to the Dream."

Where have I heard that before?

A moment's thought produced two ideas. In the floating city, Shanti's quotation had begun:

Remember the Dream
And whence it comes.

Then the cat had remarked: "The key will open the door. And then again, locks can be changed."

Neither had made much sense at the time.

Can this be the link between them? The Key to the Dream is Gemma, that's obvious, but . . .

He read on, still not able to fit the pieces of the puzzle together.

"'. . . who had been imprisoned in the steel fortress, was able to reassert the doctrines of magic and turn the Bringer of Destruction's power upon himself.

"'However, this setback merely spurred the forces of the far south to even greater efforts. Their experiments grew rapidly in size and strength, and they were soon able to abandon their use of ancient power, replacing it with the new logic they had created. Their enemies were powerless to oppose them and their influence soon spread throughout the world. The old order was destroyed.

"'The Age of Chaos began.'"

Cai reached out, his heart beating wildly, and gripped the corner of the page between finger and thumb. The paper felt thick but fragile—he almost expected it to crumble as he turned it over.

At first he thought the next page was blank, but then he saw that the words *were* there, but shimmering and elusive. He stared at it until his eyes hurt, but it made no sense, and he grew angry and confused. The swarm droned in agitation.

Cai shut his eyes and tried to calm himself. Long years of controlling his magical powers had lent him certain strengths and, though his skills were rusty now, they served him still. He made himself tranquil, enabling the sparks of energy to rise and link at his command.

I am a wizard, he told himself.

The last *wizard*, a small voice mocked.

I will *read this book*, he insisted, trying to boost his confidence.

When Cai opened his eyes and looked again at the pages in front of him, he was taken aback. The bees covered the entire surface of the book in a gently undulating carpet of black and gold.

What are you doing? he asked, hoping that their instinct had found an answer.

Drawing pictures, came the enigmatic reply.

A window opened in the crawling insect mass, and Cai watched as the queen bee moved deliberately from one end of the space to the other. As she did so, words formed on the exposed portion of the page, as though her legs had been dipped in ink. Within a few moments, however, the delicate script began to fade; the wizard leaned closer and read anxiously.

"'*Rivers of stone*.'"

Is that all? he asked quickly. The queen bee moved purposefully toward another newly opened gap, and the process was repeated.

"'Fires in the sky.'"

And then:

"'The long cold darkness.'"

It's The Destruction all over again, Cai thought, filled with dread.

The next messages were less apocalyptic—but even more obscure.

"'The One became many,'" was followed by "'random divisions . . . impassable.'"

And then a phrase that at least made a little sense.

"'Hold back the elemental fires.'"

Cai waited for another revelation, but the bees left the pages now, crawling onto the table and taking to the air. He watched them in despair.

Can't you show me any more? he pleaded.

Some pictures cannot be drawn, the swarm replied, its multifaceted voice sounding a little aggrieved.

I didn't come in here just for a few incomprehensible snippets! Cai thought privately. *There must be more to it than this!*

The bees were almost all airborne now, and the leaves of the book were as unreadable as before. It looked worse, if anything, as though the ancient tome had resented the enforced—though partial—uncovering of its secrets.

Cai turned the page. Blank sheets stared back at him, and the next few were the same. He turned back and reread the passage about Gemma's "temporary victory." Then, on impulse, he went back to the very beginning and scanned the opening lines again.

Words from myth, from storybooks and legends, flowed forth, but as soon as he finished a sentence, he realized that he could remember nothing of it, and so had to begin again. The words were bold and clear enough, but they slipped through his mind like quicksilver.

He tried again with a later page, but the same thing happened. His head began to ache abominably and his eyesight blurred.

You have seen what you were meant to see.

The thought came unbidden into his mind. He thought it was the swarm at first, then realized that they were silent. He shivered, suddenly cold, and felt the chill of marbled centuries seep into his bones.

Cai closed the book gently. He almost expected to see dust rise, but there was none. All his senses told him he would learn nothing more here; wherever the message had come from, its finality was unmistakable.

As he turned to face the blue-flame barrier, the bees anticipated his next move and streamed past him toward the arcane exit.

Hold back the elemental fires.

For the first time, Cai wondered just how he was going to get out of this room. In his ignorance, he had been able to breach the elemental wall with patterns of thought that had given leverage to his own powers. But he knew the real nature of the barrier now; the revulsion he felt at its method of construction left him unable to summon these elements of joy that were necessary to achieve a passage. The heartless logic that had designed this barrier was both impressive and revolting. By condemning the elements to eternal, hateful confinement, those ancient wizards had ensured that they inspired fear, hate, and awe—whether through ignorance or knowledge—when exactly the opposite emotions were needed to be able to pass through them.

Cai hated the sorcery that had imprisoned them, and wanted to end their agony—but knew that such an act would be far beyond his powers.

The bees reached the barrier, then swirled around, waiting for their master. He stood uncertainly in the center of the room.

Is there no other way out of here?

Although he had not directed the question specifically at them, the swarm answered.

Yes. But only if you can fly.

Cai looked up at the high ceiling and saw what they meant. A precise square hold was cut in the marble—beyond was utter darkness. The bees flew up to investigate, some of them disappearing into the darkness.

It is blocked, their echoing voice reported. *Black metal.*

The scouts reemerged.

So there was *an entrance from the tower above,* Cai thought, wondering how much Mendle had been able to read. *How does the book decide what it should reveal—and to whom?* The wizard shook his head. There were too many questions and too few answers, and he was still faced with the problem of his own escape.

How did you get through the blue flame? he asked his familiar.

Honey laughing healthy cells, the bees replied. *The swarm renews itself.*

It took Cai some time to work this out. His conversations with the bees were usually straightforward, and he regarded them as humans in that respect. Their apian nature only occasionally impinged on these communications, and when it did, the human parallels were usually obvious. This time, however, it went a little deeper. The swarm was apparently summoning up race memories, then expressing them as best they could. By going back to the very basis of their existence, the bees were able to evoke the necessary responses in their own simple emotions—and thence in the elementals. For once, they were behaving as bees—and not as a wizard's familiar.

For the first time in his life, Cai wondered whether the bees had benefited from their association. When he had first found the swarm, his own joy and wonder had been so overwhelming—the long-anticipated arrival of a wizard's first familiar was always a moment of high emotion—that he had not even stopped to consider their reaction. They had always seemed to share his happiness, but now he began to think about just how much they had given up, especially when, as now, they were forced into traveling vast distances.

Show me, he asked softly.

The swarm flew toward their master and circled his head in a dizzying swirl of gossamer wings. Soon, their buzzing was the only sound in the world and although Cai was not afraid, he *was* confused. They had never treated him like this before. Closing his eyes, he willed himself to accept whatever they were trying to do, to become one with the swarm.

He became one *of* the swarm.

Instinct awoke in him like a sudden blaze of fire. Flight became his natural state, communication a meaningless concept. All knowledge was shared. Duty, protection, and a sense of order—like the geometric perfection of a hive—welled up within him. *Honey laughing healthy cells.*

Somewhere, a man called Cai smiled at the simplicity of it all. *The swarm renews itself.* Endless generations, always changing, never changing. A selfless, joyful immortality.

You have always flown with us. The swarm's multiple voice rang loudly in his head. *But now you see brightly.*

Why have you never shown me this before?

You never asked. It was a simple statement of fact, and there was no hint of criticism.

How much more have I missed? Cai wondered privately.

He opened his eyes—and found himself looking into Wray's astonished face.

chapter 24

There was a loud snapping sound behind Cai, and he swung round to see that the blue-flame wall was as cold and powerful as ever. And yet he had gotten through! There had been no sensation of movement while he was flying with the swarm, but somehow, he had achieved the impossible.

"I thought you'd destroyed it," Wray said in a small voice.

Destroyed it? Cai thought in amazement, turning back to his gray-clad companion. "What happened?" he asked.

"For a while, nothing," the other replied. "You've been in there at least an hour." Wray paused, hoping that Cai would tell him what he had discovered, but the wizard said nothing. Indeed, he appeared dazed. So Wray pushed aside his curiosity and went on. "Then the bees started popping through and back so fast I couldn't follow them all. The wall started to go all wavery in the middle, then all of a sudden it wasn't there any more. None of it! You floated through with your eyes shut—you were so still that I thought you'd been turned to stone."

Floated?

"Then you opened your eyes and—crack!—the wall was back again," Wray concluded. "Just as if nothing had happened." His head was cocked enquiringly to one side.

What did happen? Cai wondered, still lost in thought.

"I saw the marble chamber," Wray prompted eagerly, but the wizard did not respond. "Was that the book behind you? Did you read it?" The raider tried unsuccessfully to conceal his growing impatience, and his voice took on a whining, plaintive note. "How did you move the wall? I have to know!" He took a step toward Cai, a measure of his earlier fanaticism shining in his eyes. "Tell me!"

Cai returned to the present at last, and noted Wray's threatening stance. For a moment the wizard's own eyes blazed with power and Wray was stopped in his tracks.

"I'll tell you," Cai said, "but I'm not sure you'll understand. I'm not sure I understand it myself."

"How did Wray take your explanation?" Jordan asked.

"Not very well," Cai answered. "He couldn't reconcile his earlier domination of the elementals with a need for laughter and simple happiness. He just quoted from the old references he'd found, saying that there was nothing there to indicate anything of the sort."

"The wizards who constructed the barrier would have made sure of that, I suppose," Jordan said thoughtfully.

"I lost patience with him in the end," Cai admitted.

"You're not the first to do that," Hewe remarked. "He's a slippery little toad."

"But he *has* been diligent, and has shown every sign of wanting to help," Jordan pointed out. "Perhaps, when he begins to understand what Cai really did, he'll be taking the first steps to becoming a decent human being."

Hewe just grunted.

Cai had been back with the underground's leaders long enough to explain in detail everything that had happened in the blue-flame room, and Wray's subsequent reaction. Jordan and Hewe had listened in silence, their expressions betraying no surprise, even when Cai faltered over the description of his "flight." They had been most intrigued by his passages through the elemental wall and—of course—the isolated fragments that he had been able to read in the book. Jordan's quick mind was already trying to fit the puzzle together, adding these latest clues to the ones he already held.

"The first three references are simple descriptions," he said slowly. "On the face of it, it's the same devastation that Wynut and Shanti told you about—and that you saw in your dream."

"I hope Gemma was right when she said we could change the book again," Hewe commented. "So far, it doesn't sound as if our future is very promising." He grinned, and Cai wondered at his apparent flippancy.

"Excuse my partner's fatalism," Jordan said, noting the expression on Cai's face.

"No imagination, that's my problem," Hewe admitted cheerfully. "Being stupid sometimes has its advantages."

Cai knew full well that Hewe was anything but stupid; he said nothing, admiring the way these two men could joke about the most terrible subjects. It was a form of bravery, and one he felt incapable of emulating.

"Shall I start getting a group together to travel south?" Hewe asked. "It'll take a while to organize horses and supplies—and we still have to decide who's going."

"Good idea," Jordan replied emphatically. "There's no point waiting any longer, and we might as well be prepared."

"Galar *will* be pleased," Hewe said. "I'm amazed he's been able to keep the raiders from leaving without us."

"They should make interesting traveling companions," Jordan commented dryly. "We'll need to make sure we have enough of our own men to keep them under control if necessary. How many can we spare?"

"Truthfully?"

"Of course."

"None," Hewe stated. "But that's never stopped us before." He strode out purposefully.

"What about Gemma?" Cai asked anxiously.

"We won't be ready to leave for several days," Jordan reassured him. "The messenger went off early today, so she'll probably be back before we set off. Besides, there's something else I want you to do before then, if you're willing."

"What?"

"Travel west," Jordan answered. "To Clevemouth."

Cai looked downcast.

"You'll be back before Gemma gets here," the black man added, correctly diagnosing the cause of the wizard's apprehension.

"Why Clevemouth?" Cai asked.

Jordan did not answer immediately, but instead went to look out of the window for a few moments. Then he said, "Come with me. There's something I'd like to show you."

He led Cai from the building and turned westward. Their route took them past the twisted and blackened remains of Mendle's tower, but neither of them paid the macabre ruin any attention. Jordan's long strides meant that Cai had to hurry to keep up as they threaded their way through streets and alleyways.

"Where are we going?"

"To the city wall," Jordan replied. "The tower by the western gate." He did not elaborate further. Above them, the swarm was like a small and noisy cloud, causing some consternation among the onlookers. Jordan received several greetings, which he returned cordially, but no one asked about his strange companion. Everyone in Great Newport knew that nothing Jordan did was without purpose, and so did not interfere.

Half an hour later, the two men stood atop the western tower. The great coast road disappeared into the distance before them, and a little to the south Cai could see the mass of tents that formed the Gray Raiders' enclave. To the north, the sea shimmered in the light of the setting sun.

Jordan shaded his eyes and squinted into the distance. Cai did likewise, wondering what they were looking for.

"Do you see it?" Jordan asked. "It'll be stronger soon, but it *is* there."

Cai wondered what Jordan was talking about, but then he noticed a faint green halo around the sun. As the fiery globe sank nearer to the distant horizon, he watched it through half-closed lids.

As the glare lessened, the corona became more obvious. Outside the golden glow was a ring of green, which faded into a luminous blue outer circle. Moments later, the sun turned a deep red, and the green was replaced by the varying shades of purple, but the blue remained constant. Eventually, the sun disappeared from view, but as the darkness grew, the horizon did not lose the blue coloration, stretching both north and south as far as they could see.

"A few leagues beyond Clevemouth," Jordan began, his words breaking the sunset's hypnotic spell, "there is a huge elemental wall. It's so big that it distorts the sun's rays, as you've seen. It's impossible to pass through, and no one knows what's on the other side. We know what *was* on the other side, but now—"

"Random divisions . . . impassable," Cai quoted in a whisper. The blue-flame wall paled into insignificance beside the enormity of this barrier.

"My thoughts exactly," Jordan said.

They stared westward for a few moments, spots of color dancing before their eyes.

"The wall stopped moving some time ago," the underground's leader went on. "And it remained stationary for a while. But I've just had word that it's moving again. Toward Clevemouth."

Cai did not need to be told of the chaos and distress this would cause. He turned to his companion and saw the same thought in his eyes.

Hold back the elemental fires.

"I'd like you and Wray to go and have a look at it," Jordan said quietly. "Most people won't even go near the wall now, and you two are the nearest thing to experts that we've got."

"I'll go," Cai reassured him, "but I've no idea if I'll be able to do anything. Frankly, I doubt it. How far *is* Clevemouth?"

"About fifty leagues as the crow flies, but almost half as much again by road," Jordan told him.

Cai shook his head in astonishment. *So far away, and yet so clearly visible!*

"At least you might be able to gain some valuable knowledge," Jordan said, noting the wizard's incredulity. "Who knows, if what Wray told you was true, you might be able to make *it* disappear too!" He smiled, but Cai did not notice.

I came to find Gemma, he told himself, *not to meddle in forces beyond my imagining.*

"Come on," Jordan said, placing a friendly hand on the wizard's shoulder. "We can't do anything more tonight. Let's go and eat." He led the way down the twisting stone staircase. "Is there anyone else you'd like to take with you?"

"Zana," Cai replied promptly, slightly surprised by his own certainty. "She . . . she's been my guide to this land," he added.

"Fair enough," Jordan agreed. "I was hoping to use her talents here, but we'll muddle on. Hewe will want to go with you, I'm sure." Cai was glad of this. The big man's solid presence would be reassuring. "I'd like to come myself," Jordan added, "but I'm needed here." His words were not a boast, nor did his tone contain any false modesty. It was a simple statement of fact.

They ate together in Jordan's rooms, sharing a simple but satisfying meal.

"Why have you decided to send people south *now?*" Cai asked at one point.

"Well, I've always known we'd have to go sooner or later," Jordan replied. "Part of what you told us from the book tipped the balance."

"Which bit?" Cai responded, puzzled.

"The sentence that said 'their experiments grew rapidly in size and strength,' Jordan answered. "And 'the new logic they had created.'" He paused. "That wasn't in the book when Gemma read it."

"Oh." Cai struggled with the implications of this. "So it's changed, but this time for the worse?"

Jordan nodded. "It seems to have speeded up, become more specific," he said. "With that, and with what Wynut told you, it's obvious that we're beginning to run out of time. In all honesty, there's still so much to be done here that we can't afford to send good men off on what could be a wild goose chase, but we can't afford *not* to. I don't think we dare wait much longer—even if it is a futile gesture."

"At least we might be able to gain some valuable knowledge," Cai said, surprised by Jordan's negative comment.

"You are obviously quoting a very wise man," Jordan replied, smiling. "And I accept your rebuke."

Cai grinned, and for a moment, Jordan saw the spark of gaiety and boyish recklessness that had once been ever-present in the wizard's eyes. Then, just as quickly, it was gone, and he was solemn once more.

"It's all connected, isn't it?" Cai said quietly. "All of it—the book, the elementals, the far south, the skyravens . . ." His voice trailed away, silenced by the immensity of the problem. "If only I could make *sense* of any of it!"

"Perhaps we can make a start," Jordan said.

"How?" Cai demanded.

"Do you believe in the gods?" Jordan asked softly.

chapter 25

"I don't know what you mean by gods," Cai said. "I've heard men talk of them since I've been in this land, but the idea of them makes no sense to me." He looked at Jordan expectantly.

"I'm a sceptic by nature," the underground leader began, "but I've always been fascinated by mankind's different beliefs. As far as I can understand it, gods are enormously powerful beings who somehow control our destiny, and many of them are worshipped in this country. Some have no bodies, and exist only as spirits, while others supposedly take the form of giant beasts. Some are all-seeing and ever-present, while others are more limited. There are people here who admit to a whole panoply of gods, and others who state categorically that theirs is the only one."

"There was nothing like that on the islands," Cai said, trying to come to terms with this array of super-beings. "We have the Earth-mind," he added, almost tentatively. "I thought everyone knew about that."

Jordan smiled. "Spoken like a true fanatic," he said. "No, please don't be offended," he added quickly. "It's just that tolerance does not seem to be a universal commodity when dealing with people's faiths. And I'm sure your fervor stems from a rather different source." He held up his hands to forestall Cai's next words. "Gemma has told me something of the Earth-mind, and I've heard different versions of much the same idea from others. Please correct me if I get anything wrong."

Cai sat back then and listened, wondering where this was leading. He was unable to come to any immediate conclusions, so concentrated on Jordan's words.

"The Earth-mind is a being so powerful that its dreams have become reality for us, and our entire world is contained in the dream-images of its ages-long sleep. There are many paths within the dream, and men have the power to choose between them, but the very fabric of our world and the paths themselves are formed by the Earth-mind." He paused and Cai nodded in agreement. "The Earth-mind is a single entity," Jordan added, "upon whom we all depend."

A few moments passed in silence, then Jordan went on, reciting words that Cai knew by heart, but which now sounded even more ominous.

Remember the Dream
And whence it comes.
Madness for the One
Is death for all.

Panic fluttered like a trapped bird in the wizard's heart. Ideas rose up in his mind that would have been inconceivable only a short while ago. He fought against them, but their inexorable logic drove him back. So many of the pieces fitted now.

"The Earth-mind is going mad," he whispered.

Jordan said nothing, while Cai sifted through his memories, building them into patterns he did not like, but could not deny.

"'*The One becomes many*,'" Cai quoted. "That was in the book."

"And it's a pretty accurate description of insanity," Jordan commented, matter-of-fact.

Cai found himself repeating Wynut's advice, word for word.

"A great threat hangs over the world. The threat of destruction on a terrible, unprecedented scale . . . the destruction we fear may never take place, but that alone will not save us. The very fact that the threat is *there* may be enough to doom us all."

"Something in the future—" Jordan began.

"In one of the *possible* futures," Cai corrected him.

"—is so appalling that the very idea of it is driving the Earth-mind mad."

"So even if it *doesn't* happen," Cai completed, "we still face a new Destruction."

"The Age of Chaos," Jordan said.

"'You must prevent not only the execution of the threat, but also the *possibility* of it ever happening,'" Cai quoted. "But how?"

"There are only two places where we can start," the underground's leader said. "The elemental wall first, and—"

"And the far south," the wizard put in.

"That's next," Jordan replied.

So, three days after his arrival in Great Newport, Cai set out again, accompanied by Zana, Hewe, and Wray. He left the city with mixed emotions, feeling that the journey to Clevemouth was only a side issue in the terrible events that were engulfing the world, and that the real answers lay in the far south. On the other hand, neither he nor Jordan wished to start the expedition *there* until they had heard from Gemma. With any luck, she would have returned to Newport by the time Cai completed his mission. Then they could all travel south together, facing whatever awaited them in company.

In addition, the prospect of visiting the vast elemental wall both fascinated and repelled him. It would obviously be a sight of awe-inspiring grandeur, but at the same time, the idea of power on such a vast scale was terrifying. Cai had needed the swarm's assistance just to breach a tiny barrier, and here he was preparing to face something immeasurably more powerful.

Since his discussion with Jordan, Cai had learned all he could about the blue-flame wall. He talked to those who had seen it at first hand, and listened to the various theories about its origin and nature. Some of these would have sounded preposterous just a few days ago, but they provoked uncertainty now, rather than derision. The most common was that the wall was a division between worlds. No one had any real idea of what was beyond it—believing only that it was *different*—but there were many colorful suggestions, ranging from eternal fires to vast, barren wastes of ice.

Nobody had actually gone through the barrier, but a sea captain claimed to have seen birds fly over it and dolphins dive beneath it. Cai doubted the sailor's reliability, but had listened to the tale of his voyage north to see just how far the wall extended. The ship had been forced by lack of supplies to turn back before reaching the end of the wall, and it was the captain's considered opinion that it therefore stretched the entire length of the earth. Similarly, there was no evidence of a southern limit. In the face of such obvious immensity, Cai was even more certain that he would be able to do nothing. At least the journey gave him an immediate purpose—and time to think. After all the dire premonitions of the last few days, a lull would be welcome—especially in the company of Zana, who had been glad of the chance to accompany him, and Hewe, the only member of the party who did not seem overawed by their goal. The big man's optimistic disposition and ready humor, as well as his thorough knowledge of their route and the customs of this land, made him an ideal traveling companion. Cai already counted him as a friend. The same, however, could not be said of Wray. The former raider was silent and withdrawn and reacted neither to Cai's attempts to include him in their conversations nor to Hewe's barbed comments about his continued uselessness. Cai wondered why Jordan had insisted that Wray accompany them. The man seemed intent on contributing nothing, remaining sullen and aloof.

Their journey to Clevermouth took them along the great coast road. While this was not the most direct route, it was better than trying to cross the barren, rock-strewn vales that formed the northern edge of the Western Desert. For most of its length, the road made for easy enough riding, but sometimes it twisted and turned, following the numerous bays, inlets, and peninsulas of the rugged coastline. There were villages every few leagues, scattered communities of fishermen and farmers who extracted their needs from the sea and the narrow coastal plain. The villagers were used to city merchants, and the travelers therefore caused little comment. The communities supplemented their earnings by providing simple accommodations and food for passing visitors. Cai made sure that his bees were not conspicuous, keeping them in the mobile "hive," and strapping this to his saddlebags. When they *were* noticed, though, the villagers considered them unremarkable. They were used to working with all kinds of animals.

It took Cai and his party seven days to reach Clevemouth; with each sunset, the blue-green halo became more pronounced. From the walls of the western city, the blue light remained bright throughout the hours of darkness, casting a ghostly pallor over the quiet scene.

"How far is it from here?" Cai asked Ciel, the underground organizer who had been assigned to the travelers as a guide, and who had joined them on their arrival in Clevemouth.

"Three leagues, no more," she answered.

"Will you come with us tomorrow?" Zana asked.

"If you want me to. It's little over an hour's ride, and you really can't miss it," Ciel replied dryly. "One bit's much like any other, so there's no point in heading for any spot in particular."

"You've seen it yourself, then?" Hewe asked.

"Almost everybody here has," she said. "It's quite a sight. Because it hadn't moved for a few months, though, we were beginning to take it for granted. Before the revolution, it was moving almost all the time. That's barren country out there, with few inhabitants, so the first reports were vague, but at one time the wall was over ten leagues from here." Ciel paused, thinking back to earlier days. "Some of the farmers ran from it in panic, while others were just swallowed up. Whole villages have disappeared into . . . whatever is behind it."

"I dread to think what would happen if it reached the city," Zana said softly.

"It seemed as if it would come to that at one point," Ciel said. "But since we took advantage of the chaos to get rid of the Guild here, the wall slowed down—and didn't move for ages."

"We'll try to make sure it stays that way," Hewe remarked. "And if you'd rather not come tomorrow, we'll understand."

Wray stared silently toward the west; whatever ideas stirred behind his sullen countenance, he kept them to himself.

The first thing that struck them was the sheer immensity of the wall. To compare this with the barrier guarding the book room beneath Great Newport was to compare all the oceans of the world to a bucket of water. The shimmering blue surface stretched as far as they could see, both north and south—and upward, blending into the morning sky.

The second thing they noticed was the silence. They had

left their horses when they became nervous a little while back and had covered the last half league on foot. In that distance, the only sound they had heard was their own footsteps. No birds sang, no animals called, even the wind failed to stir the bare trees and tufted grasses. It seemed to Cai that such an immense power should be accompanied by thunderous roaring or unearthly music. And yet there was no sound at all. The four travelers drew closer to the wall and stared, listening to their own heartbeats. Even Hewe was at a loss for words.

At a distance, the wall had appeared flat and straight, but now they could see that it undulated in slow waves—like a gentle swell on an impossible, sideways-flowing sea. Cai watched in stupefied fascination as branches of a tree were first engulfed, then released. They did not seem to have changed in any way; no flickers of blue residue clung to them; they simply ceased to exist and were then created again.

The base of the wall was now only about fifty paces away, and each of the four felt its presence in different ways. For Hewe, it was incomprehensible in the same way as the night sky—impossibly remote and essentially meaningless. If this phenomenon was to obtrude into his world, someone else would have to deal with it. He could only observe.

Zana's feeling was one of sheer helplessness in the face of the undeniable superiority of such a force. Before *this*, man was almost an irrelevance. She had felt much the same way when the volcano on her home isle had erupted violently during The Destruction, loosing the power of the earth upon the people of Haele. Many had died in that fiery upheaval, but others—apparently chosen at random—had survived to build their homes again on the new, much larger, island. She shivered at the memory, and at a more recent prediction. *But this time*, no one *will survive*.

Cai knew himself to be powerless before such a being. He knew, without any need to test his theory, that his talents would be totally ineffectual when matched against the strength of this wall. It would be as much use as a tiny shrimp attacking a whale—the assault would not even be noticed and would have absolutely no hope of success. As he gazed at the shimmering surface, the wizard began to realize what men understood by their "gods." Only the Earth-mind could have created such a gargantuan monument. *A monument to its own madness?*

He stood quite still now, letting all his senses register their findings. *At least we might be able to gain some valuable knowledge*. Cai remembered Jordan's optimistic advice, and smiled ruefully. *It's all I can achieve,* he thought.

By degrees, a conviction that the wall was indeed made up of elemental forces grew within him. But it was on such a vast scale that it took Cai a while to see the subtler differences between this and its tiny counterpart beneath Great Newport. The screen that he had breached had been formed by external wizardry, cruel and precise, combining the energies of several elemental beings for a particular purpose. This wall was neither finite nor precise. It existed as a whole, not as the sum of its parts. It had no purpose other than its own existence; it was implacable and impenetrable.

It was also quite mad.

That realization dawned on him gradually, seeping into his mind as a slow poison invades the bloodstream. Merely to look closely at it for too long was to invite insanity. The chilling reality of the Earth-mind's madness came one step closer, and Cai roused himself with difficulty.

"Come on," he said, his voice ringing loudly in the eerie silence. "There's nothing we can do here. Let's get—"

He got no further. As if his words had been at trigger, Wray pelted toward the wall, screaming as he ran.

While the others stared in awe, bubbling resentment had welled up within Wray, eventually boiling over into an intense fury.

I could control the elementals once . . . and now I know so much more. His days of patient research shone brightly in his memory: the ancient texts, the spells of melding and confinement, the calls for summoning. *Men are meant to control these creatures,* he thought, half-way between triumph and derision. *And now I know more than any man alive. More than this feeble wizard from the north who seeks to take my place, my power*. Cai's success at entering the chamber still rankled. Wray looked again at the massive wall before him. *But that was nothing beside this power. Control this, and you would rule the world!*

Anger, fear, and greed fed his delusions, awakening his fanaticism and making rational thought impossible. When Cai broke the long silence, Wray reacted instantly. His unbalanced mind was in control now—it propelled his body forward, his tongue forming garbled versions of the ancient spells he had learned in Newport's archives.

The others were stunned and did not react for a few moments. Then Cai followed him, running in spite of his fear.

"No!" he warned.

"Let him go!" Hewe yelled, but his words went unheeded as Cai sprinted on. Hewe and Zana glanced at each other, then followed reluctantly.

The element of surprise had given Wray a head start, and he reached the base of the wall before Cai could catch him. The raider threw himself forward, into the wall, still shouting.

It swallowed him whole. There was a brief swirl of iridescent green within the shimmering blue, and then the gentle flowing motion was restored. A terrible scream rent the air before being cut off.

Cai skidded to a halt a few paces from the wall. The bees whirled around him in a lunatic dance. Hewe and Zana approached cautiously, but before they reached him, Cai made his decision. He stepped forward, surrounded by the swarm. Their buzzing was louder than ever.

"Cai! No!" Zana called, and Hewe swore violently, lunging forward to stop him. But they were too late, and the wizard melted out of existence.

Cai was surrounded by a frozen, white mist. Frost sparkled on his clothes and hair, and he heard the bees complain about the cold, felt them grow weak. *They will die,* he thought numbly. *I must hurry*. He looked about, but could see nothing—not even the ground beneath his feet.

Another step forward, and he spied a gray blur within the white. Wray was curled into a ball, his hands over his eyes. The wizard hooked him under the arms and began to pull him backward. The swarm lent him a little of their fading strength, but he could only stagger weakly as he felt himself oppressed by unseen forces.

Cai gathered all his power for one last effort. As his muscles tensed, he told himself, *It's now or never*.

And them the mist was swept away. Cai glanced in desperate relief at the world beyond the wall and saw . . .

. . . nothing.

He screamed and toppled over, carrying the inert body of Wray with him. The swarm droned about his head, and the intense coldness gave way to the warmth of morning. He heard Zana's desperate question, "Are you all right?" but had no strength with which to answer. Then he felt himself being lifted and carried, and the sensation of cold was pushed even further back. He was laid down gently on the ground.

"I'll fetch Wray," Hewe said, his tone implying that he would be just as happy to abandon their gray-robed colleague. "Find something for him to drink." Heavy footsteps receded.

"Here you are," Zana said. After a pause, she added, "Don't you want any?"

Cai could not respond. As he made no move to take the water bottle or even to look at it, a horrible suspicion grew in Zana's mind.

"Cai," she whispered, kneeling before him and taking his hands in her own. "Can't you see me?"

The wizard shook his head slowly, his eyes focused on some point over her left shoulder.

He was completely blind.

chapter 26

The journey back to Newport was something of a nightmare for the four travelers. Cai's sudden disability had shocked them all and meant that he needed help almost every step of the way. The wizard, in particular, was astounded by his lack of sight. He had always enjoyed a wizard's perfect health, even when denying his own magical talents. The fact that he was unable to do anything about the blindness made it even more difficult for him to adjust to having to be helped. As a result, he was often irritable with Zana, who remained constantly by his side. He hated himself for his unkindness and apologized frequently, knowing that she was the last person who should feel his spite. For her part, Zana was heartsore and frustrated, but she stuck doggedly to her task, dismissing Cai's occasional cruelties as the aftereffects of pain and shock. Her friendship had not been lightly bestowed, and a few harsh words would not cause its withdrawal now.

Wray had suffered no apparent physical damage from his encounter with the elemental wall; but his mind was now a wilderness. He reacted to the others, obeying their instructions, but rarely spoke—when he did, it was in meaningless syllables that resembled the cries of animals and birds rather than human speech. Questioning him had proved pointless, and Hewe had eventually lost his temper. Wray had cowered and squealed, until—in frustration—Hewe threw the terrified man roughly to the ground. He could cheerfully have left Wray to fend for himself, but Cai insisted that they keep him with them.

"Something happened to him in there," the wizard explained. "It may be important—and we must try to find out what it was."

"Something happened to *you* because of that little toad," Hewe retorted. "And besides, what use is he now? He's as mad as a gooney bird!"

Indeed, it seemed that Cai's premonitions of insanity had come to fruiton in Wray. Apart from being unable to speak properly, his eyes stared wildly and he waved his arms about, pointing at random objects for no apparent reason. During their journey back to Newport, he stayed as far away from Hewe as possible, leading the underground's man to remark that he must have some sense left after all. When Wray *did* speak, he almost always addressed himself to Cai, making the wizard start on several occasions. It was as though Wray was trying to tell him something, but although Cai listened intently, he could make no sense of the peculiar noises.

The best healers in Clevemouth had found nothing ostensibly wrong with Cai's eyes, and were quite mystified by his blindness. He had expected nothing more, and after a fruitless day in the city, he insisted that they begin their journey back. Cai now had another reason for wanting to be reunited with Gemma. He had been a remote presence at the awakening of her healing powers and knew that if anyone could help him, she could. He thought of her more and more as the leagues passed slowly.

Hewe's strength and knowledge were even more vital to the group on the return journey, and he became their unquestioned leader in all things. Progress was painfully slow at times, but would have been much worse without him.

They were still two days' ride from Newport when Cai awoke one morning with a feeling of dread in his heart. In his dreams he could still see, so waking was particularly difficult for him, with its bitter realization every morning. But this time, it was worse than usual.

"Zana," he called softly. "Is it morning yet?"

"It's barely past dawn," she replied drowsily from her bed on the other side of their shared room. "Go back to sleep."

"Something is happening," he said. "Something terrible."

"What do you mean?" she asked, trying to wake up properly. "Where?"

The village tavern was silent.

"I don't know," Cai admitted.

"Shall I get Hewe?"

"No . . . it's just a feeling. Let him rest."

They were quiet for a while, but neither made any attempt to go back to sleep.

"Have you made any more sense of what happened to you back there?" Zana asked.

"No. I've thought about it until my head hurts, but I still can't remember anything that would help."

"Have you asked the bees?"

"Of course. But they can't tell me anything. All they remember is the cold and finding Wray curled up in a ball."

"Why didn't Wray go blind as well?"

"The only thing I can think of is that he made no attempt to see into the world beyond the wall. When I found him, he was on the ground with his hands over his eyes."

The swarm had been a great source of comfort for Cai in recent days. Luckily, they had survived unscathed and gave him a familiar contact with the dark world. He sensed them now, resting, not at all disturbed by their master's premonition.

Do you feel anything strange? he asked them, without much hope.

Movement. Signals. Far away, came their echoing reply.

Cai was about to ask them what they meant, when there was a sudden uproar from the adjoining room. First came Wray's incoherent yells, then Hewe's angry demands for peace and quiet. This was followed by the sounds of a struggle, more animal-like screeches, and the crash of a body as it hit the floor.

"I'll go and see what's happening," Zana said quickly. She got up and pulled her robe around her. Hurrying out into the corridor, she met Hewe coming out of his own room.

"I knew my sharing a room with that demented maniac was a mistake," he said, scowling. "He's gone completely berserk. The way he was waving his arms about and squawking, I'd swear he was trying to fly."

"What happened?"

"I don't know. One moment I was happily asleep, the next *he* was capering about, screaming fit to wake the dead. I asked him to stop—politely—but he wouldn't, so I had to phrase my request rather more forcibly," he concluded, rubbing his knuckles.

Zana walked past him into his room. Wray was sprawled on the floorboards.

"Is he hurt?" she breathed.

"Oh, he'll live," Hewe replied, almost regretfully. "But he may have a headache for a while. Is Cai all right?"

"Yes," she answered, kneeling beside the unconscious Wray. "But he feels that there's something bad about today."

"He's not the only one," Hewe remarked.

Far to the south, the gathering was complete. They stood in serried ranks, waiting impassively in the bitter cold. Each of the metal visages faced westward, looking out over the Kalura Range of mountains as the newly risen sun illuminated the snow-encrusted, mist-shrouded peaks. They gazed westward from their vantage point on the mountainside, seeing in the far distance the greatest peak of all, Dar Emberoth, at whose heart—so the legends said—lay the greatest jewel in all the world, a treasure beyond price, beyond imagination. But the minds behind the metal masks did not dwell on legend, did not wonder why they were waiting here. They did not question. The Great Leader would explain all to them in due course. This was the central certainty in their well-ordered lives.

Now his voice rolled out over the multitude, deep and magnificent, welcome, carrying easily to each member of the gathering. It was the voice of their god.

"You have been called here to witness the power, the strength, that will enable me to go forward in victory. I am invincible, matchless, all powerful." There was a moment's pause before the unseen speaker continued, but his audience did not shift or murmur. "You are here to see your faith justified. The faith that can move mountains. Behold!"

It started as a far-away rumble. Then, suddenly, there was an enormous flash of light, making the sun behind them seem like nothing more than a dull candle. The optical sensors in the audience's masks reacted instantly, protecting their sight from the intense glare, and enabling them to watch it grow in size and splendor. Then the fire was gone, and in its place was a vast, bulging cloud, rushing upward, that seemed to fill half the western sky. Gray and brown streamed into the air—like a monstrous tree whose roots stretched to the very center of the earth.

As one, the gathering gasped in astonishment, awed by the magnificence of the spectacle. Then the wave of noise reached them. It was a deep, guttural roaring that went on and on—as if intent on drowning out all the other sounds of the world.

As the roar finally subsided, a wind passed over the gathering. It was no more than a gentle breeze, but it was warm.

By now, the huge cloud had reached its peak and was losing its connection to the earth. As the lower portions of the heavy pall cleared, another wave of astonishment rippled through the gathering. Their perfect sight revealed that the landscape before them had been radically altered. Where a mountain had once stood, there was now only a smoking valley.

Dar Emberoth was no more.

Wray saw it first, but made no attempt to draw anyone's attention to it as he rode behind the others, nursing his injured pride and his swollen jaw. His addled mind somehow knew that Cai would want to be apprised of his discovery, and he took spiteful pleasure in withholding it from the wizard, as well as from Hewe and Zana, who could have seen it for themselves. He despised them all. *The big stupid one who treats me with such ignorant contempt has more brains in his fists than in his head. That fawning woman is of no consequence. And the wizard, who could not save his own sight when he faced what I alone have seen! He thinks he saved me! Me! Who needed no help, who plundered the elemental wall alone, unaided. Pah! I will show them. My time will come.*

He stared southward again. It was still there. Wray stifled a laugh, then winced in pain as his bruised face objected. As Zana glanced round, he turned away quickly, not wanting to give his secret away, but it was too late. Zana looked south and saw it immediately. She called to Hewe, who was riding a little ahead of them.

"Hewe, do you see something—over to the south?"

He barely turned his head.

"Desert," he said flatly.

"Beyond that. In the sky."

Hewe reluctantly turned to look. He was longing for this journey to be over, and his thoughts had been fixed on their arrival in Great Newport. Normally, travel and new companions were much to Hewe's liking, but this time had been different. After having to face his own inadequacy in front of the elemental wall, he was now finding it difficult to cope with a blind wizard and a crazed Gray Raider. However, he reacted to Zana's urgings—and reined in his mount.

"A cloud," he suggested.

"I've never seen a cloud like *that*," Zana replied as she and Cai drew alongside.

"What is it? What are you talking about?" the wizard asked.

"There's a huge cloud, over on the southern horizon," she answered. "It doesn't look natural."

"Describe it to me," he ordered.

"It looks like a giant tree," Zana said slowly. "Big at the top, but thinner below."

"It's brown," Hewe added. "And there isn't another cloud to be seen."

Behind them, Wray suddenly gabbled wildly, waving one arm about. Before any of the others could react, he spurred his mount and galloped away toward Great Newport.

"Let him go," Hewe said disgustedly. "With any luck, he'll fall off and break his neck before he gets there."

Cai shivered, a cold hard knot in the pit of his stomach. Zana looked at him anxiously.

"Does it have anything to do with your bad feeling this morning?" she asked.

"I've no idea," the wizard replied. "I've simply no idea."

As they rode on, Hewe and Zana glanced southward every so often. The day drew on, and the mysterious cloud slowly dispersed, taking on one fantastic shape after another as the winds carried it in different directions.

They found Wray shortly after midday. He was standing disconsolately beside his exhausted horse, but by this time, Hewe could not even be bothered to berate the lunatic, and just rode straight past. Wray remounted and meekly joined the party.

It was only as darkness came that Cai recalled the words that had been nagging at his subconscious ever since he had been told of the cloud.

However, this setback merely spurred the forces of the far south to even greater efforts. Their experiments grew rapidly in size and strength . . .

chapter 27

When, as last, the travelers got back to Cleve's capital, Cai was dismayed to learn that Gemma had not returned. Nor had the messenger, and although his disappearance was beginning to worry Jordan, there was little he could do. Hewe offered to go to the valley himself—he was the only one of the group who had made the journey before—but events conspired to make that impossible.

"There could be any number of reasons for him not being able to get back," Jordan said, trying to console the miserable, blind wizard.

"Rymer's a good man," Hewe put in, "and I gave him precise instructions, but the valley has strange ways of protecting itself from outsiders. Gemma once said that the only reason *I* found it was because I was meant to. Perhaps that doesn't apply this time."

"Why not?" Cai said. "She must know how desperately we need her." But then he realized that this was not necessarily the case; moreover, he remembered her most recent rebuttal of his attempted contact. *Perhaps she's still protecting the baby,* he thought hopelessly. *What do I do now?*

They learned much later that Rymer had never even reached the valley. By the time that became known, however, so much had happened that it became little more than a footnote in the annals of that momentous time. Rymer had traveled for several days, following Hewe's directions, but every time he believed himself to be getting close to the valley, the landscape seemed to change, so that his route was never clear. He wandered aimlessly for several days before eventually giving up and returning to Newport to report his failure.

Meanwhile, it was becoming clear to Jordan and his companions that they could no longer wait for Gemma. Events were moving too fast. The strange cloud had been witnessed in Great Newport, and had given rise to much speculation. The Gray Raiders had been especially excited by it, proclaiming it to be the omen that signaled the beginning of their great expedition. They grew even more restless, and soon after Cai's return, they built a huge bonfire outside their camp, burning all their possessions that would not be needed on the journey, symbolizing their commitment to the task.

"I won't be able to hold them for much longer," Jordan commented. "If we're not careful, there'll be open rebellion."

The next few days provided him with evidence that made the journey south an absolute necessity. Though there was still no message from Gemma, there had been plenty from other sources—and all the news was bad.

At first, it appeared to be rumor only, but the reports were so persistent that they had to be taken seriously. Strange tides were battering the coastline, and many sea creatures had beached themselves, apparently committing mass suicide. Dolphins, giant octopi, even whales, as well as countless smaller creatures, had died unaccountably. The island of Jed had resumed its erratic ways, appearing one day and vanishing the next. The large number of skyravens had been seen flying out over the sea, especially at night, and impossibly bright lights had been witnessed far to the north. Few seamen dared leave the safety of their ports.

Each report pointed to a time of upheaval that made the ominous words the *Age of Chaos* sound particularly apt, and Jordan eventually agreed to a date for their forces to move south. The makeup of the party was still under debate, but departure was now assured. Two separate, but equally desperate pleas, emphasized the need for haste.

The first was made by a dishevelled, exhausted rider from Clevemouth. He arrived only four days after Cai's party—but much had changed in that short time. The elemental wall had started moving again six days ago—toward his city. The progress was slow but steady, and the majority of Clevemouth's inhabitants were fleeing along the coast road. The messenger sobbed when he told them that by now his home would have been completely swallowed up by that invincible blue wall. He had seen little of the evacuation, but the few details he was able to give were bad enough. Jordan reassured him as best he could, and sent him for a meal and a well-earned rest.

"That settles it," the underground leader decided. "How soon can we leave?"

"Tomorrow," Hewe told him. "But I'd prefer it if we had one more day to prepare. There's not much left of today." He, Cai, and Zana, by now the wizard's constant companion, had listened to the sorry tale with growing horror. They knew just how overwhelming the effect of the elemental wall could be. Madness was quite literally stalking the land.

"What can we do?" Zana asked helplessly.

"Not much," Jordan answered. "We can prepare for the arrival of the refugees and try to minimize their suffering. And we can send help to those farther back on the road. The villages will be overrun soon." He paused. "We'll do what we can for them, but our only chance now is to find the root of this evil and destroy it. I just wish we hadn't waited so long. Gemma or no Gemma."

"Perhaps the raiders were right all along," Hewe suggested grimly.

"The wall seems to have gained in speed at the same time as that huge cloud appeared," Cai said quietly.

"Yes, I noticed that," Jordan replied. "At least now we have a rough idea where to head for!"

The second plea for help was delivered the following morning, when Jordan received a message that two warriors from the Lightless Kingdom had arrived in the city and needed to speak to him urgently. He hurried down to the underground tunnels, knowing that the visitors would find the meeting much easier in the subterranean gloom. Cai wanted to go with him, having been fascinated by what he had heard of this strange race. But he was dissuaded. Although he was coming to terms with his lack of sight, traveling in unfamiliar territory was still difficult and time-consuming. He found his inability to meet the people of the Lightless Kingdom frustrating, but he was promised a full report on Jordan's return.

"The basic facts are as follows," Jordan told him later. "You know that poison is spreading into their realm from the south.

Well, they've sent several parties—control groups—into the most dangerous regions, to try to pinpoint where the pollution is coming from, so that we'll have a chance of locating it *above* ground. They've had some success, but I'll come to that in a moment. A few days ago, all the southern groups reported vibrations, rockfalls, and disruption of the normal flow of the underground rivers. It caught them by surprise, so some of the details are a little hazy, but the overall effect is clear enough. The rate at which the poison is spreading has increased dramatically, due for the most part to a sudden rise in some sections of the river. A number of settlements were destroyed in the deluge, and some of the control groups have been cut off." Jordan sighed wearily, thinking of his friends below the earth. "The prophets have sent word that unless the source of the pollution is located and destroyed soon, there will be little of their land left to save. The green-sickness is already taking a heavy toll." His voice faltered, and Hewe looked away; he had never seen Jordan so close to tears before, and it was not a sight he relished.

"All the more reason for going now, then," Cai said.

"Yes," Jordan agreed, recovering his poise. "They need us to send an army south, and I was able to reassure them about that at least. I only *wish* we'd gone sooner!"

"What's done is done," Zana told him sympathetically. She too had noticed Jordan's distress and knew that the strange Lightless Kingdom must have had a profound effect upon him when he had visited its caves. "It's the future that's important now."

"You're right," he replied. Although he smiled gratefully at her, the sadness did not leave his eyes. "But sometimes we have to live with the past for a long, long time."

There was a pause while each of them found his or her own personal truth in that statement. Then Jordan broke the spell that he had cast.

"Enough of that," he said determinedly. "Let's get down to business. At least we have a clearer idea about where to go, thanks to the Lightless Kingdom."

"Where, then?" Hewe asked quickly, glad to be returning to practical matters.

"There are three possibilities," Jordan replied. "First, there's the Cascade, the place Arden told us about, where the mountain moved. That seems to be one of the starting points of the poison, and they've found a route to the surface so we can meet up with the control group. Then there's a second entrance, about seven leagues west of there, though it doesn't seem to have any connection with the pollution. They'll have people waiting at both locations."

"And the third?"

"About fifteen leagues south of the Cascade. They haven't been able to get too close to the surface there, because the pollution is too heavy."

"How close are these to where we saw the cloud?" Cai asked.

"We don't know," Jordan answered. "And until we get closer, there's no way of finding out."

"Then the sooner we get there, the better," the wizard stated.

"We? Are you sure you still want to come?"

"Try and stop me!" Cai replied, his determination obvious. "I may be blind, but I'm still a wizard . . . and I didn't come all this way just to sit around like an idiot!"

Jordan glanced at Zana.

She nodded, answering his unspoken question.

"It could be a rough trip," Hewe pointed out. He received such a withering look in return that he held up his hands in self-defense. "I never said a word," he told them, grinning.

The expeditionary force that left Great Newport at dawn the next day was composed of some eighty people. Over half that number were Gray Raiders, commanded by Galar and Tomas. Their high spirits contrasted with the serious demeanor of the rest of the party, which was led by Jordan and Hewe. The city was being left in the capable hands of their deputies, Egan and Ambros, who both felt aggrieved at being left behind—and also somewhat relieved.

Cai had insisted that Wray travel with him. The raider could still not speak intelligibly, and he was regarded with suspicion and disdain by almost everyone. The rest of their party were members of the underground, chosen for their toughness, survival skills, and fighting ability, and included healers and herbalists.

The early morning departure was watched in somber quiet by many of the city's inhabitants. To them it was a depressing sight, a sign that the upheavals in their lives were set to continue.

It seemed a pitifully small force to pit against the unknown but apparently powerful foe, but it was all that was possible. Supplying the daily needs of a larger army would have been impossible. Plans were afoot to train greater numbers of soldiers and gather stores for a second group, but that was a long-term project. Jordan knew that action was needed now.

Their route was to take them due south at first, crossing the inhospitable and sparsely populated tract of land between the two great deserts of Cleve. From there they would travel into the foothills of the massive mountain ranges and head southeast. This would take them close to the Lightless Kingdom contact points. Much of their route would be through unknown territory, but they had studied whatever maps were available, and they hoped to get help from villages along the way. The rest would have to be decided as they went.

The long column of horses moved at a deliberate pace, and there was little conversation. A group of raiders had volunteered to ride ahead as scouts, but Jordan told them to save their horses for the more arduous times ahead. They obeyed him, placated by the promise of greater action in the near future.

The cold of midwinter made it possible for them to ride through all that first day out of Great Newport. The shortest day was only six days hence, so it was important that they make full use of the light. They ate their midday meal of bread and travel-meat on the move, and their steady progress continued into the late afternoon.

Cai was riding beside Zana so that she could reach over and take his reins if necessary. When he was addressed by a female voice, he naturally assumed it was her. Then he realized his mistake.

Cai. Is that you, Cai?

"Gemma?" In his surprise and delight, the wizard shouted her name aloud, and Zana was not the only one to look at him curiously.

Gemma, where are you? It's so good to be in touch with you again!

I'm in the valley, she replied, but there was something in her tone that made Cai's jubilation fade rapidly.

Your secret place? he asked hesitantly.

Yes, she answered, *but it doesn't protect me any more! The river has become poisoned, and this afternoon I heard the siren song. Something terrible is happening, Cai.*

She sounded so miserable that Cai found it impossible to answer.

Are you still there? she asked anxiously.

Yes.

I have to go to the far south, Cai. Will you help me?

Of course, he responded. *I'm on my way south now with Jordan. I'll meet you there.*

You're in Cleve? Gemma exclaimed, astonishment and delight piercing her gloom.

You didn't think I'd stay away from you forever, did you? The self-mocking humor of his words—feeble though it was—made Gemma laugh.

I'll see you at the Cascade, then, she said. *That's where Arden and I are heading.*

We'll meet, Cai replied, *but I won't see you.*

Why? What's wrong? she demanded.

I'm blind, Gemma.

There was a short pause, then Gemma spoke again.

But you have other eyes, she said. *Look!*

Then, although Cai's body was still firmly in his saddle, at the same time he found that he was looking down on the long line of horses from above. The perspective was peculiar, shifting and multifaceted, so that it took him a while to realize what he was seeing.

I have to go now, Gemma said, a mixture of laughter and fear in her voice. *Fare you well, Cai.*

No! he cried. *Don't go!* But it was too late, and the remote contact was lost once more. Cai rode on, disoriented by the welter of new sensations.

Welcome to the swarm, the bees told him. *Our eyes are yours.*

part 4

DREAMS OF STONE

chapter 28

In the cold, early morning light of midwinter's day, the stone-clan gathered to perform their sacred duty. The meyrkats formed a wide circle about the gray monolith that stood at the center of the Diamond Desert. They were each guided by a mysterious impulse that recognized the shortest day—they called it the time when the winds change—and did not really need the instructions of Od, their unquestioned leader. Since the tribe had split into two, just after Gemma had performed the midwinter duty with them, Od had been the dominant male among the remaining meyrkats. He had a serious temperament and could be dogmatic, but he was strong and determined, and the clan felt secure in his leadership.

He was also the one they looked to for guidance on all matters connected with the standing stone. Today, however, they moved on instinct, hardly needing his telepathic messages. Nevertheless, he bustled importantly among his clan, making sure that they were evenly spaced and that the youngest of them were treating the occasion with proper respect. He was satisfied at last, and bounded over to his own appointed position, completing the circle. Then he stood up on his hind legs, head held high, with the long claws of his forepaws hanging down in front of him. After one last glance at the assembly, checking that all was ready, Od turned his sharp nose and bright, black-rimmed eyes toward the god-sky-fire-stone. He felt the glow of responsibility and a sudden pride in the clan. He had been worried that their reduced numbers might make their task difficult and displeasing to the stone, but there were no doubts now.

We sing.

As the clan reacted to his silent announcement, they each felt the music rise up within their small chests. Even the babies, the ones too young to have heard the song before, joined in, guided by the teachings of their elders and their own inner feelings.

Their high-pitched voices rose shrilly into the quiet desert air. They all knew their part in the claw-cycle—five strands of sound, interwoven in a complex, dissonant tapestry—and each sang to fulfil his promise to the god within the stone, as tradition demanded, but this year they also sang for the clan-mates who were no longer with them, the Wanderers. The stone-clan was determined to be worthy of their fellows' trust. As the sun rose in the eastern sky, the strange music went on.

Only Gemma had ever heard the meyrkats sing to the stone; to most humans, their music would have sounded harsh and unpleasant, a world away from the conventional ideas of musical beauty. And yet there was an undeniable emotional strength within its twisted dissonance, and while the actual words were unrecognizable to human ears, the message grew and shimmered in the air.

Ask my brother to move,
For the year is past.

Then, sooner than they had expected, the standing stone began to move, and the meyrkats' voices rose in volume as they rejoiced at the sight.

Slowly, silently, the rocking stone tipped over, finally coming to rest in its alternative position with a faint click. Their task done, the meyrkats' broke the circle, yelping with joy and bounding, stiff-legged, into the air. Only Od remained still, glowing with the satisfaction of their accomplishment, but wondering what effect it would have on the world beyond their territory, on Gemma and on the Wanderers—wherever they were.

As the stone-clan celebrated, a familiar deep rumbling sounded in the rock beneath their feet.

Far to the south, in answer to the subterranean, mage-born signal, another rocking stone shifted its position. But Od would not have recognized this as the result of his clan's song.

The rocking stone *here* was the size of a mountain, and the gigantic bulk moved with a terrible, ponderous grinding. The effect was like that of a small, localized earthquake; the ground shook for leagues around, causing many small rockfalls. However, one specific consequence of the shift was that it altered the course of the river that plunged into a deep pool just to the south of the mountain. Where the waters of the Cascade had flowed down a valley to the west of the mountain, they now swept into a newly opened ravine to its east. Three days later, the inhabitants of the Valley of Knowing would notice that the level of their river had dropped dramatically. A few days after that, the riverbed would be completely dry. This new and longed-for drought would bring fresh hopes that the sickness now affecting them would recede. The river was taking its deadly cargo elsewhere.

When the shaking stopped, D'vor's control party had been separated. The noise and vibration had been tremendous, and there had been several minor rockfalls in the caves and tunnels around them. C'lin and V'dal were trapped behind one of these.

J'vina was the first to react, calling out to their lost colleagues and scrambling over the newly fallen boulders, trying to find a way through.

"Be careful," D'vor warned. "The rock is still unstable."

"And don't tear the silkfish tape," C'tis added, ever the healer. "The pollution's so strong here that even a small exposure would be very dangerous."

J'vina ignored them both, clambering onward, the meyrkats close behind her. The Wanderers had been in the vast subterranean realm, known to those above ground as the Lightless Kingdom, for some months now. Some sixth sense had led them to J'vina, their warrior friend, whom they had first met in Great Newport. Since their arrival, a special bond had grown between the clan and the soldier, and now they reacted to each other's wishes on instinct. They did not share mind-talk, as they did with Gemma, but this was the next best thing.

"V'dal! C'lin! Can you hear me? Are you all right?" J'vina's efforts were rewarded with a response.

"We're not hurt!" V'dal called, his voice muffled by the intervening rock.

The other members of the control group breathed a collective sigh of relief.

"Can we get through to you?" D'vor yelled, moving carefully to J'vina's side.

"No. There's some big stuff in the fall, and the gaps are too small to get through—even for the meyrkats."

"Is there another way around?"

"Yes. Unless all the other tunnels have been blocked." V'dal, the group's guide, sounded confident. "But we may have to go quite a way back, so it could take some time. What do you want to do?"

"We'll stay here," D'vor decided, "and let you find us."

"Fine. See you soon." C'lin sounded quite chirpy, as though he was relishing the adventure.

"Be careful!" C'tis warned them.

"Anything we can do to help you find us?" J'vina asked.

"Light a fire," V'dal replied. "And call out every so often."

"In your dulcet tones, that should also serve as a warning to anything nasty lurking nearby," C'lin added.

"Keep that joker from doing himself any harm!" J'vina retorted. "We need his brawn to complement our brains."

"I'll do my best," V'dal answered, and they could hear C'lin laughing beside him. "Make us a hot drink, and we'll be there all the sooner."

"It's a deal."

So they waited, listening to the faint sounds as V'dal and C'lin left. When J'vina and D'vor rejoined their colleagues, they set up a temporary camp in a part of the cave that had remained stable during the earthquake. They lit a fire, burning a special fuel that glowed and provided heat without bursting into flame.

"Do you think they'll get through?" T'via asked. She was the sixth member of the group, chosen not so much for her practical skills, but for the fact that she was a representative of the prophets, the black-robed mystics who were the leaders of the Lightless Kingdom.

"If it's at all possible, V'dal will get them through," D'vor answered gravely. As the group's specialist guide, V'dal's phenomenal memory and vast knowledge of all the known tunnels and cave systems of their underground world far outstripped that of the others. Even here, in relatively uncharted regions, his directional sense and instant recall made him the best of navigators.

"Let's hope so," J'vina remarked, with typical fatalism. "I'm not sure any of *us* could find our way out of this rat hole."

"What do you think caused the quake?" C'tis asked as they sipped their drinks.

"The shortest day," D'vor replied. "The time when the river pattern changes. This could have been a result of the same thing." Although day and night underground tended to be defined by action and rest, rather than light and dark, crystal seams allowed a fraction of sunlight to filter through, so that their time cycle followed that of the upworld. "The rocking stone—Arden told us about it, remember?"

"Yes, but it's never caused stuff like *this*," J'vina said.

"No one's ever been so far south when it happened before," C'tis pointed out.

"No one in her right mind would *want* to be," the soldier responded.

"It wasn't always like this," T'via said softly. She was the quietest member of the control group, generally only proffering her opinions when asked, or when it directly concerned the business of the prophets. "Remember Soulskeep."

They were now a day's journey south of the cave known as Soulskeep. This had once been well within the boundaries of their land but was not deep within the poisoned regions, sealed off by metal doors and isolated by barrier zones. Only a few ever ventured near it; and no one had been south of it for many river cycles.

This was a source of much sadness to all of the people of the Lightless Kingdom, but especially to the prophets and their acolytes. T'via could remember Soulskeep only vaguely from her childhood, and longed to be able to see it again. The cave was sacred to Rael, the God Beneath, and it was there that the fungus raellim grew in profusion. Eating raellim was dangerous but rewarding for the prophets, because it produced a strange substance called earthwild, which enabled them to perceive the wishes of the god. On occasion, it could also help them see into the future. Soulskeep was a place of dread and wonder, and now it seemed that it was lost forever.

"Arden told us that Soulskeep is almost directly beneath the Cascade," C'tis put in. "And that was the center of the movement that causes the river change."

"So the way north may be very different now," J'vina said, voicing a thought that had occurred to them all. It was the way back home.

"Perhaps," D'vor said. "We'll know more when V'dal gets here."

chapter 29

The controller swore violently as he stared at the ever-changing pattern of lights and dials on the panel before him.

"It's happening *again!*" Anger and frustration were uppermost in his voice, but there was also an element of fear. His superior approached and leaned over his shoulder.

"What is it?"

"There's a blockage in the outflow ducts. The pressure's building up and I hate to *think* what would happen if it doesn't clear soon. We may have to shut part of the plant down."

"We can't do that! It's out of the question."

"But—"

"No buts! We can't shut *anything* down, and that's final. Get a maintenance team underground *now*, and tell them they've got to get those drains clear—fast!"

The controller turned to obey, wondering about the pressures that were making his superior act in what seemed such an imprudent way. For the first time, he questioned whether his own high status within the grid was actually worth it. Perhaps it would be better—it would certainly be easier—to be one of the lower orders, unthinkingly obedient, knowing only simple contentment. He punched out the appropriate emergency code, then turned back to watch the telltale gauges on the power control bank. The temperature in some chambers had already risen significantly; the pumps were laboring, forcing the outflow liquids against ever-increasing pressure. If the heat continued to build . . . the controller shuddered.

His superior had withdrawn a little, unable to make himself watch the flow of information that could spell their doom. He was silently railing against his fate. *Why now, just when we've been ordered to increase power output? I knew the duct system we installed after the dam collapsed last year wouldn't hold up. I told them, but would they listen? Of course not!* He studied the grid-map of the machinery's responses, which showed the progress of the maintenance party. *Hurry, man, hurry!* he urged silently. *We can't shut down now!*

The Great Leader's orders had been quite specific. The complex was to be brought to full output and maintained at that level until he instructed otherwise. The ever-increasing needs of the city and the experiments of their vast community must be supplied. And then, of course, there was the question of the materials needed for the development of the Great Leader's newly devised weapons. Only a few days ago, one of these had been tested in spectacular and wholly successful fashion. An entire mountain had been vaporized, blown out of existence by the mere touch of a button. Their leader had been jubilant, but that triumph had only served to increase his impatience. Hundreds, thousands more weapons must be produced, he had told them. Only then could their dreams of domination become a reality.

And only by running the power complex at its full potential could the volatile and potentially dangerous materials necessary for all this be produced.

Many of those in the grid's upper echelons had already felt the wrath of the Great Leader. He brooked no failure and punished it with ferocious severity. The head of the Power Section had no intention of becoming the next victim.

"They're not moving fast enough!" he snapped, eyeing the grid-map. "Tell them to hurry, or I'll have them all deprogrammed. And get the backup cooling systems working."

Then at last he saw the indication that the maintenance party were in the inspection vehicle and were heading in the direction of the faulty duct.

Come on! he urged the unseen crew. *Get a move on!*

The four members of the maintenance group had hardly fastened themselves into the inspection vehicle before it took off, building up speed quickly as it shot down the tunnel running parallel to the outflow pipes. Their hastily donned protective clothing was uncomfortable, but they had been left in no doubt about the urgency of their mission, and no one complained.

The discovery that any amount of waste could be pumped into the deep cave system beneath the city had been a great boon to its constructors. They no longer had to worry about contamination of their own environment or the storage of useless poison. It could be disposed of simply, swallowed up by the impervious earth.

Of course, there had been one or two problems, but these had all been overcome in time. New tunnels had been bored to ensure a fast, even flow on the first part of the subterranean journey, and various rivers had been diverted to provide the huge quantities of water needed for cooling and cleansing the city and its machinery. Where one experiment failed, another was tried, until eventually, the whole system worked perfectly. Until now.

The maintenance party was led by a senior engineer, F21M. His deputy was H73F, two levels below him in the grid, but intelligent and knowledgeable nonetheless. They were accompanied by two lower order mechanics, L290M and L384M, who could add their considerable muscle power to the task, should it prove necessary.

For most of their journey, they stared straight ahead, their steel faces perfectly impassive. They glanced occasionally at the display panels on the metal bands sealed around their left wrists. Their grid-numbers were inscribed on these bracelets, below the endlessly flashing panel that showed their position within the grid-map, and which relayed Control's instructions when necessary. Tiny red lights indicated that all was functioning normally.

The whine of the maintenance vehicle lessened as it slowed, then halted at the end of the pipe. The crew got out, and as F21M and his deputy hurried to study the controls of the monitoring station, he motioned to the other two to wait. He tried a few buttons experimentally, then shook his head.

"Looks as thought the problem is farther down," he said. "In the open rock."

H73F nodded in agreement, but did not speak.

"Signal Control," the senior engineer added. "We'll go on on foot." As his deputy obeyed, F21M and the mechanics collected their portable equipment.

"Control acknowledges," H73F reported. "The vehicle is to be sent back for further operatives."

"Good. Tell them we may need the heavy gear. And get it moving from Ground Base now."

"Yes, sir," his deputy replied. After sending the appropriate signals, she turned back and accepted her share of equipment.

"Let's go." F21M led them through the seal and into the cave system. As he did so, they became aware of the roaring, close by, of huge volumes of water.

Rockdark, the subterranean equivalent of dusk, was fast approaching, and J'vina was growing restless. There was still no sign of V'dal and C'lin, and she had suggested that they send out a search party. D'vor had forbidden it, reasoning that such a move would only decrease the chances of a full reunion, and J'vina had accepted his authority, though her impatience was ill-concealed. Any prolonged period of inactivity made her uneasy.

The meyrkats were also growing jittery, taking their mood from their warrior friend. So far, they had survived all the rigors of the Lightless Kingdom more or less unscathed. Even the poisoned areas did not seem to cause them any distress, although C'tis had not been able to work out why they did not suffer from the green-sickness that affected her own people and their animals. The meyrkats' fur was thick, but surely that would only be a marginal factor. She could only suppose that their upworld constitutions were more suitable for resisting the infection—something that Arden's earlier recovery had suggested. Even so, C'tis worried that even *their* stubborn resistance must be worn down soon—especially if they stayed too long in these heavily polluted areas.

J'vina continued to stalk the confines of their cave, shouting into the tunnel entrance until she was hoarse. The clan accompanied her on these limited excursions, adding their own piercing calls to hers.

D'vor grimaced at the racket.

"Perhaps C'lin was right," C'tis commented, grinning. "That noise would scare *anything* off."

"There'll be no light for them to travel by soon," J'vina rasped. "*Where have* they got to?"

"They'll get here, don't worry," T'via reassured her.

The warrior yelled again, then coughed and headed back to the fire, holding out her hand for a drink. The meyrkats' claws clattered on the bare rock. In the silence that followed, the control group heard a faint sound.

"It's them!"

They were all on their feet in an instant, listening hard.

"Over there," T'via whispered, pointing to one of the northerly tunnels. D'vor went to the entrance and called. To their delight, the response came at once.

A few moments later, V'dal and C'lin emerged smiling into the red glow of the firelight. Their words made light of the reunion, but they were obviously both very relived.

"Nice of you to wait," C'lin remarked, trying to sound offhand. "Did you save us any food?"

"And where's that drink?" V'dal demanded.

After these initial requirements had been satisfied, D'vor asked for news of the tunnel system. The two men glanced at each other, their faces suddenly grim.

"It doesn't look good," V'dal began. "The river level's risen a lot in a very short time, but with no predictable pattern. Some caves don't seem affected at all. We had to go back a long way in order to get around, so we've seen quite a lot." He paused, as if reluctant to go on.

"And?" J'vina insisted.

"Well, I can't be sure," V'dal said, "and there must be *other* routes that we can try, but . . . there doesn't appear to be any way to get back north."

"We're trapped?" C'tis whispered.

"I don't know," V'dal replied seriously. "But I do know that the routes I was familiar with are now all blocked by water or rock."

"There *has* to be a way around," T'via said, the horror of their situation showing in her eyes.

"Probably," V'dal agreed, trying to be optimistic.

"But it could take some time to find it?" D'vor asked.

"Yes."

They all knew the significance of that. Their food supply was limited, and there was little chance of replenishing it here, where all life was tainted. In any case, they all knew that C'tis believed the silkfish tape could only delay the onset of the green-sickness. If they remained in the contaminated areas for too long, lack of food would be the least of their problems.

"There's more water flowing north now?" D'vor asked.

"Yes. Much more." V'dal took a deep breath. "And it's heavily polluted. I tested some of the new chutes."

"Things at home are going to get a lot worse in a hurry," C'lin commented somberly.

There was silence for a while.

"We don't have much choice then, do we?" J'vina stated grimly. "We have to go south."

"Yes," D'vor agreed, unable to deny the logic of this. "It's obvious that our only hope now is to find the source of the pollution, and destroy it."

"Before it's too late," C'tis completed for him.

For a few moments, each member of the control group was lost in private contemplation. Then the dull boom of a distant explosion shattered the gloomy peace. As the rock about them shivered, they glanced upward automatically.

"Again?" T'via breathed.

"No," V'dal answered confidently. "That was much smaller. And man-made."

The echoes and vibrations died away, but the air in the cave felt subtly different.

"Water," C'tis said.

"Someone's doing a little river moving themselves," C'lin remarked.

"Then let's go and find out who," J'vina said, eager now. "We could be closer than we thought." She stood up, and her sword hissed smoothly from its sheath. "Which tunnel, V'dal?"

"Wait a moment," D'vor ordered, also rising to his feet. "We'll do this together, and in an organized fashion." He made his arrangements quickly, and the party set off into the tunnel that seemed to lead most directly toward the sound of the explosion. It was narrow, and only just above head height.

"I just hope they didn't divert the water down *this* passage," C'lin commented. "It could be a tight squeeze."

"You can swim, can't you?" J'vina said, grinning.

A damp wind blew in their faces as they moved.

F21M surveyed the results of his handiwork with satisfaction. Control would be pleased. They had removed two rockfalls and given the outflow a chance to return to normal. Desperate measures had been necessary for the second fall, but the explosive charges had been judged to perfection and had removed the obstruction without bringing down any more of the tunnel's roof. The river of waste roared past on its journey into the uncharted depths of the earth.

"Right," he ordered. "Back to the monitoring station."

As they walked along the tunnel, their powerful torches illuminated the way ahead. The beams of light showed the weirdly beautiful rock formations that decorated both floor and ceiling, and glittered in the seams of crystal. It was a beauty that few men had ever seen, but the maintenance group were oblivious to their surroundings, treating them only as a route from one job to the next.

They had been walking for nearly an hour when L290M, who was in the lead, stopped suddenly, flashing his torch down one of the side tunnels.

"What was that?"

"I didn't hear anything." F21M came up behind him and peered into the tunnel. He could see nothing unusual.

Then all four heard the unmistakable clink of metal on stone.

"Perhaps its the other unit," H73F whispered. At that moment, it became horribly obvious that the newcomers were *not* from the maintenance section.

Two immensely tall black creatures jumped out from behind stalagmites. Although they appeared to have no features on their shiny heads, they were making appalling noises and were brandishing primitive steel weapons.

"Intruders!" F21M cried, reaching for his weapon and wishing they had been issued to the others.

L290M improvised quickly, however, raising and firing the self-detonating catapult at one of the attackers. The metal bolt hit the creature squarely in the chest and exploded, leaving a huge, bloody hole. As it crumpled to the floor, a second creature fell upon the man who had fired and killed him with a single blow of its sword, almost severing his neck.

And then it seemed that the huge, black, faceless monsters were everywhere, intent on carnage. F21M just had time to see his other two colleagues killed before the first attacker loomed over him, knocking his weapon from his hand, its own sword raised for the death blow. He stretched out his left hand to fend it away, knowing the futility of his action.

From somewhere, a voice screamed, "No! We need him alive," and the blade flashed down, severing his arm above the wrist, but stopping short of his head. F21M stared with disbelieving eyes at the blood spurting from the stump, then fainted.

J'vina stood over the prostrate body of the unconscious engineer, breathing hard.

"I should have killed you, you bastard!" she hissed.

"Can you save him?" D'vor asked C'tis. "We need some answers."

"I'll try," the healer said, and gently pushed the warrior aside. "It's over, J'vina," she said softly.

"First B'van and L'tha, now C'lin," V'dal said sadly.

"There'll be more deaths before this is over," D'vor said grimly. He was feeling the loss of their comrade as deeply as anyone, but knew that there was work to be done. They would need to earn the chance to avenge their colleagues' death.

The tension drained out of J'vina in a rush. Her berserk rage left her as she stepped back and looked around at the bodies on the floor.

"I'm glad we'd put the silkfish over our eyes," she remarked to nobody in particular. "Their torches were terribly bright."

D'vor and V'dal knelt to examine their dead foes, removing the protective hoods in order to look at their faces. Cold steel masks stared back at them, dead eyes in the metal sockets. V'dal tried to take the mask off one and found that it was stuck fast. He gasped with horror, as he realized the truth.

"It's bonded to the skull," D'vor said, revulsion in his voice. "Their real faces are gone."

"Just like Mendle," V'dal whispered.

"What are those?" T'via asked in a small voice, pointing to the metal bands fixed around the corpses' wrists. They examined the bracelets, but could make no sense of the figures that appeared there. The armlets could not be removed.

"It's as if someone was trying to change them from humans into something mechanical," T'via said.

They left their grisly examination and turned back to C'tis.

"Well?" D'vor prompted.

"I've stabilized his condition temporarily, but he's in deep shock," the healer replied. "More than I can account for. With luck, he'll live for a while, but I don't know how much you'll get out of him, even if he *does* come around." She had cauterized and bandaged the wound and then used her own special powers to probe within the body of the stricken man. His nervous system had been traumatized by more than just the loss of his hand—she was sure of that.

"Do what you can," D'vor told her.

"Could the shock have something to do with this?" J'vina asked. She was holding the severed hand delicately between one finger and thumb. The metal band was still clamped to the bloody wrist.

"I don't know," C'tis answered, feeling sick, in spite of her healing experience. J'vina tossed the hand into a dark corner. The flashing red light had long since gone out.

chapter 30

"He was trying to get at this when I hit him," J'vina said, turning a curious metal object over in her hands. "Could it be some sort of weapon?"

"I don't know," T'via replied. "And I'm not sure I want to find out."

After witnessing C'lin's violent death, their examination of the various pieces of equipment had been extremely cautious.

"Where's your spirit of enquiry?" the warrior asked, rapidly recovering her normal confident attitude.

"Just be careful your enquiry doesn't get your brains blown out," V'dal warned. His words made T'via wince, but J'vina only laughed.

"A good soldier hasn't much need of brains," she said. "The other bits come in handy, though. I'll be careful." She squinted down the open-ended tube that formed one part of the contraption. "Perhaps you put something in here."

"Or something comes out," T'via suggested.

"Suppose this bit is the grip," J'vina went on, fitting it into her hand, "then the tube would point away from you like this, so you could be right. Yes! And then my finger would fit this little lever—see, just here, inside its own little shield."

"A trigger?" D'vor asked.

"But where are the bolts?" J'vina was mystified. "Well, there's only one way to find out."

"No!" D'vor shouted, but he was too late. J'vina had already pointed the tube at a nearby stalactite and pulled the lever—with astonishing results. With a muffled bang, the metal jumped in her hand and a large chunk of rock fell to the floor. Several smaller chips flew about the cave, whirring like demented insects.

There was a stunned silence.

"I think I'll keep this," J'vina remarked smugly, sounding more than satisfied with her experiment.

"Just don't point it at me," V'dal said sharply, torn between shock and laughter.

"And no more testing without prior discussion, *please,*" D'vor rebuked her.

"He's coming round," C'tis exclaimed suddenly, and they all gathered round the stranger, whose eyes were fluttering open. He groaned, and pain, fear, and confusion showed in his eyes, though his steel face remained as impassive as ever.

"My band," he croaked. "I must have it back." The words sounded unnatural, emerging as they did from unmoving lips.

"Your hand's gone," D'vor replied. "We cannot replace it."

"No," C'tis whispered. "He wants his band. The bracelet that was on his wrist."

"Lost without it . . . grid-map . . ."

"What's he talking about?" J'vina asked.

"Lost . . ." Now there was anguish in the man's strange voice, and he sounded as if he were about to cry.

"We'll help you," C'tis said kindly. "What were you doing down here?"

The metal face turned slowly to look at her.

"Your eyes are so big," he said in wonder.

"Where do you come from?" C'tis tried again.

"Maintenance."

"What's your name?" D'vor asked.

"F21 . . ." The man's voice trailed away. "I don't know," he said, sounding bewildered.

His interrogators glanced at each other.

"He's useless," J'vina said harshly. "He's not making any sense."

"Be quiet!" D'vor snapped irritably.

The warrior moved away in disgust, her patience at an end, though she harbored no ill-feelings toward her group leader for the reprimand. *It's ridiculous,* she thought. *We'll get nothing from him.*

"Wait," C'tis said quietly. "I may have something." She had been holding the man's remaining hand, monitoring the changes within his body. "There are strange substances in his blood stream, but the levels are falling rapidly. Perhaps the band was their source, and the shock is partly withdrawal symptoms."

"Who could treat people that way?" T'via said abruptly. "It's evil!"

The Great Leader decreed," came the unexpected answer. "For our own protection. Obedience is the law." He looked from face to face, as though seeing them for the first time. "You are not of the chosen." He stopped again, obviously confused. "Your faces have not been improved . . ." A new and terrible fear entered his voice as he yelled defiantly, "The grid will protect us from pain!" He wrenched his hand from C'tis's grasp and raised it to his mask. Fingers explored the cold, smooth surface, then he screamed. It was the most tormented, terrible sound that any of the control group had ever heard. It was full of the realization of ultimate terror, and ended with a whimpering sob of utter hopelessness.

There was an appalled silence.

"He's fainted again," C'tis breathed.

When the man next awoke, J'vina and V'dal were absent, having gone farther up the tunnel, trying to find out where the strangers had been heading. D'vor had not wanted to split the party up but knew that he must provide J'vina with something to do in order to stave off her increasing restlessness.

C'tis asked the group leader and T'via to keep their distance for a while, as she tried to soothe her distraught patient. He writhed and sobbed—though no tears ran down his metal cheeks—but she eventually succeeded in calming him. D'vor had told her what to ask, should further questioning prove possible, but before she had a chance to begin, the man drew a deep breath and spoke clearly.

"Eldrin. That was . . . is my name."

"Why couldn't you remember it before?" she asked softly.

"I was . . . I was different then. Someone else. They made me forget." His eyes strayed to his severed wrist, and his good hand tightened convulsively on the healer's as a wave of pain washed through him. "It was all so wonderful when we came here."

"Where?" C'tis asked quickly.

"The city. There were so many people. And the energy . . ." He looked at the healer with sad eyes. "What went wrong?" he asked in despair.

"What were you doing down here, in the caves?"

"Clearing the outflow," he replied.

"What outflow?"

"From the Power Complex and the city's waste."

"The poison."

"Yes. But it doesn't matter. It goes deep into the earth, where it can't harm anyone."

There was silence for a few moments. D'vor was very glad at this point that J'vina was not present. Her reaction to such a statement was not something he wished to contemplate.

"What would happen if the outflow was blocked?" he asked quietly, and C'tis repeated the question.

"We'd have to shut the power units down," he said. "Or they'd overheat and explode."

"And then what would happen?"

"The whole city would be destroyed—it would get so hot that rock would melt. It's unthinkable."

"But there'd be no more outflow?"

"There'd be no more *anything*."

D'vor could hardly contain his jubilation. Here was the one last desperate chance they had been hoping for. If they could destroy the stranger's city, then perhaps their own underground realm might be saved. His team would probably die in the process, but it would be a small price to pay for their people.

"How do you get to the city from here?" C'tis asked.

"The grid won't let you in," Eldrin replied.

"But if I became part of the grid?" she improvised.

"No!" he exclaimed, suddenly vehement. "You can't—and anyway, the grid is . . . not what it was supposed to be. It's evil. We've been tricked."

"Then help us," C'tis said. "We can make it good again."

Hope flared briefly in his eyes, then died away again.

"You can't," he said flatly. "Who *are* you?"

"We're the people who live in these caves," C'tis answered.

"Down here?" His astonishment was plain.

"Yes."

"Gods!" he said then, despair in his voice. "What have we done?"

"*Will* you help us?"

There was no answer for a while. C'tis sensed his inner turmoil; his mind and body were both being forced to make many painful readjustments. She fought to keep him from sliding into shock again.

"Why did you have that band on your wrist?" D'vor asked.

The stranger's internal chaos increased. C'tis wanted to tell D'vor to be quiet, but she was so intent on her work that she dared not speak, or she would lose her concentration.

"My name . . ." the man said, ". . . was changed. For identification. My place in the grid-map. Orders from Control."

"And your face?" D'vor asked.

No! C'tis shrieked silently. *Don't ask that!*

She felt Eldrin slipping away, and in desperation, she turned to signal D'vor to silence. In that moment, the stranger's body gave up its unequal struggle. His brain was numbed by the trauma, and his heart, overloaded and stressed beyond endurance, exploded.

"He's dead," C'tis said quietly.

"He's been living a nightmare," T'via consoled her. "At least he's free from that now."

Their subdued silence was shattered a few moments later by J'vina's strident whistle.

"Danger," D'vor warned, and they all leaped to their feet. "Gather whatever you can carry easily. Quick!"

J'vina and V'dal burst into the cave.

"Men coming!" the warrior gasped. "Lots of them. Like him." She stabbed a finger at the dead man. The meyrkats scrambled and bounded about her, making the floor of the cave seem alive. "But we've found where they came from."

"Good," D'vor replied. "Then let's get out of here before they find us."

They fled into the labyrinth of caves and tunnels, soon outdistancing their pursuers, and relying on V'dal—and their own instincts—to guide them back if necessary. They felt safe from attack at last, and made camp in a small, irregular cave. There they discussed their new-found knowledge. The course of action seemed obvious—even though it frightened them all.

"I just wish there was some way we could get a message

back to the prophets, and let the people know what we're planning to do," D'vor said.

"Perhaps there is," T'via said quietly, and her companions turned to look at her.

"How?" D'vor asked. "You heard V'dal say that all the routes are blocked."

"With this," she replied, holding a sliver of clear stone between her thumb and forefinger.

"Diamond crystal?" C'tis queried.

T'via nodded. "It's a piece of the major crystal that P'tra has in Midholm. Each representative in the control parties has one, but we're only allowed to reveal it in times of direst emergency."

"Well, I'm glad you've recognized the seriousness of our situation," V'dal commented dryly.

"What does it do?" J'vina asked, intrigued.

"I *hope* it will enable me to communicate with P'tra—or whichever prophet is guarding the big stone," T'via replied, her voice faltering a little.

"Image transfer? Through that tiny thing?" C'tis was astonished.

"It's the link that matters, not the size. Mind to mind, crystal to crystal."

"For Rael's sake!" D'vor exclaimed. "Why did no one tell us about this before?"

"Because there are dangers attached to its use." T'via's tone was firmer now, but she could not meet his gaze. "It drains energy from both prophet and caller. Using it over long distances *can* cause injury . . . or even death."

"Oh." D'vor's anger subsided.

"Injury?" C'tis asked.

"To my mind," T'via replied. "If the link goes wrong, I may not be much use to you afterwards."

There was a lengthy silence while they all considered the implications of this.

"I'm willing to try," T'via assured them eventually.

"Even though we're so far away?" D'vor asked quietly.

"Yes. What we're trying to do here may determine the fate of our entire race. Can you think of a better reason for taking a risk?"

No one answered.

"You're all constantly taking risks," she went on. "Now it's my turn. We *must* warn the prophets."

D'vor hesitated.

"You're sure?" he said at last.

"Of course. But I have one condition," T'via replied promptly.

"What's that?"

"If . . . if my mind *is* destroyed, don't leave me like that. I would only be a hindrance. Finish it."

"Kill you?" D'vor was aghast.

"No!" C'tis exclaimed.

"It probably won't come to that," T'via said, doing her best to smile, "but if it did, I wouldn't want to live. You *have* to promise."

"I can't," D'vor told her miserably.

"Look, if there's any chance C'tis can save me, then I know you'll try. But if not . . . you have to promise," she repeated.

After an interminable silence, D'vor made his decision.

"All right," he said softly. "If there's no hope."

"Good," T'via said, then went on, not giving the others a chance to speak. "If I do make contact, you will have to speak to the prophet. My energies will all be focused on maintaining the link." She was businesslike now. "I don't know how long you'll have, so you must work out in advance what you want to tell them, and what questions to ask. Now I must concentrate my mind. I'll call you when I'm ready."

She moved away to the far end of the cavern.

"You can't *really* mean to kill her?" C'tis whispered fiercely.

"No, but—" D'vor shook his head.

"But what?"

"It's her decision. And our promise," V'dal said calmly.

"But it's not right!" The healer in C'tis was outraged.

"Let's pray it doesn't come to that," V'dal concluded.

They sat in silence until T'via called to them.

"I'm ready," she said. "As soon as the image is clear, you can speak."

The others moved to join her, D'vor hurriedly composing his report in his head.

"Don't look so worried," she told him, smiling now. "This is what I've been preparing for all my life."

"Good luck," J'vina said.

"I'll be waiting when you've finished," C'tis added.

T'via nodded in acknowledgment, then closed her eyes.

"Ready?" she asked.

"Yes."

For several heartbeats, nothing happened. Then the crystal, which lay on T'via's outstretched palm, began to glow. A wisp of arcane vapor drifted into the air, grew, and took form. T'via sat quite still as the image coalesced before her. It was wavery at first, but the onlookers soon recognized P'tra, the prophetess. Her long robes and nightbane-black eyes were portrayed in perfect miniature. She appeared startled at first, then worried. She looked ill.

"T'via? What are you doing? What is it?"

"P'tra, this is D'vor. I have some important news. We've found the source of the poison, and there's a chance that we might be able to destroy it utterly." He had her full attention now, and the weariness and pain had left her face. "But we're cut off from home, and probably won't return. We're going to start a fire so fierce that rock will melt. Although this should halt the flow of the poison, it may well mean the deaths of those in the southern dwellings. You must move everyone as far north as possible."

"You bring good news, D'vor," P'tra replied, "but I fear it comes too late. The green-sickness is rampant now, and we will not recover. We cannot move—the poison's onslaught was too quick, too sudden. But we will await the fire gladly. Who knows, perhaps it will cleanse our realm for some future people."

D'vor could not speak. His heart was too heavy. All this effort for *nothing?*

"The link is weakening," P'tra went on. "Fare you well. You have our blessing—do what you feel is right. And look after my precious T'via. I fear she is . . ."

The image rippled, then collapsed. T'via sighed once, then slumped to the floor. C'tis hurried over and knelt at her side.

"It worked," T'via whispered, her voice full of wonder. Then her eyes glazed over, and she said no more.

C'tis tried frantically to use her healing talent within her friend's body, but met resistance at every turn. T'via's entire being was turning in upon itself, and her mind collapsed, becoming nothing more than a cold, impenetrable mass. C'tis cried out a hopeless denial, but T'via's limbs locked rigid and her whole body became still. Only her heart remained beating. The rest of her was gone.

The healer glanced at her three remaining companions, and the expression on her face told them the worst. They were stunned by this second tragedy, coming so soon after P'tra's dreadful news. J'vina came and stood over T'via's body.

"Is there nothing you can do?" the warrior asked gently.

"No. She's gone." C'tis got to her feet. "What happens now?" she asked, turning to D'vor.

She was answered by a muffled bang and swung around to see J'vina standing over their fallen colleague, the metal contraption in her hand. A small metal bolt had drilled a neat hole in T'via's chest, and stilled her heart for good.

J'vina turned away from her handiwork and faced her colleagues, tears streaming down her face. They looked at her in stunned silence.

"She was the bravest of us all," J'vina said in a choked voice. "She deserved to have the promise kept."

V'dal was the first to react. He went to J'vina and took her in his arms, holding her as she wept. No one had ever seen J'vina cry before—and her friends could offer no words of comfort. It was left to J'vina herself to break the spell.

"There's only one thing left now," she said bleakly. "Revenge."

chapter 31

Midwinter's day had come and gone as Jordan and his disparate group of followers pushed deeper into the mountains. They were making good time, asking directions at every settlement they reached and solving their supply problems at the same time. Their plan was to head for the meeting point west of the Cascade, where they hoped to get news from the Lightless Kingdom, and then decide on their course of action. Some of them would go on to the Cascade to meet Gemma and Arden; as yet, they could not see beyond that.

A few of the raiders were familiar with this part of the country, and their knowledge of the mountain terrain, combined with their assiduous and eager scouting, meant that Jordan was confident they could find the place they were looking for. The entrance itself would be well concealed, but their subterranean friends would not be hiding from the upworlders as they had done in the past, and might even be looking out for them.

The high spirits and enthusiasm of Galar's men were infectious, making it easy to sit for long hours in the saddle with half-empty stomachs, Each day brought new vistas, a feeling of achievement, and mounting expectation. Even Cai was swept along by the eager tide. His own spirits were buoyed up by the advantages of his new mode of sight and by his impending reunion with Gemma, though he knew that the events to follow would be critical. If his theories were even partly correct, the world would never be the same again—for good or ill.

"Sometimes I think the raiders are mad," Hewe commented, watching two gray-robed scouts gallop away to check out another possible route. "And then I realize we're *all* mad. It's freezing up here!"

"Uplanders always did think that coastal men were soft," Jordan laughed. "That blubber should be enough to keep you warm!"

"Blubber?" his deputy exclaimed in mock anger. "I'll have you know this is solid muscle."

"And between your ears?" Zana teased.

"Don't you start," Hewe retorted. "I thought ladies were supposed to be polite."

The bees droned noisily from inside their mobile hive.

"The swarm agrees with you about the weather, Hewe," Cai said. "I'm having to help them stay warm." The wizard was effectively blind when the bees were inside the hive, but it was difficult to keep them safe outside for long now, so Cai accepted his handicap willingly.

"They've more sense than most humans then," Hewe replied.

"That," Cai said gravely, "is the truth. Their only mistake was linking up with me!"

"I can think of worse fates," Zana said, then wished she had held her tongue. Hewe gave her an appraising glance, but Cai did not seem to have heard.

They were riding along a deep valley, traveling southeast. Stony slopes rose on either side, their peaks glittering with ice and snow. The air was thin and cold, and the cloudless sky threatened another frosty night.

"If I had to guess," Hewe said, "I'd say we're already farther east than that strange cloud."

"I think you're right," Jordan agreed, "but my major worry is whether we're on the right track to meet up with the groups from the Lightless Kingdom. We need their news."

"Perhaps the cloud was one of the far south's experiments," Cai suggested. "Wouldn't it make sense to keep those away from their center of operations?"

Jordan nodded.

"Or perhaps it *was* just a cloud," Zana said, "and nothing to do with all this."

"No," Cai told her. "It's all connected, somehow." He was about to continue when his attention was caught by the yelling of the returning Gray Raiders. They were gesticulating wildly.

"I'm surprised they don't fall off," Hewe commented,

shaking his head, as they were joined by the raider's leader, Galar.

"Looks like they may have found something," he said.

"If they're making all that fuss and they *haven't* found anything," Hewe replied, "I'll make *sure* they fall off, personally!"

Galar gave the big man a worried look, but Hewe just grinned in return.

The two riders approached, and reined in their hard-breathing mounts. They both began speaking at the same time, until Galar snapped, "One at a time! Omrick."

"We've found the entrance," the raider replied.

"You're sure?"

"It fits the description exactly, and the signal is clear enough."

"Where?" Jordan asked.

"Over that ridge," Omrick answered, pointing to a small pass between two mountains to the south of the valley. "Perhaps half a league from the top. It's easy riding. Shall we go on ahead?" His eagerness was almost painful to watch.

"No. We'll go together. Pass the word along." Jordan's command was obeyed immediately, albeit reluctantly. "We've been lucky," the black man remarked.

"Perhaps," Cai said. "But I suspect that there is more than luck at work here."

The others glanced at the wizard, but said nothing.

"Let me know when the entrance is in sight," Cai went on. "I want to be able to see it."

"Of course," Zana replied.

The long column of horses wheeled to the right and began the ascent to the pass. As Omrick had said, the ground underfoot was safe, but the steep climb left many of the weaker horses laboring. Zana told Cai when they reached the top, and he released the swarm. As always, he experienced a moment's severe disorientation as the world came into view in a giddying swirl.

Before them stood another vale, unremarkable except for the blood-red flag flying from a metal pole in the midst of a rocky outcrop. *We're getting closer*, the wizard thought. If the reports were correct, Gemma might be only a few leagues away. *Why haven't you contacted me?* he asked her silently.

Their last brief conversation had been only days ago, but it seemed like a lifetime to Cai.

The cavalcade rode down into the valley and gathered near the rocks. Jordan and Hewe, together with Cai, Zana, and Galar went ahead on foot, threading their way through the boulders until they came to the flagstaff.

"I don't see anything," Hewe said, looking around.

"The entrances aren't designed to be easily found," Jordan told him. "Spread out and search."

"No need," Cai said. "The bees can do it for us."

The swarm rose into the air and began circling the area. The wizard swayed slightly in response to the pictures they sent him, then pointed as the bees dived into a narrow crevasse.

"In there."

The group squeezed in, with Jordan leading the way.

"These people are supposed to be big!" Hewe gasped.

"They're tall, not fat," his leader replied.

Once inside, they found themselves in a dark, low-roofed cavern. The bees' droning sounded very loud.

"Hello!" The only response was a muffled echo. "Let's go on in," he said. "It may be that they can't get this close to the surface."

"Can't we have a light?" Hewe asked.

"No. We might blind them. Cai, Zana, would you rather wait here?"

"No," the wizard replied. "The bees can see better than you in this light, and I can feel my way as well as any."

"I thought they'd be waiting for us," Galar said.

"Something may have happened to slow them down," Zana suggested.

"Let's go and find out," Jordan said, and they set off, treading cautiously.

The cavern proved to have only one other entrance, which was at the far end, in the deepest recesses of darkness. Although their eyes were gradually adjusting to the lack of light, they could see nothing beyond it. Jordan was in the lead again, and he moved carefully, testing each footfall and handhold gingerly. A few paces down the tunnel, he called out again. This time there was a faint response; it was no more than a whisper, but it encouraged them to go on.

After a few more steps, a very faint light showed ahead,

and they soon emerged into a second cave, lit by thin crystal seams in the roof. Two men lay side by side on the uneven floor, and the upworlders hurried over to them.

"It's about time you got here," one of them breathed, looking at Jordan. The man's body was covered in black tape, but his pale face and large eyes were exposed, and even in the dim light, it was obvious that he was very ill. The other man was clearly dead.

"We came as quickly as we could," Jordan replied quietly. "Can you help him, Cai?" he asked, hoping that the wizard's healing skills had not also been damaged by the elemental wall.

"Don't bother," the man responded. "It's the green-sickness. Nothing can stop it now. Save your energy, and listen. I've news for you."

They gathered round, saddened by his suffering, but eager to hear what he had to say.

"We haven't got much time," he rasped. At first, his audience thought he was referring to his own illness, but then it became clear that he meant the plight of the Lightless Kingdom itself.

"The pollution's got much worse in the past few days. The river level has risen fast, surging higher than ever, and the poison is worse than ever. The green-sickness is an epidemic now. It may already be too late to stop it, but—" He paused, coughing feebly.

"But?" Jordan asked gently.

"There's one last chance," the man went on. "Most of the control parties in the south have been lost—I'm the last of our group. We were all cut off, but D'vor and his team are still operating. They got through—and they've found the source of the pollution."

"Where?" Jordan's voice was urgent now.

"It seems to be about twelve leagues south of the Cascade, maybe a little more. They were right underneath when the mountain moved. They captured one of the bastards from the city . . ." The sick man was fading fast.

"What city?" Zana whispered, but the man did not appear to hear her.

"D'vor said the blockages would cause overheating in a power complex, and that would mean there'd be a huge fire . . . so hot that even stone would melt . . . destroy the whole city, destroy the source of the pollution."

"But it would destroy more than just the city!" Cai said fearfully.

"Worth it," the man replied. "Help them. They're our only hope."

"How can you know all this, if you've been cut off?" Hewe asked.

"Crystal," the dying man replied. "B'sal here—" He indicated his companion—"gave his life to get this information for you. He was one of the prophet's best people." There was anger in his weak voice. "There's no one at the Cascade," he went on. "We couldn't get to the surface after the mountain moved. Just go to the city, help D'vor's group. They're our only hope," he repeated.

"We'll go," Jordan promised. "And we'll do whatever we can. You know how much we appreciate your help. Is there *nothing* we can do for you?"

"You're Jordan, aren't you?"

The black man nodded.

"We should have met earlier. . . . If any of my people survive this, tell them that R'ven was content to have played his part in the battle. I just wish I could live long enough to see you win."

"Your sacrifice will not be forgotten," Jordan said, then realized that R'ven could no longer hear him. Cynic though he was, Jordan offered a prayer to the god Rael on R'ven's behalf, then got to his feet and ushered the others outside. No one felt like talking as they threaded their way back through the maze of stone. As they rejoined their companions, the sun was setting behind the western mountains. Anticipating their leader's wishes, the travelers had set up camp for the night, and the ensuing discussion took place around the comfort of a fire.

"We still have to go to the Cascade, you know," Cai said. "That's where Gemma said she'd meet us."

"I know," Jordan replied. "And it may still be the quickest route to the city."

"At least this way we know where we're going for the moment," Hewe replied. "East, then south."

"True," Jordan responded. "It's what we're going to do when we get there that's worrying me."

chapter 32

As Jordan and his army were discussing R'ven's information and preparing to sleep, Gemma and Arden were savoring the very welcome comforts of the guest hut in Keld. It was clean and dry, and a fire was blazing in the grate of the stone wall. It was a distinct improvement on the hurried hours of sleep they had so far snatched in their frantic journey from the valley, when their only warmth had come from each other.

In spite of the haste with which they had left Mallory's home, the valley people had made sure that they were well provisioned, and had given them four horses to make their traveling easier. And this time, in contrast to their previous journey into the mountains, they knew where they were going. They had been delayed neither by illness nor by mistakes in navigation, and as a result, they had made excellent time. They had used every moment of available daylight, sometimes going on in darkness when the terrain was suitable.

After eight days' riding, the water level in the river, whose course they were following, had dropped quickly. Soon after that, it dried to a trickle.

"The mountain's moved again," Arden said hopefully. "Perhaps the valley will be all right after all."

"Od obviously hasn't forgotten the promise," Gemma replied, sending her silent thanks to the stone-clan. "At least *some* magic is still working." Then the other consequence of the meyrkats' action occurred to her, and her gladness faded. "But if the water's not going to the valley . . ."

"Oh." Arden's face fell. *Will it never be possible to save them both?* he thought miserably.

It was all the more reason for them to hurry onward.

In all it had taken them only twelve days to reach Keld. They had arrived at dusk, and had been greeted by the delighted villagers, who remembered Gemma as the healer of two critically ill children, and who wanted to prepare a feast there and then in her honor. She dissuaded them, accepting only a small portion of the food and precious mountain mead that they pressed upon her, and explaining that what she and Arden needed, more than anything else, was a good night's rest under a friendly roof. However, the villagers wanted to know the result of Gemma's amazing flight the previous year, and whether it had achieved the desired result. So there was much conversation before the travelers could retire to the guest hut. They were escorted by the village children, who were delighted by the fact that their visitors were married now, and who smiled and giggled until the headman, Ehren, told them to mind their manners. So the children dispersed, and Gemma and Arden closed the door behind them with some relief, but with smiles on their faces.

"I feel as though I could sleep for days," Gemma said.

"This certainly beats our tent," Arden agreed, "though I'd be happy anywhere, so long as it was with you."

They smiled at each other, secure in their love, in a world where little else was certain.

"They're good people," Gemma remarked.

"Yes, and they've special reason for treating you well," he replied. "It's a pity we can't spend more time here—I rather like being treated as a guest of honor."

"We've work to do."

"I know. With any luck, we should reach the Cascade tomorrow. Do you think Cai will be there yet?"

"I've no idea," she replied, noting the slight undercurrent of tension that was always present in Arden's voice when he talked of the wizard. *What are you afraid of, my love?* she wondered, putting her arms about him and snuggling close as they stood before the fire.

"You know, it's strange," she went on. "Since we left the valley, I haven't sensed his presence or been able to talk to him. You'd have thought that now he's so close . . ." She stopped as she felt Arden stiffen. "Cai is a very dear friend, from a long time ago," she told him quietly. "From a time when I didn't even know that you existed. You have nothing to fear from him."

Arden looked away, then turned back to meet her gaze.

"But you loved him?" It was half question, half accusation.

"Yes. But only as a dear friend," she repeated.

"Does *he* know that? He loved you too, didn't he?"

"I suppose so."

"And he's a wizard."

This flat statement puzzled Gemma. "What's that got to do with anything?" she asked. "And anyway, so are you." She smiled.

"He's a *real* wizard," he retorted. "I can't fight magic, Gemma."

"You won't have to!" she shot back. "Don't be so stupid!"

The spark of anger in his eyes was replaced by a sullen obstinacy. He did not speak.

"Arden, *please* understand. I'm looking forward to seeing Cai again," Gemma said, holding him tighter still. "He is a friend, and I hope he can help us save the valley and the Lightless Kingdom. But it's you that I love, you I want to spend my life with. What more do I have to do to prove it? If you don't know how I feel by now, then you need your head examined!" She was annoyed now.

"I'm sorry," Arden whispered after a few moments. "I *am* being stupid. It's just the idea of him that bothers me."

"Wait till you meet him," Gemma said quickly. "I'm sure you'll like each other."

Arden nodded, though he still looked doubtful, and Gemma kissed him.

"Let's go to bed," she said. "We have to make an early start tomorrow."

"And we need our strength for the journey," he added.

They both laughed. It was an old joke between them—and especially funny now, when they knew that they intended to disregard the warning completely.

They left at dawn the next morning, in spite of the protests of the headman's wife, who said they needed a good meal before starting out. The whole village was up to see them off, and Gemma had a special greeting from the two children whose lives she had saved. She and Arden rode away feeling uplifted and refreshed, more than ready for the last stage of their journey and the reunion that could mean so much to their world.

They traveled southeast at first, skirting the edges of the mountain Blencathra as they left the level plain of Maiden Moor. They had been this way just over a year ago, but only Arden had completed that journey to the Cascade.

"Let's hope there's no floating city around this time," Arden remarked.

"We couldn't have achieved what we did without their help," Gemma replied, "but on this occasion, I think I agree. I just want to get on with it! Shouldn't we be heading south now?"

"The next valley," he told her, "and then up—between those two mountains."

"Which is the one that rocks?" Gemma asked. Even after having experienced the proof of this phenomenon, she still found it hard to believe.

"The one on the left," Arden replied.

They rode on, watching the scene unfold before them, and by late afternoon reached the point where the river bed disappeared. It simply ceased to exist.

"I almost went crazy here last time," Arden admitted. "It just didn't make any sense."

Thereafter, the valley was dry and relatively smooth, great slabs of rock interspersed with soil and patches of rough grass. But it was not the valley, nor even the mountain peaks to the east and west, that drew their attention now. They could hear a dull roaring in the distance, and before long, they could see the permanent yet ever-changing swirl of mist that marked the presence of the Cascade. The last rays of the sun slanted across the vale, forming a perfect rainbow in the spray, like a magical bridge between the two mountains.

Beyond that was the waterfall itself. It was over a hundred paces high and plunged from the black cliff into a rock pool of churning white. The whole was wreathed in mist; its raging power and fierce beauty were mesmerizing.

Close to, the sound was unnerving, making the horses fretful, and they were careful to keep well away from the sheer drop into the pool.

"Once is enough!" Arden shouted above the roar. "I'll stay on dry land this time!"

"Good!" Gemma yelled back "Can you see anyone?"

"No. Let's move on a bit over to the west!" he replied, pointing through the mist into the deepening gloom of evening. "Find a quieter spot to camp!"

The horses obeyed gladly, and as they moved away from the frightening cataract, the fog grew thinner and the noise became less deafening.

"Are those campfires?" Gemma asked suddenly, pointing ahead.

"They could be," Arden replied.

"Then they're here!" she cried happily, and was about to spur her mount forward when Arden sounded a note of caution.

"We don't know it's them for sure." He paused. "Let's go carefully."

Gemma nodded, slightly annoyed by his caution but recognizing its good sense. They dismounted and walked on slowly for a little while. Then a figure appeared suddenly out of the gloom.

"Hello, young lovers," a voice said cheerfully. "Nice night for a stroll, don't you think?"

"Hewe!" Gemma exclaimed joyfully.

chapter 33

Jordan looked up as Gemma and Arden came through the flap of his large tent.

"That was good timing," he remarked, smiling broadly. "We only got here ourselves this afternoon."

"Where's Cai?" Gemma asked quickly.

"He's in his own tent," Jordan replied. "Hewe, will you fetch him? He'll only be a few moments," he went on, seeing the hesitation on Gemma's face. "Come in, you two, and sit down. We've got a lot to talk about."

"Do you know what's going on?" Arden asked.

"Not exactly, but whatever it is, we're getting a lot closer now. We'll find out soon enough."

The tent flap moved again, and Gemma jumped to her feet as Cai entered. He stood facing her, looking as young and handsome as ever, but there were lines on his face she did not remember, and his green eyes did not see her. The bees were with him, some flying close to his head, some riding on his shoulders. Their gentle droning brought back old memories.

"It's good to see you, Cai," Gemma said quietly. There was a lump in her throat.

For a moment, the wizard did not reply; it was as if he was considering the best response.

"It's good to see you too, Gemma," he said at last. "Though I wish it was with my own eyes."

After their many months apart, they felt awkward, neither knowing what to say next. Their remote conversations had often been easy and uninhibited, but now, in person, it did not seem quite so simple to pick up the threads of their old friendship. Eventually, Gemma took a tentative step forward and Cai responded by spreading his arms wide. She went to him gladly then, and fell into his embrace. The swarm buzzed over their heads.

"You're as beautiful as I remembered," he said softly.

"Have I been gone so very long?" she whispered.

"A lifetime," he replied.

There was silence in the tent. As they drew apart, Hewe and Zana came in. Gemma recognized her old traveling companion with astonishment, and hugged her fiercely, before turning to make her own introduction.

"This is Arden," she said. "My husband."

Cai did not react, but behind him, Zana stifled a gasp. Hewe chuckled.

"I'm glad you've made an honest woman of her at last," he said.

Arden got slowly to his feet, his face expressionless, and extended a hand to Cai. The wizard took it in his own, but neither man spoke. Gemma watched them anxiously, desperately wanting them to like each other.

"You're a lucky man, Arden," Jordan remarked.

"I know it," he replied, still looking at Cai.

"Congratulations," Cai said quietly. "I wish you both every happiness."

"Thank you," Arden responded. "I've heard a lot about you, Cai. I hope we can be friends."

Gemma smiled, grateful for the effort they were making on her behalf.

"I'm lucky too," she told Jordan.

"I don't doubt it," he replied. The underground leader was aware of the tension beneath this conversation, but he also knew that they had much to discuss, and night was drawing in. "Sit down, everyone. Now that we're all together at last, we much decide what to do next."

They obeyed, sitting close together. Gemma noted the slightly proprietorial way in which Zana helped Cai to sit down.

"Before we start," she said, "I'd like to try to do something about Cai's sight."

Jordan nodded. "Of course."

So she moved across and took the wizard's hands in her own. She let her senses slide away, gradually moving within his body, seeking out the malady. Memories came to her—of a massive blue wall, stunning cold, and a white fog, clearing suddenly—but she could make no sense of them. The images passed, and she continued her examination, doggedly pursuing her goal, but without success. At last she withdrew in frustration.

"I can't find anything wrong with your eyes," she said. "There's no reason for this blindness."

Cai smiled bleakly.

"That's what the healers in Clevemouth and Newport told me," he replied. "Reason or not, I still can't see."

"Then it's something *outside* your body that is causing it," Gemma said, hopelessly confused.

"It doesn't matter," the wizard said, trying not to sound impatient. "We're wasting time. And the bees are my eyes now."

Gemma returned to her place beside Arden, and her husband put an arm round her shoulders.

"Right," Jordan began. "I'll go through everything we've learned, for Gemma and Arden's sake. Tell me if I leave anything out."

He talked long into the night, and the picture he painted was a grim one. Cai's theory that the Earth-mind was going insane sounded all too plausible, and Gemma shuddered, but it was the latest news from the Lightless Kingdom that affected Arden most. He found if difficult to grasp the idea of dreams becoming reality, but he had spent several months in the underground caves and had grown to respect and even love the people of that strange realm. The thought that it might all be destroyed made even more of an impact on him because he could visualize it personally. The knowledge that C'tis, D'vor, and the others were still fighting and were so close to what seemed like the perfect solution gave him some hope. He was determined to help them in any way he could—and he said so in no uncertain terms.

"We're all going to help," Jordan assured him. "We're heading south at first light. Our problem is that we don't know exactly what we're facing. We haven't exactly got a massive army here, and the weapons this unknown city may command are probably more powerful than anything we can even imagine. Remember Mendle's tower!"

"The very least we can do is provide some sort of

diversion," Arden replied. "Which may be all that D'vor and his group need to carry out their plan."

"You realize that if they succeed, and we're anywhere near the place, we'll probably all be killed?"

"What choice do we have?"Arden said. "We can't just run away and leave them to it. And we're talking about the future of the whole world."

"We're all agreed on that," Jordan replied calmly. "But I wanted to be sure that you all knew just what we're getting into."

"Let me get this straight," Arden said later. He and Gemma were both desparately tired but knew that sleep would not come easily this night. They found comfort, as usual, in each other's arms.

"If we destroy the city, we not only destroy the source of the pollution, but we also rid the world of the threat of whatever evil is brewing there, and the *possibility* of it spreading further?"

"Yes," Gemma whispered.

"And *that's* what's been driving the Earth-mind mad, therefore it should then become sane again—and all these peculiarities like elemental walls and disappearing islands will go away?"

"That's the theory," she admitted. "But Arden, I don't believe it's as simple as that." Her voice betrayed her fears.

"It doesn't sound simple at all to me," he commented. "What's bothering you?"

"Lots of things."

"Well?" he asked, after waiting in vain for her to go on.

"This fire," she began hesitantly. "It'll destroy far more than the city. You heard what they said. So hot that *rock* will melt. What if it actually *spreads* the poison instead of containing and destroying it? What if this fire, or explosion, is the very thing that the Earth-mind fears? If *that's* what's driving it mad, then we'll be helping to create the very disaster we're hoping to prevent!"

"That's a lot of what-ifs," Arden replied, daunted by her words. "What else can we do?"

"I don't know," Gemma whispered miserably. "I don't understand what's happening, or what this *new* logic means.

I'd only just come to terms with magic—and now everything's being turned on its head again."

"Perhaps you can get the circles to help us," Arden suggested quietly. "*Cai* could help you." Gemma hugged him tighter, knowing what an effort it had been for him to admit the possibility that the wizard might be able to aid her in a way he could not. She knew that, subconsciously at least, Arden still saw Cai as a rival.

"Perhaps," she said softly. "Magic has to be important in this somehow. Otherwise, why am I supposed to be the Key to the Dream."

"You changed the book once," he reminded her. "We can do it again." *There is still hope*. "The future doesn't have to belong to Chaos."

"I keep telling myself that," she replied. "But it doesn't help much." They lay in silence for a while, then Gemma added, in a small voice, "And I'm scared."

"We all are," he told her.

"Scared for *us*. We've had so little time."

"But we *have* to do this—or the whole world may be destroyed."

"I know . . . but I don't want to lose you."

"You won't," he promised. "Whatever happens, we'll be together always."

The tent was full of dreams.

Gemma was back in the valley, looking down into the wide brown eyes of her namesake. The baby was smiling, and music sounded all around them.

Little Gem spoke, her voice a gentle singsong, childlike, yet impossibly mature.

"I wanted to see you again, Auntie Gemma. I'm sorry—I didn't mean to hurt you. Mommy says you are not someone to be trifled with. Why did you go away?"

"I had to, little one."

"You could have taken me to the mountains, up high."

"No. You're too young. Too small."

Solemn brown eyes regarded her accusingly.

Then the scene changed abruptly to Gemma's leave-taking. To her delight, Kris had come to bid farewell to her and Arden. The crippled man had brought with him a gift, a thin staff made of an unknown substance and beautifully crafted.

He had insisted that Gemma take it with her, but had not explained why. So it was added to their baggage, and they rode south, climbing toward the mountains. Up high.

The tent was full of dreams.

Arden was part of a circle of people. He knew them all well, but could not see their faces. There was something *wrong* with their faces. They were all looking in, toward the center of the circle, where a man was seeping up out of the solid ground and taking shape before them. With a growing sense of dread, Arden realized who it was.

Gemma stepped forward from the arc of the circle, and Arden screamed silently when he saw that her face was covered with a mask of cold metal.

She knelt, offering her staff of power, the symbol of all her magic, to the man who now stood before them.

Arden's dead father accepted it with a smile.

chapter 34

The four remaining members of the control group had been playing a deadly game of hide-and-seek for several days. The city had sent units of steel-faced soldiers into the caves to hunt them down, but in spite of their superior equipment, they had not been able to match the elusive skills of their prey.

J'vina led the evasive action, though she longed to stay and fight, to use her own destructive expertise and extract some measure of revenge. She recognized the importance of the greater cause, however, and devoted her talents to ensuring the safety of her companions. J'vina's single-minded intensity was frightening to see, but she was good at what she did, and the others obeyed her instructions without question.

"We certainly stirred them up," V'dal remarked during one of their brief periods of respite. "They must have valued the people we killed very highly."

"I don't think it's that," D'vor replied. "They believe we were responsible for the rockfalls that blocked their outflow—*that's* what they're worried about."

"Of course," V'dal agreed softly. "I should have realized."

"What do you think then?" D'vor went on. "Can we give them good reason, to be *really* worried?"

"I think so," the guide answered. "It's difficult to be certain—there are so many tunnels—and there are still a couple unaccounted for—but if we time it right, there are ways of effectively blocking their precious outflow."

"Good," D'vor said, with evident satisfaction. "So what do we do?"

Their attack began two days later, at rockdark. They each knew their assigned tasks and had made the necessary preparations. The patrols from the city were very few now—they evidently believed that the intruders were either dead or had somehow escaped—so they had free access to the caves and tunnels that surrounded the poisonous outflow.

As a control party for the Lightless Kingdom, they had been involved in operations to open or block tunnels several times, but this was the largest task of its sort they had ever undertaken. V'dal had planned it using his painstakingly gathered knowledge of the cave systems and rock formations around them. They had only a small amount of explosives with them and had to be sure it was used as effectively as possible. However, the recent earthquake had left several weaknesses in the structure of the stone, and V'dal was confident that their attack could therefore prove devastating. Not only would it block most of the outflow tunnels, but it would also fill many of the subsidiary tunnels, making it practically impossible for anyone from the city to reach the main falls.

Rockdark came, and V'dal set the fuses for the main charge. When the others heard that first explosion, they would light their own fuses, then escape down the designated routes. They would meet in a cave near the area where they believed the troops from the city would emerge. That was the part J'vina was looking forward to most. She waited in silence, the seven meyrkats gathered around her.

A small thump, followed by a thunderous vibration, told her that the time had come, and she smiled beneath her protective covering. She lit the fuse, watching it smoulder for a few moments to make sure it would not go out.

"This is for all of you," she said aloud. "For B'van, L'tha, and C'lin. And T'via." *Especially for T'via*. Then the warrior turned to the meyrkats. "Come on," she ordered. "We've got work to do!"

The clan responded happily, sharing J'vina's excitement, and she laughed at their antics as she led them away.

The three smaller explosions occurred almost simultaneously; each was followed by the slithering sound of moving rock, a noise that had once been a signal of fear for the control group, but which they now greeted with grim pleasure.

They met as arranged.

"Well done," D'vor said breathlessly. "Now we've got to make sure those metal-faced monsters don't undo all our good work."

Wordlessly, J'vina led them toward the enemy. No one questioned her right to do so.

Gemma knew before she reached the crest of the ridge that they had reached their goal—she could feel the evil as a palpable force in the air about her. Cai felt it too, and the bees were agitated within their mobile hive.

The sun was setting as they looked down upon the city for the first time. In a metal-filled valley, great monoliths soared skyward, vast expanses of steel and glass reflected both the dying light of the day and the myriad lamps and flares of the city itself. Smoke and steam spewed out of gigantic chimneys, and an ominous throbbing sound pulsed from the very heart of the foul metropolis. From this distance, no movement was visible; the entire complex seemed barren, utterly inhuman.

Each member of that small army looked down upon the valley in awe; none doubted that this was indeed the center of all that afflicted their world, the target of their fearsome pilgrimage.

"It's not like any city *I've* ever seen," Galar admitted in a quiet voice.

"It's like no city the whole world has ever seen before," Jordan answered.

"How can we hope to attack *that?*" Hewe wanted to know. "Where do we start?"

"It's surrounded by open ground," Arden noted. "If they have anything like the weapons in Mendle's tower, they could pick us off easily before we even get close."

"Wait until it's dark," Cai said. The bees were airborne now, and he was studying the problem with the others. "We'll have more of a chance of approaching unseen. And I may be able to cloak our progress a little." *The last wizard to start the last battle.*

Gemma had said nothing since the city had come into view, and the others turned to her now. If Cai could use wizardry, then surely so could she.

"What do you think, Gemma?" Jordan asked.

But she did not reply; her head was filled with excited voices. It was confusing, and she was not aware of her own surroundings.

The burrow falls. Clear-rush stopped.

Follow J'vee. The clan has work to do.

Black-ones-shed-skins go to fight for their territory.

Silently, Gemma called out to the meyrkats and was rewarded by their astonishment and joyful greetings.

The muffled rumblings of underground explosions reached the onlookers on the crest of the ridge, but Gemma was still preoccupied.

"Gemma, what's the matter?" Jordan asked anxiously.

"Leave her," Arden said quickly. "She's all right." He knew that Gemma's mind sometimes operated on many levels, most of which would forever be beyond him; he also knew that she was not under any immediate threat.

Where are you? Gemma asked the clan.

In the giant burrow. J'vee leads us to the battle, Ox replied. *Will you join us, clan-friend?*

If I can. Are you beneath the city?

The meyrkats evidently did not understand the word city and there was some hesitation before Av asked,

The burrow from which the shiny-faces come?

Yes, Gemma replied, images of Mendle flashing into her mind.

It is above us. We go there now, Ed answered. *Clear-rush stopped inside. Big fight with bad clan.*

Now?

Yes. It begins, Ox replied emphatically.

Gemma tore her mind away from the precious link, returning to a world where the ground still trembled. *Stars!* she thought. *We're only just in time!*

"The meyrkats!" she began. "They're below the city now, with J'vina and the rest. They're blocking the tunnels for some reason, trapping water inside."

"I thought they were going to start a fire," Hewe was confused.

"Whatever they're doing," Jordan put in, "the attack has started?"

"Yes."

People had gathered to listen to Gemma, and the news spread like wildfire. Shouts of manic joy and cries of aggression echoed through the mass of Gray Raiders, while Jordan and those closest to him wondered desperately what they should do. In the end, the decision was taken out of their hands. Now that they were so close to their goal, the raiders were in the grip of a demented fury, and although Galar and Tomas tried in vein to stop them, they were helpless before the tide of angry men. A battle chant was taken up with increasing fervor, evoking awful memories for Gemma.

"Death to the demon-spawn!"

"Galar will never hold them," Hewe told Jordan.

"I know. What an appalling mess." The underground leader turned to Cai. "We'll have to separate from the raiders. Can you hide us from the city now?"

"For a while, anyway," the wizard replied. "I'll do my best."

"Who knows?" Jordan said. "Perhaps if only a few of us get inside, it may make all the difference."

"Death to the demon-spawn!"

The first raiders broke into the open, galloping down the long slopes of the valley. Within moments, the Gray Raiders were all on the move, charging wildly in the half-light, their voices raised in a chorus of bloodlust. Some of Jordan's men went with them, swept up by the surge of battle fever.

Jordan watched the suicidal attack with dismay, then turned to Cai.

"Do what you can," he instructed. "There's no point waiting any more."

So Cai summoned up all his strength and asked his familiar for their help. He knew that what he was attempting would exhaust him, and also knew that it was the time for final efforts. If this was to be his contribution, then so be it.

The air grew darker about them as Cai's muttered words rang in their ears. An unnatural fog closed in, and the scene before them grew hazy.

"Let's go," Jordan ordered, and led his party down the slope at a steady pace. Ahead of them, more lights were coming on in the city, some brighter than anything they had ever seen. The raiders were halfway to the city by now, and must surely be noticed by its defenders soon. Cai's group rode on, the distance between them and the raiders growing wider every moment.

"There!" Hewe exclaimed, pointing through the gloom. Men were beginning to appear from the base of the nearest steel monolith. Yet more lights came on, illuminating the slope where the raiders charged. The defenders opened fire, and many horses and riders crashed headlong to the ground. As the surviving horsemen reached the metal-faced defenders, the fighting became hand-to-hand. After that, it was impossible to see what was happening.

"If you were hoping to use them as a diversion," Arden said dispassionately, "we'd better be quick. There won't be many of them left soon."

"There's a gap between the buildings over there," Hewe said. "And I can't see any guards. Shall we head for that?"

"Anyone got any better ideas?" Jordan asked. There was no reply. "Can we move faster, Cai?"

"Yes," the wizard answered, his voice sounding weak. "Better, in fact. I can't keep this up much longer."

So Jordan turned and led his companions directly down the slope. They followed him with excitement and foreboding in their hearts, knowing that they had no choice. It was now or never.

The city grew larger in their field of vision, looming over them like a mountain of steel. Each of them stared at it in horror, wondering whether it was to become their tomb.

Each of them, that is, except Gemma. She was seeing the monstrous metal valley from a different viewpoint. Large brown eyes, so much younger than her own, stared down upon the scene in fright and confusion. Little Gem, linked to her namesake now by an extraordinary bond, watched their progress from the mountaintop.

chapter 35

The controllers saw their instruments react to the vibrations within the earth.

"What was that?"

They watched the dials and lights anxiously, then one of them burst out in exasperation, "I don't believe this! The ducts are blocked again!"

A moment later, the other added, "It's even worse than before. Look at that pressure buildup! It's incredible." They stared at the panels before them, hardly daring to breathe.

"The temperature's rising fast. We'll have to shut some of the units down."

They looked at each other then, wondering which of them would have the nerve to break the news to the Great Leader. Their superior had chosen a good time to be off duty.

"Get on to Maintenance," one said quickly. "Tell them to get every operative and machine down *now*. And tell them to be quick—for all our sakes."

As the other man did his bidding, adjusting his headset as he spoke, the controller's eyes remained mesmerized by the readings on his instruments. *What can have happened?* It defied all logic, and yet it was happening. *If it goes on for too long, this place will explode into such a fireball that it will level the mountains for leagues around.*

Beads of sweat began to trickle down his face.

Ed waited patiently in his hiding place in the bright burrow that was called the monitoring station. Although everything about him was strange, he knew what the was expected to do. J'vee had discovered that the sealed door to the monitoring station could be opened from the outside by turning a circle of metal on the wall. They had let Ed in before putting their plan into operation. The meyrkat kept utterly still, aware of his responsibility. *Watch*, J'vee had signaled. *Call to us*.

The meyrkat tensed as a rushing, hissing noise filled the room. Then a moving burrow appeared, doors opened, and four men hurried to open the seal and went out into the caves. Ed stayed where he was, watching.

The doors closed again and the mobile burrow went away. Ed waited, hoping his friends would get here soon. He was rewarded before long by Ox's voice.

The clan is here. We await your call.

Ed returned his greeting, then heard the hissing sound once more.

Shiny-ones come, he reported. *Be ready*.

As the process was repeated, four more men let themselves out. This time, however, Ed came out into the open and ran across to the mobile burrow. From outside came the sounds of sudden, fierce fighting; moments later, J'vee led the rest of the meyrkats and her three colleagues through the seal.

"Good work," she said, looking around quickly. "Where did they come from?"

Get into the moving burrow, Ed told the clan. *Follow me*.

They obeyed without question, though they did not fully understand what he meant. Their excitement was obvious, however, and J'vina guessed their intent correctly.

"In here!" she called, stepping through one of the open doors. As she did so, the doors began to close of their own accord. D'vor and V'dal leaped forward to catch them, and J'vina adroitly jammed one with her sword. Her colleagues squeezed inside, and the doors slammed shut behind them.

"Now what?" V'dal wondered aloud, looking around the tiny room. "There's no way out of here."

The room itself answered him, with a jerk that made them all stagger.

"It's moving!" C'tis exclaimed as they steadied themselves. Then they realized what was happening.

"It's taking us into the city," D'vor said in astonishment.

"Good," J'vina replied. "Now there'll be some *real* fighting. I could have taken that last group on my own." Even C'tis was resigned to bloodshed now and could not deny the strange exhilaration that pulsed through her. She gripped her sword tightly, determined to play her part in the group's last desperate action.

"Whatever happens," D'vor said quietly. "We've done our best, and I'm proud of you all. Rael be with us."

The others repeated his prayer, and the meyrkats added their piping voices as if in agreement. J'vina and V'dal laughed.

Their transport began to slow down.

"Let's give them hell!" D'vor yelled as they came to a halt and the doors opened. As light flooded in, the four attackers were glad of the double layer of tape protecting their eyes. They burst out into a huge room filled with machinery and people.

To the mechanics awaiting their turn in the transport, the people of the Lightless Kingdom appeared as faceless monsters, hideous black giants who attacked instantly and without mercy. A dozen had fallen, either dead or wounded, before their fellows realized what was happening. The strange creatures whirled about, their deadly steel blades slicing through protective clothing, flesh and bone alike. Some of the maintenance crews fled in panic, but a few of the more enterprising among them found weapons and began to defend themselves. Several shots were fired, and though some of the metal bolts went wide and others felled some of the mechanics, one of the marksmen had better aim. D'vor was flung backward, landing in a bloody, crumpled heap on the smooth floor. As J'vina turned her own contraption on D'vor's assailant, the crews ran for cover.

Meanwhile, the meyrkats were adding to the confusion, darting among the flying feet, and it was they who spotted the new mobile burrow. Some of the defenders had run into it and were attempting to close doors blocked by one of their fallen colleagues. As they tried to shift the body, the Wanderers arrived, biting and scratching and calling at the tops of their shrill voices. J'vina saw them and beckoned to V'dal and C'tis, who quickly disposed of the men inside. Once the doors were clear of obstructions, they closed. But nothing happened.

"Are we trapped?" C'tis gasped.

"Press one of those buttons," V'dal suggested, breathing hard.

"Which one?" Each had a symbol on it, but meant nothing to the people of the Lightless Kingdom.

"*Any* one!"

So C'tis pushed the top button, and they immediately started to move. Upward.

The meyrkats gave excited peeps of recognition; they had been in an elevator before. Of course, the others had not, and their knees almost gave way at the first motion. They hardly had time to realize what was happening before the elevator came to a halt with a mechanical sigh, and the doors opened again. They leaped out, swords at the ready, but met no opposition. After the carnage below, the room they had entered seemed calm and peaceful.

Two men sat on the far side of the room, with their backs to the elevator. They wore headsets and showed no sign of noticing the new arrivals. In front of them were vast panels of instruments. Beyond that were enormous windows that looked out over a massive, dimly lit cavern filled with machinery and endless leagues of piping.

"We'll have to tell him," one of them said, as V'dal hurriedly motioned his companions to remain silent.

"What are Maintenance *doing?*" the other exclaimed. "There should have been plenty of men out there by now."

"It's no use, they'll never clear it in time. We must shut down now!" There was dread in the man's voice.

"All right. You get started, and I'll call the Leader."

"Now!" V'dal yelled, and the three intruders leaped forward as the two controllers spun round, aware at last of their peril. One of them died instantly as J'vina's sword took him in the neck, and the other froze as V'dal's blade came to rest on his throat.

"Show me how to shut this thing down!" V'dal demanded, ignoring the startled glances of the others.

"What?" The man removed his headset. "Shutting down?" He looked relieved as he swiveled his chair back to the panel. "First, we turn these dials . . ."

"Good." V'dal pushed the man aside and vigorously turned them all in the opposite direction.

"No! No!" the controller yelled, his face turning chalky white. "You'll kill us all!"

"Shut up!" J'vina snapped, reinforcing her words with a

single thrust of her sword. The controller was dead by the time he hit the floor.

By the time V'dal had finished, there were red lights flashing all over the panel, and loud sirens were sounding in the cavernous hall beyond. C'tis saw people scrambling along walkways and running toward the exits.

"Well, something's happening, at least," V'dal noted with a half-mad chuckle. He turned to the other two. "Get out of here and aggravate them a bit more. Get clear if you can—I'm staying, to make sure no one interferes with this." He waved a hand at the pulsating lights.

C'tis would have protested but J'vina reacted first.

"We'll not get away," she said, "but causing havoc is just what I like. Farewell, V'dal. We may not die together, but we'll be by your side in spirit. Rael be with you. Come on!" And with that she ran to the outer hall. The meyrkats bounded after her.

"Farewell, V'dal," C'tis said quietly. "I could wish I had a soldier's mentality for these last moments."

"I know." And he took her in his arms for an all to brief embrace before she turned to follow J'vina.

"Death to the demon-spawn!"

The raider's battle cry still rang out amid the fighting that raged outside the city boundaries. After their wild charge, they had been faced with defenders whose superior numbers and weapons wreaked a heavy toll before the raiders could bring their own more primitive weapons into play. Men and horses milled about in a swirl of noise and fear and blood. The Gray Raiders' cause was lost, but their fanaticism would not allow them to realize this, and they fought on against their implacable, steel-masked foes, raising their cry to the heavens once more.

"Death to the demon-spawn!"

Their numbers were gradually diminishing, and the end was in sight when two things happened. The city's defenders suddenly lost all cohesion and stopped fighting, staring about aimlessly as if their very purpose had suddenly been removed. The raiders took advantage of this, and redoubled their efforts.

But the second event brought the battle to an abrupt end. Hideously bright orange rays shone from the buildings nearby, their deadly flames turning huge tracts of land into scorched earth. Anyone caught in those ghastly beams died in agony, attacker and defender alike. It was as though the city had lost patience with the whole messy business and had decided to use its power indiscriminately but decisively.

The few surviving men turned tail and fled.

The first of many explosions ripped through the power complex. In the instant before he died, V'dal saw the fire roiling toward him and smiled. The conflagration was inevitable now.

The voice of the Great Leader boomed in every building and every street, like the voice of an unseen god. Even in the midst of their growing panic, his people stopped unthinkingly to listen to his words. The destruction of their city went unnoticed as the message of doom resounded in their ears.

"My first great experiment is over. It will end in fire, in devastation greater than we could ever have foreseen." There was madness in his voice, but also an undeniable hypnotic power. "This city will become a fiery monument to my greatness, and to the folly of those who sought to oppose me. You have served me well, and have the honor of being part of the conclusion of the first part of my triumph. I salute you all."

As the Great Leader's words sank home, panic returned in full measure. Their simple contentment had vanished forever, and the people of the city were being forced to come to terms with their fate. The terrified exodus began.

Some of the controllers were making for the launch site of the fliers, knowing that that was their best, perhaps their only, chance of escape. But the way was blocked, so they had to join the frenzied rush of the common herd as they ran toward the city limits and on toward the mountains.

Then the Great Leader spoke again.

"I have assumed override control of all functions. You cannot escape what is coming, but your sacrifice will never be forgotten. Soon, fliers will take off, bearing new weapons that will rain death upon the homes of those who have dared to attack us. *You will not die unavenged!*"

As those last words of the huge, disembodied voice echoed hollowly about them, Hewe and Jordan glanced at each other in the shadows of their hiding place.

"Newport?" Hewe asked in a whisper.

"And every other city in this land," Jordan replied. "He's completely insane."

"Insane but powerful," Arden said. "If we don't stop those weapons being used, millions will be killed."

"Not only that," Gemma added unexpectedly, speaking for the first time in ages, "but if they *are* used, the Earth-mind will go mad, whether we destroy this place or not."

"But how can we stop them?" Hewe asked. "We don't even know where the fliers are."

"We need to find *him*, not the fliers," Zana put in. She was kneeling with her arm around the exhausted wizard. "You heard what that maniac said. He's controlling everything. Stop him, and you stop the fliers."

"But we still don't know where to go," Hewe pointed out.

"The tower!" Gemma exclaimed. "That has to be the place."

"What tower?" Jordan asked, mystified.

"Gem can see it," she replied, adding to his confusion. "She'll lead us to it."

They all looked at her strangely, but followed as she strode off, Arden by her side. They made no attempt to hide now, and marched right down the center of the street.

"It's this way!" Gemma called over her shoulder. "Not far now." She broke into a run, and the others hurried to keep up with her, swords in their hands. Gemma had no weapon but carried the staff that Kris had given her. She had removed it from her baggage that morning, remembering her dream and taking it as an omen. The staff had not changed, there seemed to be nothing special about it, yet she clutched it tightly, as though it were a talisman.

Rounding a corner, they saw it—a huge tower of black metal, almost invisible against the night sky. On its side was the design of the unbalanced scales. Far above them, a light shone.

"Up there!" Gemma shouted above the clamor of the fleeing citizens and burning buildings. She sounded absolutely certain, and no one thought to question her.

As they ran toward the base of the tower and crowded in through the open door, Gemma recognized the elevator immediately and led them to it. She pushed a button and the doors slid apart.

"This will take us up," she said, "but we won't all fit in."

"Agrin, take charge here," Jordan instructed. "Make sure no one else gets into the building."

"Yes, sir." The soldier began yelling orders, deploying his troops.

"Let's go," Gemma urged. She and Arden were already inside the elevator. "Cai, can you manage?"

"Of course," the wizard replied in a quiet voice. He staggered in, helped by Zana, then Jordan and Hewe squeezed in behind him.

"I hope this thing is built to take all our weight," Hewe said. "I'd hate to get to the top and then have the rope break."

The elevator sped upward, but it still was not fast enough for Gemma, and she muttered impatiently under her breath.

After what seemed like an age, the machine came to a halt and the doors slid open, revealing a large circular room. They sprang out, their weapons at the ready, instinctively forming an arc facing the man who stood at the far side of the room. He was looking down at a wide panel of instruments.

"I thought you'd be here soon," the man said, without turning round. "Welcome to my aerie." His voice was light and high-pitched.

The six companions felt themselves grow rigid, their feet frozen to the floor. They were unable to move, no matter how they tried. As the man turned around slowly, the onlookers watched in horrified fascination, almost expecting to see the face of a grotesque madman. Arden had a sudden dread of seeing his father again—but the man who held them appeared perfectly normal. He was of slight build and had a pleasant, innocuous face. He smiled, and only then did a spark appear in his pale blue eyes.

"Don't you recognize my voice?" he asked, all too innocent, then pressed a switch. "Is this better?" The familiar voice of the city's leader boomed out, changed and amplified beyond recognition. He switched it off again.

"As you can see, I'm rather busy at the moment," he said mildly. "What did you want to see me about?"

chapter 36

They were struck dumb, and the Great Leader held them in thrall without apparent effort. Their minds seemed to have been frozen at the same time as their bodies. Only Gemma's brain was active, and she was having to fight another battle, far away.

Auntie Gemma, there's a big person here.

Not now, Gem. I'm busy.

But she frightens me. I think she's angry. She's shouting so.

Go back to sleep, sweetheart. I can't help you now.

The baby began to cry, and Gemma's heart ached. *She may be the future Key,* she fumed inwardly, *but she's not ready yet. Leave her alone!*

Like Grandma, but much bigger, she heard Gem say quietly before her attention was forced back to the circular room. Their enemy was speaking again.

"I will not deny that your ingenuity has caused me considerable inconvenience. I underestimated you. It is a mistake I will not repeat." The words were all the more chilling for the mild tone in which they were delivered. "In the end, though, it will not matter. The Age of Chaos, as you so poetically call it, is already assured. Though the world will be very different, I shall rule supreme. Your foolish attack has caused the very thing you tried so desperately to avoid. Ironic, isn't it?" He waited for a response, but finding none, continued, "No wonder your puny nations are no match for me," he went on, contempt blazing from him now. "I had expected some civilized conversation at least . . . before you die."

"Aren't you forgetting something?" Jordan spoke at last. "When this place blows up, you'll die too."

The Great Leader smiled. "Oh, I think not," he remarked casually. "We're safe in here for the time being, and by the time this place is destroyed, I will be far away. My skyraven—that *is* what you call them, isn't it?—is waiting now on the roof above us." His smile broadened. "Anyone care to come with me?" He went back to the panel, studying it in silence for a few moments before turning to face them again.

"I still have nearly half an hour before I need to leave," he said pleasantly. "Plenty of time for me to tell you what is going to happen." He was a true megalomaniac—gloating over his helpless captives.

"When the temperature in the central Power Complex reaches a certain level—long after I have gone, of course—the bedrock on which it is built will start to melt, and the whole thing will sink into the earth. When it meets the earth's own fiery core, the resulting explosion will be more powerful than a thousand volcanoes.

Zana whimpered, and he turned to smile at her.

"The resultant debris will be hurled into the atmosphere, spreading the contamination across the entire surface of the world. Some places will suffer less than others, of course, but life everywhere will be affected. The only ones who can be sure of being safe from this are those who will go with me to the underground city. Oh, it's many, many leagues away," he assured them. "I built it years ago, with the possibility of an event like this in mind." He was unbearably smug now. "And don't forget, many of my—employees—will be able to operate on the surface, in spite of the contamination. You see, transforming them *does* have its advantages. I will be absolute ruler of the world!"

"Ruler of a *dead* world!" Hewe spat. "You're insane!"

"Oh, but it won't be completely dead," the other responded, unmoved by Hewe's outburst. "Just different. However, I will admit that some places will be dead. That is necessary, and a lesson for all who remain. I cannot have anyone believing that they can attack me and not expect retribution in full measure." He paused, looking from face to face. "Great Newport . . . your precious valley . . . a few insignificant islands to the north . . . I have only to touch this button once the arming procedure is complete, and the skyravens will fly to their targets. It won't be long now."

"What if you're wrong?" Cai asked weakly. "What if the world *is* dead? You will rule nothing." *This time* no one *will survive*.

"I am never wrong!" the man retorted, angry for the first time.

"Why are you doing this?" Cai pleaded. "You are a wizard—"

"No!" The Great Leader's voice interrupted furiously. "I despise magic. I used it to create the new evolution, harnessed it to my new logic to create the siren song. That brought me the people I needed, all the minds attuned to my own. We knew that together we could create a technology that would make magic and its ridiculous tenets redundant forever. Wizardry is only for the weak, for those who need *circles* to prop them up. I stand alone!" He had been shouting, but grew quieter now. "Mendle had the right idea, but he was too impetuous. *My* victory will be achieved by absolute thoroughness, by scrupulous attention to detail."

Beside the switches that would launch the skyravens, lights turned from red to orange, and the Great Leader noted the change with satisfaction.

"It will be very soon now," he told them.

"But you *are* using magic," Cai accused, trying to flex his frozen limbs, but his captor only laughed.

"No. You are being held by a simple but selective static field, which works on the nervous system—if you know what that is." His contempt was blatant. "But I can control it precisely. Which is why you can talk and observe, but not move." He advanced on Cai and pointed a finger at his face. "*You* are the last wizard, my friend. *I* will never use magic again."

The lights had turned to green now, but the Leader did not seem to notice.

"Even if you could be the new Key to the Dream?" Gemma asked quickly, hoping to distract him. Ideas were pulsing through her mind. "If you could be the focus of all the magic in the world—wouldn't that be a prize worth having?"

Their tormentor stared at her, while the others gaped in horrified disbelief.

Auntie Gemma, the big person is angry!

Tell the big person to be calm, Gemma responded. *We will help her later.*

She saw her advantage, and pressed on.

"Have you forgotten how it feels to have the power of magic in your fingertips?" she asked. "Without the need for machines?"

Arden spoke then, though his voice was almost unrecognizable. He was living a dream.

"Father," he croaked. "The magic was in you once—don't you remember? Take the staff. Restore our love."

At his words, Gemma felt new resources surge through her. She called out to the circles, and they responded—some gladly, some fearfully, some reluctantly and in dread. Cai and the swarm, the meyrkats, the prophets of the Lightless Kingdom, Jordan, Mallory, and Arden were among the multitude of faces, familiar and unknown, human and animal, which flashed through her mind. They were ready to help. Now, if only . . .

The Great Leader stared at Gemma curiously.

"The Key?" he said slowly.

"It is my gift to you," Gemma said quickly, taking her cue from Arden's enigmatic words. "The magic was in you once. All you need to do is admit that, and you will control all the circles. Abandon your new logic. Be our leader—take my staff of power!"

Hewe and Zana protested, but Gemma could see that he was tempted and felt her muscles come back to life. She stepped forward and knelt before him, offering up Kris's staff.

The tyrant stretched out his hand, and for a wonderful moment Gemma thought she had won. But then he withdrew.

"How do I know this is the staff of power?" he asked abruptly. "I detect nothing unusual about it."

"How can you?" Gemma asked. "While you are still denying the magic within you? Open yourself to it, and you will see!"

Silence filled the room.

Slowly, he reached out again, and his fingers closed over one end of the staff while Gemma still gripped the other.

"It *was* thus," he said. "I remember now."

As the power and support of the circles flooded in to Gemma, she used it to bind him tightly, weaving a spell of sorcery that imprisoned him as strongly as bands of steel, even while he struggled and writhed, cursing and screaming.

Then the room grew still. Gemma and the Great Leader were frozen in a bizarre tableau, and of the others, only Hewe and Zana were able to move. They collapsed to the floor, their legs numb. Gemma's trap had closed about both prey and hunter.

"A stalemate," the Great Leader said through clenched teeth. "You cannot defeat me, so what do you propose to do now?"

The fire in the Power Complex was now so hot that metal was melting like butter in a desert sun. The superstructure of the enormous building had long since collapsed, spreading the flames to adjoining areas. Smoke and steam filled the air, and intermittent explosions flung wreckage into the sky. The core of the fountain of fire burned white.

The city, deserted now by almost all its inhabitants, trembled under the multiple impacts. Then the entire valley shivered as though shaking itself awake from a dream, and elementals rose up from the ground, huge swirling beings of blue flame. There were hundreds, thousands, of them, alive with pulsating light. Anyone who was still left to see them stared in awe, stunned by the beautiful, majestic visions that danced around the city. All fighting ceased, and even those who were fleeing desperately stopped in their tracks and stared.

It was as if the spirits of the earth itself had seen the mortal danger posed by the conflagration and had risen up to try to isolate it from the rest of the world. They were shielding the earth from deadly peril with their own fluid bodies. They grew together and formed a ring, a circular wall, which shifted and sparkled between the mountains and the city. No one who saw them could deny their beauty or power, but compared to the forces they were seeking to oppose, the elementals seemed flimsy and insubstantial.

Many looked into their blue flame for too long and found their own escape—of a kind.

Madness.

* * *

The big person's here again! There's lots *of her. I don't like it. She won't listen.*

Gemma was helpless. The circles had come to her aid, yet she could not escape herself without also freeing her enemy. And now Gem was becoming frantic. *There's* lots *of her.* Gemma remembered another phrase then, one that made her blood run cold. *The one became many.*

Little Gem was talking to the Earth-mind. *It's awake!* For a moment, Gemma was back in her own childhood, seeing another tiny baby who had experienced such a conversation, and who had died because of it.

Show me, sweetheart, she said, as calmly as she could. *Show me the big person.*

Instantly, Gemma was faced with something so vast, so immeasurably ancient, that she shied away. Even to attempt such a contact would mean death—or insanity at the very least. And yet the child was not harmed, only very frightened.

Age may talk to youth. And then again, innocence is power. As the cat's words came back to her, Gemma saw the truth. *She doesn't know! It's* because *she's a baby that she can talk to it!* Quickly, she instructed her tiny namesake.

Gem, tell the big person to be calm. We are trying to help her, but she must give us a little time.

I'll try, but she doesn't listen. The child sounded almost indignant.

Gemma returned her attention to the circles, anxious to be rid of her worldly enemy as soon as possible. He seemed an almost trivial problem now, compared to what could follow. If the Earth-mind added its own Destruction to the havoc of the contamination, the world would be doomed indeed.

Messages from the circles poured in.

Is it time?

Are you leaving us?

Gemma ignored them, commanding silence.

"Let me go!" The Great Leader snarled, looking down on her with eyes that were now filled with a mad intensity. "Give up this stupidity."

"The least I will do," she answered calmly, "is keep you here to die with us." *But that won't be enough*, she told herself.

Hewe had staggered to his feet and approached them, sword in hand.

"Shall I kill him?" he asked groggily.

"You can't," Gemma replied. "The power of the circles binds him—as it does me—but it also protects him from your sword."

"So I'm not in the circles?" Hewe asked.

"No. Nor is Zana—which is why the two of you can move," Gemma said. "Will you go and check the panel, make sure the skyravens haven't been launched?"

Hewe walked slowly over to the bank of instruments and eyed it suspiciously.

"The green flashing lights all say 'active—armed,'" he reported. "There are others over to the left that say 'cancel.' Shall I push them?"

"What will happen if he does?" Gemma asked her prisoner. He refused to speak, and just glared at her.

"Push them," she told Hewe, and he did so.

"All the lights have gone out," he said. "Now what?"

But something else had occurred to Gemma, and she was not paying him any attention. She had returned to the circles.

Our energy is draining fast!

What is happening? You're fading, Gemma!

Is it time?

A moment's fierce concentration proved her supposition to be correct. *Something's not right. One of the circles is missing!* She began her search, sifting through the endless bombardment of words. After what seemed an age, she found what she was looking for. Wynut's voice came into her head, a faint, faraway sound, and she clung to it, desperately trying to keep the contact alive.

At last! the wizard cried. *I thought you'd never hear us.*

We're breaking all the rules, doing this, Shanti added, his habitual testiness augmented by mounting fear. *Your foolishness will destroy us all.*

Help me! Gemma pleaded. *We need the strength of the last circle.*

We know that! Shanti snapped.

We're trying, Wynut said, more calmly, *but the link is very faint. We're not in your time and space yet, so there's only one thing that can be preventing our full contact.*

What? she asked desperately.

Elementals, Wynut told her. *We can get through anything in this world—except their power. They're pure energy, and like us, have no attachment to time and space.*

Elementals? Gemma was more confused than ever.

Yes! Shanti shot back. *They're all around you. You must get rid of them or we're all doomed.*

chapter 37

"Hewe!" Gemma called. "Go to the windows. Are there any elementals near the city?"

"I can't tell," he replied after a moment. "All I can see is the fire. Gods, but it's fierce!" He swore softly.

"We can bargain," the Great Leader suggested suddenly. "There's still time. Do you *want* to die?"

"You're in no position to bargain," Gemma retorted, angry at his interruption of her concentration.

"Come with me in the flier," he insisted. "Leave these weaklings. We are so alike, you and I—power is our natural asset. Together—"

"No!" She knew he was trying to trick her—and the suggestion that the two of them might be alike made her angrier still. "Shut up!" *Let me think*.

But he carried on, knowing that she could do nothing to stop him, and Gemma was forced to try to shut out the vile, wheedling voice as best she could.

"There *are* elementals," Cai whispered unexpectedly. "I can see them."

"How?" Gemma asked. The bees were on the wizard's shoulders still, held fast by the same trap that gripped them all. "They're in the other world," Cai answered. "That's the only place I *can* see now."

"What?" Gemma did not understand what he was saying.

"*Hold back the elemental fires*," Cai quoted. "Perhaps we can. Perhaps *he* can."

During their long journey into the mountains, Wray had kept very much to himself. He had not mixed with his former brethren, who now regarded him as a joke—mad and useless.

Yet when the raiders charged toward the city, he had been swept up by their fervor and had ridden with them, adding his own unintelligible cries to their death chant.

He had remained miraculously unscathed throughout the subsequent battle—and when the terrible beams had brought the fighting to an abrupt and fiery end, he had fled toward the mountains, with all the others who had survived—friends and foe alike.

Now his horse stumbled and fell, tumbling him on to the soft, grass-covered slope. He leaped to his feet, running until he thought his heart would burst.

The whole valley was bathed in a fierce red glow from the fire within the city, but then Wray watched in ecstasy as an enormous number of elementals poured out of the ground. They were so beautiful! He saw them gather together, encircling the city and making the fire within seem less intense, less threatening. His fear melted away and he walked slowly back down the slope, gazing in wonder at the fluid blue creatures as if seeing them for the first time.

Hold back the elemental fires, he heard someone say. *Perhaps we can. Perhaps* he *can.*

Wray walked on. He understood now. The great wall at Clevemouth had been a test—and they had accepted him. His heart was filled with a new emotion; flowers bloomed in the arid wastes of his existence, and he smelled their fragrance for the first time in his life.

Hold back the elemental fires. Wray recognized the voice now.

We are in the same circle, you and I, he informed the wizard. *That's what I tried to tell you, but I could never find the words.*

Wray! Listen to me! Cai sounded desperate. *You must breach the elemental wall. The city is cut off and . . .*

I know.

Help us! Cai pleaded. *But you cannot use force—only true friendship can save us now.*

Wray had no need of the warning. He was close to the elementals now, mesmerized by their beauty. In that moment he basked in their radiance and loved them for their freedom, their warmth and life. His previous belief that they were alien forms, to be subjugated to his will, disappeared from his mind completely. They were wondrous creatures, who accepted him as a friend.

Wray stretched out his arms in welcome, greeting the elemental spirits with every fiber of his body; he was with them in thought and feeling, in simple happiness and love.

They came to him, irresistibly drawn, and surrounded him in a gentle whirlwind, their vivid blue swirling around him in a profusion of shades and meaning. That moment gave definition to his life.

And in that moment, the elementals returned his greeting a thousandfold.

"He's done it," Cai breathed. His voice was choked with emotion and barely audible even to Zana, who stood no more than a pace in front of him. She had risen painfully and come over to the wizard, wanting only to put her arms around him and comfort him. But she could not reach him; she was repelled by an invisible barrier, and stood helplessly by while his features contorted with effort and longing.

"He's done it," the wizard repeated. A strange crooked smile passed over his face, and tears filled his green eyes. "Tell Gemma," he whispered.

Zana turned, but saw that she already knew.

Gemma got up from her knees, left the staff in the Great Leader's hand, and stood facing him. A flickering screen began to form about the evil man, becoming more solid with every moment. Gradually, it formed a perfect cylindrical container, shimmering gold and silver. It was transparent but utterly impregnable, its captive frozen within.

A moment later, the cylinder wavered, becoming insubstantial, like a ghost. And then it was gone; prisoner and prison had simply disappeared. Jordan, Cai, and Arden fell to the ground in the same instant, released from their confinement. Zana quickly moved to tend to the wizard, while Hewe stared at Gemma in amazement.

"Where did he go?" he asked.

"He's adrift in time," she answered. "Trapped by his own greed." She held up her hands to forestall any more questions. "Look after Jordan. Quickly. We must get down to the others." She helped Arden get up, and they looked into each other's eyes for a moment. What passed between them made words unnecessary.

All six crammed into the elevator and descended to the lower hallway, where Agrin and his men were waiting. Some were keeping watch from the dark glass windows beside the door, others were keeping as far from the door as possible.

"We can't go out into that," the soldier told them. "It's *murder* out there. Debris and flash fires everywhere, not to mention smoke and poisonous gases. This tower must be specially protected, or we'd all have been frying by now."

"It *is*," Jordan said grimly, "but when the Power Complex finally blows, it won't do us any good."

The finality of their situation was now doubly apparent to everyone.

"There must be *something* we can do!" Hewe exclaimed, looking to Gemma for help.

But she had retreated into her own world, the world of magic—her last refuge, and their last hope.

"Leave her," Jordan said. "There's nothing we can do—except wait."

The circles were still with her.

There must be something we can do, she pleaded. *Must it really end like this?*

If everything happened as the Great Leader had predicted, then the contamination would spread throughout the entire world, and although the evil tyrant would not be there himself to make it worse, the disaster would still be appalling. And because of that, the Earth-mind's insanity would become a certainty—bringing the Chaos that would complete the devastation. *This time*, no one *will survive*.

I would gladly die, Gemma thought, *we all would, if only we could leave some hope for the future*.

She appealed to the circles again—and this time there was a reply.

What if the fire from the Power Complex can be stopped before it reaches the earth's core?"

Gemma recognized the voice, but was more interested in its suggestion.

How? she asked.

Divert it, the voice replied. *The explosion would still destroy this place, but its effects wouldn't spread so far. Perhaps the Earth-mind could survive that*.

Would it be enough? Gemma wondered. *And where could we divert it to?"*

To the Lightless Kingdom, Arden replied, the sorrow of destiny weighing heavy in his voice.

chapter 38

Gem! Gem! Listen to me! Gemma concentrated on the little girl who was still looking down on the city from the top of the mountain, but who was also at home in the valley. *Don't be frightened, sweetheart. You must tell the big person that there is a way to stop what is making her angry—but only the big person can do it. Do you understand?*

Yes, Auntie Gemma, the child replied in a small voice, trying to control her fear.

Tell the big person that the fire need not go down into the earth. If the rocks can be moved a little, then it can go into the caves.

What caves?

The big person will understand, darling. Will you tell her?

But there are lots of her. Which one do I tell?

All of them.

I'll try.

Good girl!

Gemma felt her namesake's presence fade away and turned quickly back to the circles, seeking one of them with a leaden heart.

P'tra's face came clearly into her mind.

I heard, the prophetess said in a cracked voice, saving Gemma the terrible task of asking her permission.

It will be a nobel end, P'tra went on. *Our people are already dying. This way at least it will be quick and clean. Perhaps the fire is the invasion we dreaded for so long. But we will welcome it now. Farewell, Gemma. You are a great healer, and I know you would have saved us if you could. But the diamond crystal is fading, and our circle's strength is finished. Give our death some meaning.*

The contact was lost before Gemma had a chance to reply, but she vowed silently to do all she could to fulfill the prophet's last wish.

She opened her eyes and found that she was sitting on the floor of the tower, propped against a wall. Arden was beside her, his eyes still closed, tears running down his ashen cheeks.

The room shuddered.

I told her, Auntie Gemma. I told her. Gem sounded proud and excited.

Did she say anything?

Yes, she said, "My heart will not be pierced" . . . I think, the child replied. *There aren't so many of her now.*

Hope, almost manic in its sudden intensity, sprang up in Gemma.

"Is it the end?" Agrin asked fearfully, as the room shook again.

"No," Gemma said aloud. "The earth is readjusting—it will fight the explosion. Underground."

"You mean there's a chance?" Jordan asked quickly.

"Not for us," Gemma told him, "but for the rest of the world."

"There's someone out there!" one of the window sentries shouted. "One of D'vor's people!"

Arden's eyes shot open at that, and he leaped to his feet. Running to the door, he wrenched it open and flung himself into the street before anyone could stop him.

The heat hit him like a wall. Smoke filled the air, and he gasped, almost choking. Everything was bathed in a dull red light, and flame and ash were everywhere. He caught a glimpse of the black figure, staggering blindly, stumbling over piles of wreckage, and obviously on the point of collapse. Through the roaring of the fire, Arden heard a small voice say, "Forgive me, J'vina. I did not have your strength."

It was C'tis. Arden ran to her and grasped her around the waist.

"Come with me, quickly," he rasped.

"No. Let me die." She struggled for a moment, then grew quiet.

"Arden?"

He picked her up and ran back to the tower. The door was

open as he approached and they practically fell inside, into the welcoming arms of their friends.

"J'vina's dead!" C'tis sobbed. "She just stood there, so strong and proud, until the fire took her. But I ran away. I'm the last." She began to sob.

The last of all, Gemma thought sadly, wondering if it would have been better to leave C'tis to die outside, unknowing. She went to Arden and held him tight, understanding both his action and his hurt. C'tis had saved *his* life once.

The floor beneath them lurched and the walls trembled. A huge roaring filled the air.

"It's beginning," Hewe said.

They all prepared to meet their end, each in his own different way.

Gemma held Arden even tighter, and felt his arms respond.

"We'll *always* be together," he whispered in her ear, but Gemma was staring past his shoulder at the lookout window, and did not hear him. The window was filled with gray—cold, blue-gray. The doom-laden red had gone. A voice sounded in her head and she suddenly understood what was happening.

"There *is* a chance," she whispered, almost unable to believe her own words. "For *all* of us." Stunned, Arden looked at her, but had no chance to speak.

"Outside! Everybody! Now!" Gemma yelled at the top of her voice. "Quickly! Move!"

She dived for the door, dragging Arden with her, and together they threw it open. Some of the others cowered away, expecting another blast of heat, but instead, no more than a few paces away lay a cool, serene blanket of fog.

"Come on!" Arden shouted, and at last they all moved, following the pair in a mad scramble toward nothingness. One by one they hurled themselves into the mist, not knowing what was happening, but believing that whatever fate awaited them, it had to be better than dying in the inferno. One by one they experienced the bitter cold, saw the blue lights flash by them, and grew dizzy and disoriented.

And one by one they found themselves standing in the hallway of a quiet, old-fashioned mansion, whose tiled floor and wooden walls and staircase were miraculously unaffected by the deadly fire.

A few moments later, a small man, almost covered by a

huge, outlandish hat, appeared on the balcony above them, cackling with glee and waving his arms in the air.

"We did it! We did it!" he yelled, and flung his hat into the air as his manic laughter burst out once more.

Gemma and Arden watched the mage, not quite knowing whether to laugh or cry. All about them, their friends and colleagues reacted to their deliverance with a range of emotions. Many of the soldiers had fallen to their knees. Some were praying, some were crying openly, while others were laughing, whooping and hugging each other, practically dancing with joy. Some were staring about them, silent and white-faced, wondering whether they were dead or alive.

Cai and Zana were in each other's arms, smiling like idiots, remembering the last time they had been abducted by the floating city. How different their reactions had been then!

Cai could see again, free—as the world was free—from the enchantment cast by the elemental wall.

Jordan was helping C'tis to her feet, looking around in wonder, while Hewe was watching the performance on the balcony, a grin stretched across his scarred face.

"Is that Wynut or Shanti?" he asked.

"Who cares?" Arden replied.

Another figure, much taller than the first, appeared behind the railings.

"What's all this racket?" he demanded. "It's about time you got here. We've been calling for long enough!"

"*That's* Shanti!" Gemma and Arden said together.

The tall mage turned his attention to his smaller companion, who was still capering about, convulsed with mirth.

"Did it work?" he asked tetchily.

"Of *course* it worked!" Wynut exclaimed. "When have you ever known my calculations to *not* work!" He burst out laughing again.

"Then we're back?" Shanti asked cautiously.

"Yes. Yes. Yes!"

"And the breach is sealed?"

"Yes!"

A smile spread slowly over Shanti's features, and his long pointed nose turned pink beneath the brim of his droopy hat. Unable to stop himself, he did a little jig on the spot. Then, throwing his hands into the air, he roared with laughter. The two wizards laughed so long and so loud that they eventually had to turn away from each other, clutching their sides and trying desperately hard to breathe again.

Gemma seized her opportunity.

"Do you mean the contamination *won't* be spread by the explosion?"

"No—we've sealed it off," Wynut replied gleefully.

"Bottled it up," Shanti added.

"Squashed it flat!"

"But the Lightless Kingdom is doomed?" Arden asked. The mages became solemn in an instant, and a hush fell over the room.

"Yes," Wynut said quietly. "Their sacrifice has saved us all."

A single sob of grief sounded in the hallway, then there was silence again. Everyone turned to look at C'tis, but most turned away again quickly.

"She's fainted," Jordan said, lowering her gently to the ground.

Gemma and Arden went quickly to her side, stripping some of the silkfish tape from her arms. As soon as the skin was exposed, Gemma held her hands tightly and willed her own healing talent into action. She found many hurts and eased them where she could, but she also knew that C'tis suffered from a malady that had no cure. She would live, but it was doubtful whether she would want to do so.

Gemma looked up, having done all she could, and met Arden's gaze.

"You mustn't blame yourself," she told him softly. "You acted from the best of motives. And they were already dying, Arden. There was no hope for them."

He said nothing, knowing that she was right, but also knowing that C'tis's sob of horror would be with him for the rest of his life.

The pattering of small feet and the sound of claws scratching on wooden floor broke the silence. The wizard's cat appeared on the balcony and headed down the stairs, followed by seven meyrkats, who were having great difficulty coping with the steps. They tumbled and fell, only regaining their poise when they reached the bottom of the staircase. The effect was so comical that the tension in the room broke, and laughter echoed so loudly that only a few noticed the cat's miaouw transform itself into speech.

"A sense of balance is important in all things. And then again, falling over is just another way of *regaining* one's balance."

Gem watched the city from far above. She did not understand what was happening, but it fascinated as well as frightened her. At first, the fire had grown slowly, but then it got brighter and brighter, until she could hardly bear to look at it. Then the pretty blue lights had grown up around the edge, forming a circle. Gem had liked that, but soon some of the lights moved again, making a gap in the ring. A patch of gray fog—like a little cloud—appeared in the valley, heading toward the city. It seemed to melt into the buildings and had almost reached the big black tower when suddenly the fire was five times as bright as it had been before, and Gem had to shut her eyes. When she opened them again, she saw a huge ball of orange engulf the city, reducing it to ashes and smoke.

After that, the gray cloud had appeared to spread out, and the fire went away. It was soon so dark that Gem could see hardly anything—even the pretty blue lights had gone away.

The baby closed her eyes again and snuggled back down beneath the blankets of her cot.

The firestorm swept through the Lightless Kingdom.

Once the passage had been opened, it took the line of least resistance. Mere rockfalls and metal doors were no barrier to this heat and pressure. The awesome force turned rock to liquid and reshaped all but a few of the subterranean caverns. Rivers exploded into steam, whole lakes leaped up from immemorial stillness, adding the force of their vaporization to the onslaught. Stalagmites and stalactites that had taken centuries to form disappeared in moments; crystals shattered, sending shards flying before they melted. Tunnels roared with flame, funneling the initial onslaughts, before they too began to twist and writhe within the rock—like living snakes of fire.

Onward and outward the firestorm spread, feeding its insatiable hunger on all that fell in its path. First the poisoned lands succumbed, then the barrier zones were swept clean, and finally the conflagaration reached the inhabited lands.

Whole villages were obliterated in moments. Even before the flame arrived, the air became too hot to breathe, so the people of the Lightless Kingdom died quickly, released from the suffering of the green-sickness in one shuddering instant. With them went all the marks of their civilization; their homes, their forges and the intricate metal work, their boats and ladders, ropes and pulleys. With them too died all the plants and animals on which they depended—the dimeweed and the root crops, the bats and the silkfish.

The firestorm raged on for hundreds of leagues, seeking out each available space, until at last, its energy spent, the fire began to abate. The Lightless Kingdom was made anew, and left pristine.

And utterly lifeless.

The big person's going back to sleep now, Gem said.

You sound rather sleepy yourself, Gemma replied, smiling both at the little girl's tone and at the implications of her statement. It was the best news of all. The Earth-mind was returning to her dreaming state; there would be no repetition of the horrors of The Destruction.

There was only one big person in the end, Gem added. *I don't know where the others went.*

They went away, the adult Gemma replied lamely.

Did I help?

Oh yes, my love. We would all have been lost without you.

That's good, the child replied sleepily. *Mommy will be pleased.*

There was a moment's silence.

Sleep tight, little one, Gem whispered, thinking her namesake had really dozed off this time.

I saw the big fire, Gem added unexpectedly, perking up again. *Auntie Gemma, it was hobbible, really hobbible.*

She sounded like a child again, at last.

Don't worry, sweetheart, Gemma responded gently. *Everything's all right now. It was only a dream.*

chapter 39

The longest night the world had ever known was over. Even those who had fallen into an exhausted sleep on the floor of the hallway were aware that daylight had returned. The day they had thought they would never see had dawned.

"Can we go outside?" Gemma asked Wynut

"Of course," he replied. "Why ever not?" The two mages had been mingling with their guests all night, helping Gemma tend to the casualties, and explaining what had happened to anyone who cared to listen. Even Shanti had remained in high spirits, saying that he felt as though he had come back to life after a long "retirement." The floating city, he pointed out, had served its final purpose, helping seal the poison forever within time and stone.

For the most part, the atmosphere had been festive, with everyone rejoicing in his good fortune. Only C'tis's silent misery and the memory of her lost home had tempered their jubilation.

"Shanti!" his fellow mage called. "Gemma is going outside. Shall we accompany her? We haven't been outside this crumbly old place for decades."

"Centuries," Shanti agreed readily. "The walk will do us good."

So Gemma opened the big double doors and stepped through into the world outside. The scene that greeted her and the others almost literally took their breath away. They made room for their companions, spreading out so that everyone could take in the full significance of what they were seeing.

They were still in the valley where the city of metal had

stood. There was no sign of that evil place now, and the air about them was cool and fresh. The sky was a light, clear blue, lit by the rising sun to the east. The mountains encircling the valley were unchanged, standing snow-capped and majestic, as if impervious to the petty concerns of men.

Within the valley, however, it was a different story. The change could hardly have been more dramatic.

The wizard's rambling mansion now stood alone, on a tiny, grass-covered island in the middle of a vast, serene lake. In the dawn stillness, hardly a ripple disturbed the mirrorlike surface of the water, and the mountains were matched with their perfect reflections. They all breathed deeply, clearing their lungs of the memories of smoke and heat, and savoring the purity of all they saw before them.

It's the dream that Gem and I had together, Gemma thought, her hand clasped tightly in Arden's. Together they gazed at the lake and the mountains beyond. No landscape had ever seemed more perfect. And yet there was one flaw.

"Anybody here any good at boat building?" Hewe asked.

part 5

COMING HOME

chapter 40

The world was never quite the same for any of them in the days and years that followed. Much returned to what seemed like normality, but those who had been present when not only their own lives but the future of the earth itself was on the brink were always doomed to see beneath the surface. They celebrated their unexpected survival, but nothing could dispel their knowledge of what *might* have happened—or remove the terrible memories of that day from their minds. And it made them all the more determined that no one man should ever be allowed to wield such power again. The risk was too great.

And yet they were all human beings who needed happiness and love, and who sought them in their different ways.

Wynut and Shanti remained in their rambling mansion in the middle of the lake. They felt no need to visit the rest of the world; having seen so much during their remote and timeless travels, they were now content to stay where they were. They were happy just to be back *in* the world, where they could spend their time being pampered by their loyal housekeeper and arguing amicably over trivialities.

Eventually, when their neighbors from the nearby mountain village overcame their fear and suspicion of that remote place, the wizards received regular visitors. Their mansion became a place of refuge from the harsh realities of upland life, and also a source of help and entertainment. The villagers brought offerings of food and drink—game from their hunting, crops from their farms, fish from the wizard's own lake—and, if times were good, a bottle or two of the precious, honey-sweet mead. In return they were treated like long-lost friends and given aid and advice. Wynut and Shanti were images still, for all that they looked like frail old men, and many benefited from their healing powers. They took great delight in being able to help with the problems that the mountain people brought to them; they listened diligently and gave the gift of laughter to all their guests. Soon, their reputation was such that people came even when they had no difficulty to discuss—and these guests were treated with as much consideration as the others.

Human nature being what it is, it was to be expected that some people would take advantage of the wizards' generous hospitality, but most of the mountain villagers grew to regard them with affection. They were seen as a source of harmless fun as well as valuable aid, a pair of elderly eccentrics who devoted much of their spare time to pointless occupations such as writing books, inventing new variations to the rules of wizards' chess, and inviting their visitors to join in games of their own devising. They loved to build intricate toys that delighted the children who came to the island, and the youngsters of the region soon regarded them as wonderful great-uncles—and almost looked forward to being ill so that their parents could be persuaded to take them to the enchanted mansion.

The wizards had plenty of room for these various pursuits. Now that they were part of the world once more, time had returned to their home. All but one of the libraries was empty now—and, although that room contained many hundreds of volumes, from the most erudite to the completely frivolous, the books were concerned only with the past. The futures of the world were no longer recorded there.

The symbol carved on the door of the one remaining library was that of a pair of scales, perfectly balanced.

Gradually, the other rooms filled up with the clutter of the wizards' new contentment. Several were converted into guest rooms for the visitors who came from afar. Those few people who had met them in their earlier, timeless incarnations, and who now visited in a more orthodox fashion, were amazed at the change in the mages' characters. Gone were the acid-tongued comments, the barbed sarcasm and lapses into incomprehensibility. Instead, the old men were jovial, inclined to drink a little too much at the slightest excuse, and delighted by the results of their occasional practical jokes, wont to hold court over long and hilarious discussions on any topic that entered their heads.

It was also noted that they had stopped changing size. Shanti remained almost twice the height of his companion, but they seemed evenly matched for all that. Certainly their appetites were equally unpredictable; some days found them too preoccupied to even think of the mundane matter of food, while on others they would pack away prodigious quantities of their faithful housekeeper's excellent cooking.

In turn, they spoiled their large, mischievous cat—and it was he who best summed up their new way of life.

Immortality has been lost, he commented. *And then again, fresh fish makes up for a lot.*

Jordan and Hewe and their surviving followers returned home as heroes, but found that they had little time to bask in glory. The upheaval caused by the exodus from Clevemouth was causing problems still, and Newport's makeshift government was to go through many crises before all was well again.

The elemental wall had disappeared when the threat to the Earth-mind's sanity had been finally overcome, and Clevemouth appeared once more, unscathed but empty. The brave explorers who returned first found a silent ghost town that tested their nerves to the breaking point. The underground supervised the return to the western city as best they could, minimizing any problems and ensuring that all the refugees received fair treatment. Even so, it took some months before Clevemouth remotely resembled its former bustling self. And it took longer still for ships from the west to sail into their harbor once more. But they came eventually, demonstrating beyond doubt that the world was expanding again.

The first people to return noticed many curiosities, the most bizarre of which was the fact that food left in their homes had not spoiled, and fires still burned in the grates. It was as though time had come to a standstill while the city had been beyond the blue wall. However, such anomalies were soon forgotten in the hectic round of activity necessary in bringing the city back to life.

Meanwhile, in Great Newport, the work of building a new society went on. The account that Jordan and Hewe gave of recent events was soon known to the entire population, and although some regarded it with skepticism or even open disbelief, they could not deny that the world *had* changed for the better. The elemental wall had disappeared, the offshore islands remained constant, and the ocean's tides had returned to their normal pattern. No skyravens flew overhead, and there were no more impossibly bright lights to the north. Even so, the cynics said, that did not necessarily mean that the whole world *had* been endangered. They found the stories of the great metal city and its masked inhabitants too hard to believe.

The soldiers who had been part of the expedition to the far south were angered by this skepticism, and the subsequent disagreements caused some friction. Jordan, however, remained his usual philosophical self, and—for once—Hewe managed to be in complete agreement with him. They both knew the truth but recognized that it must seem incredible to many. Besides, they had more important matters to settle and wasted no time arguing over the past. The land of Cleve was in their hands, for the time being at least, and they were determined to guide it safely through.

Many citizens *had* accepted their tales, of course, and repeated the stories of those dramatic events, embroidering them just a little when a lapse of memory made this necessary. Songs, plays, and poems were written and performed by artists who had never been nearer to the mountains than the southern wall of the city, and thus the battle passed into history, a mixture of folktale, fancy, and a few hard facts.

Jordan found this process highly amusing, but when he found himself lauded as the leader of the world's intrepid saviors, and almost solely responsible for their success, he fought against his lionization, pointing out the crucial roles played by others. It did him little good in some quarters, though, and he often had to deny the strange and wonderful abilities that the more credulous citizens ascribed to him. Part of Jordan's problem was that everyone knew him to be a leader of honesty and vision, so when he made light of his exploits, this was put down to wholly characteristic modesty.

Hewe, on the other hand, had always been a joker, recognized for his dry wit and tall tales, and could make an audience laugh even at the most terrifying of stories. He was regarded as a hero too, but he was more like them, one of the people.

As always, the two men worked well together, inspiring

loyalty and affection in those around them, and they used their power wisely. The work of rebuilding the city went on, and plans were made for a better, more just future for its inhabitants.

In his few quieter moments, Jordan often thought back to the fantastic city in the mountains and was saddened by the waste of so many innocent lives—and of the knowledge that had been lost. Surely, he thought privately, such incredible industry and achievement *could* have been put to work for good. Why was it that such advances had been used only to promote tyranny? He kept these opinions to himself, however, knowing that this was not the time to voice them openly. The metal city had been crushed, and most men rejoiced heartily, believing the fate to be richly deserved.

After a time, the people of Cleve realized that the elementals had vanished. Jordan guessed that the blue flames had been tiny fragments of the Earth-mind, set free by its impending madness, and although he was gladdened by this sign that sanity had returned, the disappearance of the playful creatures was another loss he mourned.

The most obvious demonstration of the elementals' extinction, apart from the wall at Clevemouth, took place beneath Great Newport itself. The blue-flame room needed a new name, for its entrance was no longer guarded. The marble chamber stood open to the world, its walls and floor as immaculate as ever. Jordan and Hewe had been down to look at the ancient tome soon after their return to the city, anxious to read the new version of recent events from the pages that had given Gemma and Cai such cruel hints.

The script proved to be faint and almost illegible, but Jordan managed to decipher the words.

"However, this setback merely spurred the forces of the far south to even greater efforts. Their experiments grew rapidly in size and strength, and they were soon able to abandon their use of ancient power, replacing it with the new logic they had created. It was only by combining the talents of the Keys to the Dream, both old and new, with the total resources of the Old Order that the Age of Chaos was prevented."

Jordan began to turn the page, intrigued and wanting to read more, but the paper crumbled in his fingers, blowing away in the minute breeze of its own disintegration. The book, truly ancient now, turned to dust before their eyes.

"So the future is a closed book once more," Hewe remarked.

Jordan looked at him, unable to resist a smile.

"No imagination," he said accusingly.

"No," Hewe agreed readily. "The real world is quite enough for me!"

"I accept your rebuke," Jordan responded, bowing slightly.

"Oh, it wasn't a rebuke," the bearlike man replied with a grin. "The real world would be a lot duller without dreamers like you."

"So you've recognized my true worth at last," Jordan exclaimed exaggeratedly.

"Of course, Oh Great One," Hewe answered, happily continuing their pantomime. "I would follow you to the ends of the earth."

"And back?"

"And back," Hewe confirmed. "Especially back."

Wray was never seen again. His extraordinary encounter with the elementals had been witnessed only by a very few, and of those, only Cai understood even a little of what had happened. It was true that the wizard's view had been through the linkage of the circles, rather than more conventional sight, but he knew nonetheless that Wray had come to understand the true nature of the elemental beings at last. It saddened Cai to think that the revelation had come only moments before Wray had presumably been killed.

However, nothing was certain. The feeling persisted that Wray had not died—at least, not in the conventional sense—and that somehow his belated admission of kinship with the creatures he had once despised had provided him with some form of escape.

The last anyone had seen of the raider he was standing in the midst of a whirling mass of blue, his arms outstretched. Apparently, his own body had become translucent, glittering with the energy of his new-found friends.

Then Wray and the elementals were gone—and no man knew their final destination.

* * *

The months after the battle passed slowly for Cai. For so long, his life had been spent in the pursuit of one urgent goal after another, and now these had all been accomplished—or were out of reach forever. He had no need to travel any further, and he longed for peace and solitude. His heart was troubled, and he even felt vaguely dissatisfied at times by the restoration of his eyesight—as if it were a poor exchange for the enhanced companionship with the swarm.

So that summer found him living in a modest cottage outside one of the tiny fishing villages on the coast between Newport and Altonbridge. Zana was with him, and the wizard took her presence for granted. Now that he could see normally, he no longer needed her help as he had in the past, but she made a pleasant companion and helped keep his home from becoming a complete shambles.

At first, the villagers had been wary of the newcomers, but they soon came to accept them. Cai was happy to use his healing skills for their benefit, and Zana provided occasional advice to the owner of the village inn. Other than that, they kept much to themselves, and their privacy was respected—though local gossip made them characters of considerable interest and mystery.

As the sun rose on midsummer's day, Zana rose with it, going to sit on the porch overlooking the bay. Cai had been up for some time, as was his habit now that the days were hot, and had gone for a long walk along the beach. Zana saw him trudging back toward the cottage, his head down, deep in thought as always. The swarm made a small shadow over his head.

Oh Cai, she thought, *when will you look up and see what's all around you?*

As if in answer to her unspoken words, the wizard raised his head and briefly acknowledged her wave. Zana's heart raced, hopeful as ever. She was very much in love with him, but was well aware that she couldn't ever fill the space left in Cai's life by the loss of Gemma. Their parting had been painful to watch; even now, there were times when Zana wondered if it was not her that Cai spoke to but the absent friend from an earlier life. She wanted to shake some sense into him, tell him that Gemma would never, *could* never, be his lover now, and that if only he would stop living in the past, his life could be happy again. And yet she always held her tongue, content for now just to be with him, to be his housekeeper and companion, though she longed to be so much more.

She watched his lonely figure move slowly back toward their cottage, glad that, as always, he could take some comfort from the sea. They were both islanders, and in this she understood his feelings.

Perhaps we should go back, she thought. *Sail north. I wonder how the Star is faring*. Then she shook her head. *No, we can't go back. This is our home now.*

With this decision, a new determination welled up within her, and she told herself firmly that even if she could not replace Gemma, then she would be a more than adequate substitute and would do everything in her power to make Cai happy.

She knew what it was like to lose a first true love—after all, she had come to these southern lands in search of a man—but, she told herself there was no reason why she—why both of them—couldn't be happy with the second.

She stood up then and started across the dunes toward the beach, intending to join Cai for the last part of his walk.

Cai saw her coming and stopped in his tracks, watching her lithe movements, her long hair blowing in the gentle breeze. He stared, as if seeing her for the very first time.

I've been blind! he thought.

Do you need our eyes again? the bees asked.

Cai glanced up at them, laughing at the misunderstanding.

No, he replied, looking back at Zana. *This time I can heal myself.*

She was down on the beach now, and they walked slowly toward each other, not hurrying, but growing in certainty with every step. What might have been would never be forgotten, but it could be pushed to the back of their minds. The past was finally over—and a future of possibilities lay before them.

Cai held out his hands in greeting, and Zana's answering smile told him all he needed to know.

C'tis wandered through the empty halls of stone. The others had tried to keep her from returning alone to her own world, but they knew, as she did, that she could not survive in their upworld for long. And even though no one spoke the words aloud, they all knew that she had nothing left to live for. She was the last of her race.

Her journey seemed endless, the caverns and tunnels changed beyond recognition. She was lost almost as soon as she entered the Lightless Kingdom and walked aimlessly, hoping beyond hope to find some small sign of the people that had given her life, and who were now gone forever. She came across some colored traces smeared upon the reformed rock, but nothing was even vaguely recognizable. Bitter tears formed in her large eyes.

Nothing. Nothing at all.

She knew that the sacrifice her people had made had been worthwhile, and had been made easier by the fact that the dreadful green-sickness would have killed them anyway, but she could not reconcile these new caverns with her old life. A whole civilization could not vanish just like that. It was impossible.

The rock was still warm, but C'tis hardly noticed. She had removed the silkfish tape that had covered her for so long. She had come to think of it as a second skin, and felt vulnerable without it. There were already enough shadows down here.

Her strength ebbed, and she made no attempt to replenish it, stumbling onward through the labyrinth of stone that had once been her home.

Nothing. Nothing at all.

As her legs gave way, she began to crawl, determined to keep moving.

It was then that she saw—or thought she saw—the whisperers. Tiny fragments of multicolored light, changing with every moment, their faint susurration echoing in the silence. They led her, and she followed them, heedless of the lacerations in her hands and knees—and found that something *was* left, after all.

Though everything around it had changed, Soulskeep had somehow remained untouched. Some miracle had led the fire past its entrances, as if the shrine was sacred even to the flames of destruction.

C'tis got painfully to her feet and saw the representation of Rael, who to the people of the upworld was the Earth-mind, painted on the wall. All about it grew the raellim; crying now, C'tis reached out and broke off some of the precious fungus. *Soulskeep will not mind*, she thought. *I am the last*.

All desire to move had left her now, and she sat down opposite the representation of the god.

Now I have something to remember you by.

She smiled and began eating, feeling the earthwild seep into her blood. She welcomed the dreams, knowing that at least *they* would be peopled.

They came to her then, in welcome and in trust, smiling as the power of the raellim conjured them back into existence. Her parents and her brother, the prophets and the villagers of Midholm. B'van and L'tha. C'lin, T'via, V'dal, and D'vor. And J'vina last of all.

C'tis greeted them all, as the earthwild grew within her. In the end, she stood tall and proud beside them, offering her life as they had given theirs.

With a gentleness that surpassed all understanding, the Earth-mind accepted her offering.

chapter 41

The meyrkats stayed with Gemma for a few days. The clan that had left the desert with her all those months ago was sadly depleted, and the Wanderers were saddened by the loss of their friends from the giant burrow, particularly J'vina, who had been especially close to them. They explained to Gemma that they had been using the strength of the clan to keep the control party healthy while they were in the poisoned caves. Gemma had not known that the meyrkats were able to use the power of their particular circle in this way, and hoped that her own healing talents had somehow helped them.

She also assumed, though the meyrkats were not clear about this, that it was because the clan was part of the magical circles that they had been rescued by the floating city after becoming separated from J'vina during the final battle.

Gemma enjoyed the company of the little creatures during the short time that they had together, and they in turn were delighted to be reunited with their clan-friend. However, they all knew that they would soon have to part. There was no doubting where Gemma and Arden were headed, and the meyrkats already knew that they could not live in the Valley of Knowing.

When the time came for their farewells, Gemma entrusted the clan to Hewe. The big man was delighted by his responsibility and quite unable to resist their furry charms. He promised to lead them back to the Diamond Desert.

Will you come back to the stone? Av asked Gemma.

We will welcome you always, Gem-ma, Ox added.

I'll come, she promised, *but it will be many, many days before we will meet again.*

The clan will have a good happy-lie-all-know for you by then, Ed told her. *We will practice.*

Several days later, Hewe stood at the edge of the desert, watching the Wanderers bound gleefully toward their old home.

I wish I could be there when they reach the stone, he thought wistfully. *I bet it'll be quite a party!*

Gemma and Arden rode on alone, saddened by the spate of farewells but eager to get back to the valley. Jordan had insisted that they take two of the horses that had survived the battle, and they were glad of the gift. It would have been a long, hard march without them.

When they reached the valley, the news was better than they could have hoped for. They went first to Elway and Teri's farm, which lay at the southern end of the vale, and were greeted by Mallory's parents with joyful hearts and open arms. They told the returning travelers that the river had dried up a few days after their departure, and that since then, the sickness had retreated. Now only a few people were ill, and even they were well on the way to recovery. Although the river had started to run again only a few days later, causing alarm and fear, they had soon realized that the water was pure again—the lifeblood of the valley had returned.

In fact, the river now flowed permanently through the valley, no longer diverted every other year. The upheaval caused by the Earth-mind had made quite sure of that.

When they arrived at Mallory's home, they found that they were expected; the knowing was stronger than ever.

"We're back!" Gemma told them, amid the tears and laughter. "But this time it's for good."

She and Arden wanted to make the valley their permanent home; they could never have considered living anywhere else.

"I was hoping you'd say that!" Mallory cried. "Welcome home!"

"How's little Gem?"

"She's fine. She's asleep now, but come and have a look at her anyway."

The two women walked into the house, while Arden told Kragen and the two boys of the recent momentous events.

"Did she behave at all strangely while we were away?" Gemma asked.

"No. Why—*should* she have?" Mallory glanced at her friend curiously.

"No sleepless nights?"

"No more than any other baby. What's all this about, Gemma?"

"Your daughter is special. I've already told you that. And one day I'll have to talk to her about it."

"Well, I hope what you tell her makes more sense than what you're saying to me," Mallory responded.

"I hope so too," Gemma replied, grinning.

They had reached the infant's bedroom now and leaned over her cot. Gem awoke and opened her eyes wide, gazing at them solemnly. Then she gurgled happily, waving her tiny arms in the air.

"She's glad to see you," Mallory laughed.

I'm glad to see you too, Gemma told the baby silently.

The only response was another gurgle and a rapid blink of those huge brown eyes.

And I'm glad you can still be a child, Gemma thought. *You've done enough for now.*

As the baby looked up at her namesake, it seemed to Gemma that the knowledge of all the world was contained in that solemn stare.

What secrets are in your head? she wondered, delighted by the thought of watching the little girl grow up. *It doesn't matter. There's plenty of time.*

Gem gazed back at her, innocent and knowing all at once.

"It seems it's all settled," Arden told Gemma when she and Mallory rejoined their husbands. "There's an empty farmhouse just across the river from here that was abandoned during the drought."

"I'll get a few of the lads together," Kragen said, "and we'll soon knock it into shape for you."

"That's wonderful!" Gemma exclaimed.

"And we'll build a bridge," Vance said excitedly, "so we can go across and see you every day."

"But Gemma and Arden may want some peace and quiet, *away* from noisy children," his father remonstrated.

Vance looked crestfallen.

"Do you?" he asked in pitiful tones.

"Maybe sometimes," Arden replied, "but you can come and see us most days."

"Hurrah!" Vance shouted, more than satisfied with this answer.

"Until then," Kragen added, "we'll have to go to Lower to cross the river, unless you fancy swimming. Shall we go and see the place now?"

Gemma and Arden moved into their new home in early spring. The people of the valley had all contributed something—either by gifts or by their own efforts—and so their farmhouse was comfortable from the very first day.

Their life fell into a pattern of quiet contentment. Gemma continued her work as a healer, finding in that the best possible outlet for her magical talents, while Arden involved himself in farming and the other activities of the valley. Before long he was happily growing their own vegetables, and perfectly at home with his other tasks. They both found the simplicity of their days an enormous pleasure after the turmoil of the preceding years. They were together, and that was all that mattered.

"Are you happy, my love?" Gemma asked one day.

"You know I am," Arden told her.

"And you don't mind that we can't have any children?"

"We're enough for each other," he replied simply. "You're all I'll ever need."

"You're sure?"

"Absolutely positive. Besides, Jon and Vance are quite exhausting enough, and we can hand them back at the end of the day!"

"Just wait till little Gem gets going," Gemma warned. "I've a feeling she's going to be more of a handful than both the boys put together."

"You could be right there. Women are usually more difficult to keep under control," he responded.

"That's the sort of remark that'll get you thrown in the river," she replied.

"You see what I mean?" Arden asked, spreading his hands wide and looking at the sky as if searching for patience.

They laughed together.

"You're looking the wrong way," Gemma said. "The Earth-mind's down *there*, remember?"

Arden took her in his arms and kissed her soundly.

"I'm married to a pedant," he told her.

"*Happily* married," she corrected.

"Happily indeed," he said. "I'm happier than I've ever been in my life. Do you know what I dreamed about last night?"

She shook her head.

"My father."

"Oh." Arden often dreamed about the bad times of his childhood, waking distressed and immensely relieved to find Gemma at his side.

"But it wasn't a nightmare this time. The old bastard's been hanging over me for far too long, and this time I just told him to go away and stop bothering me. He went as quiet as a lamb!"

Arden smiled at his wife. The past had finally been laid to rest.

In the years that followed, Gemma and Arden became a dearly loved part of the valley, and it was hard to remember a time when they had not been there. Every winter they went away for a month or so, visiting the meyrkats and their friends in Great Newport, and even the mountain home of Shanti and Wynut. It took them some time before they felt at ease with Cai and Zana, but that day eventually came and saw the beginning of a happy relationship between the two couples. All these journeys fulfilled their need to keep in touch with old friends, and they enjoyed seeing how the world was faring without them. They were happy excursions, but Gemma and Arden were always glad to return home.

This was especially so once little Gem reached the age when she realized that they had been missing. She always made a fuss over them when they returned, and the sight of the little girl running toward them, her arms outstretched, never failed to move Gemma deeply. In later years, it became apparent that there were other reasons for Gem missing them so dreadfully, reasons she could not explain, and she was never completely happy until they returned.

The valley that had become their home was still a wonderful place, with its combination of serenity and beauty, but for all that, its inhabitants knew that it was slightly tainted now. It had been touched by the savagery of the outside world, its delicately preserved isolation had been shattered. Although no one ever said so aloud, they all understood that what had happened once could happen again.

Gemma and Arden lived their lives to the full, enjoying the pleasures of the place and its people, contributing their own efforts to the valley's prosperity, and trusting that their home would always remain the safe place it was now.

There was much to enjoy. The fresh greens of spring, the patchwork of summer gold, the glowing colors of autumn, and the wild, somber beauty of winter. There were the free, wild animals and birds, the satisfaction of new growth, and the beauty of the flowers and trees. There were the river and the hills, with the great mountains beyond standing stark and majestic against the sky. There was sunshine and rain, mist and wind, the fruits of the season, harvest and celebration. All blended into the wonderful whole that was the valley, casting its unique spell over all who lived there.

The spell was especially strong one summer's evening as Gemma stood in the doorway of her home, watching Arden tending to his herbs. He glanced up and saw her smiling at him. She was so beautiful that he could not take his eyes from her.

"What are you thinking?" he asked.

"About how wonderful life is," she replied. "Being here with you. A few years ago I could never have imagined that such happiness was possible."

Arden left his work and went to embrace her.

"Well, you'd better get used to it, my love," he told her softly. "Because there's plenty more where this came from!"

epilogue

"But I'm fourteen years old!" All the natural indignation of her age showed in Gem's face. "I'm practically grown-up. Why can't you tell me *now*?"

Gemma saw in her namesake all the impatience and frustration of her own adolescence, which seemed such a long time ago now. *Nobody understood me then*, she remembered. *I must treat her like an adult*. She recalled the indifference that had seemed so cruel, and which had made her own young life so painful at times. Even Cai had never fully realized how she had suffered. *I must not make the same mistakes*.

And yet still she hesitated. She had been dreading this for years.

"Please," Gem insisted. "Everyone says 'Gemma will tell you in good time,' but you're always so mysterious. And I want to know why!"

"All right," Gemma said slowly. "I'll try to explain. This won't be easy for me, little one, so please be patient." She ignored the child's grimace at the endearment and tried to organize her thoughts.

"What do you know about magic?" she asked eventually.

"Well, I know that *you* use it to heal people," the girl replied, "and that you can talk to the meyrkats."

"That's how I *use* it, but do you know what it *is*?"

"No—not really."

So Gemma told the girl about the principles of harnessing the mind's energy, then carefully explained the circles of magic and her own unique place within them. Her namesake sat spellbound.

"Oh!" she exclaimed when she finally understood. "All

those circles—through you?" She stared, wide-eyed and child-like in wonder, quite forgetting that she was supposed to be grown-up.

"Yes," Gemma replied. "The circles helped me in the battles against Mendle and the Great Leader. I would have been helpless without them."

"I wish there was magic here," Gem said longingly.

"There is, sweetheart. It's all around you."

"Really?" Gem looked startled.

"The valley is one of the circles," Gemma explained. "And a very important one."

"But nothing *ever* happens here," the girl argued.

One day you'll be grateful for that, Gemma thought, then went on, "Everyone in the valley shares the knowing, which is a form of magic that no one else has. Then there's Kris, and his warmth, and gift of prophecy. Your circle protects your home from the outside world. The valley is a magical place, believe me."

Gem considered this.

"How was I supposed to know?" she asked indignantly. "I haven't traveled everywhere like you!" Then something else occurred to her. "Are we *all* in the circle?"

"Yes."

"Even me?"

"Especially you, Gem. That's why some things have been confusing for you."

"You mean the dreams and things?"

Gemma nodded, and the girl looked worried again.

I hope you're ready for this, Gemma thought. *Because we can't stop now*.

"People always go quiet when I'm near," Gem complained sadly. "As if they're hiding something from me. Even Mum and Dad. It's not fair!"

"That's my fault, sweetheart. I needed to be sure that you were ready—and that *I* was the one to tell you."

"Why?"

"Because it's my responsibility." Gemma answered firmly. *And I didn't want to rob you of your childhood*. "Listen, carefully, Gem. What I'm going to tell you is very important, but you mustn't be frightened. I'll always be here if you need me."

"But what about when you go away?"

"Even then."

"I don't understand." Gem looked very young and vulnerable at that moment.

"The person who is at the point where all the circles meet is called the Key to the Dream," Gemma began.

"And that's you?"

"Yes," she confirmed. "But there's going to come a time when all the circles move. They'll spin around so that although they still go through one point, it will be a different one from before."

"So you won't be the Key to the Dream forever?"

"No."

"When will it change?"

"That," Gemma replied, "is up to you."

"Me!"

"You're the future Key, Gem."

Open disbelief and fear showed on the girl's face.

"I *can't* be," she whispered. "I won't know what to do."

"You'll know when you need to," Gemma replied confidently. "The circles will all be there to help you—and I'll still be in one of them, so I'll always be near you."

They were silent for a while as Gem struggled with these new ideas.

"Will I have to fight battles?" she asked eventually.

"I hope not, sweetheart. We have peace now, and there's no reason to think it won't last for a very long time—maybe even forever."

"How long have you known?" Gem asked, after another pause.

"Since before you were born."

Gemma was surprised when her young namesake accepted this statement calmly. *She's growing up so fast!*

"How did it feel . . . when you became the Key?"

"I didn't know," she replied. "I was only seven years old at the time."

"Oh."

"There was no one there to tell me what it meant," Gemma went on. "And I had to travel a long way before I found out." *At least I can spare you that.*

"Weren't you scared?"

"Yes, a little. Because I didn't understand anything. But there's no reason for you to be frightened, Gem. You've already achieved something wonderful—something no one else could have done."

The girl looked at her, questions in her eyes.

"I don't suppose you remember the very first dream we had together," Gemma said. "You were only a tiny baby—"

"I do!" her niece exclaimed. "I was on a mountain, and there was a big fire—and you told me things, and then it went out and there was a lake," she concluded breathlessly.

It was Gemma's turn to be astonished.

"That was the battle with the Great Leader," she said after a few moments. "You helped us talk to the Earth-mind, the biggest circle of all. Without you, we would all have been killed."

"Really?" A measure of confidence crept into the girl's voice.

Gemma nodded. "You're very special, Gem. Everyone knows that, and *that's* why they feel awkward sometimes."

"*Everyone?*"

Gemma smiled, knowing just what the girl was thinking.

"You will always be their younger sister, just as I will always be Arden's wife," she replied. "Vance and Jon love you, even though they do tease you unmercifully at times." Gem looked as if she could not quite believe this. "When you become the Key, you'll need your family and this valley more than ever," Gemma went on. "Your special powers will only be for really important things."

"And the circles would stop me from doing anything silly, wouldn't they," the girl said, sounding very grown-up again.

Gemma smiled at her niece's good sense. Gem had been gifted with natural intelligence and a calm temperament by her parents. Kragen and Mallory knew that their daughter's destiny was special, but they would never forget that she was still their little girl.

"Won't you miss being the Key?" Gem asked, anxious not to cause her beloved namesake any pain.

"No, sweetheart," came the gentle reply. "My life is as full as I want it to be now."

"When *will* the circles move?"

"When you want them to. You have a combination of the magical powers of the circles and of your home," Gemma told her. "So far, the valley has acted as a shield, but you can let the circles in when you want to. You can choose to meet them at any time."

Gem stared back at her, brown eyes wide with anticipation.

Is it time? Is the waiting over?

Yes, Gemma replied, smiling as she sensed the astonishment run through the circles.

You are leaving us. It was no longer a question but a statement at last, tinged with sadness, but also with excitement.

A new ear.

Both Keys shared the dream, from their separate bedrooms on either side of the river. Gemma had felt the first gentle contact, and sensed the girl's resolve. She sent her support and watched as Gem asked the valley to open her world to the circles.

They came quickly, and Gemma reveled in the multiple contact for what she knew would be the very last time. Faces from her old life and her new, the known and the unfamiliar. Voices of all tones and ages, songs of home and open sky. Landscapes of more variety than she could ever have seen—mountains, cities, plains, and oceans. Sunlight on water, starlight on snow. Sadness and joy, anger and love. Time passing, through generations. The circles moving.

There is someone I want to introduce to you all.

Gem greeted them timidly, forcing herself to look beyond the familiar people of the valley's circle.

She was welcomed by smiles on a thousand different faces. Wynut and Shanti, as absurd as ever, looking up from their latest invention; Cai, with the swarm droning sleepily above his head; Jordan, his pen poised over paper, a lamp burning low on his desk; a golden-haired man holding the hand of his violet-eyed wife; and eccentric hermit, dressed in skins and surrounded by the animals of his mountain home; Adria, pausing in her conversation with her sons; the meyrkats rejoicing in their reunited clan; and many, many more.

Gem saw them all and knew their support was hers to call upon. In her dream, she smiled.

The last image, and the clearest of all, was that of Arden and Gemma, safe and smiling, encircled by each other's arms.

"This is world-building on a major scale...
[*Guardians of the Three*] may rank as one of the most distinctive creations of modern fantasy." —*Dragon Magazine*

GUARDIANS OF THE THREE

For centuries the feline people of Ar and the powerful Lords of the East have been at peace. Legends surround the Eastern Lords and their servants, the liskash—lizard warriors—but few have ever seen them. This series tells the exciting story of the sudden rise and devastating assault of the Eastern Lords against the people of Ar, the catlike Mrem. The Council of the Three—a group of powerful Mrem wizards—must fight with their every resource to protect their vulnerable world.

Volume One: **Lord of Cragsclaw** by Bill Fawcett and Neil Randall (27462-7 • $3.95/$4.95 in Canada)
Volume Two: **Keeper of the City** by Diane Duane and Peter Morwood (28065-1 • $3.95/$4.95 in Canada)
Volume Three: **Wizard of Tizare** by Matthew J. Costello (28303-0 • $3.95/$4.95 in Canada)
Volume Four: **Defenders of Ar** by Jack Lovejoy (28453-3 • $3.95/$4.95 in Canada)

Buy **Guardians of the Three** now on sale wherever Bantam Spectra Books are sold.